AN AMISH GARDEN

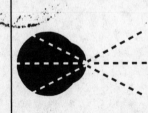

AN AMISH GARDEN

BETH WISEMAN,
KATHLEEN FULLER,
TRICIA GOYER,
AND VANNETTA CHAPMAN

THORNDIKE PRESS
A part of Gale, Cengage Learning

GALE
CENGAGE Learning®

Farmington Hills, Mich • San Francisco • New York • Waterville, Maine
Meriden, Conn • Mason, Ohio • Chicago

GALE
CENGAGE Learning®

Copyright © 2014 by Elizabeth Wiseman Mackey, Kathleen Fuller, Tricia Goyer, Vannetta Chapman.
Scripture taken from the Holy Bible, New International Version®. NIV®. Copyright © 1973, 1978, 1984, 2011 by Biblica, Inc.™ Used by permission of Zondervan. All rights reserved worldwide. www.zondervan.com.
Thorndike Press, a part of Gale, Cengage Learning.

Thorndike Press® Large Print Christian Fiction.
The text of this Large Print edition is unabridged.
Other aspects of the book may vary from the original edition.
Set in 16 pt. Plantin.

LIBRARY OF CONGRESS CATALOGING-IN-PUBLICATION DATA

An amish garden / by Beth Wiseman, Kathleen Fuller, Tricia Goyer, and Vannetta Chapman. — Large print edition.
    pages ; cm. — (Thorndike Press large print Christian fiction)
    ISBN 978-1-4104-6934-2 (hardcover) — ISBN 1-4104-6934-4 (hardcover)
    1. Amish—Fiction. 2. Christian fiction, American. 3. Large type books.
I. Wiseman, Beth, 1962– Rooted in love. II. Fuller, Kathleen. Flowers for Rachael. III. Goyer, Tricia. Seeds of love. IV. Chapman, Vannetta. Where healing blooms.
PS648.A45A39 2014b
813'.01083823—dc23   2014007333

Published in 2014 by arrangement with Thomas Nelson, Inc.

Printed in the United States of America
1 2 3 4 5 6 7 18 17 16 15 14

CONTENTS

■ ■ ■ ■

Rooted in Love

BETH WISEMAN

■ ■ ■ ■

To Jenni Newcomer Cutbirth

GLOSSARY OF LANCASTER COUNTY AMISH WORDS

ach — oh
bruder — brother
daed — dad
danki — thank you
dochder — daughter
Englisch — non-Amish person
gut — good
haus — house
kaffi — coffee
kapp — prayer covering or cap
kinner — children or grandchildren
maedel — girl
mamm — mom
mei — my
mudder — mother
nee — no
Ordnung — the written and unwritten rules of the Amish; the understood behavior by which the Amish are expected to live, passed down from generation to generation. Most Amish know the rules by heart.

scrapple — traditionally a mush of pork scraps and trimmings combined with cornmeal, wheat flour, and spices. The mush is formed into a semisolid congealed loaf, and slices are then panfried before serving.

Wie bischt — How are you?

ya — yes

CHAPTER ONE

Rosemary crossed her legs, folded her arms across her chest, and tried to focus on the bishop's final prayer as he wrapped up the worship service. Saul Petersheim was making that a difficult task. She'd made it clear to Saul that she was not interested in dating him, but the man still gave it his best shot from time to time.

"He's doing it again," Rosemary whispered to Esther. "Smiling and staring at me."

Her best friend grinned. "Are you ever going to give that poor fellow a break and go out with him?"

"We've been through all this, Esther. Saul and I dated when we were sixteen. It didn't work out then, and it wouldn't work out now." Rosemary clamped her mouth closed when she realized that Bishop Glick had stopped talking and was staring at her, along with most of the congregation. She could feel the heat rising from her neck to her cheeks, so she sat taller, swallowed hard, and didn't breathe for a few seconds.

"See, Saul even gets me in trouble at worship service," Rosemary said once the bishop had recited the final prayer and dismissed everyone. She stood up, smoothed the wrinkles from her white apron, and shook her head.

Esther chuckled. "You're twenty-one years old. I think you're responsible for your own actions at this point."

Rosemary sighed as they waited for several of the older women to pass by before they eased into the line that was forming toward the kitchen. "I guess. I just wish Saul would find someone else," she whispered as she glanced over her shoulder toward him. "Someone better suited to him." The words stung when she said them aloud.

"Saul only has eyes for you." Esther smiled. "And I don't understand why you won't give him another chance. It was five years ago."

Rosemary bit her bottom lip, tempted to tell Esther the whole story. But every time she considered telling her friend the truth, she stopped herself. There was once a time when Rosemary couldn't picture herself with anyone but Saul.

All the men had gone in the other direction toward the front door, most likely to gather in the barn to tell jokes and smoke cigars while the women prepared the meal. Rosemary shrugged. "It just wouldn't work out."

Esther picked up a stack of plates from the counter and shook her head. "I don't understand you, Rosemary. Saul is one of the most desirable single men in our district. The fact that someone else hasn't already snagged him is mind-boggling." She nudged Rosemary's shoulder. "But I really do think he is holding out for you."

"Well, he is wasting his time." Rosemary picked up a pitcher of tea and followed Esther out the kitchen door and onto the porch. As they made their way down the steps toward the tables that had been set up in the yard, Rosemary commented to Esther that the Lord couldn't have blessed them with a more beautiful day. She wasn't going to let thoughts about Saul ruin it.

It seemed like spring had arrived overnight following a long winter that had seen record-low temperatures in Lancaster County. The Zooks were hosting church service today, and their flower beds were filled with colorful blooms. Rosemary glanced to her right at the freshly planted garden, then sighed, knowing how disappointed her mother would be if she were still alive. Rosemary hadn't planted a garden in four years. She'd tried to maintain the flower beds, but even that effort had failed.

She'd filled up most of the tea glasses when she saw Saul walking toward her. She swallowed hard. All these years later, Saul still made her pulse quicken.

"You look as pretty as ever, Rosie." Saul pushed back the rim of his straw hat, then looped his thumbs beneath his suspenders. There was no denying that Saul was a handsome man with his dark hair, deep-blue eyes, and boyish dimples. He had a smile that could melt any girl's heart. Aside from her father, Saul was the only other person who called her Rosie, and a warm feeling filled her when he did. But she'd never tell him that.

Rosemary looked up at him and forced a smile, wishing things were different. "*Danki,* Saul." She turned to walk away, but he was quickly in stride with her. "Can I help you with something?" she said as she continued to walk toward the house. She kept her eyes straight ahead and masked any facial expression.

"*Nee.* Just going inside." He scratched his chin. "And trying to figure out how long it's been since I asked you out. Wondering if I should try again."

Rosemary stopped midstep. She glanced around to see if anyone was in earshot, and after waiting for one of her brothers to jet past them, she said, "I — I just don't think it's a *gut* idea for us to date. I'm very busy trying to run a household full of boys and take care of *mei daed.*" She locked eyes with his, knowing she'd do better to avoid looking at him altogether.

"Did I hear hesitation in your voice?" He grinned, and Rosemary's knees went weak. Saul wasn't just nice-looking, he was also well respected within the community and known to have a strong faith. He was sure to be a good husband and provider since he ran a successful construction company. He'd taken over his father's business when his father never fully recovered from back surgery. But there were two reasons Rosemary wasn't going to get involved with Saul. And one of them was walking toward them. Her five-year-old brother stopped in front of her, his face drawn into a pout.

"I can't find Jesse or Josh." Abner stared up at Rosemary.

"They're around here somewhere." Rosemary straightened her youngest brother's hat, making a mental note to cut his blond

17

bangs when they got home. "We'll be eating soon, and neither Jesse nor Joshua is going to miss a meal."

Saul squatted in front of Abner. "Anything I can help you with, buddy?"

Abner shook his head. *"Nee."*

Rosemary looked down at her feet for a moment. Saul was born to be a father. She'd watched him with the *kinner* in their district over the years. The man was loving and kind to anyone he came in contact with. She needed to get away from him before she threw herself into his arms or said something she'd regret. She held up the empty pitcher and focused on Abner. "I've got to go refill this and help get lunch on the table. Don't go far." Then she turned to Saul, and a sadness weighed so heavy on her heart, she couldn't even force another smile. "I have to go."

Saul scratched his chin again as he watched Rosemary' walk away. Most days, he wondered why he continued to pursue her since she always turned him away. But every now and then he would see something in her beautiful brown eyes that made him think he might still have a chance. Or like today . . . he was sure he'd heard regret in her voice.

Sighing, he turned and headed back to the barn. As he pulled open the door, the stench of cigar smoke assaulted him. He'd never cared for this recreational activity that some of the men practiced. It used to be reserved for after the Sunday meal, but somewhere along the line, a few of the men began having a smoke before they ate. Saul enjoyed the jokes and company of the other fellows, but considering John Zook had already lost one barn to a fire, Saul was surprised he allowed smoking in his new one. The men were already walking toward the door, so Saul turned around, and they all made their way to the tables.

Saul took a seat at the table beneath a large oak tree, mostly because Rosemary's father, Wayne Lantz, was sitting there. Wayne was a leader, a fair man, and someone Saul had always looked up to. Saul wouldn't be surprised if he became bishop someday. He was also the first person on the scene of any emergency and available whenever a neighbor had a crisis. Saul glanced toward the Zook barn. On the day of the barn raising, Wayne had spent more time working than any of the other men. And even after his wife died four years ago, he continued to do for others.

"Any luck with that *dochder* of mine?"

Wayne's face was void of expression as he picked up his glass of tea, then took several large gulps.

Saul had never been sure if Wayne approved of his pursuing Rosemary. "*Nee*. She still won't give me the time of day." He reached for his own glass, took a large drink, and hoped that his answer had sounded casual enough.

One corner of Wayne's mouth lifted into a subtle grin. Saul wasn't sure if the man was impressed with Saul's persistence or if he was happy that Rosemary wouldn't have anything to do with him. Wayne was quiet.

Rosemary walked up to the table carting a full pitcher of tea. She'd stolen Saul's heart the summer they'd both turned sixteen. That was the year she had blossomed into a woman, and the maturity fit her perfectly, both her figure and her personality. She'd been full of life, always laughing, and a bright light wherever she went. Saul was pretty sure she'd stolen a lot more hearts than just his that summer. He was blessed to have dated Rosemary for three months. But then one day after worship service, she'd broken up with him without giving him a good reason why. Through her tears, she'd mumbled something about the two of them not being right for each other, and she'd run off before Saul could get a better answer. She'd refused to talk about it in the months that followed.

Then her mother died the following year, and everything changed. She withdrew from everyone, and responsibility swallowed her up as she tended to her father and siblings. But Saul had seen the woman Rosemary was meant to be.

She walked around the table topping off glasses with iced tea, and when she got to her father, she set the pitcher on the table, then brushed lint from the arm of his black jacket. Wayne glanced at her and smiled, and in a rare moment, Rosemary smiled back. She left the pitcher on the table before she walked away, not one time glancing in Saul's direction. The six other men at the table were deep in conversation about a new buggy maker in town, an *Englisch* man who was building the buggies cheaper than anyone else. Saul was only half-listening when Rosemary's father leaned closer to him.

"I'd tell you to give up, but I'm guessing that isn't going to happen."

Saul shook his head and grinned as they both watched Rosemary walk across the yard to the house. *"Nee."*

Wayne ran his hand the length of his dark

beard that was threaded with gray. He didn't look at Saul, but kept his eyes on Rosemary as she walked up the porch steps.

"Will be a blessed man to win her heart." Wayne kept his eyes on his daughter. "She's so much like her *mudder,* though. Hard to tell what's going on in her head." He turned to Saul, and the hint of a smile formed. "But she will be well worth the time invested if you are that man."

Everyone had thought Wayne Lantz would remarry quickly after his wife died. Widowers and widows were encouraged to marry another as soon as possible. But Edna Lantz had been a fine woman. Saul figured Wayne was having a hard time finding happiness with someone else.

Even though Rosemary never did tell Saul why she broke up with him so suddenly, he couldn't imagine spending his life with anyone else. He'd tried to bring up the subject from time to time, but it had just put even more distance between them. But realistically, how long could he go on pursuing her?

CHAPTER TWO

Rosemary was giving the kitchen rug a good thrashing against a tree on Monday morning when a buggy turned into the driveway. Squinting against the sun's glare as it peeked over the horizon, she watched as Katherine Huyard slowed down and stopped. Rosemary bit her tongue, reprimanded herself for allowing ugly thoughts to creep into her mind, then put the rug down in the grass and walked toward the buggy. Katherine stepped out toting a basket that was most likely filled with fresh vegetables from her garden.

Rosemary glanced at the healthy weeds she was growing within what used to be a fenced garden, determined not to let Katherine get under her skin. The first few times Katherine brought vegetables, Rosemary had been grateful that she didn't have to buy them in town. But now Katherine came at least two times a week, and the woman made Rosemary feel inferior. Her tomatoes were the biggest and tastiest Rosemary had ever had. So were her cucumbers, zucchinis, squash, melons, and spinach. And Katherine was always dressed in a freshly ironed dress and apron. Even her *kapp* looked just pressed, and there wasn't a hair out of place. Rosemary blew a strand of her own wayward hair from her face as she took her wrinkled self toward Katherine. She waved, hoping the visit would be short.

"Your *daed* told me at worship how much he's been enjoying my vegetables, so I've filled the basket." Katherine flashed her perfectly white teeth as she handed Rosemary the produce. It seemed Katherine was always smiling. Rosemary wondered how that could be. Katherine had lost her husband to cancer a year ago. It had been four years since Rosemary's mother died, and only recently did her father show any signs of joy.

"*Danki,* Katherine." Rosemary accepted the gift, knowing her father and the boys would be grateful. "Would you like to come in for *kaffi* or tea?"

"*Nee.* I've got some mending to do for *mei* nieces and nephews. I try to help Ellen as much as I can."

For a few seconds, Katherine's smile

faded and she got a faraway look in her eyes. Rosemary never knew why Katherine and her husband, John, didn't have any children. Rosemary was about ten years younger than Katherine, who was in her early thirties. In a flash, Katherine's smile was back. Rosemary wondered what it would be like to switch places with the woman for a day, to have no one to tend to but herself. Even though Rosemary longed for a husband and children of her own, having even one day to herself sounded like heaven.

"Anyway . . ." Katherine bounced up on her toes, then glanced around the yard. "I just wanted to get out this morning to enjoy the beautiful weather and drop off these vegetables."

Rosemary looked around. In addition to the eyesore that used to be a garden, the flower beds were overgrown, the yard needed mowing, and Abner had left toys all over the place. There just wasn't enough time in the day to take care of everything. "*Ya,* okay. Well, *danki* again for these." She lifted the basket as she managed a small, tentative smile.

Katherine looked around again, and Rosemary shifted her stance. "I'm a little behind on my outside chores."

Katherine shook her head. "Not at all. I

think everything looks nice." She gave a quick wave and turned to leave. Rosemary had to give her credit. She almost sounded sincere.

She walked back to where she'd laid the kitchen rug in the grass, gave it a final slap against the tree, then headed inside with the rug and veggies. She was thankful that Abner, Jesse, and Joshua were all in school. But school would be out for the summer in a few weeks. The older boys would likely help *Daed* tend the fields, but Abner would be in her care all day long, which would slow her down even more.

As she pulled out a chair and sat down at the kitchen table, she wondered why she was allowing bitterness to consume her. Her mother had died, and these responsibilities were God's will for her. To tend to her family and to have very little time to herself — and certainly no time for a relationship.

The sooner Saul found someone else and got on with his life, the better for both of them.

Saul got his brother lined up first thing in the morning on Lydia Jones's house. The *Englisch* woman wanted her entire downstairs painted. Saul thought it was an awful color, a dark burgundy that made the house look even smaller than it was. But Joel was the best painter he had on his six-person payroll. He'd dropped off the other four fellows at another *Englisch* home where they were putting in laminate floors. He'd been blessed to have plenty of work the past few months, but after these two jobs, he didn't have anything else lined up, which was a little worrisome.

"Why would anyone paint the inside of their house this color?" Joel finished covering a hutch by the door with plastic as he eyed the one wall he'd painted last Friday.

Saul shrugged. "I don't know. But it's her *haus.*" He quickly inspected the work Joel had done last week. As usual, it looked good. Joel was only sixteen, but he was a perfectionist, and Saul was thankful he could leave him in a customer's home, knowing his brother would do a *gut* job.

"I'll be back for you at five." Saul maneuvered around furniture that he and Joel had moved to the center of the room. "You'll probably have half of it done by then." He sighed and stretched out the tightness in his back. Some new job opportunities needed to come up by the end of the week.

A few minutes later he was pulling onto Lincoln Highway and heading toward Bird-in-Hand. He had a few errands to run this morning, but he'd barely stepped out of his buggy at the market when it began to pour. He hurried to tether his horse, then took off running across the parking lot. He tipped the rim of his hat down in an effort to shield his face from the heavy pelts. He wasn't paying attention when he rounded a big blue van and slammed right into another person. Hard enough that it brought them both down onto the hard cement. He felt his arm sliding across the pavement, but he was more concerned that the person he'd slammed into wasn't moving.

Wayne Lantz. Saul's heart pounded in his chest as he reached over and touched Rosemary's father on the chest. The older man was flat on his back with his eyes closed.

Rosemary threw a twenty-dollar bill over the seat before she jumped out of Barbie Beiler's gray van. The *Englisch* woman was yelling that Rosemary didn't owe her anything for the ride when Rosemary slammed the door and raced up to the front of the hospital, dodging puddles along the way.

Soaking wet, she dripped across the white tile until she reached two women behind a desk. They quickly pointed her in the direction of the emergency room. She only had a few details, but she knew her father had been in an accident in the parking lot of the Bird-in-Hand market. A stranger had shown up at Rosemary's house, an older *Englisch* woman in a banged-up white car. She'd said that she was at the market when an ambulance pulled into the parking lot. Rosemary's father had been taken to the hospital in Lancaster. A young man with him had given her Rosemary's address. Even though Rosemary didn't have any reason to doubt the woman, she'd held out hope that maybe it wasn't her father who had been injured.

A few minutes later, a nurse escorted her through some double doors. The lump in her throat grew as she walked. She was worried about her father, but as the smell of the hospital filled her nostrils, she was also reminded of all the time she'd spent here with her mother. *Dear God, please don't let my father die too.*

The moment she cried out to the Lord, she felt guilty. She hadn't shown much appreciation for God's grace lately. If anything, her bitterness had pulled her away from Him. Just the same, she said another prayer for her father.

As she followed the nurse behind a curtain and into a small room, she was shocked to see Saul standing at *Daed*'s bedside. She hurried to her father's side and edged Saul out of the way.

"*Daed.*" She leaned closer to him and put a hand on his arm. "What happened?" Before he could answer, she turned to the nurse, who was writing on a clipboard. "How is he?"

"He's going to be just fine," the tiny woman with silver hair said. "The fall knocked him out for a short time, but no concussion." She raised her eyebrows and pointed with her pen to the end of the bed. "That broken ankle will keep him down for a couple of days, but we'll send home some crutches so he can be mobile when he's ready. It's not a bad break, but he still needs to stay off of it as much as possible so it heals properly."

"*Daed,* what happened?" She eased Saul even farther out of the way, wondering why he was here, but more concerned about her father. "Did you slip on the wet pavement?"

"It's *mei* fault." Saul took off his hat and rubbed his forehead. "I didn't see him, and when I got on the other side of a parked van, I ran into him."

Rosemary sucked in a breath and held it, while bringing a hand to her chest. She let it out slowly. "You hit *Daed* with your buggy?"

"That might have been better," her father said as he grinned. "Might not have hurt as much as the body slam." He laughed out loud, and Rosemary looked at the nurse, who smiled.

"He's not feeling much pain at the moment. You know, the medication."

Rosemary studied her father for a few moments, and once she'd decided that he was all right, she turned to Saul. "What in the world were you doing that made you run into *Daed* hard enough to knock him down?" She waved a hand toward the end of the bed. "And to break his ankle?"

"*Ach, dochder,* settle down." Her father shifted his position as the hint of a smile left his face. Instead, he groaned slightly, closing his eyes for a couple of seconds. "It was just an accident." Once he had repositioned himself, he nodded to Saul. "Saul's got a pretty nasty scrape on his arm."

Rosemary noticed Saul's bandaged arm for the first time, and a twinge of guilt coursed through her for not seeing it sooner. She'd been so worried about her father, and even though fear had fueled her snappy comments to Saul, no one was to blame for this accident. She just wasn't sure she'd survive if anything happened to her *daed*. It had been hard enough losing one parent.

"*Ach,* it's okay, Wayne. Not much to it." Saul held up his left arm, which was wrapped in gauze and tape. He lowered his arm, then his head. "I'm just so sorry."

Rosemary's feet took on a mind of their own, and before she knew it, she was right next to Saul. Now that she knew her father was going to be okay, a part of her longed to tend to Saul as well. Instead, she forced herself to turn to the nurse again. "Can my father go home?"

"Yes. But he won't be comfortable riding in a buggy. Do you have a driver?"

Rosemary sighed, wishing she'd asked Barbie to stay. "*Nee,* but I can get one." She reached into her apron pocket and pulled out a piece of paper with Barbie's phone number. "Can I use your phone?"

Saul stood quietly at Wayne's bedside while Rosemary called for a driver. It didn't take an overly smart man to know that Rosemary blamed him for the accident. Blame he was willing to accept. He should have been watching where he was going. At least they would both fully recover. Saul's cousin hadn't been so lucky five years ago when a car plowed into his buggy, leaving him without the use of his legs. The smell of this hospital reminded him of when he went to

32

visit his cousin in Ohio following his accident. He shook the thought away as another worry came to mind.

"Wayne, were you able to finish your planting?" Saul held his breath as he waited for an answer. Wayne usually planted acres of alfalfa. If he wasn't done, Saul would have to finish it for him.

"*Nee.* But almost. We'll make do."

Saul sighed as he shook his head. "*Nee,* I'm going to finish the planting for you. It's the least I can do. If I'd been more careful, watched where I was going . . ."

Wayne eased himself up in the bed, which, judging by his expression, was a tedious task. His pain medication didn't seem to be keeping him comfortable. "Now, Saul, don't you worry about it. You have a business to run."

Saul thought about how he didn't have any jobs lined up for the following week. He hoped something would come up, at least for the sake of his employees, but he had to make this right. "I'm free next week. I can come finish up the planting in the fields, and . . ." He glanced at Rosemary and thought about the weeds growing where her mother used to have a garden. He'd noticed it the last time the Lantzes held worship service. He wondered if Rosemary had gotten around to putting in a garden. "And I can put in a vegetable garden if Rosemary hasn't had time to do that."

"Nee!" Wayne actually lifted himself to a sitting position. "That is not necessary, Saul. I won't have you doing that. Jesse and Joshua can finish the planting in the fields, and we've gone without a garden for the past four years."

Rosemary hung up the phone. *"Daed,* Jesse and Joshua should not be on the plow by themselves. They're not old enough to be left unattended." She turned to Saul, and he couldn't help but smile. She was fearful for her brothers' safety — as she should be — but she'd also just invited Saul into their lives, intentionally or not.

"Nee, nee. I'm not having Saul work our land. This was an accident and no one's fault." Wayne scowled, shaking his head.

"Daed's right about the garden. We've gone without one for a long time. But we do need the planting finished." Rosemary sighed as her eyes met Saul's, but she quickly turned to her father. *"Daed,* it's just not safe for Jesse and Joshua to be on the plow by themselves." She shook her head. "Too many accidents happen out in the fields."

Wayne didn't say anything, and Saul knew

it was hard for him to let another man finish where he'd left off, but Wayne was wise enough to know that Rosemary was right.

"I can start Monday. Beginning next week, I don't have any construction jobs. If we still don't have any jobs by the time Monday comes around, I'll bring my crew and we can knock it out fast."

Wayne looked up at Saul and ran his hand the length of his beard. "Hmm . . . the more I think about it, I do like the idea of you putting in a garden."

Rosemary took a step toward the hospital bed, her face drawn into a frown. "*Nee, Daed.* I'll get to it."

Wayne's left eyebrow rose a fraction. "When, *mei dochder*?" Then he shifted in the bed to face Saul. "Rosemary has her hands full with the *kinner.* It would be nice to have a garden, and I think once it's in, Rosemary will be able to maintain it. But I will only allow this if I pay you a fair wage for doing it."

Saul shook his head, but before he could argue, Wayne added, "That's the offer. And if I was a man without any work lined up for the following week, I'd take it." He gave his head a taut nod.

Saul felt his face redden, and he avoided Rosemary's eyes for a few moments, but he had to know her reaction to this plan, so he glanced her way. Her eyes were cast toward the floor, her arms folded across her chest. It looked like she was holding her breath.

Saul looked out the window and rubbed his chin, then glanced back at Rosemary. He wasn't sure . . . but he thought he saw her smile.

It was just enough to give him hope.

"It's a deal. I'll see you first thing Monday morning."

CHAPTER THREE

Rosemary helped her father out of the hospital bed and into the wheelchair the nurse had brought, wishing it was anyone other than Saul who would be spending time at their home. But she figured she would stay inside and avoid him. In the end, the planting would be done, and she'd have a garden. And that would put an end to Katherine showing up with her vegetables. Rosemary would have her own garden. And if Saul did things right, maybe she'd have vegetables to be proud of.

Saul pushed the wheelchair until they were outside the hospital. Barbie lived in Paradise, so Rosemary knew it wouldn't take her long to get back to the hospital.

"Wayne, is there anything else I can do for you?" Saul hung his head for a moment before he looked back at her father.

Daed shook his head. "I can tell I'm not going to like those things." He nodded toward the crutches Rosemary was carrying. "But it could have been worse, and I wasn't watching where I was going."

"It was my fault," Saul said again. They all started moving toward the circular drive when Barbie pulled up in the van. It was still sprinkling, and as Saul helped her father into the front seat, Rosemary was thankful the area was covered by an awning. She realized that Saul would need a ride home too.

"We will drop you at your *haus* on the way." Rosemary opened the sliding door and climbed in the van, then scooted to the far side. Saul just nodded, and they were all quiet on the way to his house. After a while, Rosemary shifted her eyes to the right to peek at Saul. No smile, and his boyish dimples weren't visible. He was staring out the window.

"Joshua and Jesse can help you in the fields and with planting the garden, but it won't be till late afternoon since they're in school most of the day and have chores." Rosemary waited until Saul turned her direction before continuing. "So I don't know how much time they'll have."

Saul smiled, but just barely. "*Nee,* I'll be able to do it."

After a few minutes, Rosemary swallowed

hard and asked, "How's your arm?"

Saul offered her another weak smile. "It's fine."

Rosemary's father looked over his shoulder. "It's a nasty case of road rash. I heard the nurse say that. I also heard her say it was real important that you take the antibiotics they prescribed." He turned back around and spoke to Barbie. "Can you stop at the pharmacy before you drop Saul? The boy needs his medication."

"That's a *gut* idea. *Daed,* you have prescriptions too." Rosemary leaned forward and put a hand on his shoulder as Barbie turned the corner, nodding that she'd heard.

"I'm not taking those pills for pain. Made me feel all loopy." He scowled as he shook his head.

Rosemary glanced at Saul and wondered if he was so quiet because he felt bad about everything or because he was in pain. She bit her lip for a few moments. "Does it hurt?" She was directing the question to Saul, but both her father and Saul answered no at the same time. Rosemary suspected that neither of them was being completely truthful, and as Saul flinched, Rosemary wondered how he was going to finish planting the alfalfa and get a garden put in with his arm in such bad shape.

"We've gone without a garden for a long time." Rosemary kept her eyes straight ahead as she spoke. "Maybe just finish the little bit of planting *Daed* has left and don't worry about the garden."

Saul glanced at her but then looked forward. "*Nee,* I'm going to get the garden put in too." He flinched again, and Rosemary wondered if this was about needing the money. She knew that was why her father had changed his mind about having Saul put in the garden. *Daed* saw an opportunity to have a garden for the first time in years, but he also saw a chance to help someone.

"If that arm gives you trouble, Saul, I don't expect you to do either of those jobs," her father said. "Katherine Huyard keeps us supplied with fresh vegetables. And she doesn't have any chickens, so I try to make sure she always has plenty of eggs." He twisted around. "That reminds me, Rosemary, I want you to pick out one of the goats to give Katherine. She's been mighty *gut* to us, and her only goat died last week. She loves to make soap from the goat's milk, like your *mamm* used to do."

Rosemary was quiet. She thought about not seeing Katherine so often once the garden was finished. For the first time, she wondered what Katherine's life must be like. Lonely, she decided. No matter her bubbly personality, Katherine was bound to miss her husband. They'd been married a long time, at least ten years.

Rosemary was sure she'd let her own bitterness affect her attitude lately. Just because she was unhappy, she surely didn't wish that on others. She tried to recall the last time she laughed and couldn't. One word always came to mind. *Cheated.* God had taken her mother much too soon. And Rosemary had no time to herself amidst taking care of her father and brothers. As much as she loved them all, she often found herself wondering if happiness would ever come her way. She glanced at Saul again. And the same word surfaced. She'd been *cheated* out of a relationship with the one man she'd wanted to be with.

When Barbie parked at the pharmacy, Rosemary offered to go in and get both of their prescriptions. The men both nodded, and Saul said to let him know how much his was.

Once Rosemary was in line at the pharmacy, she asked the woman in front of her what time it was. She'd already called Esther and left a message, telling her what had happened. And she'd asked Esther to meet the boys at the house after school if they

41

were still at the hospital. But it looked like Rosemary and her father would be home in plenty of time. She would ask Barbie to get word to Esther.

Thirty minutes later, her father was asleep in the front seat, and they were pulling into Saul's driveway. It was a beautiful home, a big place that had been in his family for three generations. The farmhouse looked freshly painted, and so did the white picket fence surrounding a lovely garden. All the flower beds were filled with colorful blooms. Rosemary felt a pang of jealousy but quickly stuffed it away. She didn't want to be that kind of person. Maybe someday she'd figure out how to balance her time well enough to have a lovely home, an organized household, and flourishing flower beds. She thought about Katherine. *And freshly ironed dresses, aprons, and kapps.* But she sat taller, smug with the idea of having her own garden soon. The price was having Saul around for a week. Maybe the Lord was angry at Rosemary to put such temptation right outside her own front door. She cringed, knowing that wasn't how God worked. And despite her feelings for Saul, Rosemary knew it was a temptation she would have to resist.

Elizabeth Petersheim shielded her eyes from the drizzle as she hurried down the porch steps and across the yard. She was at the van when Saul slid the door open.

"I've been worried sick. Your father got the message you left at the shanty, but not until an hour later." Elizabeth's eyes drifted to her son's bandaged arm. "Are you in pain?"

"*Nee.*" Saul stepped out of the van, and Rosemary wondered if he'd been given pain medication at the hospital. He winced as he stood, and Rosemary's father awoke and rolled down his window.

Elizabeth and *Daed* exchanged greetings, and Elizabeth asked how he was feeling. "I will be just fine. *Danki,* Elizabeth." Her father turned to Saul. "I was running just as hard and fast as you were. This wasn't anyone's fault. Just an accident. But I appreciate your offer to finish the planting, and it will be nice to have a garden again."

Rosemary saw the look in her father's eyes, the faraway gaze he got when he was thinking about her mother.

"I'll be there next Monday after we finish the job we're working on this week." Saul was holding his injured arm now, his mouth tight and grim, like he might be gritting his teeth. "Stay off that ankle as much as you can for a few days before you start using the crutches, like the doctor said." He reached into his pocket, pulled out some money, and handed it to Barbie. She argued and tried not to accept it, but in the end, Saul convinced her to take it. Gas wasn't cheap these days. He'd already paid Rosemary for his prescription.

Elizabeth latched onto Saul's arm. "*Danki* for bringing him home, and, Wayne, please let me know if you need anything. Take care." She gave a quick wave as she tugged on Saul's uninjured arm. "Let's get you out of the rain."

It was endearing the way Elizabeth nurtured her grown son. Rosemary assumed those maternal feelings must hang on forever, no matter how old your children got. Rosemary wanted nothing more than a houseful of children. And a husband to help rear them. She looked at Saul. He waved, and just before he turned to leave, Rosemary saw him clench his jaw. She had no doubt that Saul was hurting much more than he'd let on. She waited until they were almost home before she said anything.

"*Daed,* I'll make time to plant the garden. Maybe Saul can just supervise Jesse and Josh on the plow."

Her father twisted to face her. "I know you have way too much to do, *mei maedel.* I don't think I've ever pushed you about

44

that garden. Besides, it sounds like Saul could use the money if he doesn't have any work lined up for next week. I'm sure Katherine will keep us stocked with vegetables until our garden starts producing." *Daed* smiled. "It's a *gut* arrangement, trading eggs and a goat for her produce. But even after our garden is flourishing, I'll continue to invite Katherine to gather eggs for herself. No need for her to bother with chickens when we have such a plentiful supply of eggs."

Rosemary was quiet as she pondered exactly what it was about Katherine that she didn't like. Yes, she was a bit jealous that Katherine always seemed to have herself together and be so organized and cheerful. Rosemary knew good and well that jealousy was a sin, but even as she made a mental note to work on it, something else about Katherine bothered her. Something Rosemary couldn't quite put her finger on.

Saul went straight to the bathroom and sat down on the side of the tub, cradling his arm as he bit his bottom lip to keep from crying. Whatever they'd given him in the hospital before they treated his wound had worn off, and it felt like his arm was on fire from his elbow to his wrist. He'd turned down the prescription for pain medication, thinking it would slow him down and make him sleepy. Right now, all he wanted to do was sleep. He would take the antibiotics like the doctor said and hope that he healed quickly, for sure by next Monday when he needed to start work at the Lantzes' place. He would spend the rest of the week mostly supervising and give his arm a break.

He'd seen a softer side of Rosemary, and as much as he looked forward to the possibility of spending more time with her, it was going to be a challenge to get the work done unless his arm was much better. He jumped when someone knocked on the bathroom door.

"Saul, are you okay? *Mamm* said you hurt your arm. Do you need anything?" His sister was the caregiver in the family, even more so than their mother. Saul could remember when Lena was younger and she'd told everyone that she was going to leave the community to go be a nurse or doctor. At some point she'd given up the idea, and two years ago she got baptized. But she was born to tend to others.

"I'm okay, Lena."

"I'm going to help *Mamm* get supper started. You holler if you need anything."

Saul waited until Lena's footsteps got

farther away, then he pulled his arm close to him, and for the first time since he was a young boy, he cried. The doctor had told him that it was a nasty wound, but he didn't realize how bad it was until the pain medication wore off. He'd made a point not to watch the doctor cleaning and bandaging it. Saul planned to tend to it himself and do his best to help out the Lantzes. He was thankful he'd hurt his left arm and not his right.

Rosemary had acted a little like the girl he remembered and the young woman he'd fallen in love with years ago. Compassionate and loving. She wasn't the spirited, happy person she used to be, but Saul was committed to peeling back the layers of sadness that had consumed her since her mother died. He couldn't imagine that kind of pain, to lose someone so close. But surely the old Rosemary was in there somewhere, and he wasn't going to stop searching. He dabbed at his eyes, glad no one was around to see him like this. He dreaded having to change the bandage on his arm tomorrow. Maybe he'd let Lena do it after all. For now, he just wanted to rest. Despite the aroma of something delicious wafting up the stairs, Saul walked to his room and eased down onto the bed. He would rest for just a bit before supper.

CHAPTER FOUR

Monday morning, Rosemary finished scrambling eggs and making *scrapple* while her father and the boys sat patiently at the kitchen table. Over the past week, her father had gotten used to his crutches and was getting around pretty well. Katherine had been to the house every day bringing not just vegetables, but also pies, casseroles, and loaves of bread. And in exchange, she'd picked up some eggs and accepted one of their goats. They had a dozen of the animals, so they wouldn't miss one.

She hadn't had a chance to chat with Katherine much, and that was okay. Her father usually met her at her buggy, then together they went and gathered eggs. Rosemary was thankful for Katherine's help, and even though she felt inferior, Rosemary was working to shed any bad feelings about the woman. Katherine had good intentions.

Rosemary put the bowl of eggs on the

table and sat down. After they bowed their heads and prayed silently, her father pointed his fork at both Jesse and Joshua.

"Saul will be here today to finish up the planting and to start a garden for your sister. If he doesn't bring his crew with him, get your chores done after school, then see if you can give him a hand." He looked down and scooped up a forkful of eggs.

Jesse and Joshua both frowned as they glanced at each other. At eleven and thirteen, both were at an age when they'd sometimes argue, but though they didn't look happy, neither said anything. Little Abner didn't seem to have a care in the world as he lathered up his biscuit with way too much butter. Abner had been spending a lot of time with their father. *Daed* would often sit on the couch and read, his foot propped up on the coffee table. He'd start each morning saying how useless he felt, but when Abner crawled up on the couch and snuggled in next to him with a book, both soon had big smiles on their faces.

Katherine usually came around late in the afternoons, mindful to come and go before the supper hour. Rosemary knew that she should invite Katherine for supper every now and then since the woman would most likely go home and eat alone. But would she find the inside of the Lantzes' house as untidy as the outside? She'd never known her father to be sloppy, but now that he was couchbound most of the time, he'd started leaving his glasses and plates on the coffee table. Books would pile up on the floor and end tables, and this morning he'd spilled coffee on the counter and hadn't cleaned it up. Rosemary was happy to take care of her father, but other things then got pushed aside. She glanced at the wood floors in the kitchen that desperately needed sweeping.

"I don't want peanut butter and jelly," Jesse said as he inspected the contents of his lunch pail.

Rosemary knew it wasn't his favorite, but she'd run out of lunch meat, and she was on the last of the groceries. She needed to make a trip to town. Jesse was a picky eater, and most of what Katherine brought, he wouldn't touch. "Well, it will have to do for today." She opened the refrigerator and stowed the butter. Jesse stormed off, letting the screen door in the living room slam behind him.

Once the boys were off to school, she finished the breakfast dishes and wiped down the counters and stovetop. She'd just reached for the broom when she heard a buggy coming up the driveway. *Saul.*

She looked out the window as Saul tethered his horse to the fence, but then stepped out of sight when he came toward the house. The doors were open, as were the windows, but it wouldn't cool down until after sunset. She pulled a handkerchief from her apron pocket, dabbed at her forehead, then put it back. By the time she reached the living room, her father was on his crutches, pushing the screen door open. Rosemary waited until Saul was inside and her father was finished explaining what was left to do in the fields, then she asked about Saul's arm. It was still bandaged from his elbow down to his wrist.

"Much better," he said, barely smiling. "And it will just be me doing the work. We ended up getting a pretty big painting job the end of last week, so my whole crew is working on that. It might take me awhile since I'll be working by myself."

Daed scratched his forehead as he leaned most of his weight on one crutch. "Saul, if you need to supervise your employees, or . . ."

"*Nee, nee.* They'll be fine. I've got plenty of people on the job site, so this works out *gut.*"

Daed nodded. "Hopefully Josh and Jesse can give you a hand after school."

Abner walked up to where they were standing in the living room and tugged on Rosemary's blue dress. She glanced down at him. "What is it, Abner?"

"Is Katherine coming today?"

Rosemary glanced at her father, but he was busy readjusting his crutches and didn't look up. "I guess. She comes by most days."

"Gut." Abner walked over to the couch and sat down. She hadn't been giving Abner much attention lately. There'd just been so much to do. Sometimes Abner walked to the chicken coop with their father and Katherine to collect eggs.

"Well, I'll get to it." Saul tipped the rim of his hat, then turned to leave.

"Dinner is at noon," Rosemary said as he closed the screen door behind him.

Turning back around to face her, Saul said, "Lena packed me a lunch, so I can just eat in the fields and get right back to work."

"I won't hear of it." *Daed* pounded one of the crutches against the wood floor. "It's mighty hot already for May. You'll need a break from the heat and a *gut* meal in your belly."

Saul nodded, glancing at Rosemary with a slight grin. "I'm sure whatever Lena packed won't be nearly as *gut* as Rosie's cooking."

Rosemary felt the flush rising up her neck to her cheeks, but before she could acknowledge the compliment, Saul had turned around and was heading down the steps. Having him around for the next week or so was going to be torture. She planned to stay busy, even though no amount of chores was going to completely rid her mind of him.

She spent the rest of the morning trying to get the kitchen spic-and-span in between running loads of clothes through the wringer and hanging them on the line to dry. When she'd pinned a load of towels to the line earlier, she'd seen Saul guiding the horses and plow across the far stretch of land. Now as she took down the last load from the line, she didn't see him anywhere. She was walking back to the house when she heard him call her name. She stopped and turned around, balancing the laundry basket on her hip. Her father was right. It was hot for this time of year. She ran the sleeve of her dress across her forehead and squinted from the sun's glare as she waited for Saul to reach her.

"I'm going to finish planting today, then tomorrow I'll get started on your garden. Do you have a tiller, or should I bring one from home?"

Rosemary shifted the laundry basket to

the other hip as she thought for a moment. "I think we have one. I'll check with *Daed* to make sure it still runs." She glanced at his arm. "So, you said it's much better?"

"*Ya.*" Saul was staring at her, and she hated that she could feel herself blushing again.

"I'll be serving lunch in just a few minutes if you want to wash up." She nodded toward the pump on the north side of the house, but Saul didn't move. Then he took a slow step toward her and leaned closer. Rosemary couldn't breathe. As his face neared hers, she fought the panic pounding in her chest. Even though he towered over her by several inches, he was hunched down enough that he could easily kiss her. Saul was the only man she'd ever kissed, and even though it had been five years, she could still recall the heady sensation his kisses brought on and the tenderness of his touch. She should put some distance between them and not do anything to lead him on. The logical part of her brain told her this since they couldn't have a life together, but instead she barely parted her lips and thought about how often she'd dreamed of this moment.

Saul reached up with his right hand and swatted at her prayer covering. She dropped the clothes basket and brought a hand to her head. "What are you doing?"

"Sorry!" he said when Rosemary jumped. "A bumblebee was crawling on your *kapp*. Lena got stung by one last week, and it swelled up to the size of a walnut. She was miserable for days."

"Danki," she said softly as she leaned down and picked up the laundry basket, glad her freshly folded towels hadn't spilled onto the grass. She turned and hurried to the house without looking back. Her heart was still pounding, and she was weak in the knees. There was no doubt in her mind that she would have let Saul kiss her. He would have felt the love she had in her heart for him. It had been hard enough to walk away from him when they were teenagers. She'd cried for two weeks. It would be even harder now. She needed to be careful to not get too close to him since she wasn't sure she could trust herself.

Saul ate as much of the cheesy salmon casserole as he could. Neither his mother nor Lena ever made salmon, so it should have been a nice treat. It tasted wonderful, and he'd known for years that Rosemary was a good cook, but his arm was throbbing to the point that he felt a little light-headed.

She'd been watching him during the meal, and he wondered if she thought he didn't like the meal, even though he'd commented a couple of times about how good it tasted. By the time she put dessert on the table — a raisin crumb pie — Saul was sweating like it was over a hundred degrees. It was warm, but a nice breeze blew through the screens, and it wasn't hot enough for him to be perspiring this much. He dabbed at his forehead with his napkin. Again. Then he ate some of the pie, but couldn't finish it.

"Everything was really *gut,* Rosie." He laid his napkin across his plate, hoping she wouldn't notice how much was left. Wayne and Abner excused themselves and went into the living room, so Saul stood up, and sure enough, the room spun a little. He hoped Rosemary didn't notice the color draining from his face as he headed toward the back door.

"Saul."

He swallowed hard and turned around, lifting an eyebrow. *"Ya?"*

She walked toward him and cupped his left arm in her hand. Saul flinched, but noticed that fluid was draining through his bandage. He hadn't let Lena change the bandage in three days, for no other reason than it hurt. Saul thought of himself as pretty tough — until it came to blood or wounds. Then he was worse than a five-year-old.

"This looks terrible." Rosemary gently cradled his arm in her hands. "Did you bump it or something while you were on the plow?"

Saul looked down at the yellowish color oozing through his white gauze, and he silently prayed for God to not let him pass out. He eased his arm away from Rosemary. Under other circumstances, he would have basked in the tenderness of her touch, but his feet were failing him. He sat down at a kitchen chair and forced a smile.

"It's okay. Really."

Rosemary shook her head. "It is *not* okay. Wait here." She left the kitchen and passed through the living room toward her father's room, but the door was shut. He and Abner were either napping or *Daed* was reading Abner a story. Either way, she didn't want to disturb them. She hurried upstairs to her bathroom and found her first-aid kit. With three brothers, she had doctored her fair share of wounds. When she returned to the kitchen, Saul's face was pasty white.

"Are you going to *faint*?" She raised an eyebrow, and Saul grunted.

"Of course not."

Rosemary wasn't so sure as she sat down in a chair beside him and gently raised his arm to have a closer look. "Has your *mamm* or Lena been tending to this, changing the bandage?"

"Uh . . . *ya.*"

Rosemary frowned. "I think we need to take this bandage off and have a look."

"It's fine. Really. And I've got lots of work to do."

"You won't be getting any work done if you don't take care of this. I'm going to change the bandage for you. Did the doctor in the emergency room give you any medications to take?"

"I've been taking antibiotics."

Rosemary reached for a small pair of scissors in her first-aid kit. "I'm going to snip this tape, then change your bandage."

Saul pulled his arm away. "*Nee.* No need. I'll have Lena change the bandage when I get home."

"Then go home now." Rosemary put the scissors back in the box.

"I can't. I want to get the alfalfa in the ground today. I'll take care of it this evening."

Rosemary put her elbows on the table, rested her chin in her hands, and twisted

59

slightly to face him. "Saul Petersheim, you are white as these walls, and you look like you're about to pass out."

He shook his head, grinning slightly. "*Ach, nee.* I don't know why you think that."

"Then let me change the bandage."

"*Nee.*"

"I think you're afraid."

Saul grunted again. "I'm not afraid of anything." He stood up. "Now, I'm going to get back to work."

Rosemary watched him teetering, and she didn't want Saul ending up in the hospital on her watch. "I'm going to get *mei daed.*" She stood up, folded her arms across her chest, and looked up at him. "You're not well enough to be out on that plow. Maybe you can supervise Jesse and Josh when they get home from school, but you're not going back out there."

"I'm a grown man. I think I know when I'm well enough to work and when I'm not."

"Then let me have a look at your arm."

"*Nee.*" Saul turned toward the door, pulled the screen wide, and wobbled down the porch steps. Maybe he was running a fever. She followed him, but stopped on the bottom step as he hurried across the yard.

"I'll go out with you Saturday night if you come back here and let me have a look at your arm." Rosemary brought a hand to her chest as she squeezed her eyes closed for a few moments. When she opened them, Saul was walking toward her. *What was I thinking?*

He stopped in front of her, smiled broadly, and held out his arm. "Here you go."

Rosemary huffed, spun around, and went back into the kitchen. She could hear Saul following. "You know, I shouldn't have to bribe you to get you to take care of yourself."

"You change your mind already?"

She pulled out a chair and pointed at him. "Sit." She sat next to him. This was all she needed . . . to have yet another person to take care of. She could be cleaning the kitchen floors right now. But this was Saul, and when she felt him trembling as she snipped the tape and unwound it from his arm, she said softly, "I'm going to be very gentle, okay? And if I do something that hurts, you just tell me."

Saul nodded but turned his head the other way. She recalled the time Jesse had borrowed an *Englisch* boy's skateboard and taken a bad fall. Rosemary wondered if Saul's arm would look anything like that. Jesse had slid across the concrete on his left knee, and it had been a real mess for a while. But Jesse was only nine at the time and had been much braver than Saul was being now. And she hadn't had to bribe Jesse to let her tend to him.

She glanced up at Saul, and it was impossible not to feel sorry for him. He was still white in the face, and his arm was shaky. Rosemary was a little afraid of what she might see. As she began to unwrap the dressing, Saul's breathing sped up. This was surprising to her, that he was so fearful. In every way, he'd always appeared confident, as if he had no fear.

"Are you okay?"

"*Ya*. Sure." He tried to smile but avoided looking at his arm, and Rosemary wasn't convinced that he wouldn't keel over right there at the kitchen table. She took off the last of the bandages. Saul cringed.

"It's not bad. It just needs to be cleaned up. I'll put some topical antibiotic on it as well." Rosemary spoke in a slow, calm voice, even though she was shocked by what she saw. He was missing several layers of skin, and the last thing he needed to be doing was plowing or putting in a garden. The wound was clearly infected.

Rosemary doctored him up and put on a new bandage. If he was this much of a baby, she figured he probably hadn't let Lena change the bandage in days.

"All done." She gave him back his arm. "You really need to change this bandage every day." She stood up, and he did too. "No more working here, though, until your arm is healed. You don't want to get dirt in that wound. We've gone without a garden for this long, we will be just fine. And Katherine will keep us stocked with veggies."

"I think I can finish planting the alfalfa today, then I can start on the garden tomorrow." He glanced down at his arm, then up at Rosemary, smiling. "Your touch is as tender as I remember."

Rosemary swallowed hard and looked down. By going out with him on Saturday night, she was going to send him the wrong signal.

When she didn't respond, his smile faded. "I'll probably just bring our tiller from home. We've got a really *gut* one."

Rosemary nodded and Saul walked outside. Obviously he wasn't going to heed her warning to take it easy the rest of the day. She stood on the porch step and watched him walk across the front yard until he disappeared behind the barn. All the while, visions of them together on Saturday night swirled in her head.

What have I done?

CHAPTER FIVE

Saul showed up the following morning with the tiller on a small trailer he'd hitched to the back of his buggy. Finishing the alfalfa proved to be a large task. He was glad that Jesse and Josh had shown up after school. Even though Saul had already completed the planting, the boys took the draft mules to the barn, brushed them down, and got them stowed for the evening. Everything was going well at the job site, and the crew was staying busy, so he didn't want to pull anyone away to help him with the garden. His arm wasn't as sore, but he was embarrassed about his behavior in front of Rosemary. What kind of man would accept a date as a bribe? He planned to let Rosemary off the hook today.

It was midmorning when Rosemary walked out to the garden area. Saul had cleared most of the weeds with the tiller, but he was pulling the ones against the fence with his hands. When she got closer, he saw that she was wearing working gloves.

"I told you that you cannot get that wound dirty." She put her hands on her hips. "I'm going to help you with the garden, even though this whole project is nonsense. Why grow vegetables when you can buy them in town?"

Saul used his good arm to swipe his forehead before beads of sweat trickled down his face. "There's nothing better than using the land that the Lord gave us to grow food to nourish our bodies." He walked closer to where she was standing on the other side of the white picket fence. A fence that needed a fresh coat of paint. "It's a *gut* feeling to watch the fruits of our labor become whole." He smiled as he eyed his progress so far.

Rosemary shrugged and sighed deeply. "*Ach,* well. I'm never going to share your passion for gardening, but I'm going to help you so it will get done faster. And I'll do the dirty work, like planting the bushes, so you don't get dirt in your wound."

Saul laughed. "*Bushes?* We're not planting bushes. We're going to plant seeds."

Rosemary tapped a finger to her chin for a few moments. "Katherine is already getting lots of produce from her garden. Are you sure we have time to start from seed?"

"There's still about two weeks of planting season left, really right up until the end of May. And it won't take as long as you think before you have your own red, ripe tomatoes and cucumbers and . . . anything else you might want." He paused and glanced around. "I want to get the rest of the weeds cleared first, the ones up against the fence." He looked back at her and shook his head. "But I don't need you to help me."

Rosemary opened the gate that led to the other side of the picket fence where Saul was standing. Her father was at the kitchen table with bills and receipts scattered all around. Paperwork he said he'd let fall behind. He'd encouraged Rosemary to go outside and help Saul since both Jesse and Josh had stayed after school for a class project.

"I'm going to help you anyway." She wiggled her fingers inside the gloves that had belonged to her mother, then squatted down and started pulling the tall weeds by the roots. As she tossed the first handful over the fence, she couldn't help but recall how pretty this place had been at one time. But that fond memory clouded quickly as she focused on her mother and how much

66

she missed her.

Rosemary looked up. Saul was just standing there watching her. "I said I'm going to help, but you've got one *gut* arm to help, no?" Grinning, she tossed another handful of weeds over the fence.

Saul narrowed his eyebrows and shifted his weight, still staring at her. "You don't have to go out with me Saturday night."

Rosemary avoided his gaze and tugged at another group of weeds. "I know I don't *have* to." She should have just said *okay* and left it at that, but she was wondering why he was giving her an out. "You've been asking me for years." She shrugged, not looking up as she latched onto another cluster.

He squatted down beside her, and with his good arm, he yanked about four times the amount of weeds as she had, then tossed them over the fence. "And there's nothing I want more than to go out with you. But I want you to want to. Not because of a bribe or anything."

Rosemary's heart was beating faster than normal. "I do want to." She couldn't look at Saul, afraid she'd get lost in his eyes. Their date was all she'd thought about for the past few days. Memories of the summer she'd turned sixteen were fresh in her mind, but she was resolved to not get too close to him. But if he wanted to kiss her at the end of the night, Rosemary was going to let him. Then walk away. Like she'd done before.

"Why did you do it?" Saul sat down in the dirt, and when Rosemary looked at him, he said, "Why did you break up with me when we were kids? It was a long time ago, so can you tell me now? Because I've always wondered. I thought we were so happy, and . . ." He shrugged, and as Rosemary had feared, she was lost in the depth of his big blue eyes.

"I — I just . . . it just wasn't working out." She reached for another patch of over-growth, but Saul put his hand on top of hers.

"Did I do something?"

"Nee." She took her hand back. She couldn't tell him about the conversation she'd overheard that night. He would think she was as selfish and shallow as she felt. But it would most likely stop him from pursuing her. Maybe after their date she'd tell him. She wanted — needed — just one kiss. She felt like she was sixteen years old again with every emotion she'd had back then rising to the surface. Her eyes welled with tears.

"Rosie, don't cry."

■ ■ ■ ■

When she bit her lip and didn't speak, Saul racked his brain, thinking back five years. He could picture them kissing beneath the big oak tree behind the Millers' house that day. Everything had been perfect. But not long after the meal, she'd found him, and they'd gone behind the house again. Saul had thought she wanted to sneak in a few more kisses. Instead, she'd broken up with him, giving him a lame excuse about not wanting to settle down with one person yet. But she'd cried through the entire conversation, and Saul never bought into it.

He'd tried to get over her by asking other girls out, hoping that one of them would measure up to his Rosemary. But every time Saul could feel himself getting close to someone, it was Rosemary's face he saw, and he always pulled back. She'd held his heart back then. And she still did. He lifted his shoulders and dropped them slowly.

"Whatever I did, I'm sorry. I never would have done anything intentionally to make you unhappy. So I guess you're just going to have to tell me."

Rosemary's heart ached, but there was no

way she could tell him what fueled her decision to break up back then. She was still holding on to the same reasoning now, although as she gazed into Saul's eyes, she knew that being around him Saturday night was only going to make things harder. As much as she longed for his touch, even one kiss, she needed to take this opportunity to back out.

"You didn't do anything back then, Saul." She sat down and folded her legs beneath her, plotting how to avoid a lie but still not tell the truth. She shrugged, her eyes locked with his. "I just changed my mind."

"You changed your mind?" His voice was curt. Not that she blamed him. "You just changed your mind about wanting to date me? Did your feelings just . . . *change*? I mean . . ." He shook his head. "I don't get it."

Rosemary opened her mouth in an effort to say something that would make sense to him but still stay short of the truth. She bit her tongue, knowing that she needed to talk to Esther. She'd been keeping this secret to herself for a long time, and while Esther might think she was wrong in her decision, it seemed safer to run the truth by her friend before she fessed up to Saul. She lifted herself up, pulled off her gloves, and brushed the dirt from her apron.

Her heart was heavy, but she forced the words out of her mouth. "I guess we really shouldn't go out Saturday night."

Saul stood up and just stared at her for a few moments before he leaned down and picked up his gardening spade, shovel, and a pair of work gloves that were lying in the weeds. Then he turned and walked out of the gate, even though it was still early in the day. Rosemary left the garden area and slowly inched her way toward him. Surely he wasn't leaving.

"I'm not feeling well." He tossed the items in the small trailer he had hitched to the buggy. "Tell your *daed* that I will be back tomorrow."

"Saul?" Rosemary walked up to him and touched his arm. "I'm sorry."

He eased away from her and readied his horse. Then he opened the door of the buggy, but before he got in, he looked at her, an expression on his face that Rosemary couldn't read.

"You don't have to worry about me asking you out anymore." He hung his head for a few moments, then looked back up at her. "It's always been you, Rosie. The only woman I've ever wanted to be with. But a man can only take so much." He paused, shaking his head again. "I don't know why we broke up when we were teenagers, and it's already starting again. A few minutes ago, you said you *did* want to go out with me, and you've already changed your mind. I want to be with someone who is sure that they want to be with me. I was hoping we'd have a chance to spend time together, but you're right. It's not a *gut* idea."

As Rosemary watched him direct the buggy down the driveway and onto the road, a tear slid down her cheek. *It's always been you too, Saul.*

CHAPTER SIX

Rosemary spent the rest of the day weeding the garden, her self-inflicted punishment for the way things had ended with Saul. He was right. She did change her mind about him. A lot. Some days she thought she could get past what she'd overheard his mother saying that day, but other days . . . it was just too much to bear.

She pulled her gloves off and stared at her dirty hands. Dirt had gotten in her gloves, and her fingernails were a mess. She even had two blisters. *Guess I deserve it.*

Her father was sitting in the rocking chair on the front porch when Rosemary climbed the steps. She fell into the other rocker and leaned her head back.

"*Mei maedel,* I don't know why you did all that work. Saul said he was coming back tomorrow, no?"

"*Ya,* he'll be back." *And I guess I'll stay away from him.*

"You didn't say what was wrong with him earlier. Was it his arm?" *Daed* closed the newspaper he'd been reading.

"I'm not sure."

Her father shook his head. "He had no business taking on this project with his arm like that."

Rosemary thought about how Saul would probably be working on the garden for at least another week. Or maybe not. She'd noticed that he seemed to be taking his time, but that could have been due to his arm. Either way, she wouldn't be surprised if he picked up speed after what happened today. She looked up in time to see Katherine turning into the driveway. She lifted her tired body out of the rocking chair.

"I'm going to let the oven heat up while I take a bath. Where's Abner?"

Her father stood up. "He was in his room coloring when I came outside." *Daed* smoothed his beard with his hand and waved to Katherine. "What time will the other boys be home?" he asked before she walked in the house.

"I told them to be here in time for milking and chores, so pretty soon. And I'll check on Abner before I take a bath." She paused. "*Ach,* and, *Daed,* if it's okay, I'd like to take the buggy and visit Esther later.

74

I won't be home late."

Her father nodded, so Rosemary went inside, glanced at the clock on the mantel above the fireplace, then hurried upstairs to bathe. She wasn't sure how Esther would take Rosemary's news, but her friend would be honest. Esther had come into her life right around the time Rosemary's mother died, and they'd hit it off instantly. Esther's mother had died three years before that, and Esther had been the only person who understood what Rosemary was going through. But Rosemary hadn't ever told her about Saul. She'd come close, especially when Esther questioned her about him.

She peeked into Abner's room on the way to the bathroom. Her youngest brother had a small red suitcase filled with crayons and coloring books that *Daed* had picked up at a rummage sale a few weeks earlier. Abner was busy at work, so Rosemary scurried to the bathroom at the end of the hallway.

Always rushing. But today it was her own fault for letting guilt make her feel like she needed to give Saul a jump-start on the garden. No matter the circumstances, she could tell Saul was hurt, and that had never been her intention.

She was pulling her dress over her head and running the bathwater when she remembered she was out of shampoo. Her mother had always made their shampoo, but after she'd died, it was easier to purchase it in town — like the veggies — and she'd left a new bottle on the kitchen counter. She turned off the bathwater, lowered her blue dress, then ran downstairs. Supper was going to be late if she didn't hurry, and while she'd completely lost her appetite, she had a houseful of boys who'd be hungry come four thirty. She grabbed the shampoo from the counter and turned to go back upstairs when a movement outside caught her eye. She rolled her eyes when she saw her father and Katherine heading toward the barn. *I'll never be as perfect as her.*

As she watched them nearing the barn, Rosemary thought maybe she was being unfair to Katherine. The woman had been nothing but polite and generous. But when her father and Katherine stopped outside the barn and began kissing like teenagers, Rosemary grabbed her chest and gasped.

Her father had invited Katherine to stay for supper and then insisted that Katherine not help Rosemary prepare the meal, even though she'd offered twice. "*Nee,* you're our guest," her father had said both times.

Our guest and your girlfriend. Rosemary

had already calculated that Katherine was at least ten years younger than her father, and she couldn't stop thinking about what the woman's intentions were. As upsetting as it all was, this new knowledge had kept her thoughts from straying back to Saul, at least. This was what Rosemary had been unable to put her finger on.

"Everything looks lovely." Katherine's green eyes twinkled as she spoke, and she barely looked at Rosemary before she turned to *Daed* and grinned. *So that's what all the veggies, casseroles, and egg exchanges have been about.* Katherine could walk right into a readymade family and take over. No one was going to replace their mother, especially not someone who was only ten years older than Rosemary — no matter how much pressure it would take off of Rosemary.

It took everything she had, but Rosemary forced a smile. "*Danki,* Katherine. Glad you could join us." She glanced at her father as she set a bowl of mashed potatoes on the table, fighting the frown that was settling on her face. *A little young for you, Daed.* While it was customary for widows and widowers to remarry, her father had already gone four years, so Rosemary had assumed he had no desire to remarry. And why did it have to be

Katherine?

After the blessing, *Daed* reminded the boys about manners when they dove into their food like they hadn't eaten in a month of Sundays. Once everyone had a plateful, it got quiet, and Rosemary began to think about Saul. And the look on his face when he left, knowing that she'd put an end to his pursuing her. That should have made her feel good. One less thing to worry about.

Instead, it made her want to cry. She couldn't wait till after dinner when she could go to Esther's and talk with her about everything.

Her father had an extra helping of shoofly pie, and Rosemary was pretty sure he just didn't want Katherine to leave yet. They kept glancing at each other like they were love-struck teenagers, and Rosemary wondered how she hadn't suspected anything before.

Finally, Katherine left, and Rosemary peeked out the window. Her father had the good sense not to kiss Katherine good-bye out by the buggy. Who knows if the boys could see from the living room?

She quickly cleaned up the kitchen and headed to Esther's.

Fifteen minutes later, Esther's father greeted Rosemary at the door and motioned for Rosemary to go on upstairs. Esther was an only child, and she had a huge bedroom upstairs. Rosemary knocked.

"Esther, it's me."

Her friend answered right away, wearing a white nightgown, and her dark-brown hair hung to her waist. "You're already dressed for bed? It's not even dark yet."

On most nights, Rosemary didn't even get a bath until after sundown. She had to help Abner get settled in, and despite the mess they always left, she'd usually let Jesse and Josh bathe first. It would be nice to be tucked in early and have time to read a book.

Esther shrugged. "Nothing else to do."

Rosemary bit her bottom lip, realizing it must be lonely for Esther much of the time. She walked to the double bed and sat down. Esther sat down beside her.

"What's wrong?" Esther pulled one leg underneath her as she twisted to face Rosemary.

Rosemary took a deep breath. "I told Saul I'd go out with him Saturday night." Esther's face lit up right away. "But then I changed my mind and told him I didn't think it was a *gut* idea." Rosemary closed her eyes for a few moments and shook her head. "Everything got all messed up, and I can tell he's mad, and it's — it's just a mess."

Esther frowned as she folded her arms across her chest. "I don't understand you, Rosemary. And I'm not surprised he got mad. He's been wanting to date you for years. Then you say yes, then you say no . . ."

"I know, I know," Rosemary said. Her pulse quickened. "I love Saul. I really do. And I always have. But . . ."

Esther raised an eyebrow. "What! If you love him, why haven't you gone out with him all this time?"

"Promise me that you won't hate me or think I'm a horrible, shallow person," Rosemary said.

Esther reached for Rosemary's hand and gave it a quick squeeze. "There is nothing you can tell me that would make me think less of you."

I don't know about that. Rosemary lowered her head for a moment, then looked up at her friend. "Saul and I had been dating about three months when I overheard a conversation between Saul's mother — Elizabeth — and a visiting cousin." She paused, reflecting on how she felt when she listened in on the private conversation. "I know this is going to make me sound awful, but . . ."

Esther reached for Rosemary's hand

again. "What did you hear?"

Rosemary took another long breath and closed her eyes. "Saul can't have *kinner.*" She opened her eyes, and Esther's straight face was hard to read. "And I want *kinner,* Esther. I want a large family. And a life with Saul wouldn't include that."

Esther was quiet for a few moments. "Rosemary, I don't think you're awful, and I don't think any less of you. If anyone understands about wanting a large family, it's me. I'd do anything to have some siblings, and whenever I get married, I want lots of *kinner* too. So I don't judge you or think badly of you."

Rosemary threw her arms around Esther's neck. "*Danki,* Esther. I've been so afraid to tell you."

Esther eased away. "I'm guessing Saul doesn't know that you know . . . that he can't have children."

"*Nee.* I forced myself to walk away from the relationship when we were sixteen, thinking we were young and that I'd find love with someone else." She took a deep breath, then blew it out slowly. "But I don't think I will. It's always been Saul, and it seems so unfair that I can't have him *and* the big family that I want."

Esther just nodded, and Rosemary wished

she'd talked to her a long time ago.

"My heart hurts, Esther. I don't know what to do now." Rosemary realized this was the first time that she had ever considered sacrificing a houseful of children to be with Saul. She recalled the expression on his face, the sharp tone of his voice. There had always been a level of comfort in knowing that Saul stayed in pursuit of her. A few times, she'd worried when he'd started dating other girls. She'd never wanted to commit to him, but she hadn't wanted anyone else to either. She was ashamed that she felt this way.

"Are you sure you heard correctly?" Esther tucked her other leg beneath her, then scratched her forehead.

"Ya." Rosemary remembered the words exactly and the way they stung. "I was walking past where Saul's *mamm* and Naomi were talking, carrying Abner on my hip. He was about a year old, and he still used a pacifier. When he spit it out of his mouth, I leaned down to pick it up, and that's when I heard Saul's name. I lingered. His mother's exact words were, 'It has been very upsetting for us to learn that Saul won't be able to have *kinner.*' "

"And you never asked him about it?" Esther began braiding her hair off to one side.

"*Nee.* Because he'd know I broke up with him because of that, and that would make me look awful. Plus, I didn't want to embarrass him."

"You're not awful, Rosemary. You just know what you want."

Rosemary tried to smile. "Do I?" She wanted to tell Esther about her father and Katherine, but she'd probably shared enough with her for one night.

Saul was staring at the ceiling. He'd lain down before it got dark, and now his room was pitch black. After he'd left Rosemary's, he had checked on his crew, then come home to sit in his room and pout like he was sixteen years old again. He'd gone downstairs for supper, but excused himself early.

He'd spent all this time believing that Rosemary was the girl for him. Now he would have to readjust his thinking, even though he wouldn't be getting over her anytime soon.

Lena had changed his bandage earlier, and even though his sister was gentle, all Saul could think about was Rosemary's tenderness. He'd thought it was his calling to find the Rosemary he'd once known, the happy girl with a playful spirit, the girl who drifted

83

away from him one day without any explanation. Then her mother died, and any hint of playfulness disappeared overnight.

He was wide awake when he heard his cell phone vibrating on the nightstand by his bed. He mostly used it for work, but he always kept it on vibrate out of respect for his father, who was against the use of any phone in the house. Both his parents still walked a half mile to the phone shanty when they needed to make a call. Saul picked up the phone and saw that it was after ten o'clock. He recognized the number.

"*Wie bischt,* Katherine? Something must be wrong if you're calling this late."

"*Nee,* not really." She paused. "But maybe."

Saul eased himself up in the bed and fluffed his pillow behind him. "What's wrong?" He'd formed a friendship with Katherine after her husband died. They shared a love of gardening, and Saul had a love for Katherine's pineapple cherry crisp. After Katherine's husband was gone, she was so lost that she'd busied herself doing for others — sharing her vegetables, taking neighbors meals, and helping her sister with her children. She'd become like an older sister to Saul.

"I think Rosemary saw me and Wayne

kissing out by the barn. We were so anxious to see each other that I'm afraid we didn't use much caution. The older boys weren't home, and Wayne said Abner was upstairs in his room, but I'm worried Rosemary might have seen us. She was even more standoffish than usual."

Just hearing Rosemary's name caused his heart to beat faster. He'd spent so much time loving her, he didn't know how to stop. "*Ach,* well . . . maybe it's time for her to know how you feel about her father."

Katherine was quiet for a few moments. "I don't know. I love that man so much that I feel like it is written all over my face, but we wanted to wait until closer to October or November before we shared our news. We haven't set a firm date, and we will still have to publish our wedding announcement."

Publishing usually happened four to six weeks prior to a wedding, when the bishop announced the engagement to the congregation during Sunday worship service. Based on previous conversations he and Katherine had had, Saul was pretty sure Rosemary wouldn't be happy about the news, whether she heard it now or a couple of months from now.

"She's going to have to find out sometime." Saul yawned even though he didn't feel sleepy.

"*Ya,* I know. I just didn't want her to find out like that. And I was hoping that she and I would grow closer, but she seems to resent me at every turn. I mean, she is always nice and polite, but I can tell that it's forced. I would have never thought that I could love another man again, but I do. And I love his family. I feel very *gut* about all the boys, but it's Rosemary I'm worried about."

"I'd offer to talk to her, but I'm so angry at her that maybe that's not the best thing."

"Angry? For what, that she still won't go out with you? That's been going on for years."

Saul told her about the events of the day, his heart still heavy. "If she cared about me half as much as I care about her, she would have gone out with me a long time ago. She would have given me an explanation about what went wrong when we were younger. I'm just tired of the whole thing."

"Oh dear." Katherine was quiet, and Saul felt a little guilty for shifting the conversation to his problems.

"Not a problem. I'll just finish the garden like I promised Wayne. And I'll leave her alone."

"I don't believe that for one minute. Love

doesn't just go away overnight, and I've heard you say on many occasions that Rosemary is the only woman for you, and that you'd keep trying until she could see that and love you in return."

Saul sighed. "I know. I'm just irritated."

"Saul, life is too short for regrets or to take anything for granted. If you really love Rosemary, don't give up. Things happen on God's time frame, and maybe there is a reason that you two didn't get together when you were younger. Pray hard about it, and I will too."

"I will be praying for you too, Katherine. Might the Lord's will be done for both of us."

After he hung up, he still couldn't sleep. Katherine was as good a woman as he'd ever known, and Wayne was a fine man. She'd be a good wife to him and mother to his children. But he could see where Rosemary might feel as if her toes were being stepped on. He wished they were closer so he could talk to her.

For now, praying would have to be enough.

CHAPTER SEVEN

Rosemary watched from the porch as her father stowed his crutches in the back seat of Katherine's buggy before he hobbled to the front seat. Then they both waved as Katherine pulled away. Katherine had offered to take him to the market today. Rosemary knew good and well that her father was capable of taking himself. He'd already done so several times. She shook her head, disappointed that she hadn't seen the truth before. Everything Katherine had done for their family was only in an effort to win over her father. And apparently, she had succeeded.

She sat in the rocker on the front porch for a while, glad that school wasn't out yet and the boys were gone, glad that her father had left, and wondering what things would be like between her and Saul today, assuming he showed up. But when she saw his buggy pulling up the driveway, her stomach rolled, and she jumped from the chair and went into the house. She stayed to the side of the window and peeked a few times. Once he'd tethered his buggy, he hauled the tiller to the garden.

For the next two hours, she tried to stay busy. She got the floors cleaned, made a grocery list, and tidied up her father's bedroom. But not once did she pass through the living room without looking out the window toward the garden. Saul was a hard worker, and no matter what had happened, the man was easy on the eyes. He'd always been handsome, but for the first time since they were teenagers, she was envisioning a life with him. A life without children. Could she be happy, just the two of them?

She stood at the front door for at least five minutes before she started toward the garden. Her heart was heavy about Saul, and about the thought of Katherine becoming her stepmother, which just seemed outrageous. She wanted to be happy for her father, but she was having a hard time wrapping her mind around the fact that he must be in love with Katherine. Rosemary knew her father pretty well, and she didn't think he'd be behaving so carelessly unless he really loved Katherine. Thank goodness the boys hadn't seen any of their public affection.

Saul stopped tilling when Rosemary neared the gate. The man was dripping in sweat. *I should have at least brought him something cold to drink.*

"Wie bischt?" Rosemary tried not to cringe, unsure if Saul even wanted to talk to her. He wiped sweat from his face with a rag that was tucked in his pocket.

"Ach, it's going *gut."* He paused, the hint of a smile on his face. "Mighty warm out here, though." He pointed to a thermos lying nearby on the ground. "Finished that up already."

Rosemary took a step closer, until she was right on the other side of the fence. "If you'll hand me your thermos, I'll fill it up with iced tea."

"Danki, that would be great."

Rosemary stood there a few moments, curling her toes in the grass beneath her bare feet, feeling the awkwardness. No matter the situation, she couldn't see herself with anyone but him. *Is this Your plan for me, Lord? Am I to sacrifice my dream for a large family to be with Saul?*

"How's your arm?"

"Much better. *Danki."* He stood looking at her. Rosemary wondered if he felt half as awkward as she did. Maybe he just wanted her to go away.

"I'll go then and let you get back to work." She smiled, then turned to leave.

"Rosie?"

She stopped, turned around, and waited, her heart still pounding as hard as it was when she came out the front door. *"Ya?"*

Saul scratched his chin for a moment and grinned. "I thought you were going to help me."

She swallowed hard. "Uh . . . I . . . uh, I mean, you said your arm was better." She shrugged and looked down at the grass. "And after yesterday, I was thinking you probably didn't want me around." She looked up, knowing she sounded pitiful. But she felt pitiful.

"It's better, but that doesn't mean it doesn't hurt and that I couldn't use some help."

She stared at this handsome man standing on the other side of the fence, the one who had stolen her heart when she was young. His boyish dimples, beautiful blue eyes, and broad shoulders made her feel a bit weak in the knees, and with clarity, she could almost feel his lips on hers as they'd been five years ago. And she longed to feel them again.

"Okay." She pointed toward the house.

"My gloves are inside. I'll get them when I fill up your thermos."

Saul smiled and said, "I'll be here."

Saul watched her for a few moments before he started back to work, Katherine's words replaying in his mind. *". . . there is a reason that you two didn't get together when you were young."*

Saul had prayed about it last night. He'd worked hard at being mad at Rosemary, and her wishy-washy behavior was frustrating. But he loved her, a fact he couldn't deny. He did miss the Rosemary he knew at sixteen. *I wonder if I'll ever see that girl again.*

His arm was throbbing. He'd known that pushing the tiller would be the hardest part of this job, but he was almost done, then he could start planting the seeds. For Saul, that was the best part of putting in a garden. Though gardening was normally women's work, Saul had been in charge of it at his house for years. His mother and Lena would water and maintain it, but Saul laid the seeds in the soil, a process that made him feel closer to the Lord. He finished tilling just in time to see Rosemary pass through the opened gate toting his thermos and her gardening gloves.

"Here you go." She smiled as she handed

him the thermos, and Saul wished he could pull her into a hug. It would be more than enough for now. But the ice still felt thin, and he wanted to step softly.

"Danki." He chugged down half of the thermos, put the lid back on, and blew out a breath. "I needed that."

She folded her hands in front of her. "As you know, I've never put in a garden. I used to help *Mudder* when she was alive, but even then, I didn't like it, and I'm sure I was more hindrance than help."

"Come and see." He pointed to a large bag he'd brought and motioned for her to follow him. He kneeled down, and she did too. "We are late into the planting season. Some plants tolerate root disturbance and it's *gut* to start early. Broccoli, brussels sprouts, cauliflower, eggplant, and even tomatoes should be planted before now." He turned to her and smiled. "But we're going to plant tomatoes anyway. And there are some veggies that don't like to be transplanted that do well when you direct seed them. We're late on those, too, but they're cold hardy, like corn, beans, and peas."

Rosemary sighed and shook her head. "Gonna be a long time before those little seeds become vegetables."

Saul chuckled, which felt good in light of everything. "You might have to keep accepting vegetables from Katherine for a while. She's told me how much she enjoys her visits with your family." He paused. "And during one of our conversations, she even seemed a little disappointed that I was putting in a garden for you."

Rosemary frowned. *I bet she is.*

Saul was busy sorting through the seeds and putting them in piles. Rosemary wondered how often Saul and Katherine talked. Maybe Katherine was hitting on all the single men in the community, not just her father. Maybe she preferred men ten years older or ten years younger.

One thing she knew for sure — her father's heart was involved, and if Katherine's intentions weren't exclusive to *Daed,* she needed to know. As much as she would like Katherine out of the picture, she didn't want her father hurt. Accepting Katherine into their lives was the lesser of the evils, as long as she wasn't making herself available to other men.

"Are the two of you *gut* friends, you and Katherine?" Her stomach flipped, and she was suddenly afraid of the answer.

Saul stopped his seed sorting and looked

up at her. "*Ya,* we are very *gut* friends. Katherine is a wonderful person. Any man would be lucky to have her."

Rosemary swallowed hard, surprised that Katherine was a contender for Saul's affections after all the energy Saul had spent chasing Rosemary over the years. Jealousy was a sin, but Rosemary was experiencing it. Again. And both instances had one thing in common: Katherine. Everything about her rubbed Rosemary the wrong way, and the thought of Katherine and Saul together was even more disturbing than Katherine being with her father.

"I saw Katherine kissing *mei daed.*" The bold statement was fueled by jealousy, and as soon as she said it, she regretted it.

Saul didn't look up from sorting the seeds, but he grinned. "Or maybe you saw your *daed* kissing Katherine?"

Rosemary folded her arms across her chest. *Hmm . . .* He didn't seem a bit bothered by the news. "It's very inappropriate for them to be carrying on like that. I mean, what if the boys had seen?"

Saul stood up, brushed dirt from his pants, then shrugged. "I don't think the boys would have cared. I think they like Katherine."

Rosemary walked closer to Saul. "How do

you know so much about Katherine and *mei* family?"

Saul shrugged. "I told you. Katherine and I are *gut* friends. She loves gardening, so we started out sharing gardening tips, and the friendship just grew from there." He paused, swiping at a bee that was buzzing around him. "And she brings us lots of food. I'm especially fond of her pineapple cherry crisp."

Rosemary walked closer to him, close enough that she could see the tiny scar above his right eyebrow. She'd forgotten about it until now. She remembered when Saul got hit in the forehead with a baseball bat when they were young. He was playing catcher, and Levi Esh had swung the bat a little too close and nailed him in the forehead.

"Katherine brings food to your family?"

"*Ya.* And *Mamm* and Lena take things to her too. It's called *sharing.*" Saul winked, then tore open a package of seeds with his teeth.

"I share. All the time." *Forgive me, Lord.* It was a tiny lie. She'd been so busy feeling sorry for herself and tending to the household that she hadn't made much time to do for others. She reached for the package of seeds that Saul was getting ready to rip into.

"Give me that. You're going to break a tooth." She peeled back the top of the package and wondered why Saul had used his teeth. "There aren't many in here," she said. It would be winter before these seeds produced any vegetables, and they would probably freeze over. *By then, Katherine might be living with us, and then she can take care of the garden.*

She pushed the thought aside, and when Saul squatted down in between two rows of freshly tilled dirt, Rosemary did too.

"We've been lucky that it hasn't rained. It's best to plant in dry soil, fertilize, and then water like crazy when you're done."

Rosemary watched Saul lay out the seeds, spacing them perfectly with a steady hand. You would have thought he was performing surgery or that his life depended on the exact placement of each tiny seed. His expression was stern, his mouth tight, and his eyes completely focused on the task.

"These are fast-growers. The large-seeded ones usually are, like this squash." He delicately dropped the seed in, pushed on it, and looked up at her. "They'll root pretty fast." He wiped his brow. "That's the key. We want them rooted well. Then you'll just have to water them *gut* every day."

While Rosemary didn't relish the idea of

adding another task to her chore list, she had to admit, she'd be anxious to see the first signs of growth, and Saul's passion for gardening was almost contagious. Almost.

They finished the row of squash, then Saul walked to the other side of the garden where he'd left a brown backpack. He came back holding a tiny flag with the word *Squash* written on it. He stuck it in the ground. "There. The first row is done."

They both stood up, and Rosemary felt something slither beneath her bare foot. Without thinking, she jumped and threw her arms around Saul's neck. He swooped her up as she screamed. Nothing scared her more than snakes. She buried her head in his chest and clung to his shirt with both hands as he cradled her in his arms.

"Is it gone?" She held on tighter. "Please tell me it's gone!"

Saul held her even closer. "You're okay. It's all right." He spoke softly, tenderly. "It was a tiny grass snake." He eased her down on the ground, then burst out laughing. "No bigger around than a pencil, and not much longer."

Rosemary playfully slapped him on the arm. "It's not funny!" But the more he laughed, the larger her smile grew, and before she knew it, she was bent at the waist laughing just as hard as he was, and thinking how dumb she must have seemed. It felt good to laugh. Saul stopped before she did, and when she faced him, he was staring at her.

She struggled to get control of herself, and finally she said, "What? Why are you looking at me like that?"

"There she is."

Rosemary turned in a circle, looking all around before she turned back to him. A slight smile was on his face, but his eyes were serious and locked with hers. "Who?" she asked.

"The Rosie I remember."

CHAPTER EIGHT

By Friday, Saul was exhausted from planting. It took every ounce of patience he had to go so slowly. A garden this size could have been finished days ago, but things on the job site were going well, and he was stretching out his time with Rosemary for as long as he could. It had been a wonderful week, and they'd talked and been silly. But the old and the new Rosemary still came and went, and Saul could tell that something was weighing heavily on her. Sometimes she'd put distance between them, often going back in the house early, saying that she had chores to finish. He still wasn't sure where he stood with her, and neither had mentioned anything about going out on Saturday.

He looked up midmorning and saw her coming across the yard. She smiled and waved, and Saul decided he was going to officially ask her out on a date since things had been going so well.

"Are you still working on that garden?" She giggled as she came through the gate, and Saul's heart warmed.

"It takes a keen understanding of how to plant properly." Saul walked toward her as she drew closer, and it took everything in his power not to pull her into his arms. It had been torturous to be around her all week. In a good way.

She glanced around. "Looks like we'll finish today."

Saul wasn't sure, but he thought he heard a bit of regret in her voice. "I think so."

She reached over and touched his arm. A tingle ran up his spine, and he reminded himself to not just grab her, that it might ruin everything if he spooked her. "I see you're down to a much smaller bandage. Your wound must be healing nicely."

"*Ya*. I've even been changing the bandage myself instead of bothering Lena with it."

Rosemary laughed. "I know that was a big step. I've never seen a man who was such a baby about an injury."

Saul could feel his cheeks turning red. "*Ya, I know.*" He paused, rubbed his chin. "Rosie . . ." He took a deep breath. "Would you still like to go out with me tomorrow night?" He swallowed and held up one hand, palm toward her, and avoided her eyes. "I'll respect whatever you say." He waited a few moments, then looked up and steadied his gaze as he met eyes with her. "This will be the last time I ask." He stepped closer.

She kept her eyes on his, her expression not giving away what her answer would be.

He waited, his heart still thumping.

"Well," she finally said, smiling. "You have waited a long time for a date."

"*Ya.* I have."

"Under one condition."

Anything. He cocked his head to one side and waited for the terms.

"You have to finish the garden by yourself today. That will give me time to prepare tomorrow's meal for *Daed* and the boys, something they can easily heat up. None of them knows how to cook."

"It's a deal." He knew he could have the rest of the seeds in the ground in a couple of hours, but he was willing to stretch it out, hoping she'd come visit with him during the afternoon.

Rosemary reached into her pocket and pulled out a small white nylon bag, stared at it, then looked up at him. "Can we plant this somewhere?" She took out a seed, and Saul immediately knew what it was.

"A passionflower seed." He turned it over

in his hand, wondering which species it was. He knew that some passionflowers grew wild in much of the southern United States, but others were a bit harder to root.

"Mae Kauffman gave this to me. She remembered that it was *mei mudder*'s favorite." Rosemary reached over and touched the seed, her finger brushing against his, which seemed intentional. "Will it grow?"

Saul gazed into her eyes, not wanting to disappoint her. "I think so. But we should plant it in a pot until it sprouts, then it should be planted on the south side of the house." He pointed to one of the barren flower beds. "Over there would be *gut.*"

Rosemary had a faraway look in her eyes. "That's exactly where *Mamm* used to have a passionflower. But like everything else around here, I let it die."

"That will be a *gut* place for it. Do you have a pot we can put it in? It will need lots of water to make sure it establishes strong roots."

"*Ya,* I'll go get one." She bounced up on her toes for a moment before she took off toward the house.

Saul couldn't wait until tomorrow night.

After supper, the boys went outside to finish their chores. Rosemary finished cleaning the kitchen, then took the opportunity to spend some time alone with her father. He'd been quiet the past couple of days, and Rosemary had noticed that Katherine hadn't been by.

"Saul finished the garden today," she said as she sat down beside him on the couch. He had his foot propped up on the coffee table, and he was reading the Bible.

"Gut, gut." He didn't look up as he turned the page. "It will be nice to have fresh vegetables of our own."

Rosemary wondered what that meant. Would he be glad not to have Katherine bringing veggies anymore? Would Katherine already be living here, so it would be her garden anyway? She slouched against the back of the couch, crossed one leg over the other, and kicked her foot into action.

"Daed, is anything wrong?"

He turned another page and still didn't look up. *"Nee.* Why do you ask?"

"I don't know. You're just quiet."

"Ach, just tired of this foot, of the inconvenience." He pushed his gold-rimmed reading glasses up on his nose, and neither spoke for a few moments.

"I haven't seen Katherine in a couple of days," she finally said as she uncrossed her legs and turned to face him. She thought again about what nice things Saul had said about Katherine.

Daed took his glasses off, set them on the end table, and closed the Bible. He reached for his crutches, then slowly pulled himself up. Rosemary rose also, offering him a hand, but he shook his head. He took two steps toward his bedroom and didn't turn around when he said, "I don't suspect we'll be seeing much of her anymore."

He closed his bedroom door behind him, and Rosemary just stood there, staring at her father's closed door. There was no mistaking the sadness in his voice. The decision to stop seeing each other must have been Katherine's idea, and Rosemary wanted to slap the woman silly for hurting her father. She walked to his bedroom door, lifted her hand to knock, but then just softly placed her palm against the door. *Whatever happened, Lord, please give him peace and wrap Your loving arms around him.*

Rosemary had been praying more lately, and with each heartfelt prayer, she found herself reestablishing a relationship with God that she'd come close to abandoning. Once she'd started to shed some of the bitterness she'd been feeling, it was easier to see God's will. She was beginning to believe His plan for her didn't include children, but

He was giving her a chance at love, and Rosemary could no longer fight her feelings for Saul.

Before she could move forward with her own life, she would have to make things right for her father and Katherine. Katherine had tried so hard to be nice to Rosemary, and Rosemary hadn't behaved very well in return. But would Katherine really have ended the relationship because of Rosemary's attitude? She doubted it. But something must have happened . . .

Saturday morning, Rosemary awoke excited about her date with Saul, but she was worried about her father. He had slept late this morning and said he didn't want any breakfast. In her lifetime, Rosemary couldn't recall her father ever skipping a meal, except for once — the day *Mamm* had tried a new dish, and everyone in the family learned that *Daed* didn't like liver and onions. None of them did, except for Jesse. He'd eaten the leftovers for two days.

She made Jesse and Josh promise to keep an eye on Abner, and once she'd checked on her father, she hitched the buggy and headed to Katherine's. Her mind was awhirl with various scenarios. The one in the forefront was that Katherine had broken up with her father because of Rosemary's attitude toward her, although Rosemary had never been outright rude to the woman. Or maybe Katherine had found someone else, someone younger maybe. Either way, her father was suffering, and she was going to find out why.

Katherine's yard was perfectly maintained. *Of course.* Beautiful blooms in all the flower beds and a lush garden three times the size of the one Saul had put in for her family. The yard was freshly mowed, and the white clapboard house looked newly painted. Two cardinals were perched on the porch railing, and butterflies were plentiful. It looked like one of the paintings she'd seen at an *Englisch* shop in town.

She took a deep breath before she knocked, surprised that Katherine didn't have the door open, welcoming the breeze through the screen. She glanced around, and none of the windows were open either. Katherine's buggy was here, but maybe she had gone somewhere with someone else. She rapped on the door, and when no one answered, she was about to turn and leave when she heard footsteps.

Katherine opened the door a few inches and spoke to Rosemary through the screen. "Rosemary, what are you doing here?" She suddenly pulled the door wide. "Oh *nee* . . . is it your father? Is he all right?" Katherine brought a hand to her chest as her eyes grew round.

Rosemary was too stunned to speak at first. Katherine didn't have her *kapp* on, and her red hair was in a loose bun on top of her head, with lots of escaped strands sticking to her tearstained face. Dark circles hovered underneath swollen eyes, and her dark-green dress was wrinkled like she'd slept in it.

"*Daed* is fine." Rosemary leaned closer. "Can I come in?"

Katherine pushed the door halfway closed again. "Now isn't a *gut* time, Rosemary. Please forgive me." She started to close the door, but Rosemary yanked the screen door open, then gave the door a gentle push.

"What's wrong? Did you and *Daed* have a fight? I know about the two of you, and *Daed* seems just as sad as you are. What's going on?"

Katherine opened the door wide and stepped aside so Rosemary could enter.

"I had a feeling you knew about us." Katherine walked ahead of Rosemary toward the living room, so Rosemary followed. After Katherine raised the two green shades on the windows facing the road, she lifted the

108

panes and a welcome breeze wafted into the room. Katherine sat down on the couch and motioned for Rosemary to sit near her. Katherine looked a mess, but the inside of her house was equally as beautiful — and clean — as the outside.

"I saw you kissing out by the barn," Rosemary finally said.

Katherine reached for a tissue from the box on the coffee table, blew her nose, and nodded. "That's what I thought."

Rosemary studied Katherine for a few moments, more confused than ever. "Who ended things? *Daed* seems just as upset as you are. What happened?"

Katherine covered her face with her hands, crying and mumbling. Rosemary couldn't understand her, so she waited, then asked again, "What happened?"

Katherine moved her hands, folded them in her lap, and sat taller. She didn't even try to stop the tears from pouring down her cheeks. "I love your *daed* with all my heart. I never thought I'd love again after *mei* husband passed, but the Lord blessed me with a second chance. Or so I thought." She cried harder, and Rosemary wasn't sure that she should ask what happened again, but she did. And after a few more sobs, Katherine finally started to talk.

"We had planned to be married in October or November." Katherine quickly looked at Rosemary, but when Rosemary just nodded, she went on. "We were tired of sneaking around, especially from you and the boys." She hung her head. "I'm sorry about that. We both just wanted to be sure that it was a love to last the rest of our lives before we shared the news." She started shaking her head and crying again. "And I thought it was."

At this point, it was becoming obvious that her father had been the one to end the relationship. "So *Daed* called off the wedding?"

Katherine nodded and blew her nose again. Rosemary couldn't remember seeing such sadness since her mother died. "Why?" she finally asked. *Dear Lord, please don't let it be because of me, the way I acted, or anything I did.* Guilt wrapped around Rosemary and she knew that whatever Katherine's answer was, she wasn't feeling very good about herself.

Katherine gazed into Rosemary's eyes, and Rosemary stopped breathing and braced herself.

Katherine smiled. The kind of sad smile that makes the heart hurt. "He said he didn't feel that he deserved a second chance, and that marrying me would be dishonoring your *mudder.*"

"That's ridiculous!" Rosemary was relieved that blame hadn't been placed on her, but also shocked. "Of course he deserves a second chance. He's a wonderful man." She shook her head. "*Mei mudder* would want him to remarry. That's what the *Ordnung* encourages."

"And . . ." Katherine flashed the same smile, and Rosemary knew what was coming this time. "He knew that you didn't like me, so that was a problem too."

Rosemary lowered her chin, now fighting her own tears. "Katherine, it's never been that I didn't like you." She cringed at the lie, but she didn't want to hurt Katherine further. *Forgive me, Lord.*

Katherine raised her arms, then let them fall into her lap. "Then what was it? I would like to know." A tear rolled down her cheek. "I tried to always be nice to you. I love cooking and doing for others, but I started to wonder if you thought I was overstepping my bounds with you. I just wanted to help." She waved her arm around the house. "Perfectly clean. All the time. Do you know why that is?"

Rosemary didn't say anything, just swallowed.

"Everything is always in order because I have more time on my hands than I know what to do with. When there isn't anything left to do, the loneliness sets in, and I used to start missing John." She smiled. A real smile this time. "Then your father and I got close, and I was filled with hope about the future. It didn't take long for me to fall in love with him. I thought that I could be like a *mudder* to Abner since he didn't know his *mudder*. And I'd hoped to be a *gut* friend to the boys. And to you. I've admired you so much over the years." Rosemary's eyes grew wide, but before she could question Katherine, she went on. "Such huge responsibilities you have, tending to an entire household, your father, the boys . . . and to be so young."

Rosemary couldn't speak. She was suffocating with guilt, and even though she should shed the emotion, she didn't think she could.

"So, why don't you like me?" Katherine frowned, still crying.

Rosemary took a deep breath, not wanting to lie again. "It's just that . . ." She let out a heavy sigh. "You were . . . uh . . . always so *happy*. So organized and perfectly put together." She paused. "I guess I always felt inferior." Rosemary squeezed her eyes closed, cringing. When she opened them, Katherine started laughing.

"*Danki* for giving me something to laugh about. I'm so tired of crying." She shook her head and chuckled again. "Really? That's all it takes is a happy, organized person to offend you? Well, I assure you, I hadn't been happy for a very long time until your father. And I never wanted to make you feel inferior. I only ever wanted to help." She covered her face with her hands again as though she were hiding.

Rosemary knew she'd go home and talk to her father about this, but right now there was only one thing on her mind. She reached for Katherine's hand. "I'm sorry, Katherine."

"*Danki.*" Katherine looked up and sniffled. "Edna was a wonderful woman. I'd never try to replace her. I'd be happy to come in second."

"That's not what I meant." Rosemary paused. "*Ya,* I am sorry about you and *Daed,* but I meant . . . I'm sorry for the way I treated you. I'm ashamed of myself." She looked away, blinked a few times.

Katherine squeezed her hand. "I forgive you, Rosemary. Please don't feel shame. It's the devil's sword."

Rosemary let go of Katherine's hand and

stood up. "I'm going to talk to *mei daed,* see if I can make him understand how worthy he is of your love, and I'll be praying for you both."

Katherine threw her arms around Rosemary's neck. "*Danki.* I would spend the rest of my life loving him."

The embrace lasted several seconds, and Rosemary wondered how she'd ever misread this woman. She knew how. She'd been wallowing in her own dark place, walking a path away from the Lord, and resenting those who seemed to have it all. Rosemary couldn't have it all. But she could have Saul. She hoped.

She was almost out the door when Katherine touched her arm. "One more thing." She paused, dabbed at her eyes with a tissue, then smiled. "Saul loves you very much. He always has. And he would make a wonderful husband and father."

Rosemary smiled. "I know." She hugged Katherine again before she left, surprised that Katherine obviously didn't know that Saul was unable to have children.

CHAPTER NINE

Rosemary was glad to see her father up and about when she returned from Katherine's. He was sitting in one of the kitchen chairs reading the newspaper.

"Where'd you run off to this morning?" He took off his reading glasses, and he had the same dark circles under his eyes that Katherine had.

Rosemary pulled off her black bonnet and hung it on the rack by the kitchen door. "I went to see Katherine."

Her father stiffened. "It's not your business, Rosie."

She eased a chair out and sat down. "*Daed,* she's a *gut* woman who loves you very much. Allow yourself to be happy." *Something I haven't done myself.*

"How long have you known?" He scratched his nose but didn't look at her.

"Not long."

"I didn't think you cared for her." He

sighed and reached for his cup of coffee.

"I didn't know her, *Daed*." She waited, but her father was quiet. "She just made me feel . . . inadequate. But I was wrong, and I can't stand to see you upset."

Her father pushed his chair from the table, locked his crutches underneath his arms, and moved to the living room. Rosemary followed.

"Don't you want to talk about this?"

He didn't turn around as he headed toward his bedroom. "This isn't your business," he said again before he closed his bedroom door.

Rosemary stood on the other side of the door, tempted to burst in and make him listen to her, but she knew her father, and that wouldn't work.

Well, I'm going to make it mei *business.* She walked back to the kitchen, grabbed her bonnet, found her black purse, and headed out the door. A plan was working in her mind, and she knew she'd need Saul to help her.

Saul took extra time readying himself Saturday evening, and he even dabbed a splash of aftershave on his face, something Janet Murphy had given him after he'd helped her do some yard work. The *Englisch*

116

woman didn't know such luxuries were frowned upon. It was the first time he'd used it. He didn't want to offend anyone, but he was hoping to get close to Rosemary tonight.

By the time he got to her house, his heart was racing. He hoped that Rosemary's idea didn't backfire on her, but he was glad she'd included him in the planning. All day, he'd relived the three months they'd had that wonderful summer. He'd spent the past five years hoping for another chance with her. They seemed to be moving in the right direction, and he'd been praying that tonight would go well.

Wayne answered the door when Saul knocked.

"Glad to be having you for supper, Saul." Wayne shook his hand, then eased his crutches to one side so Saul could move into the living room.

"Glad to be here," Saul said as he shook his head. "How much longer on those crutches?" He sighed, knowing that everything had happened according to the Lord's plan. If he hadn't plowed into Wayne, he never would have planted their garden and gotten a bit closer to Rosemary. But it was still hard to watch Wayne hobbling around all because Saul had been in such a hurry.

"Not too much longer. I'll be happy to get rid of these cumbersome things. Poor Rosie has been taking up the slack, taking care of things I can't do." He chuckled. "Like that poor *maedel* doesn't already have enough to do."

Rosemary walked barefooted into the room wearing a dark-maroon dress and black apron. She was smiling from ear to ear, and Saul winked at her. He wanted to tell her how beautiful she looked, but not in front of her father.

"The boys aren't here tonight," Wayne said as he motioned for Saul to sit in one of the rocking chairs across from the couch. "Ben Smoker's folks picked all three of them up for a sleepover." He shrugged. "Kind of last minute, if you ask me, but the boys were happy to go spend time with their friends. I think I heard mention of a late-night volleyball game." He sighed. "Them Smokers got that place lit up like a baseball field, enough propane to blind a person."

Saul was glad that the Smokers helped with the plan by taking the boys. And he was glad to see Wayne chuckling. Rosemary had told Saul how down her father had been.

"Supper is almost ready. You men chat while I finish up." Rosemary smiled and headed back to the kitchen.

Wayne and Saul engaged in small talk, but occasionally Wayne's attention would drift, and it was clear that his thoughts were somewhere else.

Saul kept glancing toward the window.

Rosemary did her best to keep the beef casserole warm, hoping that Katherine would show up soon, before her father hobbled into the kitchen and saw four place settings laid out. She leaned against the counter, tapping her foot on the wood floor, hoping she hadn't crossed a line. She was glad that Saul agreed to the plan, even though she sensed a tiny bit of disappointment in his voice when she'd told him. Rosemary was looking forward to some alone time with Saul as well, but she couldn't stand to see her father so upset. Or Katherine. She cringed, knowing how much she'd misjudged Katherine. She was hoping this whole thing wasn't a mistake, but when she heard her father say from the living room, "I wonder who is pulling in the driveway during the supper hour," she knew it was too late. Rosemary hurried out of the kitchen and walked into the living room just in time to see Saul opening the screen door. Katherine looked beautiful in a dark green dress and black apron, all perfectly pressed, but Rosemary no longer held that against her. She glanced down at her own black apron and swiped at a smudge of flour.

"Hi, Katherine. Come in," Rosemary said as she eased up to where Saul was standing. She took the dish Katherine was carrying and whispered, "*Gut, gut.* You brought the pineapple cherry crisp like we talked about."

It had taken a lot of convincing for Katherine to agree to come for supper, and she didn't exactly mention to Katherine that her father didn't know about the invitation. Rosemary turned to her father, who was now standing with one crutch under his arm. She tried to read his expression, wondering how mad he was, but the instant twinkle in his eye let Rosemary know she'd made the right decision.

"Hello, everyone." Katherine's eyes were still swollen from crying, but they sparkled just the same when she looked at Rosemary's father.

"Supper is ready, so let's all move into the kitchen." She carried the dessert Katherine had brought and put it on the counter. *Guess I'm going to need to learn how to make this since Saul loves it so much.* As soon as she had the thought, she hoped she wasn't being too presumptuous. She could easily visualize a life with Saul now, and there wasn't any reason that they couldn't adopt children someday. She knew several Amish couples who had. She touched her stomach with one hand and briefly thought about never feeling a new life growing inside her. But it had been five years, and she was still as in love with Saul as she'd ever been. Would it really have been fair to marry someone else, someone who would always be second to Saul?

She turned around as they all moved into the kitchen, just in time to see that Katherine and her father weren't the only ones with a twinkle in their eyes. Saul winked at her again, and somehow she knew that everything was going to be all right. For all of them.

During the meal, Saul ate like he was eating for two grown men, but both Rosemary's father and Katherine picked at their food. Rosemary had hoped that after a few days without seeing Katherine, perhaps her father had changed his mind. She caught Katherine sneaking glances at *Daed,* but her father was a tough one to read. She hoped she hadn't misread his earlier expressions. *Daed* had always told Rosemary that it was hard to tell what was going on in her head, the same as it had been with her mother.

But Rosemary had always thought that it was her father who was often the hard one to read.

"Please let me help you clean this up," Katherine said when Rosemary began clearing the table.

Rosemary thought about the last supper Katherine had with them. "That would be *gut. Danki.*"

Katherine began running soapy water in the sink while Rosemary continued clearing the table. As she reached for her father's plate, she cut her eyes in his direction and held her breath. When he winked at her, she relaxed. *Everyone is winking tonight.* She smiled at him, and after the kitchen was clean, Katherine excused herself to the bathroom, and following the plan, Saul walked out to the porch.

Rosemary whispered to her father once they were alone, "Time is too short. I know you love Katherine, and *Mamm* would want you to be happy. God is giving you another chance at love, at happiness." She paused, studying her father's guarded expression. "I've been wrong about Katherine, and she loves you very much." Her father opened his mouth to speak, but Rosemary beat him to it. "And I know you love her."

Katherine walked back into the kitchen,

and Rosemary hurried out the door to the porch. *Daed* had to know this was all a setup, but she'd prayed that he could rid himself of any guilt and be happy with Katherine.

"Well, they didn't say much to each other during supper. Do you think they'll get back together?" Saul stood up from the rocker. "It's hard to tell what your father is thinking, but he couldn't hide his happiness when he first saw Katherine at the door."

"I know." Rosemary walked to where Saul was standing. She had so much more on her mind than her father and Katherine, even though that was important to her. "*Danki* for going along with my idea. I'm sorry we didn't get to go out to supper like we planned."

Saul edged closer. "Then I guess you still owe me a date." He smiled, and as a gentle breeze swept across the porch, Rosemary caught the scent of something spicy. Saul gazed into her eyes, and she knew what was coming. They'd waited five years, and it was hard not to have regrets, but if things had happened any differently, they might not be together now. God always had a plan. On His time frame.

"*Ya,* I guess I do still owe you a date." Rosemary squinted from the late-afternoon sun rays dipping beneath the porch rafters, and Saul instantly moved slightly to his left to put her in his shadow.

"Well, I'm pretending this is a date, and I know what happens at the end of a date, or what I've always prayed would happen when I finally got to take you out." As he leaned down, his lips met with hers, and Rosemary felt sixteen again, sharing her first kiss with the man she'd always thought she would marry.

"Give me the chance, Rosie, and I'll spend the rest of my life loving you and making you happy." Saul kissed her again, and she decided there would be no more worrying about children. God would provide if it was meant to be.

They both jumped when the screen door creaked and Katherine and her father walked onto the porch. Katherine was smiling, which was enough for Rosemary.

"Shame on you for being so tricky," her father said in a stern voice as he pointed a finger at Rosemary. But then his expression broke into a smile, and Rosemary made her way to where he was standing to hug him. "I love you, *Daed.*"

"I love you too, *dochder.*" He kissed her on the cheek before he eased her away and moved toward Saul, and as the men stood chatting, Rosemary walked over to Katherine.

As they shared a hug, Katherine whispered, "*Danki,* Rosemary. I will always love your father and be very *gut* to him. I'll be a *gut mudder* to the boys too." She stepped back, latching onto both of Rosemary's hands with hers. "And I promise not to step on your toes. It's still your *haus,* and I'll fit into whatever role you would like."

Rosemary smiled as she squeezed Katherine's hands. They hadn't formally announced it, but based on Katherine's comments, Rosemary knew the wedding must be back on. "Nonsense. It will be your *haus,* and . . ." She paused, smiling as she looked over at Saul, then she leaned closer to Katherine. "I think Saul and I are going to make up for lost time, so it might be your *haus* sooner than you think."

"*Ach,* Rosemary. I'm so glad. He's always loved you, since you were both sixteen."

Rosemary took a deep breath, basking in the hope that she felt, the love in her heart that had always been there — in hiding — for Saul.

"I thought we were going for a walk," Rosemary's father bellowed, then gave a hardy laugh. "Where's *mei maedel?*"

Katherine bounced up on her toes, kissed

Rosemary on the cheek, then ran to the man who would be her partner. When they had passed through the yard and toward the open fields, Rosemary watched the man who would be *her* partner moving toward her. He kissed her again, and Rosemary counted the many blessings of the evening.

Saul nodded toward the maroon pot at the far end of the porch. "Sometimes it takes awhile for a passionflower to root, but once it does, it can thrive for years with nourishment and love."

Rosemary's heart was fluttering as she listened. Her mother had told her the same thing years ago. Their passionflower had thrived for a long time. But Rosemary had let it die after her *mamm* passed. But she had a second chance with this one and was going to make sure to nurture it so it would stay rooted in love for a lifetime.

Just like she planned to do with Saul.

"I've missed this." Saul kissed her again but then eased away. "Rosie, I'm fearful to bring this up and ruin the moment . . ." He took a deep breath. "But one thing is going to continue to haunt me. Can you tell me why you walked away before?" He paused, but spoke again before she could answer. "Because I don't want to make the same mistake again."

Rosemary swallowed back the lump in her throat. "It was never anything you did. I've been just as afraid to tell you the truth as you were to bring up this subject. Probably more so."

"You can tell me anything, Rosie. It won't make me love you any less."

He loves me. But will he still after I tell him the truth?

She looked down, but Saul gently cupped her chin and brought her eyes to his. "There's nothing you can tell me that will cause me to walk away."

"I don't know about that," she said softly.

They were both quiet, and Rosemary leaned up and kissed him on the mouth, just in case it was the last time she'd be able to. She lingered for a while, but she knew she owed him an explanation. She eased away and took a step backward, but kept her eyes locked with his.

"I–I always wanted *kinner.*" She lowered her eyes for a few moments, then looked back up at him. "And I just couldn't imagine not having a large family. I know. It was self-ish. I should have known that our feelings back then would have been enough to sustain us, but I just couldn't imagine my life without children." She closed her eyes and waited, but when Saul didn't say anything, she slowly looked up at him. "Please say something."

He took off his hat, scratched his forehead, then put his hat back on. "I want a large family too. We used to talk about that when we were together back then."

"*Ya,* I know we did." She moved closer to him, praying that he'd understand. "I was young, and I thought that if I walked away from you, I'd find someone else whom I would love just as much, someone who could have children." She shook her head. "But there's never been anyone else, Saul. Only you."

He was quiet for a few moments, then he rubbed his cheek and chuckled. "Rosemary . . ." He shook his head. "What in the world are you talking about?"

Rosemary bit her lip and tried to calm her breathing. "I know you can't have *kinner.* That day I overheard your *mamm* talking to her cousin Naomi who was visiting. I heard them saying you couldn't have children." She paused and hung her head again. "I'm so sorry. I don't know if you can forgive me. I don't blame you if you can't." She gazed into his eyes. "But I love you just as much now as I did back then. Maybe more. And we can either adopt *kinner* or the Lord will provide if it's meant to be. I just know that I want to be with you." She held her breath. "If you'll still have me."

Saul's expression was blank, and a tear slipped down Rosemary's cheek. *I've lost him.*

"Let me make sure I understand," Saul said. "You broke up with me because you thought I couldn't have children?"

She nodded as another tear slipped down her cheek. "I'm sorry."

Saul leaned over, hands on his knees, and started laughing. "I'm really not sure whether to laugh or cry." He straightened and pulled himself together. "Rosemary, as far as I know, I'm quite capable of having *kinner.* You overheard *mei mamm* and *mei* Aunt Naomi talking about Saul Bender, a cousin. He was in a bad accident back then, and his injuries left him unable to have children."

Rosemary stopped breathing. "What?" Her mouth hung low for several moments as she let this news soak in. "Do you mean that we wasted — I wasted — five years?" Her chest hurt. "It was bad enough that I left you because of it, but for it to not even be true?"

Saul didn't say anything, just shook his head.

Rosemary was sure that this was the most

bittersweet moment in her life. And was Saul going to walk away from her?

"Why didn't you just ask me?" He reached his hand out to her, but she backed away as she was swallowed up by regret.

"I don't know." She buried her face in her hands and started to sob. "I'm an awful person. We could have been together all this time."

Saul pulled her close to him and held her tight for a while before he eased her away and kissed her on the forehead, then on the cheek, then his lips met hers. "If anything had happened any differently, we might not be together now. It was God's plan for things to work out this way."

"How can you say that? Aren't you angry? At me? At God?"

"Rosie . . ." He reached for her hand and walked her to the shade of an oak tree in the front yard. They sat on the grass, and Saul brushed back a strand of her hair that had fallen forward. "If we had gotten together back then, how do you think your *daed* and *bruders* would have done on their own after your mother's death? Maybe your father would have been so busy raising the three boys, he might not have noticed the spark between him and Katherine. My sweet Rosie. Everything happens on the

Lord's time frame. Not ours." He pulled her close and kissed her tears. "We can't have regrets. We are exactly where we are today because of every event that has led us here. I just want to be with you. I love you, and I always have."

Rosemary buried her head in his chest, then looked into his eyes. "I love you too, and I always have."

Saul grinned. "And I don't know of any reason why we can't fill a house with lots of *kinner.*"

Saul was right. Carrying the burdens of the past would only weigh them down. As she sat up and watched her father and Katherine walking toward them hand in hand, Rosemary knew that they were exactly where God meant them to be.

READING GROUP GUIDE

1. Rosemary ends her relationship with Saul because she believes he can't have children. Have you known couples in this situation? If so, was it a deal-breaker?
2. Years later, Rosemary changes her mind and knows that she wants Saul as her husband, even if that means they will never have children. Do you think that Rosemary changes her mind, in part, because she is older and more mature? Or has enough time gone by that she realizes she won't find anyone she loves as much as Saul?
3. Several scenes in the story are filled with large doses of miscommunication, and things could have turned out very differently had all truths been on the table. But, as mentioned in the story, things happen

on God's time frame, and by the end, all the characters are where they are meant to be. Are there instances in your life when you met resistance, only to have it play out much better than you could have imagined?

4. In a lot of ways, Rosemary and Katherine are alike. Can you name some of the characteristics they unknowingly share?

ACKNOWLEDGMENTS

It's always fun to do these collections with such talented authors. Kathleen, Tricia, and Vannetta — you ladies rock!

To my husband, Patrick, and my family and friends — thank you for your continued support on this amazing journey. And as always — God gets the glory for laying these stories on my heart.

Many thanks to everyone at Harper-Collins Christian Publishing. I'm a lucky gal to work with such a fabulous group of people, and I'm blessed to be able to call you all friends.

To my agent — Natasha Kern — a huge thank you for your career guidance and friendship. You are just a supercool person!

It's an honor to dedicate *Rooted in Love* to Jenni Cutbirth, a woman whom I admire. She's someone who has more strength than she ever thought possible — a necessary trait when you find out that your two-year-old daughter has cancer. For a year, I watched Jenni go back and forth to the hospital, sometimes staying for days at a time for her daughter's chemotherapy and radiation. A YEAR. I was exhausted just hearing about her routine, and I jokingly appointed myself "President of the Jenni Fan Club." But all joking aside, my dear Jenni . . . you are amazing. And Raelyn is a blessed little girl to have you as her mommy. May God always shower you and Raelyn with His blessings.

ABOUT THE AUTHOR

Award-winning, best-selling author **Beth Wiseman** is best known for her Amish novels, but her most recent novels, *Need You Now* and *The House That Love Built,* are contemporaries set in small Texas towns. Both have received glowing reviews. Beth's highly anticipated novel, *The Promise,* is inspired by a true story.

■ ■ ■ ■

FLOWERS FOR
RACHAEL

KATHLEEN FULLER

■ ■ ■ ■

To my husband, James: love blooms where it's planted.

GLOSSARY OF MIDDLEFIELD AMISH WORDS

---

ab im kopp — crazy, not right in the head
ach — oh
bruder — brother
buwe — boys
daag — day
daed — dad
danki — thank you
dumm — dumb
dummkopf — dummy
familye — family
gaarde — garden
geh — go
grienhaus — greenhouse
grossdochder — granddaughter
grossmutter — grandmother
grossvadder or grossdaadi — grandfather
gut — good
hallo — hello
haus — house
Herr — Mr.
kaffee — coffee

kapp — prayer head covering
kinn — child, kid
kumm — come
maedel — girl
mamm — mom
mann — man
mei — my
nee — no
nix — nothing
schwester — sister
ya — yes

CHAPTER ONE

We need to find God, and he cannot be
found in noise and restlessness. God is
the friend of silence. See how nature —
trees, flowers, grass — grows in
silence . . . We need silence to be
able to touch souls.
— MOTHER TERESA

Rachael Bontrager let the soft, loamy soil
sift through her hands. The warmth of the
June morning rays warmed her skin through
the thin blue material of her dress. She
pushed her *kapp* strings over her shoulders
and picked several stray blades of grass surrounding the violet Verbena she'd planted a
few weeks ago. "There. Better, *ya*?" She
glanced around to see if anyone noticed her
talking to her flowers. It wouldn't be the
first time she chatted to the plants in her
garden, and it wouldn't be the last.

She moved to check for weeds in a thick

layer of Hostas and Coleus. Their vibrant hues of crimson, scarlet, evergreen, and emerald drew her closer, marveling at the beauty of the plants. She reached out and touched a ridged Coleus leaf, running her fingertips over the green edges to the lavender and magenta center. Her first plant, and it had returned since she planted the garden last year. A simple plant. Common. Yet to her, the most special.

The sound of heavy wheels crunching on the gravel of her grandparents' driveway drew her attention. She hurried through to the wooden gate of the garden, opened it, then made sure to latch it securely behind her. This year the deer were especially plentiful — and hungry.

She shielded her eyes from the bright sun as she looked up at the driver leading a team of huge draft horses closer to the house. The warm June breeze lifted the yellow short sleeves of his shirt, revealing wiry, yet strong, arms.

Rachael gulped, forcing her attention from her handsome neighbor, Gideon Beiler, to the load of manure in the wagon behind him.

"Halt!" His deep voice had a husky quality that tickled her ears. He looked down at her and smiled. "*Hallo,* Rachael."

"*Hallo*, Gideon." She swallowed again, cringing at the high pitch of her voice. "*Danki* for bringing this." The other day she'd asked his younger sister, Hannah Lynn, if they had any extra manure. Their family raised cows and goats to sell at auctions throughout the year. Hannah Lynn had said Gideon would bring it over. With her garden growing, Rachael needed more fertilizer than her horse could provide.

She walked to the back of the wagon as Gideon jumped down from his seat. She sniffed the air, expecting to inhale the pungent odor of manure. Instead, she barely smelled anything at all. She examined the load in the wagon, picking up a handful. She looked at Gideon. "This is compost."

Gideon tipped back his straw hat as he neared. Rachael looked up at him, her neck craning to meet his warm brown eyes. He was at least six inches taller than her five-six height. He pushed his wirerimmed glasses closer to his eyes but didn't look directly at her. "*Ya*."

"From your place?"

He nodded. "We had a little extra from our garden this year."

She glanced at the load in the wagon. "A little?"

"Uh-huh." He finally looked at her.

"But . . ." He shrugged his shoulders.

When she first met him last year, after moving to Middlefield from Indiana to help care for her grandfather, he barely looked at her, much less said anything. But since he lived next door and worked at his family's farm, they couldn't avoid each other. Lately she realized she didn't want to.

She kept that to herself. Over time he'd learned not to be so shy around her, but that didn't mean he was interested in her as more than a friend.

And she had more to worry about than having a boyfriend. Focusing on the load of fresh compost, she said, "Do you mind dumping it in front of the *gaarde*?"

"Is that where you're gonna leave it?"

She shook her head. "I'll get the wheel-barrow and move it all behind the *grien-haus*." It wasn't exactly a greenhouse. Not yet. But once she finished it, she could garden year-round, focusing on fresh vegetables that were so expensive during the winter months.

"I can do that for you," he said.

His kindness didn't help keep her thoughts on an even keel. "That's all right. I know you're busy with the farm."

"They won't miss me for a few minutes." He grinned, displaying a deep dimple in each suntanned cheek.

She gripped the edge of the wagon and tried to get a grip on her senses too. "I'll, uh, get the wheelbarrow."

He nodded and leapt onto the back ledge of the wagon. She returned a few moments later.

Gideon tossed a shovelful of compost into the rusted three-wheeled barrow. "Looks like this thing has seen better days."

She regarded the wheelbarrow. Gideon was right. The barrow was old, like everything else around her grandfather's home. One tire kept losing air and she had to fill it using a bicycle pump at least once a week. Purchasing a new one was low on her list of priorities. Keeping food on the table and paying for gas and propane to keep the lamps lit and the stove going — that's what mattered most. Which was why her garden was her most important possession in the world. Fortunately their community helped with her grandfather's blood pressure and heart medications, or they wouldn't be able to make ends meet.

When the wheelbarrow was nearly full, Gideon plunged the shovel back into the shrinking pile. He jumped down, his huge boots thudding on the gravel drive. He grabbed the handles in his large, strong hands and pushed it through the open garden gate.

Rachael brushed a few stray flecks of compost from her arm and smiled. Whoever married Gideon Beiler would be a lucky woman. Her smile faded. Too bad it wouldn't be her.

Gideon nearly tripped on a small stone in the winding path through Rachael's garden. *Great.* That was all he needed to do, trip over his gigantic feet like he used to when he was a *kinn.* Although he was twenty-five, the memories of being teased for his gangly frame came up at the worst times. Like now, when he was trying to be nonchalant around Rachael. *Keep cool,* his Yankee friend would say. But he had never met Rachael Bontrager.

The partially built greenhouse was at the back of her fenced-in plot, near a large patch of perennials thriving in the shade of a huge oak tree. He'd never been this far back in her garden before. Gideon dumped the compost and stepped back, studying the structure. Although it wasn't complete and the design was crude, he could see the genius behind it. Recycled wood pallets were nailed together to make the floor, and the back wall was constructed from used, mismatched windows. More windows and two old doors were neatly stacked and leaning against the short fence, which upon further inspection, was also made of various pieces of wood.

"Obviously it's not finished yet."

He turned at her sweet, lilting voice. He glanced down, meeting her light-green eyes, which reminded him of the beach glass he'd picked up on a fishing trip to Lake Erie a few years ago. They were a stark and beautiful contrast to her dark-brown hair, which was nearly black against the white of her *kapp.* He focused on the greenhouse again, not wanting her to catch him staring.

"*Ya,*" he said. *Ach,* he sounded *dumm.* Why couldn't God have blessed him with the gift of smooth speech? And while He was at it, coordination and decent eyesight would be nice. He shoved his glasses up the bridge of his nose for the tenth time that morning. "When did your *grossvadder* start making it?"

"Winter. And he's not building it. I am."

He looked at her. "Where did you get the materials?"

"I guess you haven't seen my *grossdaadi*'s barn. It's stuffed with all kinds of spare parts, scraps of wood, nails, screws . . . all the things he picked up from odd construction jobs." She touched the back wall, running her fingers across the chipped white paint. "He can't bear to part with anything." She turned to Gideon. "So I decided to put some of it to *gut* use."

She never failed to surprise him. While most of his time was taken up working their small farm with his father, sometimes he would take a break and sit on the front porch, eating lunch or just enjoying the rest. Often he'd see her working in the garden, from dawn to dusk it seemed, except for when she went to the flea market on Mondays. Even there she was working, selling plants and flowers to both Amish and Yankee customers.

"*Mei daed* made sure I knew how to use a hammer and nails," she added. "It comes in handy. I don't have all the particulars figured out yet, but it will come together." She grinned. "I can't wait to have fresh broccoli in the winter. I love broccoli."

His gaze stayed on her, and all he could do was nod.

"Broccoli salad, broccoli and rice, chicken and broccoli —"

Did she realize how perfect she was? Resourceful, sweet, beautiful? He wished he could tell her that and so much more.

Instead he grabbed the wheelbarrow. "I'll

get the rest of the compost."

"Uh, okay," she said.

He hurried away, his cheeks heating. When would he stop acting like a nervous *dummkopf* around her? And more important . . . when had he started seriously caring for her?

Rachael sighed as Gideon rushed off. Gideon Beiler, short on words, always in a hurry. Then again, why would he stick around to hear her waxing poetic about all things broccoli? Not exactly interesting conversation.

She never should have let him help her move the compost. She was capable of doing it herself. As it was, he gave it to her for free and didn't charge for delivery. She shouldn't have taken further advantage of his kindness.

Knowing he would refuse if she offered him money, she looked around the garden, desperate to find something to show her appreciation. But there wasn't much here, except for the planted perennials, and she couldn't give him a dug-up plant. Then she spied one of the flower baskets she'd made to sell at the flea market on Monday. When she heard him returning, she grabbed the hanging basket.

After he dumped the compost, he picked

up the wheelbarrow by the handles. "One more trip should do it."

"Here." She thrust the basket in front of her. Pink Petunias. *Just what every man wants.* She cringed.

He stared at the basket, now inches from his chest. "Um, nice flowers."

"They're for you." With every word, she dug a deeper hole. One she wanted to disappear into. "I mean, they're for your *family,* er, your *mamm.* She likes flowers, *ya?*"

"Ya." He took the basket from her and set it in the wagon. "She'll like them." He pushed the wheelbarrow.

"I just wanted to thank you . . ." But he was already several feet away, his long legs covering a lot of ground.

Rachael looked at the patch of violet Verbena near the gate and rolled her eyes. "I should stick to talking to plants."

CHAPTER TWO

God writes the Gospel not in the Bible
alone, but also on trees, and in the
flowers and clouds and stars.
— MARTIN LUTHER

After he delivered the compost to Rachael,
he went home and put the flower basket on
the front porch, then headed for the huge
white barn behind the house. The sounds of
lowing cows and bleating goats, chomping
on sweet timothy grass in the nearby pasture, barely registered in his thoughts. He
passed by his mother's vegetable garden
near the small wooden deck attached to the
house. While his mother was a good gardener, the small patch paled in comparison
to Rachael's larger, distinct garden. It was
stunning, like the woman who cared for it.

He entered the section of the barn where
the calves were raised. This spring they'd
had five, along with fifteen goats. He and

his *daed* would sell them at auction in the fall, and until then, they — with the help of his seventeen-year-old sister, Hannah Lynn — would make sure they were fat and healthy.

As he approached their pen, the calves, with their thin legs and awkward gait, hurried toward him, filling the barn with their hungry moos. The smallest one was almost pure white except for the two black patches on either side of her flanks. She slipped on the loose straw on the barn floor, tumbling forward and landing on her face.

Gideon chuckled and knelt down. "*Kumm* here."

The cow scrambled to her feet and went to Gideon. He nuzzled her damp nose. "It's not fun when your legs don't work right, *ya?*"

But the cow didn't seem to care that Gideon could sympathize with her. She and the other calves were ready for their food. He dumped a bag of grain in the trough, and the mooing quickly faded into crunching as they munched on their morning snack.

"About time you got here." Hannah Lynn walked into the barn.

Gideon turned around, brushing his hands together. Dust from the grain danced in the air. He looked at his younger sister, smelling the morning's work in the stalls on her. She had on a pair of his old boots, the tops reaching the hem of her blue dress. The boots were about three sizes too big, but she insisted on wearing them. "I'm not that late," he said.

"You've been gone over an hour. I thought you said you'd be right back."

"Took longer than I thought."

Hannah Lynn crossed her arms and leaned against the barn pole. "So . . . how's Rachael?"

Gideon picked up a broom and started sweeping the barn floor. Not that it needed it — they all kept things in good shape around here. He shrugged as he pushed the broom. *"Gut."*

"Ask her out yet?"

He nearly lost his grip on the broom. He wished his sister would mind herself instead of him.

She sighed. *"Nee,* I take it."

"You can take it however you want." Gideon pushed the broom harder. A cloud of dust collected in the air.

"I know. It's none of my business." Hannah Lynn uncrossed her arms and straightened. "I'm just watching out for you."

"I don't need your hovering, little *schwester.*"

"Then why don't you start courting Rachael already?"

Gideon stopped sweeping. "It's not that simple."

"Why not?" Hannah Lynn said, taking the broom from him. "You like her. She's available, at least from what I've been able to find out." Hannah Lynn leaned her chin on the top of the broom handle. "She keeps to herself, though. Kind of like someone else I know." She poked him in the shin with the broom bristles.

"Are you done?"

"What are you afraid of?"

"I'm not afraid." He snatched back the broom. "What I am is busy."

"You are afraid." Hannah Lynn moved to stand in front of him. "Afraid she'll say *nee.*" Her eyes widened. "Or maybe you're afraid she'll say *ya.*"

He leaned the broom against the rough-hewn wall. "That's *ab im kopp.* Why would I be afraid of that?"

"Because then you'd have to actually *geh* out with her." Gideon turned away. His sister didn't understand. She was seventeen. What did she know about relationships? Or rejection. Or yearning —

"Gideon." Hannah Lynn snapped her fingers in front of his face.

158

Her expression came into focus. "You need to stop spinning your wheels," she said.

"That's not what I'm doing."

"That's exactly what you're doing. You care for Rachael. I'm sure almost everyone in the district knows."

"That's comforting."

"*Mei* point is, you can't just wait for the right moment. Or for things to happen. You have to act. If you like Rachael as much as you seem to, then she's worth going after."

Gideon scrubbed his hand over his cheek, feeling the stubble of whiskers he'd shave off in the morning. A sign of his singleness.

"You know what *Mamm* always says."

"*Mamm* says a lot of things."

Hannah Lynn straightened her posture, clasping her hands together like their mother often did. "You *geh* after what you want. And if it's God's will, you'll get what you need."

"Nice imitation."

"She's right."

Gideon sighed. He was tired of pretending, of acting nonchalant around his sister, who clearly saw through the façade anyway. "I don't know."

"Don't know what?"

He felt his cheeks flame. "I don't know . . . anything." He had very little experience asking out the girls in his district. Even his sister didn't know about the time he'd asked Julia Keim to a singing. He could still remember how her face had contorted as she tried not to laugh. He'd been nineteen, and he hadn't asked anyone else since.

Hannah Lynn was tall for an Amish woman, almost six feet. Yet she still had to look up to him. "Make it simple. Ask Rachael to *geh* on a buggy ride. If she says *ya,* problem solved." She turned and started to leave.

"What if she won't?"

She stopped and turned around in the doorway. "Then you'll know where you stand. And you'll have done something, instead of pining away." She disappeared out the door.

Behind Gideon, the calves mooed softly, finishing the last bits of their meal. Gideon reached over the top of the pen and patted the smallest one on the head. He wished he wasn't so transparent. Or that his sister wasn't right, not to mention she sounded more confident at seventeen than he was at twenty-five. The only thing standing in his way was fear. And unless he wanted to spend his life alone, he had to stop being a coward.

160

■ ■ ■ ■

Rachael spent the rest of the morning working in the garden. In a few days she would go to the flea market, and she still had a few flower arrangements to put together. She found that combining different plants and flowers in a simple container appealed to her customers more than selling the individual plants.

For the next hour, she worked on preparing a medium-sized pot at her potting bench, another structure she'd cobbled together with spare parts. Her grandfather never threw anything away, and in Rachael's mind, that was a good thing. She'd found a small cast-iron tub sink, the white enamel peeled off in places, and nestled it inside a wood frame. Underneath she nailed an old pallet to the legs of the frame, which served as an extra shelf. A coat of white paint from a half-empty can she found in the back of the barn added the finishing touch.

She placed the terra-cotta pot inside the shallow sink and filled it with light-green creeping Jennie, which draped just over the pot's edge. In a few weeks, with proper tending, the plant would hang like a leafy curtain until it trailed to the ground. Next to the creeping Jennie she added two magenta Impatiens, which gave the arrangement a pop of color. Then she placed the final touch — Swallowtail Coleus. A sturdy plant, despite its delicate, thin branches. The Coleus would grow straight up, balancing out the rest of the plants.

She stepped back and looked at her handiwork, pleased with the simple arrangement. Her stomach growled and she realized it was lunchtime.

When she went inside to make lunch, she found her grandfather in the kitchen, leaning on his cane, stretching to reach a cup from the cabinet. She hurried to him. "I'll get that." Rachael pulled a coffee mug from the cabinet and placed it on the counter. She frowned at him. "You should have waited for me to do this."

"I can get a cup, Rachael." He moved to pick it up, but she took it from him.

"I'll get your *kaffee*," she said. "You *geh* sit down."

He muttered something she didn't understand, but she thought she heard the word *bossy*. As he walked to the table, the thudding sound of his cane was a counterpoint to the slight drag of his left foot on the floor. He plopped onto the chair.

Rachael washed her hands before pouring

him a cup of still-warm coffee from the percolator pot on the stove. She took it to him. "I'm sorry. Time got away from me this morning."

"I don't know how many times I have to tell you, I'm fine." He took a sip of the coffee, a bit of the brown liquid dribbling on his chin and catching into his nearly gray beard. "You worry too much."

"I'm supposed to be taking care of you."

"So you keep reminding me. Every day." He set the cup on the table. "Rachael, I appreciate you coming here. But it's been a year since . . ." He stared at his cup for a moment.

Since the stroke. She shook off the memory of when they'd received a call from Lydia, Gideon's mother, who had happened to be outside when she saw Grandfather collapse as he was walking to the barn. If it hadn't been for Gideon's family, her grandfather might be dead. "Hungry?" she asked, walking to the pantry, pushing away the horrible thought.

"*Ya.* But I see what you're doing."

"Getting the bread?" She opened the door and pulled out a loaf of homemade bread she'd baked two days ago.

"Changing the subject. I'll take eggs and bacon, by the way."

He'd asked for the same thing for breakfast. She'd made him oatmeal instead. "You mean tuna salad, *ya*?"

"I'm tired of rabbit food."

"Rabbits don't eat tuna. And you know the doctor said you have to watch what you eat." Rachael took two plates from the cabinet and set them down. She picked up a head of lettuce from one of three large bowls on the counter. They were filled with fresh vegetables, some that she'd picked from her garden. "That includes fat, salt —"

"And everything that tastes *gut*." He put his right hand on the table. His left remained in his lap. "What I wouldn't do for some ham, eggs, hash browns, bread slathered with butter . . ."

Rachael ripped a few pieces of lettuce and placed them on the bread. Her grandfather's crankiness was a good sign. When she'd first arrived to help after his stroke, he'd been depressed, had some mild memory problems, and found it difficult to balance. Now he was as ornery as he'd ever been. She opened and drained a can of tuna, then placed the fish on the bed of lettuce.

"What about apple pie?" he asked.

She glanced at him. "Not on your diet,

Grossdaadi."

"It has apples in it." He winked.

Rachael smiled and brought him his sandwich. "Do you need anything else?"

"I need to talk to you." He patted the chair next to him. "Sit."

She sat, alarm pooling inside her. "Are you okay?"

He pushed at the plate. "*Ya.* That's what I'm trying to tell you. I'll be just fine by myself now. I know it was touch and *geh* for a while, and I'm glad your parents could spare you to come and help me out." His voice turned gruff. "It's been nice to have another person around for a while."

She wanted to reach out and pat his hand, but he wouldn't appreciate it. He never showed affection, an unusual quirk she'd accepted. A widower for over five years after being married for almost fifty, he'd lived alone for a long time. Her parents, who had moved to Indiana shortly after they married, couldn't move back to care for him. But she could. And she wouldn't let him be alone again.

"It's time you went home, Rachael."

She just wished he didn't make it so hard sometimes.

"I'm not going home." Rachael stood and went to the sink. She rested her hands on

165

the edge of it. "My place is here."

"Your place is back with your *mamm* and *daed*. Your *bruders* and *schwesters*. Don't you miss them? Don't you want to be with your friends instead of an old *mann*?"

She spun around and looked at her grandfather. How could she think about what she wanted when he needed her? She had no intention of going back to Indiana, not anytime soon. "I belong here."

"Humph." He picked up his sandwich. "You're as stubborn as your *daed*."

"I'll take that as a compliment."

When they finished lunch, she could see he was tired. "You should take a nap."

"Nee." He started to get up from the table. "I think I'll *geh* out to *mei* barn. I haven't been there in a while."

"But —"

He held up his hand. "You're already telling me what to eat. You're not gonna tell me how to spend every second of *mei daag*." He grabbed his cane. "I need some air."

She started to say something, then bit her bottom lip. He was right. She couldn't order him around like he was a child. But she couldn't stop worrying about him, either. She peeked through the back door of the kitchen and watched as he hobbled to the barn, saying a quick prayer that he wouldn't do anything overly strenuous. Or overly foolish.

When he disappeared into the barn, she closed the back door and finished cleaning the kitchen.

Later, she stepped onto the front porch, breathing in the fresh air, the scent of flowers wafting from the garden mixed with the earthy smell of the Beilers' farm next door. She thought about what her grandfather said. But she didn't want to go home, even though she missed her family. She belonged in Middlefield right now, helping her grandfather, making sure he had fresh vegetables to eat and didn't overwork himself. She couldn't stop him from tinkering in the barn, but she could be here if he needed her help.

If she set aside her worry, she knew she wasn't being fair to him. After her grandmother died, he would spend hours in the barn, going through the things he'd collected over the years, sometimes forgetting to eat or get adequate sleep. His deteriorating health had led to the stroke that nearly killed him. But as long as he didn't do too much, there was no reason why he shouldn't be surrounded by his collections, the things that made him happy. Still, he didn't need to be alone.

Indiana could wait. Her father had asked her, his oldest child, to be there for his father. She would keep that promise to make sure her grandfather was safe and healthy.

And possibly surprise him with a small sliver of apple pie for tonight's dessert.

CHAPTER THREE

By cultivating the beautiful we scatter the seeds of heavenly flowers, as by doing good we cultivate those that belong to humanity.
— ROBERT A. HEINLEIN

Once he'd finished the day's work, Gideon sat down with his parents and sister for their evening meal. After bowing his head in silent prayer, he picked up a dish of steaming mashed potatoes and plopped a large spoonful onto his plate. He passed them to his father.

"There's a hanging basket on the front porch," *Maam* said. "Beautiful pink Petunias. Hannah Lynn, do you know where they came from?"

His sister shrugged. "I saw them when I came home from Rebekah Yoder's. I thought you bought them."

"They're from Rachael." Gideon kept his

eyes on his food as he swirled the potatoes in the creamy gravy.

"Rachael, hmm?"

Gideon looked up and glared at his sister. "She gave them to me when I took over the compost."

"And she thanked you with flowers." Hannah Lynn's brown eyes danced with teasing behind her glasses. "How sweet."

"They're for *Maam.*" He glared at her. Hadn't she pestered him enough for one day?

"That was nice of her." His mother took a fried chicken breast from the platter in front of her. "She has such a gift for gardening. I'm amazed at how much work she's accomplished in a year." She looked at Gideon. "I baked some oatmeal cookies today. Maybe I'll take a plate over to her tomorrow."

"I'm sure Gideon wouldn't mind taking them for you." Hannah Lynn grinned.

He scowled at her.

"I'll do it. I haven't had a chance to visit with Rachael in a long while. Eli seems to be doing better, from what I've seen of him at church. Having Rachael there to help him is such a blessing."

Gideon took a bite of his fried chicken, saying nothing. But he felt Hannah Lynn's foot nudge him from across the table. He pushed back.

"Ow."

"Not at the supper table, you two." Their father didn't look up. He didn't have to. His tone said it all.

"She's a nice *maedel* too," his mother continued, as if nothing had happened. She piled her plate high with buttered green beans. Bits of bacon clung to a few of the shiny pods. What Rachael Bontrager was to gardening, his mother was to cooking. Gideon's parents' plump frames attested to that. Unlike him and Hannah Lynn, they were both on the short side. "But she does seem to keep to herself."

"That's what I said," Hannah Lynn commented.

He ignored her and took the bowl of green beans from his mother. "*Ya.* I guess." At least his mother seemed oblivious to his feelings for Rachael.

Mamm sprinkled a little salt on her chicken. "You should invite her to a singing, Gideon."

Then again, maybe not.

"*Ya,* Gideon." Hannah Lynn smirked. "Invite her to a singing."

"We've got two heifers due to birth any day," his father said, giving Hannah Lynn a stern look before turning to Gideon. "We need to make sure we're prepared."

"We are." Gideon appreciated his father's quick switch of topics. Discussing his love life — or lack of it — with his mother and sister was turning into a nightmare.

After supper, Gideon went outside to bring the cows into the barn from the pasture. He made sure the horses were comfortable for the night, filling their water troughs to the brim and adding a thin layer of extra hay over the trampled straw in their stalls. Chores done, he went inside, pausing at the edge of the backyard where their property abutted the Bontragers'. There were no trees or bushes to obscure his view of the house and Rachael's garden, which was partly obscured by two tall, wide oak trees. He didn't see her, only heard the echo of hammering.

She was probably working on the greenhouse. He should offer to help her build it. She shouldn't have to work so hard. Or work alone.

Just as he started to step across the property line, she appeared, carrying an empty glass. He froze, watching as she paused to pull a few weeds from the square vegetable patch on the right side of her garden. Tiny shoots of tomato and pepper plants peeked through the soil. He squinted through his glasses. The sun hung low in the sky behind her, the muted colors of sunset providing the perfect backdrop. His heart thrummed. Her independence and work ethic appealed to him just as much as her beauty. With her grandfather being ill, he knew she was in charge of all the chores and keeping the Bontrager household running smoothly. He helped out when she let him, mostly with cutting wood for the stove in the living room. But more often she refused his offers. She was the most capable woman he knew, and he'd never heard her complain.

"You're staring."

He groaned at the sound of Hannah Lynn's voice. "Back to pester me again?"

"I can't help it." She grinned, looking up at him. "You're too easy to tease."

How well he knew that. "I don't appreciate it." His private moment ruined, he turned and headed for the house. He heard Hannah Lynn coming up behind him.

"I'm sorry." She stepped in front of him, blocking his path. "You're right. I shouldn't tease you about Rachael."

He looked down at her. "*Danki* for finally realizing that." He started to walk away from her.

"I should be helping you instead."

He paused, turning. "What?"

"I know how you can tell Rachael how you feel."

He took Hannah Lynn by the arm and led her toward the front porch. "Keep your voice down."

"She can't hear me." Hannah Lynn shook him off. She moved to the top of the porch steps. She was now even with his line of sight.

Now he wished she'd go back to teasing him. He shook his head. "*Nee.* Absolutely not."

"Won't you at least hear me out? Do you want to court Rachael or not?"

Hannah Lynn could be relentless, like a dog guarding his bone. If he didn't listen to her now, she'd never let it drop until he did. He looked over his shoulder. Rachael was gone. "You know I do. But that doesn't mean she'll agree to *geh* out with me."

His sister's grin widened. "By the end of next week, she will."

The following Monday morning dawned cloudy, but it was the warmest day they'd had so far. Before Rachael left the house, she grabbed the last oatmeal cookie from the plate Gideon's mother had dropped off last week. She would return it with some brownies, using her *grossmutter*'s popular recipe. Maybe she'd set aside one for herself before she took them over. She did miss sweet treats, and it had been difficult to keep her grandfather out of the oatmeal cookies. She'd relented and let him have one, which he savored.

She went to feed her grandfather's horse, which had his own pocket of space in the barn along with *Grossdaadi*'s various collections. When she finished giving him his oats and fresh water, she patted the horse's gray head and left the barn, glancing at the Beilers' yard. No one was outside. Just the cows and goats.

She hadn't seen much of Gideon since he'd brought over the compost. For the rest of the week she'd tried to catch a glimpse of him, but she never did. Yesterday he disappeared right after the church service. She even tried to think of an excuse to go over to his house, but everything she came up with seemed ridiculous. Her feelings for him had grown stronger over time — and more pointless. If he liked her, he would have let her know by now.

Rachael made her way to the garden. But when she opened the gate, she noticed the latch was a bit loose. Short on time, she made a mental note to tighten the screws when she returned from the flea market. She made sure the gate was securely shut behind her and went to the unfinished greenhouse. Nearby was her potting bench, along with several iron shepherd's hooks holding her hanging baskets.

She decided to take four of them, two containing purple Petunias and two filled with multicolored Impatiens. They seemed to be the most popular flower for hanging baskets. She stood on a small stool and reached up to grab two of the baskets. When she stepped down and turned around, she noticed something lying on her potting bench.

She neared, peering at the single stemmed flower that hadn't been there the night before. Rachael set the baskets on the ground and picked up the flower. A purple Iris. She touched the small, plain white card attached with a thin pale-blue ribbon.

My Compliments.

Rachael looked around the garden. Nothing else had been disturbed. She studied the Iris. It was a beauty, with the darkest purple petals she'd ever seen. A slash of lemon yellow peeked out from the interior of each petal. This wasn't from her garden.

She fingered the card. *My Compliments.* What did that mean? The short sentiment was written in uniform print, the letters almost square in shape. Plain. Masculine.

Her hanging baskets forgotten, she went inside, carrying the flower. She walked into the kitchen, where her grandfather sat at the kitchen table, holding the newspaper in one hand. He peered up at her over his reading glasses. "Ready for me to drive you to the flea market?"

She sighed. They'd argued about this last night. "I'm driving myself. There's *nee* sense in you hanging around for hours, waiting for me to sell flowers."

"I refuse to be trapped in *mei* own *haus.*"

"I *know.*" Rachael rubbed her temple. "What if you come with me next week?"

He looked at her before focusing on the newspaper again. "I suppose that will be fine."

She let out a breath. She'd deal with next Monday when it arrived. She started searching the cabinets. After the third one, her grandfather asked, "What are you looking for?"

"*Grossmutter*'s vase. I thought I put it in here." She crouched down and opened the cabinet under the sink. "There it is." She filled the glass cylinder with water, put the Iris in it, and placed it on the table.

"Nice flower," he said. "I didn't know you

were growing Irises."

"I didn't know you knew what Irises were."

"I do know a little about flowers. Your *grossmutter* kept a *gaarde* too. Not as big as yours. But enough for us." He looked at the Iris. "She liked Tulips the best."

Rachael nodded. Every spring dozens of yellow, red, and orange Tulips bloomed in the flower beds that edged the front porch. She untied the card from the Iris stem.

"Someone give that to you?" he asked.

She shrugged. "It was left on my potting bench. There's *nee* name on the card." She glanced at the battery-operated clock on the wall. She didn't have time to talk about this now. "I have to *geh.* I'll be back this afternoon. Please don't *geh* anywhere other than the barn while I'm gone."

He sighed. "I promise. But I'm only doing this as a favor to you."

"Understood." Satisfied, Rachael started to leave.

"Secret admirer," her grandfather mumbled.

"What?"

"*Nix.* You better hurry or you'll be late."

She went to the barn to hitch the horse to the buggy. *Secret admirer.* The fact that her grandfather had mentioned it was surprising. But the idea was silly. She had been invited to a couple of singings over the past year, but she'd made it clear that she wasn't interested. Eventually the *buwe* stopped asking. The only man she wanted to go to a singing with had never asked her.

But he was also the only one who had easy access to her garden. Could he have left the Iris?

Rachael paused. *Would he?* Her pulse thrummed at the thought.

She frowned, dismissing the thought. If he were interested in her romantically, he wouldn't go to this kind of trouble. He was shy, but also plainspoken, a quality she appreciated. He wouldn't leave her a flower with a vague card. He would simply ask her out.

She put the mystery out of her mind as she loaded her plants and flowers into the back of the buggy. When she finished, she guided the horse down the driveway at a brisk pace. She needed to arrive as soon as she could, since business at the flea market was at its peak during the morning hours.

But as she drove to Nauvoo Road where the flea market was located, the fragrant scent of flowers and potting soil filling her buggy, she thought about the Iris again.

Could it be from Gideon? Deep in her heart, she willed it to be true.

CHAPTER FOUR

Arranging a bowl of flowers in the morning can give a sense of quiet in a crowded day — like writing a poem or saying a prayer.
— ANNE MORROW LINDBERGH

Business at the flea market was brisk. Rachael had set her small stand of flowers, plants, and hanging baskets near the outside entrance of the flea market hall, and within two hours she had sold everything but two petite Croton plants.

A young Yankee woman walked by Rachael's stand, wearing huge round, black sunglasses. Her lime-green purse, practically the size of a duffel bag, was slung over her shoulder. She paused in front of the Crotons.

"What are these?" she asked, pointing to the plants.

"Crotons." Rachael picked one up.

"They're very easy to care for and make great indoor plants." She touched one of the leaves. "As they grow, the leaves change from green to red, and the yellow spots turn a pinkish color."

The woman lifted up her glasses. "That sounds pretty. But I have a black thumb. I've killed every plant I've ever owned, so I just gave up on the gardening thing."

Rachael smiled. "There's no such thing as a black thumb." She took the other plant and handed them both to the woman. "Here. Try growing these. Make sure they get plenty of sunlight and don't overwater. I promise you'll be happy with them."

The young woman eyed them for a moment. "Okay. How much?"

"No charge."

Her eyes widened. "I couldn't take them for free. Let me pay you something."

Rachael shook her head. Although she could use the few dollars these two plants would bring, she enjoyed the woman's surprise even more.

"Thank you. I'll take good care of them." She took the plants and grinned. "At least I'll try."

"I know you will. Enjoy them."

As the woman walked away, Rachael folded up her table, still smiling. First the surprise flower, then she'd sold all her plants and had managed to put a smile on someone's face. What a great morning.

She returned home, ready to make lunch for her grandfather. He wouldn't be happy with the simple cucumber salad, sliced cheese, and fruit she planned to make. Still, she would ignore his usual grumblings, which lately had included complaining that his clothes were getting looser. After so many months, she was getting used to it.

But as she pulled into the barn, she saw movement among the piles of Grandfather's belongings. Rachael pressed her lips together, parked the buggy, and jumped down.

"Grossdaadi!" As she neared, she saw he was in the middle of lifting a heavy board, one that she'd barely been able to move herself last week.

He let the board drop and turned around. "Rachael," he said, putting his hands behind his back and giving her a half smile. "You're back already? I was just checking *mei* inventory."

"You were doing more than that. You're supposed to be taking it easy."

He lifted his chin, his beard reaching just past the collar of his shirt. "I have been — for a year." He grabbed his cane and limped toward her. "I can't spend the rest of my life doing crossword puzzles, taking naps, and walking out here wishing I could do something other than watch the day pass by. I need to work."

"But what if you have another stroke?"

"I won't." He patted her shoulder awkwardly. "And I promise I won't do anything I'm not supposed to."

"You already are. You shouldn't be lifting that board."

Grossdaadi held up his good hand. "Fine. If you'll stop nagging me, I won't lift any more boards."

"And if you need to move something, ask me." Rachael went to unhitch the horse from the buggy. "I'll do it."

"You do enough around here." He turned and started walking out of the barn. "Too much, if you ask me. I'll be in the *haus.* Where I always am."

Rachael leaned her forehead against the horse's neck. *Lord, what am I supposed to do?* She understood her grandfather's frustration. But she wanted him to be safe. Yet she didn't want to be his jailer either.

She finished unhitching the mare and led her to her stall. After feeding the horse his lunch, Rachael went back in the house, expecting to find her grandfather in the kitchen. When he wasn't there, she checked his bedroom. Cracking the door open, she peeked inside. He was lying on his bed, his back to her. Slowly she closed the door.

Somehow they had to find a balance. Maybe he was right — what harm could it do if he spent some time fiddling around in the barn? As long as he didn't overdo it, he should be fine. When he woke up, she'd apologize for being so strict. She wanted him to be happy and healthy, to enjoy life now that he was getting better.

She just hoped she was making the right decision.

The next morning, Rachael went about doing the chores inside the house — paying particular attention to the bathroom and kitchen. When she finished, she retrieved the push mower from the barn and began tackling the backyard.

She waved at her grandfather as he made his way to the barn. Their talk last night had been short, but she could see he was happy. This morning he didn't complain about his oatmeal and she heard him whistling from his bedroom as he got dressed, which made her smile.

A couple of hours later, the grass in the front and back yards now neatly trimmed, she entered the garden, determined to do more work on the greenhouse. The ground felt cool against her bare feet as she walked to the partially built structure. She'd work on attaching a couple of old windows together to start the bottom of the second wall. She wasn't sure how she would connect that wall to the other one, but the answer would come to her. It usually did once she started working on a project.

Rachael passed by the potting bench, almost ignoring it, until she spied a flash of color on the plain wood bench. Another flower, this time a gorgeous sprig of lavender. She picked it up, inhaling its sweet fragrance. Purple, her favorite color. She tried to think if she'd told anyone that. Had she mentioned it to Gideon? She didn't think so. Rachael read the attached card, written in the same neat, square handwriting. *Admiration.* Once again the secret admirer idea popped into her head. Yet she realized there was nothing overtly romantic about this card, or the Iris card.

"Another flower?"

She turned to see her grandfather approaching. His steps were slower than they had been earlier in the morning, but she saw a sparkle in his light-green eyes that hadn't been there in a while. She held up the flower. *"Ya."*

186

"Smells nice. Lavender?"

She eyed him for a moment. So, he knew about Irises and lavender? Plus, he'd planted the talk of a secret admirer in her head. Suddenly she realized what was going on. She went to him and kissed his whiskered cheek, ignoring his awkward grimace. She'd kiss him whether he liked it or not. "*Danki* for the flowers. I love them both."

He shook his head. "What are you talking about?"

Rachael grinned. "I know they're from you. I don't know how you managed to get them, but then again, I always knew you were resourceful. The notes are nice, but you didn't have to do this."

His bushy gray brows furrowed. "Rachael —"

"I am glad you remembered purple is my favorite color." She sniffed the lavender again. "This is very sweet."

"It is?" Her grandfather leaned against his cane.

Rachael looked at her grandfather, love swelling in her heart. "You don't have to thank me for helping you."

"You've gone *ab im kopp.*"

Her smile faded. "What?"

"I didn't leave those flowers for you. The thought never crossed *mei* mind."

187

"Oh." She dropped her hand to her side.

"And I didn't know purple was your favorite color." He shrugged. "Wouldn't matter anyway. I'm color blind."

"You are?"

"*Ya*. Can't tell if your dress is blue or green."

"It's yellow," Rachael said.

"See?" He pointed to his straw hat. "Got knocked in the head when I was a kid. Been living in a gray world ever since. Although I do remember that the sky is blue and the grass is green." He chuckled.

"But . . ." Rachael looked at the lavender. "Who else would do this?"

"I don't know." He turned and walked away. "Maybe you do have a secret admirer."

Rachael rubbed a petal of lavender between her fingers, releasing its scent. "I can't imagine who that would be."

"What about Gideon?" her grandfather called over his shoulder. "He knows you like flowers."

"Everyone knows I like flowers."

He waved her off. "I'm heading inside. *Gut* luck solving your mystery."

Rachael put the lavender back on the potting bench. She stared at it for a moment, then tried to put it out of her mind. She picked up a hammer from the toolbox

188

underneath the bench. Then she opened a mason jar filled with nails and rummaged to find the right size. But she couldn't concentrate on the greenhouse. All she could think about were the flowers, and her grandfather's suggestion that Gideon might be the one who left them.

She blew out a breath and set the hammer down. *Only one way to find out for sure. I'll* geh *over to the Beilers' and ask him myself.*

CHAPTER FIVE

Hope is the only bee that makes honey
without flowers.
— ROBERT GREEN INGERSOLL

Rachael walked to the edge of the property line between her house and Gideon's. The warm air carried the sweet scent of freshly mowed grass mixed with the musky smell of the cows next door. She looked at Gideon's house, a simple structure much like her grandparents' — white, without shutters or other decorations, except for a small flower bed at the base of the front porch. She smiled, noticing her hanging basket suspended from the extended roof covering the porch.

Then dread filled her stomach. Asking Gideon about the flowers was a bad idea. Not to mention awkward. What was she supposed to say? *Hallo, Gideon. Did you give me the flowers? Does that mean you like me?*

But she couldn't let this go. She had too much to do, too much responsibility to be distracted by the mysterious flowers. Her palms dampened as she gripped the lavender, took a deep breath, and walked over to Gideon's.

Again, doubt assaulted her, making her emotions sway back and forth. Maybe he wouldn't be home. Maybe she should just turn back and forget about this. Maybe —

"Hi, Rachael."

She stopped at the bottom of the Beilers' porch steps. "*Hallo,* Hannah Lynn." She looked up at Gideon's sister, who was four years younger than Rachael and several inches taller. She was one of the tallest Amish women Rachael had ever met.

"What a pretty flower." Hannah Lynn bounded down the steps. "From your *gaarde*?"

Rachael studied Hannah Lynn for a moment. If she knew anything about this flower, Rachael couldn't tell by her expression. "*Nee,* it's . . ." She sighed. "Never mind. Is Gideon here?"

"He and *Daed* left for an auction early this morning. I was just going out to work in the barn." Hannah Lynn frowned, wrinkling her freckled nose.

"You don't like working with the cows?"

"Not really. I can think of a hundred other things I'd rather do." Hannah Lynn shrugged. "But when *Daed* and Gideon are gone, it's up to me."

"I won't keep you, then."

"I'll tell Gideon you stopped by."

"All right." Rachael paused. "Actually, don't tell him. It's not important."

"Are you sure?"

"*Ya*. Have fun with the cows."

She scrunched her face again. "I definitely wouldn't call it fun."

Rachael waved to Hannah Lynn as she walked away. Rachael went inside her garden and closed the gate behind her. As it latched shut, she noticed a deer peeking through the woods directly behind the rear fence.

"Shoo!" She ran toward the deer. It ducked back into the trees. Rachael shook her head. She'd seen more deer stalking her garden lately. She loved the beautiful creatures — except when they helped themselves to her garden. She'd had the same problem with her garden in Indiana.

She walked over to the greenhouse, laid the lavender on the potting bench, and picked up her hammer. Best to just let all this nonsense go and focus on the task at hand.

But as she hammered the first nail into the window sash, connecting it to the pallet floor, an idea came to her. She paused. Smiled. Problem solved. By tomorrow, she would know if she really had a secret admirer.

"Was that Rachael?" Gideon asked Hannah Lynn as she came around the back of the house. He wiped his dusty hands on his pants.

"Where?" Hannah Lynn's eyes grew round. Innocent. She was a terrible liar.

"I just saw her. She was talking to you by the front porch." That familiar twinge of excitement tickled his belly. "What did she want?"

Hannah Lynn looked around, her eyes widening. She pulled him to the side. "She knows, Gideon."

"That I left her the flowers?"

His sister huffed. "*Nee,* that you are running a farm. Of course I'm talking about the flowers."

"Then why did she leave?" A sick feeling formed in the pit of his stomach. "She's upset, isn't she?"

Hannah Lynn shook her head and grinned. "*Nee.* Not at all. She was holding the lavender when she came over. And from the look in her eyes, she's confused."

"That doesn't sound so *gut.*"

She elbowed him in the side. "Confused and interested. That's the important thing. I told you this was a great idea."

He scratched his chin, not sure what to think. He'd balked at his sister's corny idea of leaving the flowers with a note attached to each one. It wasn't something he would think about doing. But she had been insistent that Rachael would appreciate them. "How do you know she's interested?"

"She wouldn't have come over to talk to you, then chicken out at the last minute and decide she didn't want to talk to you."

"What?"

"Just trust me, Gideon. I know what I'm talking about."

Women. He'd never understand them. "Okay. So she's interested." The tickle returned in his belly and he couldn't resist smiling. "Guess I better ask her out now."

Hannah Lynn gripped his arm. "*Nee.* Not yet."

"Why?"

"Because we have to finish the plan."

He raised a brow and turned to Hannah Lynn. "We? I thought the whole idea was to get her attention. Now I have it."

Hannah Lynn rolled her eyes. "You really

think a couple of flowers are enough? You have to woo her, Gideon."

"Woo?"

She fingered the white ribbon of her *kapp*. "Keep letting her know she's special to you."

"I think you've been reading too many of those novels you keep bringing home from the library." Gideon turned and headed toward the pasture.

Hannah Lynn ran to catch up with him. "I'm just trying to help, you know. The least you could do is show me a little appreciation."

He stopped. Turned and faced her. "I'm sorry. *Danki* for your help. But I think I can take it from here."

She moved to stand in front of him. "Gideon, if you could see how happy she was —"

"I would have if you'd told me she was here."

"I didn't want to ruin the surprise." She took a step back. "Look, you have three more days. Three more flowers. Then you can reveal who you are." She clasped her hands together. "It will be so romantic."

"I think you're enjoying this more than me," he said. But he had to admit that he liked the idea of surprising Rachael at the end of the week, now that he knew she was okay with getting the flowers. He wished he could see her face when she found them in her garden. But he didn't want to risk getting caught. Now that didn't seem to matter as much.

"Maybe I'll just give her the rest of the flowers in a bouquet," he said.

"Gideon, just stick with the plan. Please? She will definitely *geh* out with you after this."

He took off his hat, letting the air cool his dampened hair. It was still morning, but he'd worked up a sweat already milking the cows. "All right. I'll put the Geranium in the garden tomorrow morning."

"*Nee*. She'll be expecting that. You'll have to find a different place."

"Like where?"

Hannah put her hands on her hips and sighed. "You'll figure it out. I shouldn't have to think of everything." She turned and headed back to the house, her bare feet disappearing into the lush green grass with each step.

He put his hat back on and looked over at Rachael's house again. He saw her grandfather coming out the back door, heading for the barn again. He'd done that every day this week. He guessed Rachael thought her grandfather was okay enough to start working again.

Once more, Gideon thought of all the responsibility Rachael had resting on her slim shoulders. If he could, he would help her carry that burden. He realized Hannah Lynn was right. Even if he initially thought leaving Rachael secret flowers was silly, they made her happy. And he would do anything to make sure she stayed that way.

The next morning, Rachael awakened an hour before dawn. She snuck out of the house and hid in the back of her garden, where she still had a view of the greenhouse and potting bench. She waited. And waited. And waited some more, until her legs began to cramp from her crouched position. As the sun rose higher in the sky, she couldn't wait any longer. She needed to make breakfast before her grandfather fixed himself biscuits and gravy. Or eggs and sausage. Or something he knew he wasn't supposed to have but would try to sneak by with anyway.

Her shoulders were slumped as she went inside the house. She had looked forward to another flower, guessing as she fell asleep last night what kind of bloom she would receive today. Now she realized she'd been prideful to assume she'd get another. She should be grateful for the two flowers she had and not expect any more.

She put the disappointment out of her mind and set about the day's chores. After making breakfast, she headed to the garden again. She didn't have much to do, just pull a few weeds from the patch of Begonias in the corner and water the tomato plants in the vegetable patch. The straw mulch she'd mounded around each plant had kept her weeding to a minimum this year.

When she finished, she went inside and retrieved a freshly laundered load of dresses from the spin washer. Most of her neighbors did their wash on Mondays, but since she went to the flea market on Mondays, Wednesdays were her wash days.

She held the woven clothes basket on her hip as she made her way to the line behind the house. Rachael set the basket on the ground and reached for a clothespin from the cloth bag attached to the line. She froze.

Attached to the bag with a wooden clothespin was a bright red Geranium. She smiled as she unfastened it and read the card. *Sincerity.*

She left the clothes and took the flower inside, adding it to the other two in the vase on the kitchen table. The purples contrasted beautifully with the vivid red of the Gera-

nium. *My Compliments. Admiration. Sincerity.*
What did it all mean?

Rachael pondered the puzzle as she went back to hang up the clothes. She paused at the clothesline when she saw Gideon heading toward the barn. She started to wave, only to notice he wasn't looking in her direction. "Gideon!" she called.

Instead of answering back, he disappeared into the barn.

She frowned. He must not have heard her.

Deep in her heart, she harbored hope that he was the one leaving the flowers. But that possibility seemed to disappear with each passing day.

Would he act that way if he was interested? Would he ignore her if he was the one leaving flowers with such lovely sentiments?

She picked up her light-blue dress, shook it out, and pinned it to the line. Whoever was leaving the flowers was doing a good job of keeping his identity a secret. She wondered if he would ever reveal himself.

CHAPTER SIX

And the heart that is soonest awake to
the flowers is always the first to be
touch'd by the thorns.
— THOMAS MOORE

For the next two mornings, Rachael rose early and waited to see if she could catch whoever was leaving her the flowers. And each morning, she never saw who dropped them off. In her mailbox on Thursday she found a stem of pink Stock sitting on top of the mail, a lovely flower with multiple rosy-pink buds that bloomed along its thick green stem. *Lasting Beauty.* That one made her blush, and for the first time, she really believed that these weren't just sweet sentiments, but romantic ones.

Friday's flower appeared on her grandfather's hickory rocking chair on the front porch. A stunning sunflower. Not like the companion plant that she had planted in her garden. Those were giant sunflowers, their sturdy stems acting as trellises for the climbing pole beans.

But this sunflower was a small, delicate blossom, similar to ones she'd seen in some fancy flower arrangements in a floral shop back in Indiana, usually in the fall. *Dedication,* the card said. Her secret flower deliverer certainly was dedicated.

That afternoon she added the sunflower to the rest of the bouquet. Then she started on an early supper — fresh green peas and baked chicken breast. Her grandfather walked in just as she was putting the chicken in the oven.

"More flowers." He sat down at the table and picked up the card, which Rachael had left near the vase. He held it closer to his eyes, then farther away. "Don't have my glasses on, but it looks like it says *dedication.*"

"It does." Rachael measured out two cups of peas and poured them into a pot.

"Did all the flowers come with a card?"

"Ya." She added water to the pot and turned the burner on. "All of them just one word or phrase." She paused, a thought coming to mind. "I think I know why."

Grossdaadi put the card down. "You do?"

She sat down by her grandfather and

picked up the card. "I knew roses had meanings," she said. "But it just dawned on me that other flowers probably do too."

"That's nice. What's for dessert?"

"Applesauce." She studied the card. "I should have figured this out before now."

"Don't suppose we could have some peach cobbler on the side?"

She glanced at him. *"Nee."*

"You're as stubborn as your —"

"*Mei daed.* I know." She peered at him. "I also know where he gets it."

"Funny. You should respect your elders, Rachael."

But she could see the teasing in his eyes, their hue the same as her own. "Believe me, I'm trying."

A knock sounded on the back door. Rachael rose and answered it. Her heart flipped with surprise — and something much deeper — when she saw it was Gideon. After all this time, why was he here?

"Hi, Rachael." He glanced down at his feet, as he usually did when he was around her.

She followed his gaze. His boots were encased in mud and dirt. He smelled like a farm, and she didn't mind it one bit.

He looked at her again. "Do you have a minute?"

Rachael tilted her head to the side and twisted the end of one of the ribbons dangling from her *kapp.* "Sure. Come on in."

"I . . ." He looked down at his boots again. "Okay." He took off his boots and left them on the back porch. "I won't stay long," he said as he walked into the kitchen.

Her grandfather was already getting up. "Gideon," he said with a nod.

"*Herr* Bontrager. Nice to see you're feeling better."

"I am, now that I've been sprung from my cage."

"*Grossdaadi,*" Rachael said, dismayed. She glanced at Gideon. He probably thought she was some kind of tyrant.

"I'm teasing." He picked up his cane and limped toward the kitchen door. "I'll leave you two to talk."

Gideon took a step forward. "You don't have to *geh.*"

Grossdaadi looked at Gideon. Then at Rachael. "Oh, I think I do."

Rachael wanted to shrink into the kitchen floorboards as her grandfather disappeared. She glanced at Gideon and tried to chuckle. She sounded like a squawking bird instead. "I have *nee* idea what he's talking about."

But Gideon didn't seem to be listening.

Instead he was looking at the flowers. "Nice." He dipped his head toward the vase. "Your *gaarde* must be doing well."

"They're not from my *gaarde*." She looked up at him, threading her fingers together. This was it. She'd left him an open opportunity to tell her he'd given her the flowers.

"Oh." He shifted on his feet. "They're nice, anyway."

Her heart skipped. The flowers weren't from him. At least now she had confirmation. And now that she knew the truth, suddenly she didn't care who gave her the flowers. Because if they weren't from Gideon . . . then they meant nothing to her.

She gulped down her disappointment. "What did you want to talk about?" she asked, her voice flat.

"Monday morning. I have a few things to do in town. I thought if it was okay with you . . . I could . . . give you a ride? When you were finished at the flea market, I'd pick you up and bring you home." He glanced at the flowers again before looking at her. "I didn't see the sense in both of us taking a buggy when we're going to the same place."

"Oh." She pursed her lips to the side. "Well, that's . . . practical."

He nodded. "So . . ." He rocked back on

his heels. Looked around the kitchen. Anything, it seemed, to keep from making direct eye contact with her.

Inwardly she sighed. She might as well face it — Gideon wasn't interested in her. He was acting the same around her as he always had — shy, a bit awkward, but in an endearing way. Nothing had changed. His offer came from being neighborly, not because he had feelings for her.

She felt so foolish. All this time, when she thought there might be something between them, he was being hospitable. Embarrassment rolled around within her. For the first time, she felt uncomfortable around him. And she didn't think that sensation would change by Monday.

"I wouldn't want you to *geh* to any trouble." She backed away from him.

"*Nee* trouble," he said, finally meeting her gaze.

"Still, I don't think it's a *gut* idea." She looked up at him. Paused at the furrow in his brow.

"You don't?" he asked, his eyes widening.

"Don't what?"

She turned to see her grandfather come into the room again. She groaned inwardly. All she needed was for him to say something humiliating again. She looked at Gideon, expecting to see him paying attention to her grandfather.

But Gideon's eyes were still on Rachael.

She frowned. He seemed almost . . . upset.

"Thought I left my glasses in here." He walked to the table.

Rachael knew that wasn't true. Sure enough, her grandfather sat back down at the table. She guessed he figured they'd had enough time alone. He looked around the table for a second, then patted the pockets of his pants. "Well, imagine that." He pulled out his reading glasses and put them on, peering at her and Gideon over the rims. "I had them on me all along."

"Amazing," Rachael muttered.

Grossdaadi leaned back in the chair. "Don't mind me. You just keep talking."

"We're finished. I was just about to leave." Gideon looked at Rachael one more time, his eyes confused behind the lenses of his glasses.

"So soon?" *Grossdaadi* said. "Stay, Gideon. Join us for a cup of *kaffee*. It won't take long for Rachael to perk some." He turned to her. "Right?"

"Right," she said, her voice tight.

Gideon paused, looking at *Grossdaadi*.

"You wouldn't turn down an old *mann,* would you?"

"Nee," Gideon said.

"*Gut.* Rachael, two cups of *kaffee,* if you don't mind."

Gideon moved from the door and sat across from *Grossdaadi.* Rachael moved to start the coffee. She glanced at Gideon, who was sitting on the edge of the chair, his broad shoulders a little hunched. He didn't look too happy to be there.

She filled the coffeepot with water and hid a sigh. He wasn't the only one.

CHAPTER SEVEN

Flowers grow out of dark moments.
— CORITA KENT

This was the last time Gideon was listening to Hannah Lynn. It was her idea to come over and offer to give Rachael a ride. "Then you can give her a whole bouquet of roses," she'd said. "And declare your love."

"Love?" he'd asked, frowning. "I want to ask her out, not scare her away."

"Just trust me, Gideon. I've been right so far."

And he had trusted her. He'd even followed her advice and mentioned the flowers without giving away his secret. But it didn't matter. He couldn't even give her a ride to the flea market, and that could hardly be considered a date.

Obviously she thought the flowers were from someone else. All he wanted to do was leave at that point. But he couldn't be rude to *Herr* Bontrager, especially after what he'd been through.

Gideon glanced at Rachael standing at the stove. Instead of joining them, she stared at the coffeepot, like she was willing it to boil. It felt like his insides were curdling. He'd purposely stayed away from her this week, like Hannah Lynn suggested, concerned that he would slip up and "ruin the secret." Made all the effort to get the flowers she told him to, write the cards, and sneak over to her house. And that had been fine with him, when he thought Rachael appreciated it.

But now that he could see she thought the flowers were from someone else . . . he felt sick inside.

"How's the farm doing?"

Gideon hadn't realized he'd been staring at Rachael until her grandfather spoke. He turned to him.

"*Gut, Herr* Bontrager."

"Call me Eli."

"Eli. Just waiting for two of the cows to birth. They still have a few weeks to *geh.*"

"Then you'll have lots of fresh milk." Eli looked at Rachael. "You know what milk makes me think of?"

She didn't look at him. "What?"

Gideon had never seen Rachael like this

— her tone as flat as a flapjack, her back completely straight, her hands gripping the edge of the counter as the percolator began to bubble.

"Ice cream."

She turned off the burner. "You can't have ice cream."

"I can dream about it." He laughed, but it died away quickly when Rachael gave him a hard look.

Silence filled the room for a moment, broken only by the sound of Rachael pouring the coffee into the mugs. She set one in front of each of them without a word and returned to the stove where she had left the third. She picked up a spoon and stirred the contents of the pot. Peas, he guessed from the smell.

His heart ached at the awkward tension between them. He'd gulp down the coffee, go home, and tell Hannah Lynn her flower idea was a complete failure.

"So, what isn't a *gut* idea?" Eli took a sip of his coffee.

"What?" Gideon and Rachael said at the same time.

"You said something wasn't a *gut* idea, Rachael." Her grandfather met her gaze squarely. "What is it?"

Gideon sipped the hot coffee, almost

burning his mouth. He glanced at Rachael. Her eyes were as round as pie plates. But she looked at her grandfather and spoke.

"Gideon offered to take me to the flea market on Monday. I told him I didn't want to be a bother. Besides, you offered to take me, remember? That's why it wasn't a *gut* idea." She quickly took a drink of her coffee, only to suck in a breath and nearly drop it on the counter.

"Are you all right, Rachael?" Eli asked.

"Fine." She gasped. She folded her hands tightly together. "*Kaffee* is a little hot."

Her voice sounded like it had gone through a cheese grater. He shouldn't have stayed. "I better get going. Told *Daed* I wouldn't be gone long."

"All right." Eli sipped his coffee again. Slowly. "We'll see you Monday."

Gideon cocked his head. "Monday?"

"*Ya.* To pick up Rachael."

Gideon paused. "But what about you?"

"I can *geh* with her anytime."

"But —" Rachael said.

"She'll be ready." Eli looked at her. "*Ya?*"

Rachael nodded. What else could she do? He hadn't had much interaction with Eli before Rachael had moved in, but just from this conversation, Gideon could see that he was a force to be reckoned with.

Gideon dragged his fingertips across his forehead, ready to refuse, not liking the idea that Rachael was being cornered into catching a ride with him. But he didn't want to embarrass either one of them further. "All right. See you Monday, Rachael."

"Right. Monday."

Gideon slipped on his boots and walked home, wishing he'd never started all this in the first place. At least before, he could imagine Rachael liked him. Now he knew for sure . . . and maybe he knew this all along. That had to have been what kept him from asking her out before. He knew, deep down, he wasn't what she wanted.

Hannah Lynn met him just as he crossed over into their yard. "Well?" she asked, her eyes bright with anticipation.

"She said *nee.*" He blew past her, ignoring her shocked expression. He wanted to forget everything that had happened . . . at least until Monday.

Monday morning, Rachael paced the length of her garden. She had wakened early, unable to sleep, dreading the ride to the flea market. After Gideon had left Friday, she wanted to give her grandfather a piece of her mind for meddling in her business. But he had calmly finished his cup of coffee, giving her a satisfied look. She didn't know what he was up to, and at that point she'd been too stressed to care. They didn't speak for the rest of the night.

Since there was no church on Sunday, she had managed to avoid seeing Gideon. For the first time since she could remember, she didn't go to her garden, not even to sit and pray, as she had done when she first arrived and her grandfather was so sick. She wanted to hide, to find a way to get out of the nearly half-hour drive to the flea market.

But she was being stupid. Nothing had changed between them. They were still friends. Just because he didn't feel the same way about her that she felt for him didn't mean that she couldn't accept a ride from him.

Yet that didn't stop her mouth from going dry when he pulled into the driveway with his buggy.

She swallowed as she stood outside the fence of her garden. She had everything ready — her table, the plants and flowers and hanging baskets she planned to sell, plus a couple of container planters she'd prepared on Saturday night. She touched the back edge of her *kapp* as he pulled the four-seater buggy to a stop.

He climbed down from the buggy. She

looked up and met his eyes, but he averted them quickly. He seemed as uncomfortable as she felt.

Suddenly she realized she didn't like this. She didn't want to lose Gideon as a friend, or the comfortable feeling they'd had with each other before the flowers started appearing. She forced a smile, then, finding out it wasn't that difficult, gave him a genuine one. "*Danki* for taking me to the market," she said.

He looked at her. She thought she heard him let out a breath before he smiled back. "Glad I can help."

And with those two sentences, everything was right between them again.

"Do you think you'll have enough room for all of this?" She peeked into the back of the buggy.

"*Ya.* You might have to hold a couple of plants in your lap, though."

"That'll be all right."

He came up beside her and slid the square fold-up table in the back. "We can put as many plants as possible on the seat. The table will keep them from falling on the floor."

He turned, but she hadn't moved away yet. They bumped into each other, his hand brushing against her arm.

Rachael held her breath. He'd never stood so near to her. All feelings of friendship flew out of her head and her heart.

Gideon's pulse raced as he gazed down at Rachael. Being this close to her, he could almost count every freckle on her cute little nose. He'd nearly sent Hannah Lynn over to tell Rachael that he couldn't take her to the flea market, but he wouldn't go back on his word. He and Rachael were still friends. He'd have to find a way to accept that.

But now, with only inches between them and neither one moving away, he wondered how he could. Would it be possible to tuck his emotions so deep inside his heart that they'd never resurface? If this moment was any indication, he knew he couldn't. But he didn't want to lose her friendship, either.

"Gideon." Rachael leaned toward him.

Mesmerized by her soft voice, he asked, "What?"

"Hold still." She brushed her hand against his shoulder. "You had a little dirt there." Her eyes remained locked with his.

"Oh. *Danki.*" He couldn't look away. Suddenly he didn't care about rejection. He had to let Rachael know how he felt — even if it meant risking their friendship. "Rachael." Without thinking he touched the end of one of the white ribbons of her *kapp.*

"*Ya?*" If his gesture bothered her, she didn't let on.

"I . . ." He licked his lips, the words stuck in his throat. He pushed past it. "It was me —"

"Rachael!"

They both turned at the frantic, garbled sound of her grandfather's voice. He held out his hand and collapsed on the porch.

"*Grossdaadi!*" Rachael rushed toward him.

Gideon followed. They both crouched by the old man. His eyes were closed, his face pale as paper.

"Dear Lord!" She leaned over him, tears sliding down her face. "Is he . . . ?"

Gideon held his hand above Eli's nose and mouth. Seconds turned into hours as he waited to feel the exhalation of air. Finally, a faint rush of air brushed his palm. "He's breathing."

"Thank God." She grabbed his hand. "*Grossdaadi . . . Grossdaadi!*"

"I'll call an ambulance." He raced to the call box next to the road, situated between both their houses. As he punched in the emergency number, he turned around to see Rachael hovering over her grandfather's still body. *Lord, be with Eli. He and Rachael have been through so much.*

216

When he heard the dispatcher's voice, he told her about Eli and gave her the address. He hung up the phone and ran back to the porch. Eli's eyes were now open, but his gaze was transfixed on the porch ceiling.

"He's not saying anything." She looked at Gideon, terror in her eyes. "What's wrong with him?"

His stomach dropped. "I don't know, Rachael. I'm sorry, I don't know."

CHAPTER EIGHT

Don't send me flowers when I'm dead. If you like me, send them while I'm alive.
— BRIAN CLOUGH

Rachael paced in the emergency unit's waiting room. The blare of the TV sounded behind her, the nasally voice of the woman reporting the news pounding in her head. She'd been allowed to ride to the hospital in the ambulance with her grandfather, but since then she had been relegated to the waiting room while they examined him in the back. She'd checked with the receptionist several times, but so far there was no word on her grandfather's condition. The only hope she clung to was that her grandfather had been responsive in the ambulance, and even had enough energy to bicker with one of the emergency workers.

Unable to stand being inside anymore, she walked out of the hospital and down the steps leading to the emergency room drop-off. The sun beat down, its rays assaulting her with heat instead of warming her as they usually did. She sat on the edge of one step and dropped her head in her hands. Nothing mattered to her right now but her grandfather.

She closed her eyes and prayed. *Lord, please don't let him die. I'm not ready to lose him. He can be stubborn and nosy and downright foolish sometimes, but I love him. And I don't want to let him* geh.

She opened her eyes. She didn't know how long she sat on the concrete step, praying for her grandfather's healing, trying not to think the worst yet preparing herself to accept God's will. Finally she stood and went inside, barely noticing the coolness from the air conditioning.

She sat back down, ignoring the inquisitive look from a Yankee woman in the waiting room. Just as she settled back in her chair, the double doors to the emergency treatment rooms opened. A nurse dressed in a dark-blue hospital uniform walked out.

"Rachael Bontrager?"

Rachael jumped from her seat and hurried to her. "Yes?"

"The doctor wants to speak with you."

The knot in the pit of her stomach tightened. She followed the nurse down the hallway, the doors automatically shutting behind her. A few feet away she saw a man wearing a white coat, a stethoscope around his neck. He was writing notes on a thick clipboard when Rachael approached.

"Miss Bontrager, I'm Dr. Carr. I've been treating your grandfather."

"How bad is it?"

The doctor removed his dark-framed glasses. "He's going to be fine. We're still running a few more tests, but from what we can gather, he hasn't had another stroke."

She let out a breath of relief. "Then what happened to him?"

"All we've been able to ascertain is that he was dizzy right before he fainted. That can happen for a number of reasons. He was dehydrated, so we're giving him IV fluids right now."

"Dehydrated? But we have plenty to drink around the house. Water, tea, and of course, coffee. He drinks a lot of that."

"That could be the culprit. Too much caffeine can cause dehydration."

She had no idea. "But he's been a coffee drinker all his life. It's never affected him this way before."

The doctor nodded. "It's possible, given his advanced age, that his body can't tolerate the caffeine as well as it used to. But we'll rule out other possibilities. Don't worry, we'll do a thorough examination of your grandfather." He smirked. "If he'll let us, that is."

Rachael crossed her arms. "Is he giving you trouble?"

"He's . . . lively." The doctor flipped the chart closed. "He also wants to talk to you. Exam room number two. We'll be moving him to the main hospital in a couple of hours. We want to keep him overnight to finish up the tests and make sure he's well enough to go home."

"All right." She could feel the tension release from her shoulders. The doctor's words bolstered her confidence. If her grandfather had passed out from dehydration, she'd make sure he drank twenty glasses of water a day.

She walked into the hospital room, stunned at all the machines near her grandfather's bed. She'd never been in a hospital, and she couldn't help but stare at the tubes and wires running from his arms to the various beeping machines. A nurse adjusted a clear tube leading from the middle of his arm to a pole. The hook at the end held a bag filled with what looked like water. The nurse looked at Rachael.

"They should have a room ready for your grandfather soon, Miss Bontrager."

"I'm right here," *Grossdaadi* grumped. "Don't talk about me like I'm not."

"Don't worry, Mr. Bontrager." The nurse touched his shoulder. "We're all aware that you're here."

"Gut." He looked at Rachael. "So when are you taking me home?"

The nurse passed by Rachael. "Good luck," she said, shaking her head and leaving the room.

Rachael sat down on the chair nearest to the bed. "They're keeping you overnight, *Grossdaadi.*"

"That's what the doc said. But I'm not staying. I want to *geh* home."

"I know, but let them figure out what happened to you."

"I know what happened. I got dizzy. That's it."

"You passed out." She looked down at his hand lying against the white sheet. Gnarled, rough, with ridges of veins on the top. "You're also dehydrated."

"I won't be after this." He held up his arm where the clear tube snaked out from underneath a bandage. She assumed that was the IV the doctor mentioned. Everything hit her with full force. Her grandfather

222

was back in the hospital, uncomfortable, and hooked up to machines. Despite everything she did to take care of him, she'd failed. "I'm sorry," she whispered.

"Sorry?" He turned to her, frowning. "What are you sorry for?"

"This is *mei* fault."

"What?"

"I shouldn't have let you work out in the barn. I should have made sure you drank enough water. I should have —"

"Rachael." In a rare show of affection, he took her hand and didn't let go. "I want you to listen to me, all right?"

She looked at him, squeezed his hand, and nodded.

He stared at her for a moment. "I've said you're just like your *daed.* And part of that is true." His green eyes began to tear. "But you're most like your *grossmutter.* She used to worry about me, you know. Afraid I would fall off the roof when I used to do roofing jobs. Worry I'd have an accident on a construction site. She'd tell me I ate too much, or ate too little." He leaned his head back against the pillow. "And I used to give her a hard time too. Now I'd give anything to hear her nagging at me again."

"She did it because she loved you."

"I know." He let go of her hand. "And I

know that's why you're hovering over me all the time. But I want you to realize what your grandmother, for whatever reason, couldn't. She wasn't responsible for me. Neither are you."

"But I promised *Mamm* and *Daed* I'd take care of you."

He looked up at the ceiling. "Can't exactly blame your *daed* for worrying. He got that trait from *mei* Martha. But your parents shouldn't have put that burden on you."

"You're not a burden."

"*Ya,* I am. I'm also a grown *mann.* I can take care of myself. And when the time comes that the Lord wants me in heaven, I'm ready."

Rachael's eyes stung with tears. "I'm not," she croaked.

"Well, I don't plan on going anywhere for a long time." He looked at her again. "Tell you what. When I *geh* home, I'll follow the doctor's orders. *Nee* more complaining about rabbit food or arguing with you about taking a nap. But you have to do something for me. Two things, actually."

"Anything."

"First, stop worrying. That won't make either of us live longer."

"Okay. I'll try." She knew it wouldn't be easy, but having this conversation with him was already providing her some relief. "What's the other?"

"Quit spending so much time alone. That's not natural for anyone. You're always working in that *gaarde,* or doing chores, or worrying about me. You need to be with people your own age, not an old crust like me."

"I don't mind it."

"You will, eventually. I know you're working hard to make sure we have what we need. But the Lord will provide. He always has. So make some new friends. *Geh* to a singing." He gave her a sly grin. "I know someone who would be glad to take you."

A knock sounded on the door. The nurse came inside. "Mr. Bontrager, your room is ready. An orderly will be here to transport you in a few minutes."

"Humph." Then he looked at Rachael. She lifted a brow. "All right," he said.

The nurse smiled. "You're sounding better already."

After the nurse left, Rachael closed the door and looked at her grandfather. "I'll stay with you tonight. I'm sure you'll be going home tomorrow."

"That's the spirit." He smiled and shifted to a higher seated position in his bed. "So do we have a deal, *grossdochder*?"

Rachael grinned. "We have a deal."

CHAPTER NINE

Help us to be faithful gardeners of the spirit, who know that without darkness nothing comes to birth, and without life nothing flowers.
— MAY SARTON

The next morning the doctor gave Rachael's grandfather the all clear. "He's good to go," Dr. Carr said. He looked at *Grossdaadi.* "Remember to drink plenty of water, Mr. Bontrager. And cut back on the caffeine."

He frowned. "Can I at least have dessert every once in a while?"

Dr. Carr looked at Rachael. "I don't see why not. Everything in moderation."

Rachael got up from the chair she'd slept in last night. While her grandfather had snored peacefully last night, she'd been in and out of sleep. She was as eager to get home as he was. "I'll *geh* call us a taxi," she said. "I'll be back in a minute."

"*Gut.* That will give me time to get out of this *dumm* hospital gown."

She shook her head. "Glad to see you're back to normal."

He grew serious. "Me too."

Rachael opened the door and started down the hallway toward the nurses' station. They'd already given her permission to use the phone.

"Rachael."

She turned around to see Gideon coming down the hall. Her heart thumped in her chest. She'd never been so happy to see him. Emotions overflowed inside her as she walked toward him.

"What are you doing here?" she asked when she reached him.

He looked down. Not at his shoes this time, but at her. "I came to take you home."

Relief flooded her, bringing all the emotions she'd held together over the past twenty-four hours to the surface. Before she knew it, she was in his arms.

Gideon held Rachael, not worrying if anyone in the hallway was watching them. He rubbed her upper back with his hand. "It's all right, Rachael."

"He's going to be okay," she said against his chest.

"That's what they told me." He'd called last night and early this morning, checking on Eli's status. After some cajoling on Gideon's part, the nurse revealed that Eli was being released that morning. Gideon hired a taxi right away.

He resisted the urge to kiss the top of her head. "God is *gut*," he said, his voice low.

Suddenly she moved away from him. She wiped her fingers underneath her beautiful green eyes. She looked exhausted. He didn't blame her — he'd been scared when the ambulance pulled out of the Bontragers' driveway. He'd wanted to hire a taxi and follow them. He wanted to be there for Rachael. But he couldn't. Instead he went back to the farm, feeling helpless except for the prayers he offered while he was working.

"I'm sorry." She brushed back the strings of her *kapp*.

"Don't be." He looked down at her. "The taxi is waiting outside."

Rachael was quiet on the way home, but Eli was a steady stream of chatter. Gideon didn't hear half of what he said, keeping an eye on Rachael. Everything would be okay, yet he wouldn't stop worrying about her. Not until they were home.

A little more than thirty minutes later, the taxi pulled into Rachael's driveway. "Oh nee," she said, saying her first words since they'd left the hospital. She looked at Gideon. "I don't have my purse."

Eli reached into his pocket. But Gideon stopped him. "Don't worry about it." Gideon handed the driver his fare, and he and Rachael helped Eli out of the car.

"I don't know about you two, but I'm bushed," Eli said. "Didn't sleep a wink last night."

Rachael half-smiled. "You were sawing logs, *Grossdaadi.*"

"Was I? Well, I'm headed inside."

"I'll be right there to fix your lunch," she called after him.

"There should be a zucchini casserole in the kitchen from *Mamm,*" Gideon said. "Hannah Lynn was supposed to drop it off while I picked you up, so it should still be warm."

"Sounds delicious." Eli looked at him. "You two take your time, *ya?*"

Gideon's cheeks heated. He hadn't fooled Eli. Seemed everyone knew how he felt about Rachael, except Rachael.

He expected her to follow her grandfather inside. Instead she watched him limp up the steps. "He's going to be okay," she whispered.

"*Ya.* He will."

"I have to keep reminding myself of that."
She looked up at him. "*Danki* for picking us
up. I'll repay you for the taxi fare."

"I won't accept it." He looked at her. The
sun was high in the sky, partially covered by
the flat, streaky clouds that had gathered
across the sky over the morning. "You
should *geh* inside and get some rest."

"I can't. I still have to take care of the
horse —"

"Already done."

She gave him a weary smile.

"Now. *Geh* inside. I'll check on both of
you tomorrow."

"You don't . . ."

He steeled himself for her refusal. This
time he would ignore it. She needed his
help, and he was glad to give it.

She gazed at him. "I'll see you tomorrow."

Stunned, Gideon waited until Rachael was
inside. When he saw the hazy glow of a gas
lamp shining through the window, he let
out a long breath. Eli would be okay. Rachael would be okay.

And as he walked back home, he still
remembered the feel of her in his arms.

Bright sunlight prodded Rachael to open
her eyes. She stretched out, letting the
sunbeams warm her for a moment, still

stuck in the twilight of sleep, and remembering that she dreamed about Gideon.

Suddenly she bolted upright. Looked around the living room. She'd fallen asleep on the couch. She vaguely remembered eating a bit of the zucchini casserole, then sitting down for a moment. Lying back, just resting her eyes for a few minutes before she went upstairs to her room.

Instead, she'd spent the night in the living room, sleeping more deeply than she had in weeks.

She looked out the window. By the position of the sun in the sky, she knew she'd overslept. She went to her grandfather's room. The door was slightly open, and she could hear his snoring, softer now than when he was in the hospital.

Rachael went into the bathroom and splashed some water on her face. She looked in the mirror, taking in her askew *kapp* and wrinkled dress. Knowing the horse would be hungry by now, she quickly repinned her *kapp* and straightened her light-blue dress.

In a hurry she went through the back door and to the barn to feed and water the horse. Her bare feet were soon drenched from the grass. Had it rained last night? She didn't remember hearing a thing. As she came out of the barn, she glanced over at the Beilers', a little disappointed she didn't see Gideon.

She could still remember how it felt to be in his arms, to lean against him. He made her feel secure. Comforted. Like she wasn't alone. She wanted to have that feeling forever. He'd been different with her at the hospital. Sure of himself. He'd known exactly what to do and what to say.

As she walked to her garden, she realized that yesterday had only cemented her feelings for him. And even though he wasn't the one who had given her the flowers, she still had to tell him how she felt. She owed it to both of them.

Relaxed for the first time in a long while, she moved toward the garden gate . . . and froze. But it wasn't the wide-open gate that caused the sick knot to form in her stomach.

The plants she'd planned to take to the flea market Monday were still on the ground outside the garden fence. In the chaos of her grandfather's hospitalization, she'd forgotten all about them. As she neared, she could see that the tender leaves and stems were bent, even broken in some places. "Oh *nee*!"

She looked at her vegetable patch. It was flattened. Puddles of water gathered in small pockets in the soil. The tomatoes and bell peppers she'd planted two weeks ago were destroyed. Her cucumber frame lay on the ground. She picked up a cucumber. It was covered in pockmarks. The cornstalks were broken, partially mature ears of corn lying useless on the ground.

She ventured farther into the garden. The flowers were also victims. Her Impatiens, Pansies, Geraniums . . . all crushed. All ruined.

Rachael sank to the ground. The evidence was clear. Rain wouldn't have done this kind of damage. But hail would have. Sometime during the night it had hailed, destroying almost everything.

All the time, effort, and yes, money she'd put into the garden — gone because of one storm. Instead of fresh vegetables in the summer and shelves lined with canned vegetables in the winter, they would have very little. The peace she'd felt just a moment ago disappeared.

She put her face in her hands and wept.

Soon after wolfing down his breakfast, Gideon made his way to Rachael's to check on her and Eli. A fierce storm had come through last night, and the hail had sounded like rocks hitting the roof. He expected his father to ask him when he'd be back, but he

234

didn't say anything. It seemed his whole family was realizing how important Rachael was to him.

He pushed his hat onto his head and rushed through the damp morning grass, through his front yard and then hers. He didn't bother going to the house. She would be in her garden. She always was.

But as he drew closer, he could see the plants they'd left outside the garden Monday. He also noticed that the flowers in two of the hanging baskets were ruined. He wiped his face with his hand, thinking about the hailstorm last night. The flower baskets weren't a good sign.

He stepped into the garden, hearing the soft sounds of her crying before he saw her hunched over, kneeling on the ground. He took in the disaster of her garden — once a neatly manicured, nurtured little plot of paradise. Now it looked like a herd of cattle had trampled through it.

He went to her. Stood beside her. She didn't move, just continued to cry. Gideon reached out, only to pull his hand back. Maybe she wanted to be alone. Maybe he was intruding.

Then she looked up at him, her eyes pooling with tears. He knelt beside her and rested his hand on her shoulder.

"Are you all right?"

She wiped her face with her hands and sniffed, lifting her chin. *"Ya."* She stood, shrugging his hand off her shoulder. "It's all ruined."

"Rachael, it will be okay."

"Nee." She moved away from him. "It won't." Rachael turned her back to him. "I've got a lot of work to do."

He walked closer to her. "Let me help you."

She shook her head, turned, and walked past him. He followed as she went to the small storage shed right outside the garden where she stored her gardening tools.

"I'll have to see what I can salvage." She picked up a large bucket from the floor.

"Rachael —"

"There's still time to plant some more tomatoes and peppers." She grabbed a rake off the wall. "They'll come in late, but it will be better than having none at all. I'll have to rebuild the cucumber trellis —"

He stepped in front of her. "Stop."

She looked up at him. "I can't stop. There's too much damage to repair. I'm wasting time arguing with you."

"Then don't argue." He took the rake from her. "Let me help."

"You have your own work to take care of."

"*Daed* and Hannah Lynn can manage. It won't hurt Hannah Lynn one bit to get out there and milk the cows." He smiled a little, hoping to cheer her up.

She reached for the rake. "*Geh* home, Gideon. I can do this myself."

"I know you can." He refused to let go. "But you don't have to. I'm here, Rachael." He cleared his throat, his emotions getting the best of him. "I always have been."

Her fingers released the grip on the handle. *"Danki."* Her voice, small and vulnerable, twisted his heart. "You're a *gut* friend." She moved past him and walked out of the shed.

A friend. Normally he hated to hear that word. He'd always wanted to be so much more. But that wasn't what she needed now. She needed a friend — and he would be there for her.

CHAPTER TEN

Flowers are happy things.
— P. G. WODEHOUSE

Three hours later, the sun blasted its heat straight above them. Gideon took off his hat and wiped the sweat from his forehead with the back of his hand. They'd made good progress. Rachael had picked over the plants she thought she could save or at least attempt to nurse back and pointed out which ones needed to be thrown away. She even managed to find a bright side. "They'll make *gut* compost," she'd said shortly after they set to work.

Now he was raking a bare patch of soil where a group of green and white Hostas used to be. He couldn't believe how much damage the hail had done. He was also learning more about plants and flowers than he'd ever known before.

"Thirsty?" Rachael came up behind him.

He turned. The pain so evident in her eyes earlier that morning was gone, replaced by determination. Without thinking, he brushed her cheek with his thumb. There was nothing there, but he couldn't help himself. "You had some, uh, dirt . . ."

She brushed at her cheek, which turned a rosy shade. "I'm going inside to get some cold tea. Do you want some?"

"*Ya*. The sun is brutal today."

"I'll be right back." She looked up at him and smiled before she went into the house.

For such a rotten start to the day, it was turning out to be a pretty good afternoon.

"Gideon!"

He heard Hannah Lynn's voice in the distance. He leaned the rake against the fence and went to the gate.

"*Daed* sent me to find out what's taking you so long." She looked at the garden. "Wow. What happened?"

"Hail. Tell *Daed* I'm helping Rachael. I'll be home when we're finished here."

"All right." Hannah Lynn hesitated. "So . . . are you two . . ."

"Friends. We're friends."

"Oh." She frowned. "I thought for sure the flowers would work."

"I can't get mad at you for trying." He leaned forward. "But from now on, I'm doing things *mei* way."

"Got it." She held up her hands and backed away. "I'm done meddling in other people's business."

"I doubt that," he muttered.

"What?"

"Nix." He turned and grabbed the rake, returning to work.

A few minutes later, Rachael appeared. "Fresh brewed," she said, handing it to him. "I only had a few ice cubes in the cooler. It's not very cold."

"It will do." He took a long swig of the drink. Then he looked around the garden. "Do you have a piece of paper and a pencil?"

"In my shed. Why?"

"Thought it would be a *gut* idea to make a list of what you need to get this garden back in shape." He set aside the rake and headed for the shed. She followed. "Where's the paper?"

"Here." She pulled out a small notepad and short pencil from a little yellow pail hanging on a nail on the shed wall. He wasn't surprised she was that organized.

"How about we walk around the garden and you tell me what you need? Then I'll *geh* to town tomorrow and pick it up." When she opened her mouth, he held up his hand. "Don't even try."

"Try what?"

"To tell me *nee*. Or talk me out of it. Or say that you can do it yourself." He leaned over her. "I'm doing this whether you like it or not."

"Okay." She crossed her arms over her chest. "First thing I need is five hundred pounds of potting soil."

He held the pencil over the pad, his eyes widening. "How much?"

She grinned. "Gotcha."

By suppertime, Rachael was exhausted. Gideon had left an hour ago, saying he had to put in a couple of hours at the farm before sundown. Before she could say she was sorry, he told her not to be. It was as if he had sensed her guilt before she'd spoken it.

But it had been like that all day with him. She stood at the edge of the garden. They had accomplished so much together. This morning she was devastated by what had happened. Now she had hope that her garden wasn't a complete disaster. She still wouldn't have as many vegetables as she'd planned for, but they would have enough.

She heard footsteps behind her. Turning, she saw her grandfather coming toward her.

He stood next to her and whistled.

"I know," she said. "The hail really hit the *gaarde* hard."

"*Ya.* I saw the mess earlier. I'm impressed by what you and Gideon did today." He looked at her. "You make a *gut* team."

Rachael looked at the garden again. It was stripped down and there was still a lot of work to do. But instead of seeing everything she lost, she focused on what she and Gideon had accomplished. It had been nice to work alongside someone, especially him. Her grandfather was right. They did make a good team.

Peace entered her soul, a peace she hadn't felt since coming to Middlefield. She'd faced two of her biggest fears — her grandfather getting sick again and her garden being destroyed. In spite of everything, she could still count the blessings. Danki, *Lord.*

"Well, I'm hungry." Her grandfather tapped the ground with his cane. "How about I cook supper tonight?"

She grimaced. *"Nee."*

He frowned. "What about our deal?"

"Oh, we still have a deal." She put her arm around his shoulder. "But you're a terrible cook."

"True. How about I check on the horse and you make supper?"

"That sounds better."

As her grandfather made his way to the barn, Rachael looked at the garden one more time. She'd done enough work for the day. Tonight she would relax. Maybe even read a book, something she hadn't had the energy or the patience to do in a long time. She took one last look at her garden and smiled.

She walked to the shed and was about to shut and lock the door when she noticed a piece of paper on the floor. She picked it up. Gideon's list. He must have dropped it when he left. She'd go to the Beilers' tomorrow and give it to him. She stepped out of the shed and closed the door, then snapped the padlock in place.

She decided to double-check the list to make sure she didn't forget anything. She didn't want Gideon making multiple trips to town on her account.

Then she stopped reading. She brought the list closer to her eyes, studying the handwriting. Plain, neat, square letters. Handwriting she'd seen before.

Her pulse thrummed as she ran into the house and to her room, opened up the drawer on the side table, and pulled out the note cards that had been attached to the flowers. Rachael laid them on the bed and placed the note next to them.

The handwriting was identical.

She smiled. It widened as she reread the flower cards. *My Compliments. Admiration. Sincerity. Lasting Beauty. Dedication.* All written in Gideon's unique hand.

Her heart warmed. Hadn't he proven all of these to her? His admiration of her garden. His sincerity when he spoke. The lasting beauty of his friendship. His dedication to being there when she needed him most.

Not only did the flowers speak what was on his heart, his actions did too.

She stacked the cards together. She would see Gideon tomorrow, and this time he was the one in for a surprise.

CHAPTER ELEVEN

For there is a sound reasoning upon all flowers. For flowers are peculiarly the poetry of Christ.
— CHRISTOPHER SMART

Gideon rose well before dawn to milk the cows. He was on the third one when his *daed* walked into the barn.

"Nearly done?" *Daed* asked.

"Ya." The splashing sound of the milk hitting the bucket filled the barn.

"You must have started early."

"I wanted to finish so I could check on Rachael ... . er, Eli."

His father smiled. "I know who you meant." Then he grew serious. "How is she?"

"Fine." He patted the cow's flanks and picked up the bucket. He walked over and poured the milk into a larger trough. "I promise I won't be gone all day."

"Don't worry about it." *Daed* pulled his hat over his brow. "We'll take up the slack for a little while."

"Danki." He handed his father the bucket. "Have at it."

His father smirked and took the bucket. Gideon was almost out the door when *Daed* called after him.

"Does she make you happy?"

He looked at his father. They'd never talked about Rachael before, even though he obviously knew about Gideon's feelings for her. Were things between him and Rachael exactly the way he wanted them? No. But he accepted that now. He treasured their friendship. No matter what, he wanted Rachael to be a part of his life. "*Ya*. She does."

"That's what counts. *Geh* on. And take your time over there."

Gideon grinned and left the barn. He stepped outside into the warm sunshine. He tilted his head toward the sun, taking in its warming rays, which seemed to seep straight into his soul.

He headed for her house. When he got to the gate, something on the ground caught his eye. A yellow rose. He'd nearly stepped on it. He picked it up, recognizing it from the variety of roses she had on several trellises on the west side of her garden. They had survived the hail assault. It was small, a little underdeveloped. A card was attached.

He smiled. She'd discovered his secret after all. He looked at the card.

Friendship.

His heart sank. She couldn't be clearer than that.

But that didn't change his mind or how he felt. He opened the gate and latched it behind him. A thought occurred to him. Although no one could predict something as destructive as a hailstorm, he could help protect her garden from deer and other pesky critters by fixing the latch on the gate so that it would close on its own.

Out of the corner of his eye, he spotted another rose lying on top of the dirt bed he'd smoothed out yesterday. This one was pink. The card said *Joy.* This one was a little better. He smiled, glad she was happy.

He lifted his head at a shrill whistle coming from the back of the garden. He walked to the partly finished greenhouse. A hand appeared in the window, holding a white rose. Just as he started toward the greenhouse, the hand and flower disappeared. He ran to the other side of the wall.

She wasn't there. He looked on the ground. Gideon chuckled as he picked up the white rose. He read the card. *New Beginnings.* So roses had meanings too, just like the other flowers. But what did *New Beginnings* mean?

"Gideon."

He turned to see Rachael coming out from behind the oak tree. Her smile hit him square in the chest, the look in her beach-glass eyes nearly buckled his knees. "Rachael," he said, his voice gruff with emotion.

She looked at the flowers in his hand. "I see you got my messages."

"I see you figured out *mei* secret." He walked toward her. "I hope you liked them."

"I did. A lot." She moved closer. "And I'd hoped it was you."

"You did?"

She held a flower. A small red rose. "Here. To complete your bouquet."

"I have to say, I've never had anyone give me flowers before." He looked at the rose. "What does this one mean?"

"Love."

Rachael's mouth grew dry as she waited for Gideon's reaction. For a moment, she thought she'd made a mistake. What man would want flowers? When he didn't say anything, dread pooled inside her. She'd been too eager to surprise him. Then she used the word *love.* Now she was probably scaring him away.

"There are different kinds of love," she said, trying to fix this. "Friendship love, for example." She giggled, but it faded when he didn't smile.

"Is that what you're trying to tell me? That you love me . . . as a friend?" He pushed up his glasses.

"Uh, not exactly."

He held the roses at his side. "Rachael, I need to be straight with you."

She gripped the red rose. One tiny thorn pressed into her skin, but she barely felt it.

"The flowers weren't *mei* idea. They were Hannah Lynn's."

"They were?" The dread tightened inside.

"She thought it would be a nice surprise. I think it ended up being more of a game to her. She found the flowers and told me what they meant."

"I see." Rachael turned around, her cheeks flaming. And here she thought he'd put a lot of thought and effort into finding just the right words. The right flowers. Instead he just let his sister do it. He was the delivery boy.

"Rachael, look at me." When she didn't turn, she felt his hand on her shoulder.

"Please."

She spun around but didn't look up at him.

"I shouldn't have let Hannah Lynn talk me into it."

She wondered if he realized how he was twisting the knife. "It's okay."

"*Nee,* it's not. I never wanted you to get the wrong idea."

Too late for that.

"But I'm not *gut* with words." He dropped his hand from her shoulder. "I usually say the wrong thing."

"Gideon, I've never known you to say the wrong thing."

"I'm pretty sure I have now. You look upset."

She pressed the rose against her chest. "I'm not upset." She tried to laugh, but it came out sounding like she was choking on a lemon. "And the flowers . . . I just wanted to show you how much I appreciated what you did for me yesterday."

"They're nice." He took the rose from her. "I like this one most of all."

His words took her off guard. "You do?"

"*Ya.*" He moved closer. "It says what I've been meaning to tell you for a long time." Gideon touched the end of her chin with one of the rose's soft petals. "I care for you,

Rachael. Not as a friend. You mean a lot more to me than that."

Her heart flipped over as he took her hand in his. "Gideon, you're wrong."

"What?"

"You are *gut* with words." She tilted her face to him. "You just said the perfect thing."

He bent forward and kissed her, pressing his lips so sweetly against hers she thought she might float away. Then he pulled her against him, and she felt him rest his chin on the top of her head.

"I thought I'd scare you off," he said, his voice sounding a little breathless. "That's why I never said anything."

"And here I thought I scared you off." She took a step back. "How long have you felt this way?"

"Pretty much since I met you."

She laughed. "Purple."

"What?"

"Purple roses. Those mean love at first sight." Her laughter faded. "If I had one, I'd give it to you."

He took her face in his hands and kissed her again. When they parted, she glanced down, seeing the rose between them. "We crushed it," she said.

He glided his thumb across her cheek. "Don't worry, we'll grow more. In your *grienhaus.*"

"But it's not finished yet."

He smiled. "It will be soon. Because we'll build it together. Remember what I said? How you don't have to do things alone? I meant it."

She stepped away from him, suddenly inspired. "I was thinking about how to seal the old windows once the walls are built. *Grossdaadi* has a box of caulk in the barn. Don't ask me why, but he does. Also, we need to build shelves inside —"

He kissed her silently. When he pulled away, he said, "Let's just enjoy the moment, okay? I've waited so long for this . . . we can put the *grienhaus,* and everything else, on hold. At least for a little while."

She snuggled against him, the greenhouse becoming a memory in the back of her mind. He was right. She'd waited for them to be together too.

As she leaned against his chest, Rachael thanked God for her blessings. For so long she focused on her work, on worrying about how she would do everything, instead of concentrating on what was right in front of her — family, Gideon, and love. She vowed to change that, to enjoy life, no matter what happened. With God and Gideon by her side, she could face anything.

READING GROUP GUIDE

1. Do you think Rachael was too over-protective of her grandfather? Why or why not?
2. Could Rachael have reached out more to her community? In what ways?
3. Should Gideon have followed his sister's plan to "woo" Rachael?
4. What could he have done differently?
5. Rachael let her worries over her grandfather and her garden take over her mind and heart, keeping her from fully trusting God. Have there been times in your life when fear and worry kept you from putting your faith in the Lord?

ACKNOWLEDGMENTS

Thank you to everyone who helped make this book possible: my editors, Becky Philpott and Natalie Hanemann; my agent, Tamela Hancock Murray; and of course my family for their unwavering support.

ABOUT THE AUTHOR

Kathleen Fuller is the author of several best-selling novels, including *A Man of His Word* and *Treasuring Emma,* as well as a middle-grade Amish series, The Mysteries of Middlefield.

■ ■ ■ ■ ■

Seeds of Love

TRICIA GOYER

■ ■ ■ ■

This book is dedicated to two great churches: Easthaven Baptist Church in Kalispell, Montana, and Mosaic Church of Central Arkansas in Little Rock. More than fellow church members, you are friends. And you've taught me what a loving community is all about!

GLOSSARY OF WEST KOOTENAI AMISH WORDS

aenti — aunt
danke — thank you
dat — dad
Englisch — non-Amish
Englischman — non-Amish man
gut — good
ja — yes
kapp — prayer cap
kinder — children
liebling — darling
mem — mom
ne — no
oma — grandmother
opa — grandfather
vell — well
wunderbar — wonderful

CHAPTER ONE

Eli Plank sipped a cup of strong coffee as he sat down to write his *Budget* report, which had to be mailed today in order to make the next printing of the paper. One of his earliest memories included watching his *dat* reading *The Budget* each night after dinner. It was a staple in Amish homes. A way for men and women from all around the country to connect, telling of the joys and hardships of their local Amish communities.

For as long as he could read *The Budget* himself, Eli had always sought out the news from the West Kootenai community first. The local scribe's column often read like an adventure novel, with elk taking down clotheslines and wild turkeys showing up in buggy sheds. The Amish families who'd traveled to West Kootenai were the adventurers among them — like modern-day Lewises and Clarks. Now he was one of them. Eli wondered if the area would live up to the expectations he'd set in his mind. And he also wondered how many days his mother could go before writing him of his need to return to Indiana, settle down, and find himself a wife.

He sat at the small handmade wooden table. Next to him the large window was open. The cool wind carried in the scent of pine and a stirring of dust from the four-wheel-drive truck that had just rumbled down the road. Yesterday his first visitors had shown up at the cabin. A trio of Amish kids who lived just down the road. They'd brought over cinnamon rolls from their *mem* as a welcome to the area, and a note to let him know that church would be at their house this week. They'd pointed to a small yet tidy ranch house down the road.

"That's where we live, not far at all yet," the youngest one — a girl — had proclaimed. "And on the other side of that is the Carashes' house. They're *Englisch*. Sally is my best friend."

Eli had only been in the small West Kootenai community two days, but it was long enough to discover this was an Amish community unlike any other he'd been in. Three things stood out: the way the Amish and *Englisch* mingled as friends, the snow still on the mountains though it was May, and the pretty blonde Amish woman who barely glanced his way as he offered a hello in the general store. She was lovelier than most of the young women back home — yet he wouldn't tell *Mem* that. The last thing he needed was *Mem* writing to give him courting advice. She seemed overly worried that he was already twenty-four years old and had yet to find a suitable woman to pursue.

Instead of glancing his way, the young woman had been focused on bags of planting soil, asking the store clerk, Edgar, a slew of questions about hard freezes and soil content. Growing up with his family's seed business, Eli knew gardening. He now kicked himself for not stepping forward and offering her some advice. Then again, he'd only be guessing. It wasn't as if he'd ever gardened in these parts. He was certain that planting in the high mountains had to be quite different from Indiana. And it wasn't until the woman walked out the door with her purchases that he saw the same trio of kids who had stopped by his cabin waiting for her.

"That's Sadie. She's been through quite a loss," Edgar had informed him. "Yet those kids keep her connected to real life. Otherwise I think she'd spend most of her thoughts on her garden." Edgar sighed. "Though I'm not sure if it's the one she's planting or the one of her childhood that she thinks 'bout the most."

Edgar hadn't said any more about the woman, and Eli hadn't asked. Yet he'd been pleasantly surprised to know she lived right down the road. He'd have a chance to see the woman again this morning. After all, being neighborly as he was, Eli had offered to walk the woman's younger siblings to school . . . seeing that there was a bear in these parts and all. It was the kids themselves who'd stopped by last night to tell him the news. A bear . . . now that was something to write home about!

THE BUDGET — West Kootenai, Montana
May — Unseasonably warm weather (or so the locals tell me) with clear skies reflecting off the mountain snow. Schoolchildren were running around barefoot during morning recess, even though the frost had barely melted. Seems to me that in Montana, if the sun is shining, that's good enough reason not to wear a coat and shoes, or so they think.

Montana is everything I imagined it to be. Arrived two days ago with three other bachelors and found the West Kootenai area to be just as lovely as everyone describes. Mountain peaks surround the high-mountain valley. Green pastures and the songs of birds hidden in tall pine trees. Everything smells like pine . . . and dust. Very few roads around these parts are paved. If I walk fifty feet in any direction there's always something to explore — rivers, ponds, mountain trails — and words cannot describe the expansive Lake Koocanusa.

Now I know why so many bachelors come to these parts every year. I, like the rest of them, used the excuse that we must live in this area for six months in order to receive our resident hunting license in the fall. I am looking forward to hunting season, no doubt, but I'm also thankful to live here too. There are numerous bachelor cabins all over the area. I have the smallest one and don't have a roommate yet. Maybe this means that local families will take pity on me and invite me to dinner and good conversation often. One can only hope.

Spent a few days giving the bachelor's cabin a good cleaning before unpacking my things. As I washed a film of dirt off the cabin windows with a hose, I thought of the ladies back home who'd often come to help *Mem* clean before Sunday church. Wishing they could show up here for even one hour. Tomorrow I start my job at Montana Log Works. My hands are more used to tilling weeds than shaping logs, but I suppose I can just look at these pines as the big brothers of the plants *Mem* tends back home.

I just came from Pinecraft, Florida, for the season, and I haven't adjusted to the weather yet. The balmy days filled with ocean breezes are gone. Even though it's late spring, Montana's still clinging to winter. The nights get downright cold, and the cold seeps deep here. You're not going to find me without my shoes and jacket.

It's good to see some familiar faces in the area. I'd met the Sommers family (Abe) when they still lived in Indiana. Linda Tillman (Rudy) is a cousin of my mother's too. She brought a fresh loaf of bread to my cabin and got the whole place smelling *gut.* Of course, I'm most excited to meet the bear cub that the neighbor kids are talking about. Yet we all know that when a cub is around, the mother isn't far. I'm heading out in a few minutes to walk the neighbor kids to school. The kids and I have high hopes we can spot it. One doesn't have to look far to find adventure.

This reminds me of God's Word, which says, "Fear of man will prove to be a snare, but whoever trusts in the LORD is kept safe."

Trust is a good word to cling to today for all of us. Trust that being neighborly and introducing oneself to a new friend can warm your heart even more than the Montana sun on a crisp spring day.

      — Eli Plank, the bachelor scribe

CHAPTER TWO

The small tomato plant trembled in Sadie Chupp's hands as she stepped out into the cool Montana morning.

"Don't worry. It's only for the day," she whispered to the plant. "Tonight you'll be back in your warm glass cave." She gently closed the door to the greenhouse behind her.

The small plant sprouted from heirloom seeds passed down for generations. From her mother's garden journal, Sadie had discovered that the seeds she used came from *Oma*'s grandmother. And who knew before that? How many generations of plants had been nourishing the bodies of those in her family? How many tomatoes had been sliced upon a fresh garden salad, canned, or made into tomato gravy?

"Of course, that was in Indiana . . ." Sadie swallowed down her emotion. In a way, she felt like that little plant — frail and unprepared for a new life in Montana. Hit by the elements on all sides.

Sadie had only been in Montana five months, arriving just after Christmas. The calendar read May, but the air still held the chill of winter. And as she gazed onto the tall mountain peaks that surrounded their small valley, snow still clung to them. Whenever Sadie mentioned putting in a garden, many folks in this area urged her not to put anything in the ground until after Memorial Day, and even then to harden the plants, setting them out a little each day and then bringing them back into the protection and safety of the greenhouse overnight.

Sadie set the tray of tomato plants on the ground. The air smelled of earth and dew. Of spring creeks and honeysuckle.

She sighed, wishing that life could be managed as well as a garden. Wouldn't it be easier if there was a way to harden yourself — to prepare for big changes? To prepare for cold, dark nights?

Life hadn't worked that way for her, especially in the last year. She'd always looked forward to turning twenty years old — with hopes of finding a lifelong partner. But her twentieth year stripped away so much that she held dear.

Too many times lately life changed for the worst in a moment. First, when she lost her parents in a car and buggy accident, and then when her siblings decided to sell their family home only a few months after their parents' deaths. She couldn't stand the idea of watching another family living in the only home she'd ever known, and so she'd come here — to her uncle's small ranch in the Amish community of West Kootenai, Montana.

She'd come to heal and to be far from the "attentive" coddling of her older sisters. In their eyes, she'd always be the baby of the family, in need of help and advice. Even from this great distance, her sisters wrote almost every week and became anxious when she didn't do the same. Maybe that's why she enjoyed her Montana family. They gave her space, didn't press, and didn't mind that she spent hours each day in the greenhouse.

Just ten years older than her, Uncle Melvin had always seemed more like a brother than an uncle. And even though she enjoyed being with his family — feeling fully loved by them — Sadie still wondered if God would ever give her a place of her own, a home to put down roots, and someone to share a life with.

A half dozen small brown finches sat on her aunt's clothesline and twittered as they flew from the ground, to the line, to the ground again, excited for the start of the new day. Their feathers were puffed up, making them look like fuzzy balls, and Sadie was thankful for her thick sweater. The air was chilly still compared to the greenhouse, but the thermometer said it was sixty-six degrees, just slightly above the temperature she'd read that tomatoes liked.

Out of all the possessions her parents had owned, Sadie had asked for — and received — two family treasures: her *mem*'s heirloom tomato seeds and her garden journal. Her mother rarely shared her intimate thoughts in conversation — and she never wrote them down. Instead she had been diligently taking notes on what worked best for her plants. That's where Sadie had first learned about hardening. It's also where she'd read that tomatoes preferred to be grown at temperatures between sixty-five and eighty-five degrees, which was asking something of this Montana mountain environment.

Tomatoes also loved direct sunlight, so she'd found the brightest spot in her uncle's yard. Sadie pressed her lips together and could almost imagine the taste. It would be months yet, but it was something to anticipate after eating the ones from the grocery store that were low in quality, poor in taste, and high in cost. Then again, she doubted any tomato could compare to the ones her mother used to grow.

The tomatoes from her mother's garden were always softer than the ones in the store, with green shoulders near the stem. *Mem* had told her that over the years, scientists had worked to make the store variety of tomatoes more uniform in color when they ripened. They also had to be able to be hardier in growth and be firmer to withstand being shipped around the country. As it turned out, all these changes also compromised the taste. And that's what made *Mem*'s heirlooms so special. A flutter danced around her stomach seeing the small green plants living on, thriving. The wind picked up, stirring their leaves as if they were dancing.

"Excited about being outside, are you?" Sadie chuckled.

She rose and moved toward the greenhouse that her neighbor let her use while they spent the spring and summer away visiting family. She picked up another tray of plants. Her plain black shoes crunched on the pine needles and maple leaves and the new sprigs of light-green grass that struggled to push through both.

Her younger cousins' happy voices carried through the trees, pausing her footfall. She stepped into a clearing to get a better view. Her cousins hurried out of the house, preparing for the mile walk to the little Amish schoolhouse, but something was different. They were more excited than she'd ever heard them on a school day.

Isaiah's laughter split the air, followed by Noah's. Then came six-year-old Rachel's voice as she called out to her brothers.

"Wait up!" Rachel called desperately, and Sadie's heart sank. Little Rachel tried to keep up, but her small stride was no match for the boys' long-legged sprint.

"Oh, those boys." Sadie brushed a stray strand of blonde hair back from her face and tossed her garden gloves to the ground. She rushed through the treed area that separated the two houses in the direction of the dirt road. Her toe snagged on a large rock, tripping her. She caught herself and it only fueled her anger.

As the youngest sister of six siblings, she knew what it was like to be the one lagging behind. What it was like to be left out. Her older siblings hadn't even asked for her thoughts when they decided to sell their parents' farm. Didn't they think she'd have an opinion?

As Sadie approached the front of the houses, she noticed the boys a little way up the dirt road, chatting with the bachelor she'd met briefly in the general store yesterday. Little Rachel jogged with her metal lunch pail in her hand, trying to catch up. Sadie strode toward them with a quickened stride and approached the boys at the same time Rachel did. Heat rose to Sadie's cheeks, and she struggled to catch her breath.

She crossed her arms over her chest, willing her pounding heart to calm. Willing her voice to stay low as she narrowed her gaze on her young cousins. Her throat tightened, tense, and the words pushed out between clenched teeth. "How many times have I told you that you need to wait for Rachel? You can't leave her behind like that."

Ten-year-old Isaiah and eight-year-old Noah looked back with surprise. But it was the Amish bachelor who gasped. His eyebrows lifted, and his eyes widened. Green eyes, she noted. Handsome eyes, too, but she pushed those thoughts away.

"I–I'm sorry," Isaiah stammered. "I was gonna wait. I just wanted to meet up with Eli —"

"It's my fault," the bachelor — Eli she

now knew — said. His voice was slightly shaky as if he was startled by her. He pointed to the small bachelor's cabin just up the road, nestled into a cluster of tall pine trees. "Last night the boys came by my cabin and told me they saw a bear cub near the Sommers' place up the road. They were excited to show me the spot this morning. I apologize." Eli pulled his hat from his head with a flourish. Light-brown hair stuck up in back like a rooster's comb, striking her as funny. She pressed her lips together to keep from smiling and then blew out a slow breath.

Sadie's attraction to him stirred in the pit of her gut. "They were excited, eh? Well, sir, excitement is no excuse for bad manners." Heat rose to her cheeks, and she resisted the urge to fan her face. "And I'm afraid that I haven't been a very good example." Sadie offered an apologetic smile. "I'm sorry for getting excited and not introducing myself. I'm Sadie. Sadie Chupp."

"Nice to meet you, Sadie." Eli shook her hand like an *Englischman* would, and warmth crept up the back of her neck. She quickly pulled it away.

"I'd love to chat, but the *kinder* can't be late for school, can they? Especially if they have to keep an eye out for a bear cub along the way."

"*Ja,* we must hurry. But not too fast for your sister." Eli bent down to one knee, not even minding the dirt road. He gently tugged on the young girl's *kapp* string. "And what was your name?"

"Rachel." She smiled up at him, displaying her missing front teeth.

"Well, Rachel, you and I can look on the left of the road and the boys can look on the right. If a cub is out there, we'll be sure to see him."

Rachel nodded eagerly and they began to walk. Suddenly she turned back and waved. "Bye, cousin Sadie."

"Cousin?" Eli placed the hat back on his head. "I thought Sadie was your sister." He glanced at Sadie out of the corner of his eye, but didn't linger on her long.

"*Ne.* She's our cousin from Indiana," Noah explained. "Her parents died, and so she came to live with us, but she has her *mem*'s tomato plants, and we're not to touch them — they're important."

Eli looked at Sadie with compassion and she shrugged. "Well, there you have it. If you ever want to know someone's life story, just ask a *kinder.* Have a good day then." She waved them away, uncomfortable with the attention. Maybe that's why she'd grown to like gardening more and more . . . In a garden, one didn't have to face one's grief and people's concern on a daily basis. She could hold it all inside if she wished. Or she could let it out — teardrops moistening the soft soil — if she wanted.

The bachelor stood still, his eyes large and full of questions, but he didn't say a word. Isaiah tugged on Eli's sleeve. The man turned, flanked by the kids as he walked away. He had a long, determined stride, and all three kids scuffled to keep up. Seeing that lightened her heart. It also made her feel even worse for the way she'd treated them — treated him.

Sadie turned back and trudged to her aunt and uncle's house, wishing she hadn't let her temper flare up. Wishing she hadn't chased the kids down. And wishing they hadn't said anything about her parents' deaths. For now there was yet another person in the community who would offer her compassionate looks, yet who'd be afraid to come too near because they didn't know what to say or do.

Grief not only built an emptiness within . . . sometimes it built a barrier of loneliness too. A barrier that few dared to cross.

Sadie finished up her task of setting out

the plants and then walked toward the house. She'd offered to help Linda with the deep cleaning — the kind that only got done when the whole neighborhood would be showing up for church the following Sunday.

Linda was already busy at work, dusting the banister that led upstairs to the kids' room — and Sadie's small half room — when Sadie entered. She could tell by the look on Linda's face that her aunt had watched her interaction with Eli and the children. *Aenti* Linda tried to hold back a smirk as she brushed her cleaning cloth along the wooden handrailing.

"Seems like the kids were extra excited. They do like getting to know the new bachelors in the spring. The boys have had more than one *gut* fishing buddy over the years."

"*Ja,* Eli seems nice enough."

"Eli, is it?" Linda glanced back over her shoulder. "Ah, yes. I remember now. I knew about Eli Plank even before he'd shown up in these parts."

Sadie waited for Linda to continue, but her aunt didn't elaborate. Was she just teasing? Sadie refused to ask about the man. Refused to put any ideas in her aunt's head that she was taking an interest. The last thing she needed was word to get back to her sisters.

"You should have given your letter to Eli — or the kids — to drop by the store on the way to school."

"Letter?" Sadie walked to the kitchen and dipped her hand into the soapy water in the kitchen sink basin, deciding to start with cleaning the wood paneling in the kitchen first.

"*Ja,* the letter you promised to write to your sisters every week. By my calculations, it's been two weeks. I'm surprised I haven't heard from Marie telling me that she'd already bought a train ticket to come and check on you."

"And leave her vegetable garden for her children to tend? We both know that won't happen."

"She's concerned about you, you know."

Sadie sighed. "I know."

"They all are."

"*Vell,* what else can I write about that I haven't written in the other twenty letters? Montana's beautiful. I'm enjoying the kids, and I started *Mem*'s tomato seeds in the greenhouse with hopes for a fruitful year."

Aunt Linda raised an eyebrow. "You could tell her about the bear that everyone's talking about."

Sadie cleared her throat. "*Ja,* and then

283

my sister Carol would be here for sure, ready to take me back to civilization."

"You could tell her about the Amish bachelors." Linda winked.

"*Ne*. That would excite my sisters even more than a bear. Wouldn't they be happy then for their youngest sister to finally find a man to care for her, since I need so much caring-for in their eyes?"

"They're just trying to help, Sadie."

Sadie took long strokes as she scrubbed the paneling. "I know."

"That's why God gave us families — and community. No one is meant to live life alone, to carry their grief alone."

Sadie didn't say anything. What could she say? She would open up if she found the right person. Someone who'd listen and who didn't try to find a solution for everything. Someone who could understand why some days were harder than others, and that sprouting new life was a way of healing from loss and death. Sadie didn't know if someone like that existed. But if he did, well, that would be worth writing home about.

CHAPTER THREE

Eli Plank plopped the last bite of chocolate chip cookie into his mouth and settled down under the shade of the aspen tree. He'd just finished up lunch at the Kraft and Grocery, eating with Abe and Ike Sommers, and he now hoped for a few minutes' peace to kick up his feet before his lunch break was over. He'd only been working at the Log Works half a day and already his back, shoulders, and arms ached. He'd used different muscles today as he peeled logs — muscles he didn't know he had.

Eli folded his arms behind the back of his head and relaxed onto the cool grass, crossing one leg over the other. And it was only then — with his mind freed from other distractions — that he allowed his thoughts to drift back to this morning.

There were few things that made Eli feel like a fool, but the way he got tongue-tied when Sadie Chupp strode away this morning made him want to slink behind one of the pine trees that lined the dusty road. Why hadn't he thought of something to say — offer condolences? How long ago had she lost her parents? From the look on her face it was still fresh. Her heart-shaped face was one of the prettiest he'd seen, but he couldn't help but notice the dark circles around her eyes and the worry lines creasing her forehead.

It also made sense why she'd acted so protective over little Rachel. It was as if Sadie's heart had been rubbed raw by the troubles of life and was now overly sensitive to the pain of others.

Eli's whole life he pictured himself married to someone similar to his *mem.* Someone most content when quietly tending her garden or rolling out piecrust with a low hum under her breath. That was before he caught the fire in Sadie's gaze as she approached them. It had caused his heart to leap in his chest. That was also before he noted the pain in her eyes as she walked away, and he wondered what he could do to help. He wanted to hear Sadie's story — the one that was reflected in the depth of her eyes.

"Hey, Eli! Lunch break's over!" The voice shouted behind him, and he turned to find

Jonathan Shelter waving in his direction. Jonathan was his supervisor at Montana Log Works, and a friendly fellow. A patient one too. Jonathan hadn't said anything when Eli showed up five minutes late. Maybe because of Eli's tale of seeing fresh bear tracks on the road. Jonathan had also been patient when he had to explain more than once how to skip-peel the lodgepole pine with drawknives — mostly because Eli couldn't get Sadie's sweet face out of his mind. Thoughts of pretty women and sharp knives didn't mix. Work had to remain his sole focus.

He returned to the work area and put on his heavy apron once again. He pulled a long lodgepole log from the pile. It was heavier than he thought, and it took some effort to set it in the notched-out sawhorse. Then, taking up the drawknife in both hands, he scooped it under the layer of bark, pulling the knife toward him and peeling off a chunk. His job was to do this again and again, leaving a layer of color, but removing the bark. Eli's draws were steady but seemed slow-moving compared to the other workers. They moved at twice his speed with skill and ease, making it look as easy as peeling an apple.

Earlier Jonathan urged Eli to take his time.

Jonathan promised that he'd get used to it and speed up after a few days.

Eli pulled, pulled, pulled the knife — one swoop at a time — watching the bark curl up and fall to the ground. It was different work than he was used to, but in a way it felt good. It was different than gardening, different than writing . . . and made Eli feel as if he was one step closer to being able to care for his own family someday. Not that he'd give up his other work.

He enjoyed being the "bachelor scribe" for *The Budget* and sitting down with a paper and pen. Not to be prideful, but more than once readers had written in to tell the paper that Eli's reports were the first they looked for when they picked up a copy of the newspaper. Readers enjoyed his adventures, and his *dat* didn't mind him traveling and writing as long as he'd keep his promise about three things — to return and get baptized into the Amish church, to find a good woman to marry and bring her home, and every now and then to mention his *opa*'s seed company. He'd easily promised the first and the last, but how could one promise to find true love? Eli hadn't promised that. He'd thought that would be the hardest one to keep until his eyes met Sadie's.

But enough of that now. He had a half day's work to put behind him. He just hoped his aching arms would hold out. He often put in a day of hard work in the garden or the fields, but this repetitive movement was different.

Four hours later, after he got off of work, Eli was only partly surprised to find Isaiah and Noah Chupp waiting by the rack where the Amish bachelors parked their bikes. Jonathan Shelter had brought Eli a bicycle to use while he was up in these parts. It was a mighty kind gesture.

"Do you have time to help us find the bear?" The words spouted from Isaiah's mouth.

Eli's stomach rumbled, and he pulled a handkerchief from his pocket and wiped his sweaty brow. Dirt and wood particles came off, and he guessed he was completely covered with sawdust. "I'm not ready for dinner yet. How about I just meet you in the morning? And —"

"Or you can walk with us now and eat dinner at our place . . . ," Isaiah offered.

"Oh no, I couldn't do that. I'm sure your *mem* doesn't want company stopping over."

Noah pointed his finger into the air. "*Vell,* you'd not be the only one. She does wash for many bachelors, and when they happen to bring their laundry by near dinnertime, she always invites them in."

"Oh *ja,* I heard about that . . ." Eli chuckled. It had actually been on a list that one of the previous bachelors had left pinned to the wall of the log cabin, right next to photos of some of the big game they'd caught. Someone had started the list a few years ago of the best creeks to fish in, where the shooting range was, and local ladies who took in wash. Eli smiled, remembering there was a note that said if one dropped off laundry to Mrs. Sommers's or Mrs. Chupp's place around dinnertime, they'd often get invited in.

Still, would Sadie think it too obvious if he showed up at her uncle's place for the second time that day? He wouldn't mind seeing her pretty face again, yet with every place he visited, he told himself not to tie up his heart unless it was somewhere he could settle, plant roots, build a life, and start a family. As pretty as Montana was, it was too early to even consider making it home. And as pretty as Sadie was, he still had much to learn about her.

He rubbed his jaw, still unsure.

Isaiah must have noticed Eli's hesitancy. He stepped closer, peering up into Eli's face. "*Ja,* really. I overheard *Mem* just last night in the barn telling *Dat* that they needed to put a new posting up on the bulletin board at the Kraft and Grocery. She said it would be good for cousin Sadie to spend time with people her own age, especially some of the bachelors."

Eli brushed wood chips off his sleeves, then rolled them up. He guessed he could wear this outfit for work again tomorrow. No use washing sweaty clothes just to get them sweaty again. But he did need the rest of his clothes washed. "*Vell,* if they were going to put up a sign at the store . . ."

Noah's eyebrows lifted. "So, can we go now?"

"We can head to my cabin and maybe keep our eyes open for bear tracks on the way. But as I wash up and gather up my dirty clothes, I want you to head home, you hear? I don't want anyone to think that you put me up to this."

Noah pouted. "But we —"

"You reminded me of your *mem*'s laundry service, that's all. And I was needing my clothes washed, *ja*?" Eli swallowed hard, knowing his words committed him. "And let's not assume that dinner will be part of the evening . . . understand?" Yet what Eli didn't say was that he hoped it would be, maybe even more than the boys. Both for the food and the company.

"We understand." Isaiah placed a hand on his brother's shoulder and quickly nodded, as if urging Noah not to argue.

Eli took the handlebars of the bicycle and freed it from the rack, but instead of riding it, he pushed it down the road with Isaiah on his left and Noah on his right. He'd always enjoyed being around his nieces and nephews, and having these local boys befriend him so quickly made West Kootenai seem more like home.

"So, do you think we're going to see the mean mama bear this time?" Isaiah's blondish-red eyebrows nearly met in the middle as he raised them.

"I don't know." Eli shrugged. "I talked to some of the locals, and most think that the yearling's an orphan. A mama wouldn't let her little one be caught out in the open so much — and get into so much trouble."

Noah's eyes widened. "We can adopt him! Do you think *Dat* will let us keep him as a pet?"

"Not on your life." Eli tried to hide his smile. "Little bears grow up to be big bears, and you can't tame a wild creature like that."

Noah shrugged. "I think you could . . . if you tried."

"Better not even try." Eli paused. "It's fun and games when we're together like this — and when you're with an adult — but don't ever go near a bear alone, got it?"

Noah nodded, his shoulders sagging. The mood grew more somber when they walked all the way to the bachelor's cabin and didn't see any signs of the bear.

Eli parked his bicycle by the front porch's railing. "I'll meet you at your house in a little bit. Just give me fifteen minutes to clean up, *ja*?" He leaned down and placed his hands on his knees, meeting Noah eye-to-eye. "No spilling the beans, you hear? It's our secret."

With those few words the boys' furrowed brows softened. Their eyes widened and their mouths circled into *O*s. A boy with a secret was just as exciting as bragging rights over seeing a bear, he guessed. The only question was *if* they'd keep the secret . . . or if they'd warn their pretty cousin that one of the bachelors would be stopping by and was hoping for a dinner invitation. Would Sadie be excited to see him knocking at their door — laundry or not?

CHAPTER FOUR

Sadie sat at the rough-hewn log table next to Rachel, and both nibbled on crackers Sadie had snuck from the cupboard. Her aunt had a pot of soup simmering on the stove and fresh bread already sliced for the dinner table, but Sadie wasn't the patient type. As soon as the first rumble of hunger came, she wanted to eat . . . now.

Rachel occupied herself by drawing pictures of flowers from one of the seed catalogs that Sadie was flipping through. *Aenti* Linda had walked down to Susan Carash's house to look at some fabric Susan was offering for one of the quilts Linda was sewing. Knowing her aunt, Linda would come home with all that Susan offered. *Aenti* Linda was frugal. Nothing went to waste in her home if she could help it.

Rachel pointed to illustrations of plants and vegetables. "Can I cut out the pictures?"

"*Ja,* but not from that catalog." Sadie

flipped through the pile. "I want to keep those, but you can cut out from this one." She held up a glossy-covered copy of *Pioneer Creek Seeds*. The fancy script on the front made her stomach tighten. "The Largest Variety of Heirloom Seeds Anywhere," it read. Sadie tried not to smirk. She'd met the owner, Paul Hostetler, on more than one occasion. His seed company hadn't been far from her parents' farm, and he'd come by a few times, taking an interest in her mother's heirloom tomatoes.

He'd stood at the edge of the garden, praising her *mem*'s fine gardening skills — her neat rows, fine organization, and healthy-looking plants. He'd seemed nice enough, but her *mem* was able to see behind the smile. Recognize his true motives.

"He's interested all right, interested in taking money from our family's heritage," Sadie's mother had explained. "I do the work and he reaps the rewards. I don't think so."

"He's a nice man," her *dat* had countered. "He brings you a few of his own seeds every time, does he not?"

"*Ja*, but he has plenty to spare. You're right when you say that he is a nice man. A nice *Englischman*." Although most of Mr. Hostetler's family was still Amish — including some of his children — he and his wife had left the Amish community. They carried on, talking to the Amish families in Pennsylvania Dutch, but no one fell for his kind ways. In addition to his seed company, he was also an assistant pastor in one of the *Englisch* churches. He'd walked away from their Amish traditions to more liberal thinking, and no one from their community let him get too comfortable with them, lest he think he could have a foot in both worlds.

Sadie puffed up her cheeks and blew out a breath at the memory. Her *mem* had been so protective of those seeds, which made the plants she was growing in the neighbor's greenhouse mean so much to her. She'd planted them all — down to the last one — since her sisters already had their own favorite store-bought seeds that they were using. Even though store-bought seeds were sterile and couldn't be used year after year, they usually produced a bigger yield, which was important if you were raising a large family. Sadie was the one who would carry on the legacy, and she wanted to do whatever she could to help those tomatoes thrive.

A knock sounded at the front door, and Sadie jumped. She stood and moved to the door at the same time she heard the back door open and then slam shut again. Isaiah and Noah ran into the house.

"Who's here?" Isaiah asked with wide eyes. The way he blinked quickly made her feel as if he already knew the answer.

"I'm not sure. I was just going to find out."

Noah glanced around. "Where's *Mem*?" He moved to the door ahead of Sadie, as if blocking her path.

"Your *mem* is down the road."

The knock sounded again, louder, and Sadie placed a hand on her hip. "Are you going to let me pass?" She tapped her toe on the rag rug.

Noah wrinkled his nose. "Maybe we should just have him come back when *Mem*'s here."

"*Him?* You know who's here?"

Noah shrugged and moved out of the way.

Sadie hurried to the door and opened it. Her jaw dropped open when she noticed the handsome Amish bachelor standing there. His hat was in one hand and a laundry bag was in the other. The sleeve of a dirty work shirt hung out the top of the bag. He was smiling at her — not only with his lips but with his eyes. Her heart did a small flip in her chest.

"Uh, hello," she said breathlessly.

He cocked an eyebrow. "You okay? You're breathing like you were just in a race."

She took a deep breath, telling her heart to calm. "Oh, that, well." She glanced over her shoulder at her cousins, who wore guilty looks on their faces. Then she turned back to Eli. "I'm sorry. I had to race Noah to the door. I'm not sure why, but he was determined not to open it unless my aunt was home."

"Well, yes, I did need to talk to her — your aunt. I heard that she takes in laundry, and I was wondering if I could bring mine once a week?"

"*Ja,* she does — we do — I'd be happy to take it for you. We ask that you give us two days before picking it up." Sadie reached her hand out.

"Sure, that's fine. Two days then. I have other things to wear until then." He passed the bag over, and she had to use both hands to hold it. Sadie urged herself not to wince at the smell of dirty socks. Since she and her aunt traded off, Sadie made a mental note to take the baking in the morning rather than Eli's laundry. "We'll be sure to get this done. Have a *gut* night."

"Uh, you too." Eli blinked once, and his lips turned down slightly. He turned away from the door, and Sadie wondered what was bothering him. Had she said something wrong?

"No, wait!" The words shot from Isaiah's mouth, and he sidled up to Sadie. "You can't just let him leave like that. *Mem* always invites the bachelors in for dinner."

Suddenly, Sadie understood. This was a setup! She crossed her arms over her chest and took a step back. Then she glanced at Eli. He paused and turned back as if waiting to hear her response. She noted humor in his eyes as if he, too, was waiting to see how this would play out.

Being invited to dinner was clearly what the bachelor hoped for and what Isaiah hoped for too.

"*Ja,* she does invite some in." Sadie tapped her lower lip with her fingertip. "But not all of them." Sadie offered a slight smile and raised her voice for her cousins' benefit. "Only the ones *she* likes. She doesn't know Mr. Plank well, so I'm sure she wouldn't mind if I wished him a *gut* day . . ."

"Sadie!" This time it was Rachel's voice that called out. Sadie hadn't realized the girl had followed her to the door and was standing next to her. "*Mem* says that we are to offer what we have to anyone who comes to the door."

Sadie noticed a slight smile on Eli's face, so she continued in good humor. "Anyone?"

Rachel enthusiastically nodded, her *kapp*

strings bouncing. *"Ja."*

Sadie swung the door open wider. *"Vell,* I suppose that means you, Mr. Plank."

"Wunderbar, thank you. I'm so glad you came to that decision. I am hungry. And something smells *gut.* Chicken soup maybe?" He stepped in the door and then paused. Eli leaned down and spoke low so only Sadie could hear. "You don't mind, do you — really?"

"Ne. Not at all." She glanced up and met his gaze. "My cousins are right. My aunt is always very welcoming."

"And you?" he asked a bit louder. "Are you always welcoming too, Sadie?"

"I used to be." Sadie sighed as she closed the door behind him. "My siblings used to say I attracted friends like flowers attracted bees." She shrugged. "But that seems like ages ago. Now I . . ." Sadie halted her confession. What did she know about Mr. Plank? Was he trustworthy?

"What, Sadie?" Eli waited, his green eyes peering down at hers. "What were you going to say?"

"I was going to say . . . I'm sure that my aunt should be home any minute. You're right, that chicken soup does smell good." Sadie hurried to the kitchen, but not before she saw curiosity in Eli's eyes for the second time that day.

CHAPTER FIVE

It was less than thirty minutes later when her aunt and uncle arrived home. Both seemed happy to meet Eli and have one of the new bachelors in the area joining them for dinner. Like Sadie expected, her aunt had returned with a nice bag of fabric and a smile.

"Look, Sadie." *Aenti* Linda showed her the colorful strips. "We can make a quilt together. Did I ever tell you that it was your *mem* who taught me how to quilt?"

"*Ja.*" Sadie's stomach sank, and she took the sack from her aunt's arms. She wondered if the ache would ever lessen. "And I do think *Mem* would have loved this red gingham," she managed to say.

"Oh, and I was going to mention, Sadie, you better bring your plants in." Her aunt lifted the lid from the soup. Steam and the wonderful aroma of dinner burst into the air. "Dinner can wait a few minutes. The wind is really picking up out there — a cold wind from the north —"

"In?" Eli asked. "Do you have tomato plants hardening?"

"*Ja,* did the kids tell you?" Sadie looked at him, surprised.

"No, but that's what *Mem* would be doing now. Can I help?" He moved toward the back door without waiting for her answer.

"*Ja,* sure."

They hurried out the back door. The wind had indeed picked up. Eli hurried over to the trays of plants that once had been sitting in full sun and scooped them up. "And where's the greenhouse?"

She bit her lower lip, hoping he didn't drop them. Sadie reached out for the trays and then pulled her hands back. *Trust him, Sadie.* She'd already insulted him twice today. Surely the strong bachelor could carry a few trays of new sprouts to the greenhouse.

"It's, uh, over at the neighbor's property. The owners went to stay with family in Arkansas for the winter and said I could use it." She led the way.

"That's kind of them." Eli followed her. "And from what I can tell of this place, it's just what someone around these parts would do — share what they have with others."

She hurried down the worn path between the tall, thin lodgepole pines, making her way to the greenhouse. She opened the door and stepped inside. It was warm and the air was moist, a welcome change from the outside.

He placed the seed tray on the shelf nearest the door. "This is a great greenhouse. Too bad it doesn't have more plants growing inside of it."

"*Ja, vell,* I was worried about being too industrious. I'm not sure about the Montana soil, the growing conditions and such, but I had to plant my tomatoes. Filling two seed trays with these seeds has been a tradition that's been passed on for a hundred years — maybe more."

Eli had a pensive look on his face, and she expected him to ask about her heirloom seeds. Instead, he glanced around and a smile crossed his face.

"What if I helped you?"

"Excuse me?"

"I know it's a short growing season in Montana, but most people around these parts don't plant until Memorial Day anyway — or at least that's what Edgar at the store said. If you want to pick out a few things that grow good in these parts — maybe zucchini, potatoes, carrots — I'll buy the supplies for a deer fence. From what I've seen and heard, that's important around here. Then I can come help once in a while — till, pull weeds . . .

"You *garden*?" Sadie didn't mean for the words to blurt out, but growing up Amish, she'd learned gardening was usually the chore of an Amish woman.

His cheeks turned pink. "Well, I . . ." He ran his hand down the side of his face, and his words trailed off.

"I'm sorry. I didn't mean for that to sound rude."

"I know it's not common, but our family runs a large vegetable farm back home. My father works with my mom's *dat* — my *opa* — and they have quite a business. I grew up hearing talk of heirlooms and hybrids, of loam and types of soil. But if you'd rather not . . ."

"I would. I'd like it . . . just as long as you don't mind that my tomatoes get most of my attention. I really can't tell you how special they are." She tried to keep her voice from quivering as she said those last words, but it was no use.

"*Ja*, of course."

And before he could say anything else,

305

Sadie motioned him to the door. He stepped out and she followed him, shutting the door tight.

"A garden is a way of showing that you believe in tomorrow," she mumbled.

"What was that?"

She repeated it. "Oh, it's just something that my *mem* used to say. An old proverb."

Eli chuckled. "Sometimes I wonder if my *mem* ever said anything that wasn't a proverb." He cleared his throat. " 'Pray for a good harvest but continue to hoe' — that's another one."

" 'The best things in life aren't things,' " she added, pointing her finger.

Eli smiled. "And one of my favorites, 'The dearest things in life are most near at hand.' And that's saying something for a man who's lived in a half dozen or so locations in an equal number of years." His gaze was intent on her, and Sadie looked away, glancing down at her feet as she stepped over a log. She could feel heat on her cheeks.

Sadie hurried her footsteps. "I'm sure they're wondering on us. I don't want to keep dinner waiting."

Eli didn't comment. He simply picked up his pace and stayed by her side.

Uncle Melvin and *Aenti* Linda welcomed in

Eli as if he was a long-lost friend, and it wasn't until they were all sitting around the dinner table, with her aunt ladling up chicken noodle soup, that Sadie realized that was exactly how her aunt and uncle saw him.

After a silent prayer, her Uncle Melvin lifted his head and turned his attention to the bachelor. "Eli, it's *gut* to have you for dinner. I've read your letters in *The Budget.*"

The Budget? Sadie's eyebrows furrowed.

Eli shrugged. "Oh, it's just nonsense mostly, but people seem to like the silly things I write about."

"I hope you don't write about this meal." *Aenti* Linda chuckled. "My homemade noodles turned out less flavorful than usual."

"Oh, I won't. I have made it a point never to talk about food or conversation, lest people are afraid to invite me over." Eli patted his stomach. "And because of that rule I'm well fed, which not every bachelor can say." Eli took a spoonful of soup and smiled. "But if I were to write about it, I'd say this soup is delicious, the noodles especially."

A smile crossed her aunt's face, and everything started to make sense. No wonder Eli was so good with words. They came from a scribe.

"So, are you enjoying Montana?" her uncle asked.

Eli nodded. "*Ja,* so different from Pinecraft, where I just came from. There the young Amish women wear flip-flops for shoes," he said. "And there are no horses and buggies. Instead, everyone rides on bicycles, and they especially like to ride to the beach."

Her cousins' eyes grew wide as if Eli was speaking of something from a fairy tale. Eli told them that he'd been working down there, encouraging local stores to carry his grandfather's seeds, until the draw of living in Montana to gain one's resident hunting license lured him.

"Of course, there's a lot to see and do until hunting season. I'll call it 'researching' — the hiking, the fishing." He chuckled. "And I was wondering, Sadie, if I could write more about your heirloom tomatoes? That's a special thing."

"*Ach.*" She waved a hand and tried to hide her smile, but her insides warmed — heat moved from her chest to her limbs. "There isn't much special about a tomato plant."

"*Ja,* there is, and I can't wait to hear."

They chatted about other things, mostly just listening about what the kids had done at school that day, and after a while Sadie felt comfortable opening up. She glanced to her uncle and aunt. "I think we'd all agree that my *mem* was as proud of her tomatoes as she was her children." Sadie laughed.

"That's an understatement, *ja*?" Uncle Melvin stroked his beard and lifted his gaze to the ceiling. "I was a lot younger than your *mem,* and sometimes she would babysit me. I remember once I didn't latch the gate to the cow pasture after doing chores, and the cows got into the garden." Uncle Melvin smiled and shook his head. "I heard the wails and thought she'd hit her foot with her hoe. Come to find out one cow had made his way into the garden. A few plants were trampled, but thankfully it wasn't worse."

Sadie dipped a piece of her bread into her chicken noodle soup and then bit it off. She couldn't help but grin.

"*Ja.* That was *Mem.* In the spring and summer, that's where I'd find her when I woke up in the mornings." She picked up her spoon to take another bite but paused with it halfway to her mouth when another memory stirred. She set down her spoon and then tapped her chin. "I just thought of something I hadn't thought about in a while. I must have been five or six and I came downstairs and was startled that *Mem* wasn't feeling well. She tried to shrug it off, but I knew if she wasn't in her garden with her tomatoes, then something was surely wrong, so I ran to the fields for *Dat.* Turns out her appendix had burst and the doctor said we got her to the hospital just in time." She glanced to her uncle and noticed his quick nodding.

"*Ja, ja* . . . I remember that."

Sadie picked up her spoon again. "I suppose my tomato plants mean so much because they've been passed down, sort of like our Amish heritage. I couldn't imagine leaving the Amish — who would do that? And I couldn't imagine not having my tomatoes."

She glanced over at Eli. He shuffled in his chair as if he was sitting on a pile of dry pine needles. What made him so nervous? She noticed a general weariness about his shoulders, and she guessed his first day at Montana Log Works hadn't been easy.

With dinner finished, Aunt Linda and Rachel began clearing the table. Sadie turned to him. "You must be tired . . . after such a long day."

"*Ja,* I need to get home, especially since I have to be back at work bright and early." He rose and the three kids trailed him to the door. "Thank you for dinner —"

"Can we look for the bear tomorrow on the way to school?" Noah interrupted.

Eli leaned over and placed his hands on his knees. "Actually, I think if we don't look for him, we're more likely to see him."

"Really?" Isaiah asked.

"*Ja.*" Eli nodded. "So why don't we do that? Why don't we be on the lookout and then report in?"

All the children, even Rachel, seemed to approve, and Sadie couldn't help but smile.

Eli turned to Sadie next. "And if it's all right with you, I'll come by tomorrow night and look at your garden plot. I'll ask Edgar at the store what would work best for deer fencing." He turned to Sadie's aunt and uncle. "You don't mind, do you?"

"No, not at all," Uncle Melvin replied for them both. "It's kind of you to make such an offer, but I can't let you pay for it." Uncle Melvin reached for his wallet.

"How about I exchange laundry instead?" his aunt offered. "And you know, Eli, that you're welcome at our table anytime you like." Aunt Linda looked to Sadie and smiled as she said those words.

"Both sound wonderful and worth any money, time, and effort I put into helping. And . . ." Eli cocked one eyebrow as he placed a hand on the doorknob. "And the greatest reward will be to place a slice of one of Sadie's tomatoes on a bacon, lettuce, tomato sandwich. How long do we have to wait?" He winked.

"Seeing that they're just baby sprouts, awhile," she answered. "But it will be worth it, *ja*?"

Eli left with a wave. There was a quickness to his step as he hurried down the road in the direction of the bachelor's cabin. The whole family stood on the porch, watching him go, until he crested a hill and disappeared from view.

"So he's coming back tomorrow then?" Uncle Melvin asked.

"*Ja,* to measure for the deer fencing, which I do have to admit I'm excited about." Sadie smiled, crossing her arms over her chest and feeling them tremble. She followed the family into the house and then moved to her room, placing a hand on her cheek and finally allowing a full smile to emerge — the smile that Eli's nearness caused but one she'd held back.

Somehow Eli Plank had wormed his way into all their hearts in a very short time. Her brow furrowed slightly as she remembered another man — that *Englischman* from Pioneer Creek Seeds — who also had an easy demeanor and a way with words, but she pushed those thoughts out of her mind. This was not the same situation. Eli was just trying to settle within the community, that's all.

She just hoped Eli didn't make a habit of getting close to people and then walking out of their lives for good, because after tonight that would bring heartache to them all . . . especially her.

THE BUDGET — West Kootenai, Montana
My young friends and I have been trailing that bear cub over these Montana hills. We've yet to see his mother, and after talking to locals, either it's a yearling that was shooed away by his mother too soon or he lost her to some tragedy. If you can imagine a child having free rein of a candy store without a mother to supervise, that is what this cub is like. He's tossed around some trash cans and trailed after kids on bikes, much to the chagrin of locals. Personally, my favorite part of the day is riding my own bicycle to and from work, hoping to spot Goliath — a name the local children gave the cub after the Bible's favorite bad guy.

Without another bear around to play with, the little whirlwind of energy likes to climb trees, tackle brush, or dig up roots,

313

which makes my work of skip-peeling seem mundane in comparison. If you're not aware of skip-peeling, a drawknife is used to hand peel a log, leaving some of the cambium layer on the log's surface. This is different than a clean-peel where it's peeled, well, clean.

With Memorial Day weekend coming, many of the locals are preparing their gardens. They have their seed packets ready. All except Sadie Chupp. This industrious gardener borrowed her neighbor's greenhouse to get an early start on her plants. From Indiana, Sadie's garden experience is in her blood. Just as her heirloom tomato seeds are passed down for generations, obviously the know-how to care for these plants has been passed on, too, because while most of her neighbors are still plotting their gardens, Sadie has planted her first tomato plants into the rich Montana soil. It makes me think of God's Word that tells us not to grow weary of doing good, for at the right time, we will reap a harvest if we do not give up.

— Eli Plank, the bachelor scribe

CHAPTER SIX

With Eli's help, it only took a few weeks to get Sadie's beautiful garden in. They started by prepping the soil and building a deer fence around it. The garden ended up being bigger than Sadie had planned, but when Uncle Melvin asked for beets and Aunt Linda for peas, they had to add in the cucumbers, cabbage, and squash that the kids also asked for.

The cool breeze of the morning stirred Sadie's *kapp* strings. She opened the makeshift gate and noticed that small sprouts had popped up seemingly overnight. Sadie sighed, because so did the weeds. Back in Indiana, most women did their garden work first thing in the morning. Of course, back in Indiana most gardens were near the roads, and no Amish woman wanted a neighbor to drive by in a buggy and see a garden full of weeds.

Here, her garden was behind the house. It

was surrounded by a deer fence and not visible to any of their neighbors. Then again, her guess was that even if neighbors saw a garden with a splattering of weeds, they'd give it no mind.

Still, Sadie couldn't leave the weeds unattended for long. She moved to her uncle's shed and found her garden gloves and also grabbed a piece of cardboard that she could use to kneel on. She opened the gate and entered, thankful for the sun shining on her face and *kapp.* Still, she could think of many other things she could be doing on this beautiful Saturday morning than weeding, like joining the rest of the family for a walk down to Lake Koocanusa.

She placed the cardboard on the ground and settled down. "It figures that he was happy to help me plant, but not so keen on weeding."

"Was that me you were talking about?"

Sadie turned and there stood Eli with a Styrofoam coffee cup from the Kraft and Grocery. In his other hand he held a garden hoe. He loudly swallowed the last of the coffee and then walked over and tossed the cup in the trash can. His hat was pulled low over his brow, but even then she could see the twinkle in his eyes at catching her complaining.

"*Vell,* the truth is, I didn't mean for you to overhear my grumbling."

"Of course not." Eli chuckled. He unlatched the gate and entered, closing it behind him. Having him closed up in the garden with her felt both intimate and dangerous.

"What are you going to do with that hoe?" she asked.

He took a step closer. "I'm going to get these weeds, of course."

She rose to her knees. "It's a little invasive, don't you think?"

"They're weeds, Sadie. Just weeds." He moved down the row toward the new sprouts of carrots and with quick movements began jabbing at the weeds.

Seeing that caused her stomach to knot up. "You know, I don't really mind just weeding them by hand."

Eli paused and looked at her. "But why? That takes so much more time. If we just get this done quickly, then we can do something else, something more fun with our day."

"But . . . Eli, why aren't you listening to me?" Sadie sat back on her heels and glared at him. She held back from standing, striding over to him, and taking the hoe out of his hands.

"Listen, Eli." She struggled to keep her voice strong. "I know your way might be faster, and from all the help you gave me during the planting and such, you no doubt have a lot of experience, but this is the way my *mem* did it — pulling weeds by hand. Our time in the garden was a peaceful time. It was one of the few times I had her alone. It was a good time to connect. In the kitchen, things were always busy as she cooked for our large family, but she seemed to relax in the garden. It just seems, well, it just seems that's how it should be."

He paused and turned to look at her. "I– I'm sorry, Sadie. I had no idea."

She nodded and returned to sitting sideways on the cardboard, tucking her skirt and apron under her legs. Sadie was an adult, but whenever she was in the garden, she felt ten again, watching her mother and working so hard to make sure she was doing everything right.

She closed her eyes for a moment and reached down and grabbed a handful of soil, feeling its warmth in her fingers.

Sadie heard the movement of Eli coming toward her. He hunkered down near her. Close enough to offer support, but far enough away to still be appropriate.

"I've been wanting to ask about your

parents, Sadie, but I've been afraid to. I didn't want to make you sad."

"Thanks . . . for wanting to ask. I know it's hard for people to know what to say."

"I want to say the right thing — do the right thing."

Sadie wrinkled her nose and looked up at him. "Well, today, the right thing is to pull the weeds with your hands and not chop them with that hoe."

"*Ja, ja,* okay." He cleared his throat and then moved over to the fencing, leaning the hoe against the meshed wire. Then, with a tenderness she'd yet to see from him, Eli kneeled in the warm, soft dirt and began pulling weeds.

She sat there for a minute, trying to imagine another person being so understanding, so patient with her. Her older siblings would have demanded that she grow up. Even *Aenti* Linda would have made a comment that there wasn't just one right way to do things. Seeing Eli pull those weeds, and that he knew which ones to pull, made her tear up. What did she do to deserve a friend like this? She'd lashed out at him and demanded of him, yet Eli had continued to turn the other cheek.

She closed her eyes and blew out a deep breath.

"Lord, I know my loss does not give me a free pass to strike out at others. To demand my way." The prayer was barely a whisper upon her lips. "Heal me, Lord, so I can plant goodness into the lives of others. So I can be a blessing and not a stray weed . . ."

Eli paused his movements and looked back at her. "What was that?"

Sadie glanced up. "Oh, nothing." Something tickled her cheek. She brushed it away. "Or, what I should say is that I didn't mean to disturb your work. I was just sending up a prayer, that's all. Asking God to change me . . . to remind me not to be so demanding. I'm sorry if I've come across harsh, Eli."

He turned on one knee and looked at her. "You're anything but harsh, Sadie. You're passionate about some things, and I like that. I appreciate the way you stood up for Rachel the first time we met, and I actually like that you see this time in the garden as a time of connecting instead of a rush to get things done. I can learn a lot from you."

Sadie sighed loudly and placed her balled fists on her hips. "Would you just stop that?"

"What do you mean?"

"I mean, can't you get upset a little? Do you always have to be nice?"

Eli cocked an eyebrow. "Are you saying you *want* me to get upset?"

"I'm saying that in real life people get upset. You could defend yourself, Eli. You could raise your voice just a little bit. Otherwise how am I going to know . . ."

"Know what?"

"Know that you're real and not just a figment of my imagination. My *mem* used to tell me if something seems too good to be true, it probably is. So you . . ." She squinted. "Maybe I have really lost my mind in grief and you're just my imaginary friend."

Eli frowned. Then he picked up a dirt clod and threw it squarely at Sadie. It hit with a thump in the center of her chest and burst into a thousand pieces, splattering dirt all over her clean white apron.

Sadie's mouth opened in surprise and shock.

Eli crossed his arms over his chest and jutted out his chin. "Is that real enough for you?"

"Ja." She picked up a dirt clod, sailing it in his direction. It hit his neck, and Eli jumped to his feet in surprise.

"Why, you throw like a boy!" he proclaimed.

She picked up another dirt clod and fingered it. "I'll take that as a compliment. And you weed like a girl. It seems that we make an unlikely team."

"That may be so, but don't get carried away with pelting me. Why don't we finish up weeding and then head out? As fun as this is, there is a lot more of the area to explore."

Sadie nodded and then dropped the clod to the ground. "Sounds like a deal. Besides, if my *aenti* returned home and saw me covered in dirt, she'd begin to wonder about you. And so far they like you. We wouldn't want to change that, would we?" She winked.

It only took an hour for them to finish up the weeding, and then Sadie put the garden gloves and cardboard back in the shed.

"Now that the work is done, do you have time to play?" Eli asked.

"*Ja.* What do you have in mind?" A chipmunk chattered in the tree overhead as if commending Sadie for stopping her work to have some fun, but she gave it no mind.

"*Vell,* I happen to know two box lunches are waiting for us at the Kraft and Grocery, and then I thought we'd hike over to Alkali Lake."

"Where's that?"

"Oh, there was a note about it posted in my cabin. It's by the shooting range. I've heard the local wildlife really like the water and you can see moose, elk, and even bears gathering there in the afternoons."

"Do you think it'll be safe?"

"We'll make sure to stay far enough away so we can see them, but they won't bother us."

She placed a hand over her heart, noticing its beating had quickened. "*Ja,* I think it's something I'd like to do, especially since you'll be there to fight off any wild animals." She glanced over at Eli.

"There's only one thing, though," she said. "If you're going to write about our adventure for *The Budget* — which I have no doubt you'll do — can you not mention that I'm the only one with you?"

"Is there a problem, Sadie? Afraid of becoming popular?"

"*Vell,* I do have brothers and sisters back home, and I've already gotten letters from them asking about you, wondering if I'm going to be the one who — well, never mind."

"No, you have to tell me."

Sadie ran a hand down her throat. "*Ne,* really. Forget I said anything." She placed a hand over her stomach. "And we better hurry." She strode out toward the road. "That lunch sounds wonderful."

She heard Eli's footfall behind her and

hoped he didn't question her again. After reading his last post for *The Budget* she'd indeed gotten a slew of letters, six to be exact. And all of them asked the same questions. *Are you dating Eli? Will you be the one to remove his "bachelor" status?* She didn't respond. Why should she? It was foolishness really. Her name was mentioned one time in the report of an Amish scribe and suddenly her family was picturing themselves at her wedding.

They'd only gotten one hundred yards from her aunt and uncle's place when they saw movement across the road ahead of them. It was a ball of brown fur about the size of a large dog, yet it bounced like a puppy when it ran. It zipped from one side of the road to the other and then hurried up a small slope, disappearing into the trees.

Sadie froze. "Did you see that?"

"*Ja,* it was the bear cub."

Sadie laughed. "It's so cute, smaller than I thought. The way the kids talk about 'Goliath,' I imagined it being the size of a sheepdog, not a golden retriever."

"Do you want to follow him, Sadie?"

"Follow him? No. Isn't that dangerous?"

"I don't think it will be. C'mon."

Her feet stayed firmly planted. "But what about the lunch? The picnic?"

"We'll get the lunch in a few minutes, but why go look for wildlife when we have it right here?"

"Okay, *ja.*" Sadie took a deep breath as she followed Eli up the sloping hill. "Do you have any idea where we're going?" she called after him. He paused and waited for her.

"No idea. I haven't headed out this way before." Eli's smile was as large as the Montana sky, and Sadie knew why. This was going to be something all right — something special for the Amish bachelor's next *Budget* report. She pressed a hand to her forehead. She could expect even more letters this time.

CHAPTER SEVEN

Eli straightened his shoulders as he led the way, first up the slope and then into the trees. Over the last few weeks he'd spent more time with Sadie, wishing he'd see the same spark of life flashing in her eyes that he'd seen the day they first met. But he was thankful to have Sadie's friendship.

In the garden, Sadie's voice had quivered when she'd asked him to put down the hoe. Emotion had filled her voice, and he was thankful to hear it.

Eli had mentioned Sadie to his grandfather on the telephone just a few nights ago. He didn't enjoy standing in the cold phone shed, and he wasn't going to make a habit of calling home, but he had a few gardening questions that couldn't wait.

"I don't understand. It's like she's just doing what she thinks she ought to be doing. I've seen her fired up a few times. I've seen a spark of anger — of humor — in her eyes. But the grief she's enduring from her parents' death is still a dark curtain, holding her back. Maybe she's afraid to care too deeply again — to open herself up to the people around her."

"Sometimes that happens." His grandfather sighed.

"But what do I do about it?"

"What can you do except be her friend? And pray for her?"

"But isn't there something I can say?"

"Eli, you've worked in a garden your whole life. You should know that things take time. A planted seed begins the process of growth once you place it in the soil and water it, but this growth can't be seen immediately."

Eli remembered his grandfather's words as he heard the heaviness of Sadie's breath. She strode along behind him, trying to keep up.

He glanced back over his shoulder. "Am I going too fast?" Eli slowed down.

She shook her head and moved past him, taking the lead. "*Ne,* look! There he is!"

Just ahead of them, the bear was scurrying up a pine tree. It was a bit wider than the lodgepole pine, and when the bear reached the lower branches, he settled onto one.

327

They gazed up at him, but the bear's focus was on something in the distance. He was about the size of her cousin Rachel with dark-brown fur and claws that clung to the tree.

"That must be his safe place." Sadie's eyes were bright, her cheeks flush.

They dared to step a little closer, and as they did, a stench grew.

"What is that?" Sadie coughed and waved a hand in front of her face.

Eli gagged. "I wonder if he dragged bags of garbage back there. It smells horrible — like something died."

Sadie pinched her nose. "It smells like dead fish."

Eli took a few more steps until he was able to look over a clump of brush and get a good look at the base of the tree. He noticed fish bones and various scraps.

"Looks as if our guy here hasn't been cleaning his plate."

"But why does he bring the fish here?" Sadie scrunched up her face.

"It must be a habit — maybe instinct or something his mother taught him." Chills traveled up his arms. "But cubs usually only act this way when they feel threatened that their lunch is going to be taken away. When they know there is a bigger bear around."

Sadie's eyes grew wide. Her jaw dropped. "What? Are you joking with me?"

"I'm not joking. I'm sure I heard that, read that, somewhere. I —"

Eli's words were interrupted by a movement in the distance. His heart leapt to his throat. He grabbed Sadie's hand and tugged her.

With quickened steps, he turned and moved toward the road. Partly because he believed it could be true, but mostly because he'd seen a look of fear in Sadie's eyes. He wanted this to be a fun day. He guessed that scaring Sadie out of her mind wasn't her idea of fun. Her fingers tightened around his.

They moved side by side until Sadie pulled her hand from his grasp and rushed past him. Another noise like the sounds of rumbling within the brush sounded, and he expected her to cry out in fear as she ran down the hill. Instead, laughter spilled out of her mouth.

"Run! C'mon, Eli." Her *kapp* strings trailed behind her, and she giggled as if she was ten again. He followed, and couldn't help but laugh. She didn't slow down until they reached the dirt road.

When Eli caught up with her, Sadie was bent over, hands on her knees, breathing heavily. His stomach did a flip seeing her there, not because he'd been worried about a bear, but because he realized this moment changed everything.

Over the last few weeks he'd told himself they were just friends. Even as they were planting the garden together, Sadie had been kind but she'd kept her distance.

Maybe the best way to help Sadie get over her grief is to remind her how beautiful life can be, laughter can be.

"Eli." She glanced up at him, tucked a few strands of blonde hair back in her *kapp.*

"*Ja?*"

"I have a question for you. A serious one."

"What is that?"

"Do you have any idea how fast a bear can run?" She glanced back over her shoulder as if she expected the cub to be following them.

"Does it matter?" he asked. Then he started jogging again, picking up speed. "Just as long as I can run faster than you!"

Her laughter rang out then, deep from the pit of her stomach. Harder than he'd ever heard her laugh, and as Eli paused to let her catch up, his mind wasn't on the bear cub, their picnic lunch, or strolling over to Alkali Lake. Instead, all he could think about was making Sadie laugh tomorrow, and the day after, and the day after.

THE BUDGET — West Kootenai, Montana
Down a winding dirt road that is full of potholes is a small lake. I've heard it said that the locals often go there to view wildlife. A friend and I sat for an hour quietly watching the lake, but we didn't see one creature, not even a bird. An hour before that, though, we saw the famous bear cub, Goliath. Sometimes what matters is not what you go looking for, but rather what you find when you're not looking. That's what my time here in Montana has been like. I'm eager to see what tomorrow brings.

We've had a whole mess of rainy days, and that caused the local youth to move their Sunday singing into the Kraft and Grocery. Some of us visiting bachelors sat around and watched them, humming along. Mostly we were there for the pie that was passed around.

At church last Sunday, Jared and Elizabeth Brubacher and family were visiting from Ohio. Lester and Wanda Coblentz came from Dorado Springs, MO. Sad that their vacation was spent indoors keeping dry. As soon as they headed back on the train, the sun came out. Go figure.

The book of Ecclesiastes speaks of sunshine being sweet. Getting up this morning, I have to agree it is. Of course, a few verses later, there in chapter 11, it says that people ought to enjoy every day of their lives. So today I'm also thankful for the rain.

— Eli Plank, the bachelor scribe

CHAPTER EIGHT

Sadie kneeled beside the row of carrots and shook her head. She glanced around at the fencing, wondering what had gotten in and how. Something had been having lunch in her garden!

She heard a whistling behind her and recognized one of the hymns from the youth sing a couple of weeks ago. Sadie tried to push her annoyance to the side for a moment and just enjoy the smile on Eli's face.

"Why, someone's sure happy today," she called to him.

"*Ja,* I am. *Opa* called my work and left a message. I just got off the phone with him. Today is my grandparents' anniversary, and he got *me* a gift."

She stood and opened the gate for him, smiling wide. "It's their anniversary and you got a gift?"

"*Ja,* my grandmother bought him a greeting card and inside was a train ticket to

Montana. He's coming in a few weeks, and there's something even better than that."

"What's that?"

"My grandmother told him to look for a small cottage while he's here, someplace to spend the summers. It would be great to have them around, even if it's just for a few months a year."

"Have them around?" Sadie fingered the metal of the fence. "Does that mean you're staying?"

"Well . . ." Eli cocked his head. "Have I given you any indication that I'm going somewhere?"

"*Ne,* but that's what you do, isn't it? As the Amish bachelor, you travel from place to place."

Eli removed his hat and ran his fingers through his hair. "Well, that's what I've done, but things can change . . ." His voice trailed off.

Sadie sat there for a moment, still. *Breathe, Sadie.* She bit her lower lip. Did Eli's desire to stay have anything to do with her?

She was about to ask when movement by the back door of the house made her pause. An Amish woman stepped out of the back door and set a large jar with tea bags on the porch railing for sun tea. Even from this distance the woman's movements were familiar. She was taller than her aunt and thinner too. Sadie sucked in a breath. Her oldest sister had followed through with her threats! Carol had come to Montana. And she hadn't let Sadie know she was coming. Had Aunt Linda known? Why had they kept it a secret?

Sadie sat back on her heels. She didn't know what to say. What to do. The best thing was to just pretend that Eli was a friend and that her heart didn't race whenever he was near. Then — after her sister left — she could explore her feelings further. She'd never be able to open up to Eli with her sister watching her every move.

She gingerly leaned forward and tugged at a weed, trying to act natural. Trying not to feel like the child she always felt like in her sister's presence.

"Sadie?" Eli cleared his throat. "Are you okay?"

She forced a smile. "*Ja,* why?"

"Your face — it got all pale. You're not feeling ill, are you?"

"*Ne* . . . I —" She leaned forward again to tackle another weed. How could she explain that her life was not her own? Even all the way in Montana, her oldest sister had come to check on her . . . and no doubt check on her tomatoes too.

She returned to their conversation. "That's wonderful about your grandparents' anniversary. Do you know how they met? I always love hearing those stories." She prayed she sounded convincing. She hoped he couldn't tell that her stomach was tied up in knots.

"My grandfather said he was nine years old when he saw my grandmother for the first time. She was thirteen, a grown woman in his eyes." Eli chuckled. "Her brother was marrying his sister, and the most exciting part about the wedding was knowing that he'd probably see her more at family events."

"My *mem* and *dat* met at a volleyball game." Sadie offered a sad smile. "They'd both gone with someone else but caught each other's eyes. They died on the way back from a volleyball game, too, many, many years later . . ."

"I'm sorry about that. I read about the buggy accident in *The Budget.*"

How many times had she heard the words *I'm sorry*?

In her opinion, people were awfully sorry about things they couldn't control. Yet the people who should be sorry for selling the farm without asking her — her siblings — hadn't offered an apology once.

"Sadie, I . . ." Eli looked into her eyes and then fell silent.

A lump filled her throat, and she attempted to swallow it away. She didn't know what he could say to make things better.

"You don't need to say anything, and thank you for caring. I'm glad you're here because I need your help. Can you take a look at the fence? Maybe there's something I'm missing." She needed other help too. But how could she explain her sister? Her siblings?

Eli looked around, puzzled. "Why? What's wrong?"

"Something's been chewing the tops off the carrots."

He bent down and looked at them, shaking his head. "The little varmints."

She rose and led him around the eight-foot chicken wire fence. "This fence works for keeping the deer and bears out, and I can't imagine squirrels and rabbits being able to get in. I don't see any holes where they could've dug under. At the store, I talked to that rancher lady, Millie Arnold. She said that she uses an electric fence." Sadie cocked an eyebrow. "But that's not possible here. And Edgar offered to give me some extra galvanized hardware cloth that he had, but it seems like so much work.

These few plants aren't worth it."

Eli nodded, but she could tell he didn't believe her. She knew it wasn't the truth either. The plants meant she was carrying on her heritage. She jutted out her chin, happy that she'd be able to show the beautiful plants to Carol. She and Eli had worked hard. She just hoped that a few hungry creatures wouldn't ruin everything.

He studied the fence for a while and then looked up at the wide Montana sky as if trying to formulate a plan.

"Those tomatoes are worth a lot, Sadie, and we both know it." Eli tapped his chin. "I have an idea . . ."

She cocked her head. "What?"

"You promise not to laugh, *ja*? I mean, your *mem* was an expert gardener, and what I'm going to suggest isn't very traditional."

"I promise I won't laugh. Well, as long as you don't tell me to put up a scarecrow." She fingered her sleeve, curious. "I've never liked them, ever since one of my older brothers dressed up as one and jumped out and scared me. Serves me right for being the youngest."

"Not a scarecrow, but close . . ." Eli crossed his arms over his chest. "Pinwheels. This place gets a lot of wind. The movement will keep any pesky critters away."

She placed a hand over her mouth, holding back a laugh.

Eli feigned a frown. "I told you not to laugh."

"I'm sorry. I can't help it."

"Will you try it?"

She shrugged. "I might."

"If I buy them for you, will you put them up?"

"Only if you help me," she said.

"*Ja,* okay then, it's a date."

Eli stepped forward and reached out a hand, as if he were going to place it on her shoulder, then dropped it again. "What? Would you like me to plan something more romantic?"

A shiver raced up her arms, and she suppressed a smile. The kids were home from school, her aunt was cooking dinner, and her sister was no doubt watching them through the kitchen window, critiquing their every move.

"Eli, I'm thankful that we are friends." She glanced up, and her eyes fixed on his. Their green depths penetrated her. "But —"

He took a step closer and a chill of excitement traveled down her spine, but she refused to allow herself to respond.

"But? But what, Sadie?"

Instead of answering, Sadie swallowed.

"Pinwheels, you say?"

His lower lip curled down, an obvious sign of his disappointment. She wanted to explain, but how could she? She didn't know why her sister was here or what her agenda was. How could she ever plan her future when there was always someone who'd go out of her way to step in and try to plan it for her?

Eli released a heavy sigh. "I'll see if someone can take me to Eureka — or even Kalispell — to pick up the pinwheels."

She pursed her lips as she looked up at him. "Why, that's a very tender gesture, Eli."

"Nothing but the best for you, Sadie." He winked. "Speaking of which, my grandfather also mentioned that he'd love to see your garden when he gets here. He's willing to help however he can."

"I'll appreciate the help," she answered, wondering if Carol had come for the same reason. "This is the first time I've grown tomatoes in a greenhouse, and the first time I've tried to grow them in this colder climate. The soil is different. I'm not sure why I didn't think of all those things before planting." A weariness came over her, and she wondered why she'd ever come to Montana. No matter how far she went, she'd never be able to leave behind her grief. And she'd never get beyond her role as the youngest one in the family.

"Sometimes I wish I would have just stayed in my old community," she said. "It might have been easier to just live the life I already had, as hard as it may be, than to forge a new one."

"Do you really think that, Sadie? Because I've been watching the care you receive from your aunt and uncle. And it seems to be reciprocated."

"*Ja,* I do, but I just wish I knew where I belonged."

"And where would you like to be? What kind of place would you like, Sadie?"

"It may seem silly, but one just like that one." She pointed to the house next door. "Just a simple place with a garden spot and a greenhouse. A place where I can watch my children walk to school, where my husband would work close enough to sit at the table with me for every meal, and a greenhouse out back — with light and a heater — so no matter how cold it is outside, or how the snow piles up, I can still have something growing inside."

"I love that." Eli smiled. "I love how you nurture life."

"It's when I feel closest to God, I suppose. I get a glimpse of the joy of those days of creation when life bursts forth from the soil."

She also liked being part of something her family started, something she was honored to carry on. Sadie opened her mouth to say that, but stopped when she saw Eli's eyes focused on the house next door.

"And what type of place do you want to settle down in?" she wanted to ask him. *"And most importantly, with whom?"*

Sadie tried to act surprised as she and Eli entered the house and she found Carol standing at the sink peeling potatoes.

"Carol!" Her voice rose, and she offered a quick wave. "You're here. I didn't expect it."

Her Aunt Linda cleared her throat. "Neither did I. I heard a knock at the door and there she was." She turned to Sadie, her eyes widening, mimicking her expression. "Your sister even hired a driver to pick her up in Whitefish."

Carol put down her vegetable peeler and hurried to Sadie, wrapping her arms around her sister's shoulders for a quick hug. "I guessed you'd try to talk me out of it, but some neighbors were coming this direction, and I tagged along. I knew you wouldn't want me to come all this way, but I miss you, I really do. And I just wanted to check to see if everything was all right."

Sadie took a step back. "Everything? Like the tomatoes?"

Carol clicked her tongue. "I wondered if *you* were all right." She glanced over to Eli.

He stood at the threshold of the kitchen, waiting to be welcomed into the conversation.

Sadie quickly introduced him, and Carol acknowledged him with a quick nod. "It doesn't seem right that I've learned more about what my baby sister is doing through *The Budget* than I get in her letters. I was her age when she was born, and I've always felt like a second mother." She lowered her chin and peered down at Sadie. "I suppose being written about comes when you're . . . friends . . . with a scribe."

Sadie wrapped her *kapp* string around her finger. "I've written you —"

"You've written, but I've lived on this earth long enough to know that what one *doesn't* say matters more than what they do." Carol glanced over at Eli. "Isn't that right, Mr. Plank?"

"*Ja.*" He ran his hand down his smooth face. "That's an honest assessment. But you have to ask the reason why." He looked over at Sadie. "Sometimes one's trying to hide the truth, but other times one's just waiting for the right time to reveal it. After all, once words are spoken, it's hard to take them back."

Carol's eyes widened, showing her surprise at Eli's response.

"I know I'd regret it if I didn't invite Eli for dinner," *Aenti* Linda cut in.

"Actually, I think I'll head home and get some things done around the house. I have another *Budge*t report that I need to send in too."

"Is it hard?" Carol moved toward the doorway as if this was her house and it was her job to usher Eli to the door.

"Is writing the report hard? *Ne,* not really. I just pretend I'm writing home to a friend."

"Not that part. I mean, is it hard that everyone knows about your life? Have you ever considered how hard that would be on a family someday?"

Sadie stood fixed in the kitchen as if her feet were glued to the floor. On one hand, she couldn't believe her sister was so bold with her questions. But on the other hand, she understood. Carol had come because if Sadie opened her heart to Eli, then all of her life would be open to the world. It was something she hadn't thought about, but obviously Carol had.

Before Sadie could reprimand her sister for her bold words, Eli stepped through the front door. "I'd like to say I know what I'm doing, but I can't say I do. I don't have a wife. I don't have children — although I want them someday."

"*Ja,* that's what I thought." Carol returned to the kitchen and began peeling potatoes again. Sadie wished the floor would open up and swallow her. Even if she did have feelings for Eli, it didn't matter now. Who would want to marry into a family with someone so confrontational? Then again, in just a few minutes' time, her sister had brought up questions Sadie hadn't thought to ask.

Maybe Eli will always just be a friend, she told herself. It was enough work just keeping on top of the garden. Now with her sister here, how could she test her feelings for Eli too?

After Eli had disappeared down the road, they shared small talk about the trip and about family members back home. It wasn't until after dinner, and when everyone else had gone to bed, that Sadie had the nerve to confront her sister. They sat side by side in two rocking chairs on the front porch. Even though it was nearly ten o'clock, the sun hadn't fully set yet. That was something about Montana — and living so far north — that she was still getting used to.

"That wasn't kind, the way you treated Eli today." Sadie tried to keep her voice calm. "He's a good man. He's been a huge help with the garden." The creak of the rocking chair punctuated Sadie's words.

"One must desire more than good gardening skills in a husband, Sadie. You must think more of your life to come than your emotions of the moment. It would have helped *Mem* and *Dat* . . ."

"Helped *Mem* and *Dat* how?" Sadie's brow furrowed. "I don't understand."

"*Dat* was a good man, but he wasn't very good with money. Their debt was high — he owed on accounts all around town. We didn't find out, of course, until after their deaths."

Sadie gasped. "High debt. Is that why —"

"Why we sold the house? *Ja,* of course. It broke my heart to sell it."

"But you didn't tell me."

Carol glanced over, her eyes full of compassion. "You were going through so much already. We didn't want to burden you. We didn't want you to think less of them . . ."

Sadie focused on her sister's face. It had been hard for Carol to confess the truth. Sadie could see it all over her face. Carol —

her other siblings — had been trying to protect her. She thought of Eli. Carol was no doubt trying to protect her still.

Carol touched her *kapp.* "But that's in the past. It does my heart good to see that you're all right. And tomorrow I'm eager to see the garden. To see *Mem*'s tomatoes. I'd love some of the seeds to take back home. I'm only staying a few days. It's a quick trip."

"*Ja,* I'd be happy to give you some seeds once the fruit comes in. Once I dry them."

Carol stopped her rocking, looking startled. "I–I don't understand. Are you saying that you planted *all* the seeds?"

"*Ja . . .*" A boulder formed in the pit of Sadie's stomach.

"Did *Mem* ever tell you to leave some aside, in case it isn't a *gut* crop?"

Sadie didn't answer. Instead she just folded her fingers and looked to her lap.

Carol was quiet. The only sound was crickets chirping in the field beside the house. "*Ja,* well. I'm sure everything will be fine," Carol said finally. "You said it was a beautiful crop coming in, right? There shouldn't be any problems. No problems at all."

CHAPTER NINE

By the time Carol left, Sadie was sad to see her go. During the evenings, after everyone else went to bed, they sat on the porch, talking about their lives in a way they never had before. And for the first time, Sadie felt like an adult in her sister's eyes. The only thing they didn't talk about again was Eli. Sadie was afraid to bring the subject up. It was easier to talk about everything else. It was easier to talk about tomatoes. Sadie was thankful that the tomatoes were coming in well. So well, she could almost taste them.

While most of the other plants were still in the early stages of growth, Sadie's tomatoes were large, round, and a few had already ripened. This morning she headed outside with a small bowl, preparing to pick the first tomatoes of the year. She'd waited for this day for so long.

She'd invited Eli to come down for lunch, and she couldn't wait to see the surprised look on his face when she placed a fresh salad before him, with her tomatoes gracing the top. She had to thank him too. He'd spent his whole Saturday looking for pinwheels, and he'd even hired a driver to take him to Kalispell, but his efforts had paid off. Eli had presented her with a large bouquet of pinwheels that they'd placed throughout the garden.

The bright, spinning, colorful wheels had done a fine job of keeping the critters away. Every day Sadie had grown accustomed to thanking God for bringing Eli into her life, and not just because of all the help he'd offered in her garden. Yet she still had many questions. Would he be a good husband? Could they have a good future together?

Sadie's footsteps stopped short when she saw her uncle standing at the fencing, peering intently into the garden.

"Oh, don't you think of it, Uncle Melvin. Those tomatoes are called for. You hear? I promise to make you something good — something yummy — from the next batch."

"Sadie, have you taken a look at your garden lately? Something's not looking right."

"Are you talking about the carrot tops? They got nibbled down a few weeks ago, but ever since Eli got the pinwheels, there hasn't been a problem."

"*Ne,* I'm not talking about the carrot tops. I'm talking about the tomatoes." Her uncle's voice was tinged with panic. "At first I thought it was just mud on your tomatoes, but look at those dark spots. I think I've seen that before — heard neighbors talk about it. It looks like your first batch of tomatoes has blossom-end rot to me."

Sadie's heart skipped. "What?" She'd heard of that. It could ruin produce quicker than anything else. She hadn't been in the garden in a day or two, but surely things couldn't have gone wrong in that short of time — could they? She opened the make-shift gate and hurried inside.

Sadie sank onto her knees in front of the tomato plants, not caring if her dress got dirty. She placed the empty bowl on the ground and gently lifted a tomato stem. Sure enough, on each of her three best tomatoes was a black spot on the blossom end — opposite the stem.

"I've heard it happens sometimes to the first fruit of the season."

"What is it exactly?" Tears sprang to her eyes. "Is it a pest? Disease?" She looked to Melvin, horrified. "Is it going to ruin *all* the plants?" A pain started in the pit of her stomach. When she was planting her seeds, she considered setting a few to the side, just in case something like this happened, but her mother's words had come back to her. *"Nothing ventured, nothing gained, Sadie. One cannot be too stingy when it comes to gardening. If you expect a big harvest, you have to give a big investment."* The only problem was that she'd given it all — and now she might lose it all.

"If you want, I can stop by the store and talk to Edgar at lunch," her uncle offered. "He's been in this area his whole life. And —"

Sadie rose and moved to the gate. Her knees grew soft and her heart ached. She could not lose these tomato plants.

With fumbling fingers, she closed the gate, locking it tight. "I'll be . . . back." They were the only words she could get out.

"You okay?"

"*Ja,* just going to see Eli. I need him to ask his grandfather about this. He seems to know about these things."

It only took fifteen minutes for Sadie to walk to Montana Log Works, half the time it usually took. On the way, Susan Carash, their neighbor, had slowed down her truck, asking if Sadie needed a ride. As much as Sadie wanted to get to the factory as quickly as possible, she didn't want to explain her garden, her fears, or why she was crying, so she declined.

Sadie heard the sounds of machines and the voices of men as she entered the Log Works. It smelled of wood and glue. The lighting was dimmer than the bright sunshine outside, and it took a minute for her eyes to adjust.

There. Halfway across the building, Eli was using a sharp knife to peel the bark off a lodgepole pine log. She didn't dare rush up to him with that big knife in his hand, so she waited. It took less than thirty seconds for someone — his boss, she supposed — to alert Eli of her presence. The man talked to Eli and then pointed to the door. Eli's smile fell when he saw her.

Eli placed the knife on a shelf and took off his leather apron, then hurried over. His hair was stuck to his brow with sweat and concern filled his eyes. "Sadie, is everything all right?"

"Something is wrong. We did something wrong, Eli." Her voice was sharper than she meant it to be. "The tomatoes —" Sadie's voice caught. "Well, the first tomatoes have something horribly wrong with them. There are big black spots of decay on the end not connected to the vine. Uncle Melvin says it looks like blossom-end rot."

Eli's eyes widened. "Don't worry, Sadie. I'll call my *opa* tonight. I'll come and see them later, and then I'll call —"

"No!" The word shot from her lips. "Can't you do it sooner?" She looked to the office that was connected to the workshop. "Can you ask to use the phone? Tell them it's an emergency. I can pay whatever it costs for the call."

"An emergency?" Eli scratched his head, making the back of his hair stick up like a rooster's comb, but even the sight of that didn't make her smile. "Do you really think —" he started and then paused. Then, with a tender look in his eyes, Eli reached a hand toward her arm. "*Ja,* hold on one moment."

Sadie nodded and moved back to the open doorway, standing so that part of her was in the sunshine and part of her was in the shade. After members of her family successfully passed down the seeds for generations, she'd be the one to ruin it all. And she'd gone out today with hopes of a harvest. There hadn't been even one healthy tomato.

A few minutes later, Eli met her at the door and then motioned for her to follow him outside. "I talked to my *opa,* and I have good news. From how you described it, it does sound like blossom-end rot, but it's not a disease or parasite. The problem is a low level of calcium in the fruit. When the fruit grows faster than the amount of calcium that can be absorbed from the soil, the tomato starts to decay."

"What does that mean? How can we fix it?"

"First, my *opa* says that you have to stop watering it so much. He said try to feed the area with manure or compost too. He also says you can add in some crushed eggshells, but all these tricks usually help more during the planting. He says it could help now some, but there isn't a guarantee."

"So basically, I'm killing my precious plants because I'm watering too much?" Sadie lowered her head.

"That, and the problems with the soil — it's a deadly mix. Oh, and because it's a colder part of the country, the roots take longer to go deep, so that makes it harder for the plants to get calcium too."

"So what do I do?" she asked again.

"Water less, add eggshells and manure, and pick off the affected fruit. He says that just because those tomatoes were damaged doesn't mean any other fruit will be."

Sadie breathed out a heavy sigh. "That's *gut* news."

"Oh, and there's one last thing."

"What's that?"

"*Opa* said the best thing you can do is pray. He says the One who created gardens cares about yours."

Sadie smiled. "I like that, and the next time you talk to him, can you tell him *danke*?"

"*Ja.*" Eli nodded and then took her hand. "And in just a little while you'll be able to thank him yourself. He should be here before we know it. You're going to love him, Sadie — and he's going to love you."

THE BUDGET — West Kootenai, Montana

Many of you have written to ask about Goliath — the yearling bear cub that was stirring up trouble around these parts. It turns out that the trouble got the attention of local Fish and Wildlife officials. They showed up asking questions about the young bear. Many of the locals agreed that he was a pest and asked for the bear to be moved.

The officials agreed that something needed to be done — especially with young children around, but they said that moving a bear was expensive, and most of the animals that are moved return in short order. They said that putting the animal down was probably the best option, much to the uproar of the community.

Our guess is that Goliath heard murmurs of his fate and decided to head to the hills. (My personal belief is that the snow is melting, and he now has fresh berries and other things to dine on without the bothersome people in his way.) No matter the reason, no one has seen the bear cub in many weeks, and we're hoping it stays that way.

On a better note, the gardens in the area are turning out nicely. Ruth Sommers planted enough zucchini to bake bread for all of northwest Montana — or so she claims. Personally, I'm looking forward to summer days passing so I can get a slice of that myself. Other gardens are progressing nicely, and many of the gardeners have admitted to me that they've ordered from Pioneer Creek Seeds. I couldn't be prouder of that, and I'm sure my father and grandfather are too.

Sadie Chupp's heirloom seeds went through a little bump in the road when she discovered they had blossom-end rot. Her overzealous watering was one cause, but from what I've heard, the other tomatoes are coming in fine. I'm looking forward to a tomato sandwich in the near future.

Also, I've moved from skip-peeling logs to assembling furniture. My boss called it a promotion. My back agrees.

We're going to have an Amish auction here soon, and everyone has rolled up their sleeves to get things ready. Quilts have been arriving daily at our store/post office, and I've had a sneak peek at some of them. It seems that many Amish communities around the country have represented themselves. In addition to funds going back to the women for their hard work, our local Amish school will benefit, and children like Isaiah, Noah, and Rachel Chupp thank you.

Oh yes, and you might have noticed my use of "our" in the previous paragraph. "Our store, our school." I've traveled many places, but until I arrived in West Kootenai, I'd always considered Indiana to be home. After living here awhile, I can say that this place is growing on me.

Sending OUR best wishes from the mountains.

— Eli Plank, the bachelor scribe

CHAPTER TEN

It took two weeks of watering less, incorporating eggshells and manure into the soil, and praying — lots of praying — but Sadie's heart leapt with joy when she walked out to the garden one morning and noticed the new tomatoes had begun to ripen and were blemish-free.

Sadie let out a long breath. A weight lifted from her shoulders. Thankfully she wasn't going to be the one who ended the heritage. Instead, she hoped that this would just be part of a humorous story she told to her children and grandchildren someday. She just needed these tomatoes to ripen for a few more days, and then she could harvest their seeds. Then — and only then — would she really be able to breathe a sigh of relief and laugh at herself.

"I can't believe I ran up to Montana Log Works to tell Eli about my 'crisis,' " Sadie mumbled to herself. She shook her head, wondering what Eli's coworkers must have thought of her. *Great Tomato Catastrophe, indeed.*

She walked to her uncle's shed to grab her garden gloves, and once inside, she heard what sounded like someone moving around outside. The door behind her creaked open.

Sadie turned. Even though it was early, she expected it to be Eli. He usually visited her after work, but sometimes he surprised her in the early morning too.

Instead, it was Rachel who trembled in the cool morning air, still wearing her nightdress and head scarf.

Sadie quickly took off her sweater and hurried over to the young girl. "Oh, *liebling,* come in. It's chilly out there."

"I had a dream, Sadie."

Sadie wrapped the sweater around Rachel's shoulders. The girl's forehead creased with concern.

"Was it a bad dream?"

"*Ja.*" Rachel lowered her head. "It was *Mem* and *Dat.* They were in an accident."

"Was it a buggy accident, Rachel, like my *mem* and *dat*?"

"*Ja.*"

"Just because something tragic like that

359

happened once doesn't mean it'll happen again."

"But what if it did happen? Would you stay here with me?"

"*Ja,* of course. I would never leave you alone."

"But what if you were married with your own kids?" Rachel's lower lip trembled. "*Mem* says that Eli loves you — that she can see it in his eyes."

Sadie took Rachel's shoulders and knelt before her. Fear filled her face. She was concerned about the nightmare, but it was her aunt's belief that Eli loved her that caused the most shock.

"Your *mem* said that . . . that he loved me?"

"*Ja,* I heard her and *Dat* talking. They said they'd be very sad if you married and returned to Indiana. And if you do, who will be here to take care of me?"

"Oh, *liebling,* you don't have to worry about that. I don't think that anything will happen to your parents. Also, I have no plans of going anywhere. Do you understand? And as far as I know, Eli plans to stay here too."

"Do you mean that?"

Sadie nodded, but was she jumping to conclusions? Eli claimed to like it here.

He'd said more than once that Montana was starting to feel like home. But what did that mean for him? What did that mean for *them*?

"Just go to bed and rest your little heart. Pray to God, and remember that He can sweep all your worries away like the swish of a broom."

Sadie didn't know where those words came from, but as she waved Rachel back toward the house and pulled on her garden gloves, she realized she needed those words too. She could either question if Eli did indeed care for her as much as she cared for him, or she could trust that God knew Eli's heart and had a plan for both of them. He also had a perfect home in mind for her, whether here or another place.

That was one thing she was learning from Eli. To ask for help and then accept it, not only from those around her, but also from God.

Still, she wondered. *Are Aunt Linda's observations correct? Is there truly love in his eyes when he looks at me?*

Sadie hoped that tonight she would have some answers. Eli had asked her to join him for dinner. It wasn't uncommon except for the fact he'd asked her four days ago to save this specific night. Did he happen to know that it was the anniversary of her parents' death? Surely he couldn't know. Still, God did. Maybe God knew she'd need special care today.

Eli guided Sadie to a table in the back of the restaurant portion of the West Kootenai Kraft and Grocery. The eyes of the other Amish women bored into her. They were hardly discreet. Sadie sat and smoothed the skirt of her cape dress, wishing there was another place to spend time with Eli — to get to know him better — but their only choices were her aunt and uncle's living room under the gaze of the kids, or here in the restaurant, the one public gathering place in the community. At least here everyone only stared and didn't try to interrupt their conversation.

They sat facing each other, and instead of looking into his eyes, she traced the wood grain pattern on the log table with her finger.

"I came in for lunch, and Annie and Jenny were making up some strawberry pies. I wonder if anyone would mind if I ate dessert first."

She laughed. "Or *only* ate dessert. Strawberry pie sounds good. They couldn't have picked their own strawberries, could they?"

"Maybe if they started them in a greenhouse . . ."

"*Ja,* I suppose that's possible." Sadie smiled. "You should see my tomato plants. They're taller than they would be in Indiana, I suppose."

"So you're adjusting to life here then?"

The question didn't surprise Sadie. She'd seen the tender look in his eyes lately. She'd seen his concern.

"I am. It's taken some getting used to . . ." Her voice trailed off, and she glanced up, staring into his eyes. "Sometimes I think it's all a dream, you know? I picture getting on the train and making my way back home. I picture *Dat* in the barn and *Mem* at the stove — in our old house, of course. *Mem* would always wave me in when I walked in the door, as if welcoming me, telling me to come closer, and urging me not to let in any flies." She chuckled. "If there was one thing that drove *Mem* crazy, it was a fly in her house."

Eli leaned back, inhaling slowly. He seemed fixed on her every word. "I can't even imagine, Sadie. I have my parents and both grandparents on *Dat* and *Mem*'s sides. I've never lost anyone close. I can't really imagine," he repeated.

"It's God's will, I suppose." She said the

words without conviction.

"*Ja,* we can accept it, but that doesn't mean we shouldn't grieve. I've had a talkin'-to with God over far less things."

She smiled unexpectedly at his words, and she tried to imagine that. Eli seemed so levelheaded.

"Oh, you did, did ya? And did you write about that, too, in *The Budget*?" Sadie cleared her throat, and then she attempted to talk in a deeper voice. "I got mighty angry at God today. I picked up a few smooth stones and chucked them at majestic, tall pine trees as I spouted angry words."

Eli's smile faded at her words. "Does it bother you, Sadie, that I share my life with the world? I know it bothers your sister."

"I've been thinking about that." She paused for a minute and then shook her head. *"Ne.* I mean, I don't think so. I hope it doesn't hurt your feelings, but I've never been one to read *The Budget.* That was something that *Dat* —" Her words caught in her throat. "That was something that *Dat* did."

He reached across the table, as if to pat her hand, but she pulled it away. She needed to know if Eli was serious, truly serious, before she allowed any display of public affection.

Eli nodded and pulled his hand back. "I'm sorry."

She wasn't sure if he was sorry about how memories of her parents stirred up emotion yet again, or that he'd tried to hold her hand in public. Sadie just shrugged and then picked up the menu as if it was the most fascinating reading material she'd ever come upon.

"I'm not sure what you think about the time we've been spending together, Sadie. I'd like to hope that you consider me a close friend, maybe more. But I did want to mention again that my grandfather is coming to the area. *Opa* has always wanted to see Montana, and my being here is a *gut* excuse."

"That's wonderful." She clasped her hands on her lap and smiled, truly excited for him.

"*Ja*, I'm eager to see him. Many folks tell me we're like two peas in a pod. But I just wanted to warn you before he arrived."

"Warn me?"

"*Vell*, I've told him about you, Sadie. He likes to garden and . . ."

She could tell from the way his eyes darted to his water glass, then back to her, that wasn't all he wanted to say.

"And . . ."

"And what?"

"And I told him that my feelings for you were starting to grow."

She blinked her eyes several times before she answered. "It's *gut* to know that," she said softly. "For a while I wondered if —"

"Ready to order?" the waitress interrupted.

They both ordered slices of strawberry pie and coffee. Sadie couldn't think of ordering anything more than that — not with the butterflies dancing around in her stomach. Then she saw it, the love in his eyes that Aunt Linda talked about. Suddenly fear pounded in her heart. Was she really ready for this conversation? Was she ready to open her heart?

Their pie and coffee arrived a few moments later, but instead of picking up his fork to take a bite, Eli turned his gaze to her again. "Now as I was saying —"

"You were saying that your grandfather is quite a gardener," she hurried to say. "I'm so thankful that he was able to help me with my tomato plants. Have you told him how much they've grown?"

Eli scowled. He leaned forward and lowered his voice so only she could hear. "Sadie, you know that before we were interrupted, my mind wasn't on tomato plants."

She pressed her lips together into a thin line. Of course she knew that, but how could she tell him that the thing that scared her most was getting her hopes up? She couldn't risk a broken heart.

"Will your grandfather be here long?" she asked, shaking off thoughts of what would really happen if she allowed herself to get caught up in dreaming of a life with Eli.

He sighed. "A week or so. Long enough to get to see a lot of the sights. Long enough to get to know you a little. More than anyone else, I respect my grandfather's opinion."

Opinion about what? she wanted to ask. *About whether I'm worth risking your heart over?* But she didn't ask, and she could tell from his face that he was frustrated at trying to take the conversation to a deeper level, only to have her draw it back to gardening.

In her own mind, Sadie truly wondered if she was worth the risk. Was there even a large enough piece of her heart left to give to Eli?

Eli acted as if he had more to say, but instead he dug into his pie with gusto.

"I suppose all I wanted to tell you is that I hope you don't mind if my grandpa asks you a few questions. He wants to know your heart, Sadie. He most likely wants to know if you're right . . . for me."

"Right for you?"

"As in marriage. Don't you understand that's what I've been trying to say?"

"Marriage?" The word played on her lips.

Eli leaned forward and took her hand, obviously not caring what anyone thought. "Yes, Sadie, and you don't have to answer me now, but look into my eyes. Know my heart. I don't want to go anywhere unless I have you by my side."

CHAPTER ELEVEN

The day had turned to dusk as Sadie sat on the swing waiting for Eli. Her heart brimmed with joy. Eli cared for her — he really did. He cared so much that he asked his grandfather to come all this way to meet her, or at least that's what he finally confessed.

Even though it was only eight o'clock, the rest of her family had gone to bed. Most nights, her aunt, uncle, and cousins were in bed before sunset, especially since her uncle woke them at 4:00 a.m., summer or not.

She brushed her shoes on the porch as she swung. He'd told her he'd come, and she had no reason to question why he wouldn't. Eli always kept his word. That was one thing she cared about most — loved most — about him. Sadie smiled. *Ja,* it was turning into love all right. And soon maybe marriage.

Up ahead, two figures crested the small

rise. They were about the same height, but the one on the right of the road walked with a lightness to his step. The older man walked with more of a shuffle, yet Eli's *opa* seemed to be in good shape for someone his age.

She walked to the gate and waved, then waited for them to get closer.

"Sadie, I have someone I'd like you to meet." She could hear the joy in his voice. "*Opa* told me he'd chatted with your mother many times, and she was a wonderful gardener."

They entered the gate.

"I think she was envied by everyone in LaGrange county . . . not that the Amish envy." The older man stretched out his hand and shook Sadie's. "It's an honor, dear." It wasn't the usual way the Amish did things, and it reminded Sadie of when she and Eli first met.

"You can call me *Opa,*" he said. "It seems only right, don't you think?"

Heat rose to her cheeks. She'd be a welcome member of the family if that's what Eli chose. She released his hand and motioned to the house.

"Come inside. I'd love to hear more," she offered. "It's always a joy to talk to someone who knew my parents. I've told Eli about

Mem's garden, and it's wonderful to know you thought highly of it too."

She led them to the house and opened the door wide. "I have coffee made and cookies, or if you'd rather have milk, I —" She turned, and her words lodged in her throat. There were two things she noticed immediately about Eli's grandfather once he came inside. First was how similar the two men looked, with green eyes and chiseled features. Of course, Eli's grandfather wore a beard, as did all Amish men. But the second was that he was wearing *Englisch* clothes.

Her smile faded, and *Opa*'s eyes widened. He looked down at his jeans and western shirt and then turned to Eli. "You did tell Sadie that I wasn't Amish anymore, didn't you?"

Eli looked to Sadie and cocked his head. "I believe so. Didn't I? Surely I must have. I've talked about you, *Opa,* so much, with so many people in the area, well, I did mention that, didn't I, Sadie?"

"No." The word fell flat from her lips. "That's something you forgot to mention." She tried to act nonchalant as she placed the cream and sugar on the table and then got three coffee mugs from the cupboard. Her hand was shaking slightly as she set the mugs before them, but she tried to pay it no mind. She hoped *Opa* didn't notice. He gazed up at her, and she smiled. What else could she do?

Sadie stood tall, posture straight, as if her whole worth in his eyes would be summed up in how well she held herself.

"You probably want to know why I have Amish family but I'm no longer Amish," *Opa* said. "Both my wife and I were raised Amish, and we lived that way for many years. Then there were circumstances . . . people came into our lives who loved God. Who were more concerned about the character of one's heart than one's *kapp* or beard. The more time we spent with them, the more we began to see that God didn't require us to follow our Plain ways so strictly. We're still a simple people, and I run a simple business. It's not as if we turned our back on the Amish."

Sadie nodded, but she didn't know what to say. She wished she could slow her pounding heart. Wished her mind wasn't so muddled.

What do I do now? What would my brothers and sisters say? It wouldn't be good. Not at all. Sadie bit her lip and stood there silently.

Eli looked at her with a curious expression. He took a sip of his coffee, peering at her over the rim of his coffee cup. He could tell something was wrong. She could see it in his eyes. But what could she offer? Sadie couldn't even sift through her own feelings.

Was she mad at Eli for not making it clear that his grandfather wasn't Amish? Yes. Did she now question her feelings for Eli? She had to admit she did. For as long as she remembered, she'd only imagined herself marrying a *gut* Amish man from a *gut* Amish family. She hadn't ever considered the alternative. She wouldn't even want to imagine what her *mem* and *dat* would say if they were still alive. And the fact that they weren't and she couldn't go to them for advice made her even more flustered.

She sat down at the table across from Eli and *Opa*.

It doesn't matter that he's not Amish, Sadie told herself. People left the Amish for various reasons. As long as Eli had a strong faith and commitment to the Amish, that was all that mattered, right?

"Sadie, Eli told me that some of your tomatoes got blossom-end rot, is that right?" *Opa* asked.

She was thankful he changed the subject. Her tomatoes were something she could easily talk about — and it gave her time to think.

"*Ja,* I had never seen that before. Thank you for telling Eli what I needed to do about it."

Opa took a bite from his cookie and nodded. "I'm glad I could help, and if you're interested, I'd be happy to stop by tomorrow and look at the rest of the garden to see if there are any other problems. It's always a challenge when you start gardening in a new place."

She poured herself some coffee but didn't drink it. "*Ja.* I mean, *ne.* I mean, no, I don't mind."

"Have you ever considered selling your seeds, Sadie? From what I hear, they are a very special heirloom variety. Seeds like that need to be saved up, treasured, and doing so is one of my hobbies."

Sadie's brow furrowed, and she shook her head. "My *mem* refused anytime someone tried to buy seeds from her. Sometimes she would give them to neighbors. There have been *Englischers* who've approached her. Some were very insistent, but to us, these seeds are our heritage." She thought again of the man from Pioneer Creek Seeds. Sadie remembered her mother's words.

"No, I'm sorry. I can't sell the seeds," she said. "These tomatoes are special. They're all I have of my family."

He nodded and then smiled. "I wonder why I even asked. I understand, Sadie. I've heard those same words before. Your *mem* told me the same thing many times." He chuckled. "It's almost like hearing her words come through your mouth."

"You asked my *mem* about selling her seeds?" Sadie's throat clenched down. Her stomach ratcheted up. She was certain she was going to be sick.

"Excuse me?" She leaned forward, studying the man's face. "What did you say your name is?"

"Paul, Paul Hostetler. I'm sure I met you once back in Indiana when I was visiting your *mem.* You were just a little thing then, but maybe you have heard about our business, Pioneer Creek Farms?"

"You." Tears sprang to her eyes as she looked from Paul to Eli and then back to Paul again. "Is this what it's all been about, Eli? Is that what everything's been about? My tomatoes? My seeds?"

Eli leaned over to take her hand, but Sadie pulled it away.

He stood and walked over to her, but she rose and moved toward the cupboard, putting space between them. "Don't think you can sweet-talk me." Her lips trembled as she spoke. "Either of you . . . I can't believe you've come all this way. I can't believe you've given me so much attention for . . . my seeds. They must be valuable indeed."

Suddenly the realization of what she was saying must have hit Eli because his eyes widened and his jaw dropped. "Sadie, are you saying what I think you're saying? That I've been spending all this time with you so I can warm you up to buy your seeds?"

"Isn't that true?" She jutted out her chin. "Your grandfather tried to persuade my mother, but she didn't fall for it. But me?" Sadie placed her hands over her face, and then she shook her head. "I'm such a fool, and you knew it when you approached me, didn't you? You knew how to help. You knew what to say . . . how to care." Sadie's voice rose. She lowered her hands and gazed at Paul. "No wonder you were so eager to help me with the blossom-end rot. You didn't want to lose what your eye was focused on."

"Sadie, listen to yourself. My grand-father . . . he had no intention of trying to trick you." Eli ran his hand through his hair and then turned to his grandfather. "Won't you tell her? I don't care about seeds. Tell her that this is not what it's all about."

Instead of trying to urge her, *Opa* only sighed. "Eli, I'm afraid that if I say anything it's only going to make things worse. It's clear that Sadie here has heard plenty about me. Anything I'd say would be taken with a grain of salt." Sadness filled the man's face. "I think I remember how to get back to your cabin. If you'd like to stay and talk to . . . your friend . . . I can find my way back."

"No." Eli stepped away and shook his head. "I don't think there's anything else to say. Sadie has already made her decision. She's already judged us before she's heard a word." Eli looked at her, and then he shook his head. "Good night, Sadie. I'm sorry — I'm sorry you feel the way you do." He then turned and motioned for his grandfather to follow him to the door. And then without a word, they slipped into the night.

Sadie watched them go, and anger surged through her. Anger at them and anger at herself. She'd fallen for it — fallen for him, and to what reward? Only to have her heart broken again.

Sadie rushed forward, locked the front door, and then dimmed the lantern light. She needed time to think. She needed time to pray, and deep down the only thing that brought her joy was that tomorrow she'd be able to pick the first harvest from the garden — and save those first seeds — and prove she wasn't a complete failure after all.

CHAPTER TWELVE

Sadie hadn't slept a wink. She'd tossed and turned all night, considering everything that had happened the night before — her words, Eli's words, *Opa*'s words. Had she jumped to conclusions? What if Eli had been telling the truth? What if he hadn't made the connection? And . . . what if his *opa had* been more concerned about his grandson than the seeds? If that was the case, she'd just ruined everything in one fell swoop.

As soon as the morning light came, Sadie headed outside to pick her tomatoes. Suddenly nothing mattered as much to her as picking the first ones, heading inside, and following the step-by-step instructions in her mother's garden journal on how to save the seeds.

There was a gentle pink glow of light extending over the mountains. She walked out onto the porch, noticing something moving across the yard. A bear! Goliath!

She'd recognize his playful gait anywhere. And along with him, he was trailing something — part of her fence! She cried out, but the bear didn't stop. Instead, he picked up speed, and the fencing uncaught from his paw. Seeing the opportunity, the bear darted away with all his might.

Sadie sucked in a breath. The garden! Her stomach dropped as she noticed the deer fencing strewn across the yard, but then she saw the garden plot. It was rooted up as if someone had taken a shovel to it.

"My tomatoes!" Sadie rushed forward. "Goliath!" She seethed and clenched her teeth.

Anger built up in her, and she sank to the ground. Her tomato plants were strewn about, and the green tomatoes that the bear hadn't eaten lay smashed. Sadie gathered up the green, smashed tomatoes and hurried into the house. She placed them in a paper bag and then rushed outside. Isaiah's bike was the first one she saw, and she jumped onto it. Her skirt ripped as it caught on the chain, but she tugged it hard and gave it no mind as she rode toward the bachelor's cabin.

Sadie didn't know what she'd say until she got there. She rushed up the porch stairs and pounded on the cabin's door.

Less than ten seconds later, the door opened. Eli's eyes widened in surprise. "Sadie, are you all right?"

"That bear. That stupid bear! First the blossom-end rot and then him. He got in. He ate my ripe tomatoes. He made a mess of everything. The plants are dug up. Even the green tomatoes are smashed." The tears came then.

"Oh, Sadie." Eli pulled her into his embrace. His warmth enveloped her, and she felt safe in his arms. For the first time in a long time, she felt safe.

"Did anything survive?" It was *Opa*'s voice, and she could hear him approaching. Sadie held up the paper bag and then watched as he gingerly poured the contents out onto the table.

"Four small green tomatoes." He sighed. "If they weren't smashed, we could have let them ripen in the windowsill, but like this . . . I'm afraid it's not going to work, Sadie. I'm afraid they're lost."

"But maybe if we could go back. Maybe if we can check out the plants to see if there is one we can salvage —" Her words were desperate. "Otherwise everything is lost."

"*Ja,* we can look. We'll see what we can do." *Opa* sighed. "But I have to tell you, it doesn't look good."

Sadie sat down on the couch and let her tears fall. She cried because of the tomatoes. She cried for her parents. She cried because she'd lost the heirloom seeds — the most valuable things they'd left to her. And the whole time she sat there crying, Eli sat with his arm wrapped around her. He was tender, despite how she'd treated him. He was loving in a way she didn't deserve.

And as they sat there side by side, *Opa* sat before them in a chair. *Opa* prayed for her — prayed for them — not loudly, but even his whispers held conviction.

It was only as she paused and looked up that she realized that both of them were dressed and booted up as if they were ready to head out into the morning.

"I'm so sorry." She wiped her face with her hand. "Were you going somewhere?"

"*Ja,* as a matter of fact, we were going to see you."

"Really, after what I did? What I said?"

Opa offered her a hankie, and she wiped her nose, looking from Eli to *Opa,* and then back to Eli again. "I'm so sorry that I didn't believe you."

She rested her chin on his shoulder, and she could feel Eli swallow against her ear.

"Your grandfather is a good man," she finally said. "He's just trying to do what's right . . . to hold on to something before it's lost." The words were for her as much as him.

Eli sighed. "I understand, Sadie. It's all you have left of your parents."

"I should have given your grandfather the seeds. I'm afraid I've ruined everything."

"What do you mean?"

"I mean I've lost it all, my heritage."

"No, no, you haven't, Sadie. That's what we were going to tell you."

"What do you mean?"

"My grandfather got something in the mail — back in Indiana. My grandma packed it in his bag as a surprise, not only for him, but us too."

"What do you mean?" Sadie sat back and then watched as *Opa* moved to his suitcase, removing a white padded mailing envelope. He pulled out a letter first, handing it to her.

"Read this letter from my wife," *Opa* said with the slightest of smiles. "Out loud."

Dear Paul,

I should have told you this came a few days ago, but I thought you'd like the surprise. We've been praying for Sadie Chupp — such a special girl — and God has answered our prayers in an unexpected way. There was a large package that came in the mail, with a small package inside. I've included both. The smaller package was addressed to you from Mrs. Samuel Chupp . . ."

Sadie paused. Her hands began to quiver. "My . . . mother. I don't understand."

"Keep reading, Sadie." Eli's voice was gentle.

The letter included was from a man who bought a large box of garden supplies at an auction. He bought it last fall and just pulled it out this spring. In addition to clay pots, garden tools, and some seed packets, he found this small envelope. It looked as if it was prepared to be mailed but never shipped. The only right thing to do was to mail it.

Sadie paused from her reading. "And what was inside?" Her heart double-beat in her chest, and deep down she already knew.

Opa opened the envelope and pulled out a smaller one, handing it to Sadie.

"You have to read the letter first," he insisted. "Your *mem*'s letter."

Sadie opened the envelope and pulled out a piece of paper. The letter was dated June

1, just a few days before her parents' death. The tears came.

Dear Paul Hostetler,

If you don't remember me, I'm Samuel's wife, and I have the garden that you always appreciate on Mooring Road. My tomatoes have done very well this year — the best ever. And as I've been drying seeds, saving them, God has been putting you on my mind.

Now, Mr. Hostetler, I'm a good Amish woman, and I believe that God has called me to live the Amish way, but lately God's been pointing out to me how selfish I've been with Englischers, especially with you. Is there anywhere in the Bible that says we're supposed to only love our neighbors who are like us? I think no.

So I've enclosed with this letter some of my heirloom tomato seeds. Use them, sell them, it does not matter to me. I just know that God has richly blessed me with life, a home, and family . . . and my garden. How can I not share?

And maybe, sir, when you are in the area, stop by. It would be great to see you again, and maybe you could give some gardening tips to my daughter Sadie. She's eager to learn, but not always from me. If you have a daughter I'm sure you understand.

Mrs. Samuel Chupp

Sadie didn't know whether to laugh or cry when she read her mother's words, and so she did a little of both. And then as tenderly as she could, she poured out the small seeds into her hand. Tomato seeds. They were tiny — not much larger than grains of sand — but they were so much more than seeds to Sadie. They were a handhold to the past. They were a renewal. And a promise for the future.

Sadie closed her hand around them and looked up at Eli's face. "What I tried to hold on to, I lost. What was given up — shared — is the only thing that was saved."

With tenderness, Eli ran a finger down her cheek. "Isn't that true about everything, Sadie? Especially about love."

"I'm sorry I didn't trust you," she whispered.

He rested a hand on her shoulder. "I'm sorry I didn't tell you the truth sooner about my hope for our future. I want to earn your trust again, and I want you to know that I'm going to stick around and prove that."

"Are you saying that you're going to give up your stint as the travel-writing bachelor?"

"My hope is to give up the traveling part, and maybe — well, I won't try to push too hard, but the only part I want to keep of that title is 'writer.' And gardener. In fact, I'm counting on you to guide me in a few areas. I hear it's harder to grow things in these parts." He winked.

"*Ja,* from what I've heard, it only works when one gets a good start in a greenhouse."

"Well, that's not a problem then."

"You have a greenhouse?" Her brow furrowed. "Where?"

"I think you know it well." Eli smiled. "It's the one you've been using."

"It's another reason my grandfather came to visit," he explained. "I told him about your neighbor's place, and *Opa* contacted the owner to see if he'd be interested in selling. It turns out, he was."

Laughter bubbled from Sadie's lips at the sight of *Opa*'s smile.

"I told your neighbor that I want to expand my seed business. I get requests all the time from those in the Northwest who want seeds that fit their climate. I'm looking forward to coming here now and then to learn from the locals. And in the meantime, I've asked Eli to care for the place when I'm not there."

"So you'll be my neighbor, Eli?" As gingerly as she could, Sadie poured the seeds back into the envelope.

"*Ja.* What better position to be in to court you? I can't really think of one."

"Court me?" Her jaw dropped. "I was just hoping you'd forgive me."

"Can't I do both?"

"Of course. I'd love that."

"*Gut.*" Eli stepped close and gave her a quick hug. "Then let's write that on your schedule, along with cleaning up your garden."

"I'll take all the help I can get," Sadie said and smiled. "And I'll count on you helping me track down the bear."

"Do you think it's time for relocation?" Eli smirked.

"*Ja.* I think so. It seems like every wild thing needs to find a place of his own to call home, and I know we've found ours." She reached for Eli again and accepted his hug. "Yes, in your arms, Eli, I've found my home."

THE BUDGET — West Kootenai, Montana
It's been a busy few weeks around the West Kootenai area. After Goliath decided to romp around in Sadie Chupp's garden, folks around here decided he needed a new home. One can't mess with heirloom

387

tomatoes around the West Kootenai and think he can get away with it. The locals believe it was the colorful, flashing pinwheels in Sadie's garden that drew the bear, and then when Goliath got there, he decided to have breakfast. Personally, I don't agree with that notion. Can't a bear just be hungry every once in a while?

A dozen of us bachelors got together, trapped the yearling, and turned him over to Fish and Game. When all of us told them we'd pool our money to pay for his safe relocation, they agreed. I'm only partly upset that my first few paychecks from Montana Log Works went to pay for a bear's new home rather than mine, but I'll try not to be jealous.

The most talked-about event, though — even more than the bear — was how Sadie received an envelope of her mother's seeds the very day she thought she'd lost all of her own plants, all of her heritage. The story is too long to relate in this short report, but suffice it to say that her mother's generosity is coming back to bless Sadie now. Sadie had enough seeds to share with her siblings — something she was happy to do. Many members of her family will be enjoying these tomatoes for years to come.

This reminds me what the Bible says, "For whoever wants to save their life will lose it, but whoever loses their life for me and for the gospel will save it." So many times in life we try to protect what we value, but we are doubly blessed when we give it away.

Have you given away your love today? Have you shared your faith? If not, what are you waiting for?

— Eli Plank, the scribe who will soon not be a bachelor, thanks to Sadie Chupp

READING GROUP GUIDE

1. Sadie Chupp finds herself in the small Amish community of West Kootenai, Montana, after losing her parents. How does this community help to heal her heart?

2. Eli Plank calls himself the bachelor scribe. What do his letters to *The Budget* reveal about his character and personality?

3. Why do the heirloom seeds matter so much to Sadie? What do they symbolize for her?

4. What kind of trouble does a mischievous bear cub cause? What do this bear's antics reveal about Sadie?

5. Near the end of the book, Sadie discovers something surprising. How does the "found" letter change her ideas and allow her to open her heart?

ACKNOWLEDGMENTS

Thank you to the HarperCollins Christian Publishing team: Daisy Hutton, Becky Philpott, Natalie Hanemann, Katie Bond, and Laura Dickerson. I also want to thank all the unsung heroes: the managers, designers, copy editors, salespeople, financial folks, etc., who make a book possible.

Thank you to Amy Lathrop and the Litfuze Hens, Caitlin Wilson, Audra Jennings, and Christen Krumm, for supporting me and helping me stay connected with my readers . . . and for the gazillion other things you do!

Thank you to my author-friend Melissa K. Norris for sharing all your wisdom about heirloom tomatoes!

I'm also thankful for my agent, Janet Grant. You're my rock star.

And I'm thankful for my family:

John, thank you for encouraging me and helping me every step of the way. Cory,

Katie, Clayton, and Chloe, I am in awe of how you love and serve God together. Leslie, my missionary daughter. Your love for Jesus shines. Nathan, someday you'll have a book published. I hope you mention me! Alyssa, Bella, and Casey. God's gift of adoption is amazing! Grandma Dolores, you may not have passed down seeds, but your heritage of love and godliness is something I treasure.

Finally, thank You, Jesus, for making being part of Your forever family possible.

ABOUT THE AUTHOR

USA Today best-selling author **Tricia Goyer** is the author of thirty-five books, including the three-book Seven Brides for Seven Bachelors series. She has written over five hundred articles for national publications and blogs for high-traffic sites like TheBetterMom.com and MomLifeToday .com. Tricia and her husband, John, live in Little Rock, Arkansas, where Tricia coordinates a Teen MOPS (Mothers of Preschoolers) group. They have six children.

■ ■ ■ ■

WHERE HEALING
BLOOMS

VANNETTA CHAPMAN

■ ■ ■ ■

For Uncle Joe,
who still keeps a garden

There is a time for everything,
and a season for every activity
under the heavens.
— ECCLESIASTES 3:1

GLOSSARY OF SHIPSHEWANA AMISH WORDS

ach — oh
boppli — baby
daed — father
dat — dad, father
danki — thank you
Englischer — non-Amish person
freind — friend
gem gschehne — you're welcome
Gotte's wille — God's will
grandkinner — grandchildren
gut — good
haus — house
kaffi — coffee
kapp — prayer covering
kinner — children
mamm — mom
mammi — grandma
nein — no
Rumspringa — running around; time before an Amish young person has officially joined the church; provides a bridge

between childhood and adulthood.
schweschder — sister
Was iss letz? — What's wrong?
wilkumm — welcome
wunderbaar — wonderful
ya — yes

CHAPTER ONE

Shipshewana, Indiana
Mid-May

Emma Hochstetter stepped onto the back porch and pulled in a deep, cleansing breath. The colors of the May afternoon were so bright they almost hurt her eyes. Blue sky spread like an umbrella over her family's tidy homestead, which was dotted with green grass, three tall red maples, and an entire row of bur oak trees. And the garden — Mary Ann's garden.

Her mother-in-law could be found out among the garden's rows every morning and every afternoon. The place was a work of beauty. Emma would be the first to admit it. It was also a lot of work, especially for two old ladies living on their own. Emma wasn't in denial that she was now officially old. The popping in her knees each time she stood attested to that. Turning fifty the past winter had seemed like a milestone.

She now woke each morning grateful to see another day, which might have seemed like an overreaction, but they'd had a hard year.

"Done with the laundry?" Mary Ann called out to Emma from her bench in the garden. She'd recently turned eighty-four, and some days it seemed to Emma that her mother-in-law was shrinking before her eyes. She was now a mere five-one, which meant she reached past Emma's chin, but barely. Her white hair reminded Emma of the white boneset that bloomed in the fall, and her eyes reflected the blue, bell-shaped flowers of the Jacob's ladder plant.

"*Ya*. Just folded and hung the last of it." Emma walked down the steps and out into the garden.

"Gardens will bless your soul, Emma."

"I suppose so."

"They are a place to rest, to draw near, and to heal."

"At the moment this garden looks like a place to work." Emma scanned the rows of snap beans, cabbage, and spinach. The weeds seemed to be gaining ground on the vegetables.

"Remember when the children used to follow behind me, carrying a basket and picking up the weeds I'd pulled?"

"I do." Emma squatted, knees popping,

and began to pull at the crabgrass.

"The girls were cute as baby chicks. Edna leading the way with Esther and Eunice following in her steps."

"All grown now, *Mamm.*"

"Indeed."

"We should probably think of cutting back on the size of this garden."

Mary Ann fell silent as Emma struggled with a particularly well-rooted dandelion. The weed pulled free and dirt splayed from its roots. They both started laughing when two fat worms dropped from the ball of dirt and crawled back toward the warm, moist hole.

"I guess we know what Harold and Henry would do with those."

"My boys always did prefer fishing to gardening." Emma brushed at the sweat that was beading on her brow and resumed weeding. The temperature was warm for mid-May, nearly eighty. With the sun making its way west and a slight northern breeze, the late afternoon was a bit more pleasant. Perhaps the heat was why everything in the garden was growing with such enthusiasm.

Summer had barely begun, and already their vegetable plot had become a place of riotous chaos. The flowers tangled into one another in an unruly blend of scents and colors — reds, blues, yellows, oranges, and pinks. Shipshewana had experienced an early spring, bountiful rains, and mild temperatures. Emma struggled to keep up, and the garden became more a place of labor than of healing.

Still, she continued to work on the row of snap beans.

Mary Ann sat on her bench and watched.

"Gardens are a reflection of God's love for us," Mary Ann said.

"*Ya,* indeed they are."

"You missed a weed, dear. Back near the bean plant." Mary Ann pointed at the bunch of quack grass with her cane.

Emma smiled and reached for the grass. She no longer thought of Mary Ann as Ben's mother. After living on the same property for over thirty years, she was just *Mamm.* Sweet, dear, and at times, more work than an infant.

Emma prayed nightly that she would live forever, that she wouldn't leave her alone.

"The weeds aren't easy to find because the plants have grown so large." She used her apron to wipe the sweat from her forehead. "Everything is running together."

"Evil can overtake good —"

"I'd hardly call a weed evil."

"Especially when you don't spend a little time each day tending to what is important." Mary Ann's eyes twinkled in the afternoon sunlight. She might have been referring to Emma's recent absence.

"I'm glad I went to Middlebury and spent the week with Edna. All three of her children suffering with the flu at the same time? *Ach!* We had our hands full with laundry and cooking and nursing."

Mary Ann moved her cane left and then right. She gazed off past the barn, and her voice softened. "Do you remember the year Harold came down with a bad case of the influenza?"

"He was nine."

"While you were tending him, I spent many an hour out here, praying for that child's soul and body — that the Lord would see fit to leave him with us a bit longer."

"Harold would call out, and his blue eyes, they'd stare up at me and nearly break my heart. The fever was dangerously high. I can still recall how hot his skin was to my touch."

"Difficult times."

Emma had reached the end of the row. She turned to the next and stifled a sigh. Most afternoons she enjoyed her time in the garden, with Mary Ann sitting on the bench and sometimes dozing in the sun. But today weariness was winning, that and a restlessness that resembled an itch she couldn't reach. Perhaps her impatience came from comparing her own life to her daughter's.

The trip to Middlebury should have been a nice reprieve from the work of the farm, but she came back nearly as tired as when she left.

Certainly it had been a delight to spend time with Edna, her husband, and the grandchildren while a neighbor had stayed with Mary Ann. But looking around her daughter's tidy farm and newer house, she found herself wondering if they should sell the old place. Perhaps it was too much for two old women to maintain. Something smaller would be good. Her daughter's place was half the size and much more manageable.

"*Mamm,* this garden is too big."

"No garden is too big, dear."

"We can't possibly eat all of this food."

"Which is why we share with those in need."

They'd joined a co-op several years ago. In exchange for the vegetables, they received fresh milk, eggs, and occasionally cheese.

Both Emma and Mary Ann were relieved that they didn't have to look after a cow — Emma had never been good at milking, though she'd done it enough times as a child. And chickens required constant tending. She also didn't favor the idea of purchasing their dairy products from the local grocer. Fresh was best. Still, what they put into the co-op far exceeded what they received.

"Maybe it's grown past what we can manage. Instead of adding a little every year, maybe we should hack something back." Emma stood and scanned right, then left. The garden, which had once been a small vegetable patch, now took up one entire side of the yard. "We could plow up that row of flowers over there, maybe plant some grass instead. And we do not need ten tomato plants."

"Help arrives when you call."

"Yes, but —"

"Hello, Danny."

Emma had turned her attention back to the row of blooming plants and was reaching up to trim back the joe-pye weed, which threatened to take over the Virginia bluebells that were already in bloom. Her hand froze at Danny's name. Slowly, she brushed the dirt from her fingertips by running her hands across her apron, inadvertently leaving a stain of brown slanting from right to left against the light gray material. She swiped at the hair that had escaped from her *kapp,* tugged her apron into place, and turned to face the man who had first courted her.

CHAPTER TWO

Danny enjoyed the sound of Emma's voice, even when it was only two words. There was something about seeing her in the garden that set his day on a solid foundation.

Emma.

He'd loved her so many years ago, when he was only a boy. Then he'd gone away, and she had married. Her life with Ben had been a good one, by the looks of things, and he understood fully how much she must miss her recently deceased husband. Danny's own life was solitary, though he was grateful to be surrounded by a good community.

On various occasions, he'd heard Mary Ann insist that he was one of God's many blessings, that the Lord Himself had sent Danny home to Shipshewana to be their help and neighbor.

Emma didn't seem as sure.

They'd had a hard year. Emma's father-in-law, Eldon, and husband, Ben, had both passed within a few weeks of each other as winter turned to spring the year before. Danny was glad he'd returned when he had, in the middle of the winter, when the snow was still falling and the land lay fallow. He'd thanked the Lord more than once that he'd had a few months to spend with Ben before he'd died. Long enough to know there were no ill feelings between them.

"Gardening, I see."

Emma glanced up after she'd pushed some stray hairs back into her *kapp*. He'd only glimpsed the brunette curls that were now mostly gray. But Emma's caramel-colored eyes looked the same as when she was sixteen.

She must have stopped growing about that age, because she still only reached his shoulder. And though she'd put on a little weight over the years — what woman didn't after five children — she carried it well. Emma looked healthy, and in brief moments, she looked happy.

When she glanced his way, the dismay in her eyes amused Danny, and it also kicked his pulse up a notch. He wasn't a young man and wasn't sure why he reacted this way when he was around Emma.

"Indeed." She smiled tightly. "Every

afternoon, as the sun creeps toward the horizon, you're bound to find us here."

"We love our time in the garden," Mary Ann said.

Danny raised an eyebrow, but Emma only shook her head and threw an endearing look at Mary Ann. The garden was her passion, not Emma's. Mary Ann obviously did enjoy her time in the garden. Then again, she was sitting on a bench, not sweating over a vegetable patch.

Emma had confessed one night that she was grateful she could still work in the garden. And she was grateful Mary Ann was still sitting on the bench.

Since Danny didn't know how to respond to either of them, he placed his walking stick next to Mary Ann's bench and turned back to the task at hand. Without asking what she needed, Danny moved to the other side of the row Emma was working on and held back the plants she was trimming.

They worked in silence for another ten minutes. When they'd reached the end of the row, he wiggled both eyebrows and asked, "Where to next? Carrots and onions, or another floweredy row?"

Danny knew the name of every bloom in their garden, but sometimes he felt self-conscious about the years and years of knowledge stored in his mind. Like the stack of notebooks in his office, he didn't think what he'd learned and seen should be displayed in every conversation. Sometimes it was good to be the clueless old guy who lived next door.

Emma wasn't buying it. She snorted and said, "Don't play ignorant, Danny. I saw your piece in *The Budget* on using indigenous plants throughout your yard."

"Ya?"

"I'm pretty sure you have an encyclopedic knowledge of gardening, among other things."

When Danny only blinked, Emma dusted her hands on her apron and turned in a circle. "I need to work the ground around the carrots and add a bit of fertilizer."

"Want me to bring some from the barn?"

"*Nein.* I have some in the bucket at the end of the row, but there's no need for you to —"

"I'll fetch the bucket and meet you at the carrot patch."

Emma glanced at Mary Ann, but she appeared to be ignoring them. Her cane was raised, and she'd plunged it into a boisterous stand of flowering mint. She was attempting to coax a butterfly into settling on the polished oak walking stick.

So they turned to the vegetable section, and that was when Emma froze. She pressed her fingers to her lips. Danny followed her gaze and saw a young lad, probably fifteen. He was sneaking out from the back of Emma's barn. As his scrawny frame came around the corner, he looked right at them.

For a moment, their eyes connected, and then he sprinted away, like a young buck in flight.

Emma dropped the gardening tools and rushed after him.

Danny caught up with her when she was halfway to the road. "We'll never catch him."

"Probably not."

"Amish?"

"Ya."

"Any idea what he was doing there?"

"Nein, and I don't need this right now."

"Best go see if he took anything."

They reversed direction and headed to the barn.

"The door isn't latched, and I always make sure to fasten it."

"He probably doesn't know you bring in the horses every evening. In some counties, they're left in the pasture."

"This early in the year? *Ach!* It's still too cold in the evenings."

As he walked into the darkness of the

barn, Danny's mind was flooded with memories of Ben, Eldon, and his own father. For so many years, their families had been intertwined like the mint mixed with the tomatoes in Emma's garden. The barn smelled like the memories of those he'd loved — wood chips, hay, oats, and leather.

"Do you keep any money in here?"

"Nein."

"What's in the office?"

"Old files. Ben's things. Nothing anyone would want to steal."

"He was here for something."

"Maybe he was hiding out."

"Maybe." Danny crouched down near a bit of stray hay.

Emma shrugged, but Danny pointed toward the farthest stall. The door was cracked open a hair's width. Danny held up his hand for her to stay put.

Instead, she strode in front of him, across the barn, and to the stall. When Emma saw the bedroll, camp stove, and extra set of clothes, she backed up until she'd reached the opposite wall and stood against it, as if for support.

"Do we have an Amish runaway living in our barn?"

"Or he could be a hobo."

"Whatever he is, what are *Mamm* and I going to do about it?"

CHAPTER THREE

The boy had upended one of the pails she used to carry horse feed. Apparently he was using it as a table. Her stomach tumbling, Emma walked back into the stall, sat down on the pail, and looked around in disbelief.

"What are you going to do?"

"Do? I suppose I'll call Bishop Simon, and he'll decide whether to call the police."

Danny leaned against the stall wall, crossed his arms, and rubbed at his clean-shaven jaw with his right hand. "Or . . ."

"Or? We have an *or* here?"

"Just saying." He spread his hands out in front of him. Big hands.

Danny brushed at straw that clung to his dark pants. Suspenders draped over his pale-green shirt. He pushed back the straw hat covering his mahogany brown hair sprinkled with gray. When he did so, Emma noticed his bangs flopped close to his chocolate-colored eyes. The gesture made

418

Emma think of the boy he had been. Perhaps that was the problem. She suffered from memory misplacement.

He was a big guy — over six feet and trim. It was one of the reasons folks were surprised when he decided to be a writer. Danny would have made a great farmer, or a farrier, or even a cabinetmaker. All of those occupations would have made sense. But a writer? An Amish writer?

She sighed and returned her attention to the horse stall. "You haven't said anything."

"I wouldn't want to put my opinion where it has no place."

"Out with it." The words escaped as a growl. She sounded moody, even to her own ears. It occurred to her that she never used to snarl at folks, unless they were tracking mud through the kitchen.

"What if you left him some food instead?"

"Why would I do that?"

"Because he's obviously living here, and he must be hungry."

"But I don't want him to live here. I want him to leave. My barn is for my horses."

"You're right."

"People don't live in barns."

"Most don't."

"And he must have a home. His parents are probably worried sick."

"Maybe."

Emma closed her eyes and pulled in a deep breath. When she'd spoken to her daughter Edna about her moodiness, Edna had smiled and reminded her of *the change.* She had thought she was through with that. Maybe not.

"I don't want him to stay. I want him out of my barn and off my property."

Danny pulled down on his hat. He looked Amish, but there were times Emma wondered. All that traveling must have affected his way of thinking.

She stood and swiped some hay off the back of her dress.

"Seems as if he was careful with the cookstove," she admitted. The boy had placed it inside one of the midsized tin troughs.

"Indeed."

"Don't know what he could have been cooking."

"He probably caught a rabbit."

She brushed past him into the main portion of the barn. A young boy, a boy her own *grandkinner*'s age, eating rabbit he'd caught from the field? And nothing else?

"I'll bring him some leftover ham and bread from last night's dinner, leave it in his stall, but only this once."

"It would be a kind thing to do."

"And he can reciprocate by moving on."

"Maybe he'll see the food and trust you, tell you what's happening and why he's here."

She humphed as they stepped out into the late-afternoon sunlight. Old people made that sound, and she was not that old.

Danny touched a hand to her shoulder, and Emma froze. Her feet became like cattails in an iced-over pond. Her heart thudded in her chest. She refused to look at him as he leaned close and whispered, "Perhaps *Gotte* has sent him to you, Emma. Perhaps *Gotte* has sent this child to us."

Against her better judgment, she turned and looked up into Danny's eyes. His expression was a curious mixture of intensity, hope, and amusement.

What was she to say to that?

How was she supposed to respond?

Emma had no idea, so she turned and trudged off toward the garden.

Later that evening she told Mary Ann about their guest in the barn.

"I think Danny was right." *Mamm* squinted her eyes as she glanced across the room and out the window. "We should try to help this one who is lost."

"We don't know that he's lost. Maybe he's lazy."

"Few children are actually lazy, though they are often confused. Sometimes one looks like the other."

Emma stood to gather their dinner dishes. With only the two of them, cleaning up had become much easier. She checked the large kitchen table to be sure she had all the dishes, and the memories almost overwhelmed her. She could see their brood of five, plus Ben's parents, crowding around the table. The children often jostled one another as they made room on the long bench or in the chairs. As if they were still there, she could see — actually see — them settle for prayer. The boys bareheaded, the girls with their *kapp* strings pushed back and stray locks peeking out. The deep baritone of her husband's voice when he'd ask who was hungry.

Mary Ann reached out and covered Emma's hand with her own.

It startled her from the past.

"It's okay to feel what you're feeling, *dochder.*"

About the past?

About the vagrant in her barn?

About Danny?

"I don't know what you mean, *Mamm.*

422

Unless you're referring to my feeling tired. I'm not as young as —"

"*Gotte* isn't done with you yet."

"I suppose not, since I'm still here."

"He has plans, Emma."

"*Ya?* Has He let you in on any of them?" She couldn't help smiling as she added dish soap to the warm water and plunged the first plate into the suds.

"You're laughing, but He has. I believe He has." Mary Ann stood and carried her glass to the sink. At a time in life when most folks slowed down, she was still quite spry. Too thin. Emma remarked occasionally that she'd like to give some of her extra girth to Mary Ann, if that were possible. It seemed no matter how she changed their meals, Mary Ann became a little smaller each year, and she became a pound or two heavier.

"Share with me, then. I'm interested to know what my future holds."

"No one knows that, dear." *Mamm* picked up a dishcloth and began to dry.

There was something about her tone that caught Emma's attention. All this talk of the future and God's plans. It was different from their normal evening banter.

"Danny says perhaps *Gotte* brought this boy to us. That maybe that's why he's here or why we found him."

"The boy could have gone anywhere," Mary Ann said.

"There's no telling how long he's been hiding in there. I don't look in that back stall often."

"But today you saw him."

"I did, which is strange, *Mamm.* If he were hiding, it seems he would have been more careful."

"Maybe he wanted you to see him."

"That doesn't make sense. He ran the moment our eyes met." Emma let her hands soak in the warm water. All that was left to wash was the pan she had used to stew the chicken and potatoes. She wanted to enjoy the dishwater before it grew cold and soiled.

How long had it been since the boy had enjoyed a warm bath?

She closed her eyes against the question. It wasn't her responsibility to worry about the welfare of a stranger.

And yet the Scriptures spoke often about strangers. Didn't they? Something about the welfare of strangers and angels unaware?

Mary Ann hung up her dish towel, then stretched to kiss Emma on the cheek. She'd always been affectionate, but in the last few years, she'd become more so. Maybe she realized the importance of expressing her feelings while there was still time.

"Pray on it, my dear."

With those words of wisdom, Mary Ann turned and left the room.

CHAPTER FOUR

The next day proceeded as most Tuesdays had since the children moved away. Emma and Mary Ann ate their breakfasts, cleaned two of the downstairs rooms, and then donned their shawls for the Stitch Club, which took place at a neighbor's home.

Laura's home was on the other side of town. It wasn't a far drive, and though the day was cloudy, it felt good to be out and about. Emma guided their buggy through Shipshewana, past the Blue Gate where Edna had worked her first job as a waitress. They stopped at the light, and she glanced over at the Davis Mercantile. While she didn't need any more fabric, it was always nice to drop in and say hello. The light changed, and she resisted the temptation to stop, directing her sorrel mare past Yoder's and onto Laura's street.

The group was working on a quilt for the June auction. The women numbered a baker's dozen, and they were all excited to be in the last stages of the project. Stretched on the quilt stand, which took up a good portion of Laura's sitting room, was a large double-wedding-ring quilt. As they stitched it together, Emma wondered about who would purchase it. Newlyweds? Or a couple who had already spent a lifetime together? Amish? Or *Englisch*? Would someone buy it for themselves or for a loved one?

The Lord knew. Before they began stitching each week, Laura reminded them to pray for the recipient. As soon as they had silently done so, the room became a bevy of activity.

Emma's daughters had not been able to attend, since school was now out of session and they were busy with their children. Instead, she and Mary Ann would stop by Eunice's house on the way home. Her eldest daughter, Eunice, lived next door to Esther, her youngest, which made for easy visiting.

They'd finished piecing the quilt together and were now ready to begin the actual quilting, as they'd basted the top to the back the week before. Once the quilting was finished, they'd bind the edges and be done! Perhaps three more weeks.

The conversation around the quilt fluctuated from letters folks had received, to items read in *The Budget,* to the occasional phone call shared with a loved one. Finally, they descended into gossip.

Emma wasn't proud of this, though it probably wasn't the type of gossip a bishop might frown upon. She thought of it as gossip because the conversation was based on what had been heard and tidbits passed along the grapevine, versus cold hard facts.

She only listened, though she'd been known to participate. Her thoughts kept wandering to Danny and the boy in her barn. Suddenly Emma realized someone might know something about the boy, so she focused her attention on the conversations swirling around her.

Nothing related popped up. Certainly this group would know if the boy was a runaway from any of their families.

There was a lull in the conversation. Laura cleared her throat and asked if anyone had seen or heard from Nancy Schlabach. An uncomfortable silence filled the room.

"I sent my youngest girl to take them some fresh eggs." Verna pulled off her glasses and pinched the bridge of her nose. "She told me Nancy was sporting a black eye. Didn't offer any explanation about it."

"Like before, I'm sure she would give some illogical account of what happened."

Laura shifted her chair to the right and bent over her row of stitches.

"I know the bishop has been by to see Nancy and Owen." Emma ran her fingers down the strings of her prayer *kapp* as the group stopped what they were doing and stared at her, waiting for more details. "I asked Bishop Simon because I was worried, and I thought maybe there was something we could do."

"And? What did Simon say?"

"That the church leadership was meeting with Owen, trying to convince him to enter a rehab program. He hadn't agreed to it, and Simon suggested it might be necessary to move Nancy and the boys."

Verna spoke up. "The problem is that they've no family here. When they moved from Ohio, they thought the land they were buying would be forty-five acres of heaven. But farming is hard work, and their property was a mess when they bought it." Verna replaced her glasses and picked up her quilting needle. "I've spoken to her about staying at our place, but she won't. She knows we have children to the roof rafters. Still, we would make room for her."

"*Ya*, we all would," Laura murmured.

Each woman in the circle nodded in agreement. Each of them would gladly offer shelter to Nancy and her two small boys.

Mary Ann had barely said a word since they arrived. She glanced up from her stitching. "Nancy needs a sanctuary."

"Sanctuary? What type of sanctuary?" Laura stowed her needle and sat back in the chair.

"A place of healing. A safe place."

"*Ya,* we could use that in our community. Oaklawn has been a real benefit to Goshen, Elkhart, and South Bend. Perhaps they will build a facility here."

Verna sighed and bent even closer to her stitching. "Supposing the Mennonite Alliance did plan a facility like that here, it would take a year or more to complete. Nancy needs help now."

"God provides sanctuary," Mary Ann reminded them.

Emma remembered what she'd said the day before, about gardens being a place of blessing. Where a person could rest, draw closer to God, and heal. That was the sort of place Nancy needed. A garden of God's design.

So many people were hurting in the world. Emma felt rather ashamed that her thoughts had been ungrateful of late. Mary Ann was right. More time in prayer and no doubt she would have a better perspective.

■ ■ ■ ■

Eunice was sitting on the front porch, rocking baby Silas, when Emma and Mary Ann pulled into the driveway. Her six-year-old older daughter, Miriam, sat nearby, playing with three wooden horses.

"Let me hold that little man." Mary Ann settled into the rocker, and Eunice placed the baby in his *mammi*'s arms.

Emma didn't know who looked more content, the child or Mary Ann.

"Where's Esther today?"

"The boys wanted to go into town and do some shopping with the money they earned from helping tend to Doc's garden."

"It's a wonder he has one at all, as much time as he spends in his office."

"Georgia loves the fresh vegetables, but the arthritis in her hands makes gardening nearly impossible. It must be hard for the doctor to see his own wife suffering so. The boys were only too happy to make a little spending money."

"Only eight years old and already the twins are hard workers." Emma pulled Miriam into her arms when she skipped over to show the women the horse she was playing with. Even at her young age, she already had a real preference for anything to do with animals.

"So tell me about this boy in your barn."

Emma wasn't surprised she'd heard. It was the way of life in their small community. She told Eunice all she knew, and then added, "The food I left last night was gone when I checked on him this morning."

"But he wasn't there?"

"*Nein.* His stuff still was — a small duffel bag too small to hold more than a change of clothes."

"It is strange that he'd pick your barn."

"Have you checked yours lately? Could be that we all have Amish teens stowing away, and we just don't know about it."

Eunice laughed but then grew somber. "Just be careful, okay, *Mamm*? And tell Danny if you need anything."

That was the way of things too. Her family now accepted Danny, counted on him, as if he'd never walked away from their community. She'd asked Danny about that once, about how he could bear to leave. He'd told her that at the time it had seemed what he ought to do, what he had to do, but that now he couldn't imagine being anywhere else.

As they were walking back toward their buggy, Eunice tucked her arm into the crook of her mother's. "I saw Danny's piece in *The Budget.* So he is still writing."

"*Ya.* I suppose."

"Do you ever talk to him about it?"

"*Nein.* What's to say?"

"You could ask where he's been, what things he's seen. Maybe he wants to share his experiences with someone."

"I believe he shares them with his notebooks, piled high around his desk."

"Well, we're all relieved that he decided to come home, that he changed his mind about selling his parents' land. It's *gut* to have an Amish man living next door to you. Someone we trust."

"Must have been a hard decision for him."

"Why do you say that?" Eunice had helped her *mammi* into the buggy. Now she stood in the afternoon sun, studying her mother.

"He didn't stay when his folks passed. Only came home for a week or so."

"I'm sure he had his reasons."

"*Ya.* Then a year later he shows up, pulls the For Sale sign out of the yard, and settles in. I guess he had a hard time deciding whether he wanted to continue with his travels, with his studies, or move home."

"What's important is that he's here now, and you can depend on him if you need someone."

"I can depend on my *kinner* too."

"*Ya, Mamm.* But Danny is right next door. Don't be proud. Let him know if you need something. And call me from the phone shack if you want Aaron to come over and speak with the teen in your barn."

"Your husband has plenty to do without worrying over a teenage boy."

Eunice stared down at the baby in her arms. "He'll be that age before I know it. And I would not want him sleeping in a barn, but if he was . . ." She stepped closer and kissed Emma on the cheek. "I'd want him in yours."

Later that afternoon, Emma and Mary Ann were once again working in the garden when Danny arrived. He was wearing the same dark pants but a pale-blue shirt. Danny looked comfortable in whatever he wore. Had he worn *Englisch* clothes while he was away? Did he miss that life? And why did he appear every afternoon to help in their garden? Perhaps he needed the exercise of gardening after sitting at his desk all day. Emma had seen a few of his articles in *The Budget* over the last six months, but she had an idea he was working on something bigger.

She didn't want to ask what it was. Somehow it seemed rude unless he brought up the subject.

Besides, if he wanted her to know, he would tell her. Wouldn't he?

They finished pulling carpetweed and prickly lettuce from around the mint, then moved on to care for the butterfly weed. Though its name indicated it was a weed, it was far from it. The plant's orange blossoms hadn't made an appearance yet, but they would soon — before July. Once they did, the butterflies would descend on it, and what a sight that was.

Working in the flowers did much to ease Emma's worries. She was even considering inviting Danny to dinner when he straightened up, stretched his back, and motioned toward the barn.

"Any sign of your guest?"

"*Nein,* but the food was gone this morning."

"Bedroll still there?"

"It is. I'm wondering if I should sneak up on him in the middle of the night so we can have a talk."

"If he's ready, that would work. If he's not, he'd run, and this time you might not see him again."

"I'm not sure I want to see him again. This mission of mercy is your idea."

"We are to be peacemakers," Mary Ann chimed in. "Full of mercy and good fruits."

"Yes, *Mamm*. But —"

"I've been thinking." Danny ran his fingers through his hair. He'd be needing another cut soon. Who did that for him? Most Amish men had their hair cut by their mother or sister or wife. Danny was that rare occurrence — an only child in an Amish home. He had none of those people in his life. He'd have to go to a barber and pay good money for what family would normally do. "It's supposed to dip into the forties again tonight. Our lad didn't have much of a bedroll."

"He's not our lad."

"I have a nice sleeping bag at home. Never use it anymore."

"You could offer him a room in your house." She said the words in jest before she considered how they might sound.

Danny crossed his arms and stared at her. "You're right. I do have an extra room."

"I didn't mean —"

"Still need to catch him first."

"He's not a fish, Danny. He's a boy with a family and some sort of past he needs to deal with."

"I'll go and fetch the sleeping bag. It's a *gut Englisch* one, rated to zero degrees. He'll

She wondered what other things he had learned on his travels. As always, her thoughts circled back to the main question — could he be satisfied living in their little town?

Then Emma stepped into Danny's house, the home that had been in his family for two generations, and she promptly forgot all of her questions.

CHAPTER FIVE

Emma had been in Danny's home before, when he'd first come back.

She and Ben had gone over to welcome him, and she'd carried with her a plate of oatmeal cookies. That was over a year ago. She'd had no need to stop by since. Most days he found a reason to come to their house, though she still hadn't figured the *why* that was tied to that.

"I guess you spend the majority of your day at your desk?" Emma worried her *kapp* strings. The thought of all those words, all the places that Danny had visited, overwhelmed her. Did he write about Shipshe? Did he include *them* in his articles?

"A good bit, yes."

"Going through the notebooks?"

"*Ya,* I have a *gut* memory, but checking against my notes I find that I sometimes remember things differently than they actually happened. Reading what I wrote while

I was there, it brings people and places into focus."

The house was small since his parents only had the one child. Many Amish couples start with a home big enough for three or four and add on rooms as the family grows. Danny's parents never had a need to add on, and the last time Emma had been in the house, it had needed updating.

She now stood in a home that looked as if it was recently built.

The paint was fresh, white trim and a light-beige color on the walls. Danny had taken out half of the furniture, so the rooms appeared larger. He'd also spent some time scrubbing and shining the wooden floors.

"I didn't realize you'd been remodeling over here."

Danny laughed as he put his hands on his hips and looked left, then right. "Let me show you the kitchen."

She could see some of the kitchen from where they stood in the sitting room, but she followed him eagerly.

"What would your *mamm* say?" Emma walked over to the new stove and ran her hand across the front panel. "Still gas, *ya*?"

"Sure. Of course. So is the fridge, but it's one of the newer models."

The appliances weren't over-the-top. They

were what a bachelor would need. He'd chosen well. Emma had looked at a refrigerator like his, but decided it was a bad use of their money since the one they had still worked.

"Writing must be paying well!" The words popped out of her mouth, and she immediately wished she could yank them back. It was none of her business how Danny Eicher managed to afford his home improvements.

"It pays all right, probably as well as farming. *Mamm* and *Daed* didn't leave much as far as money in the bank, but they left the land, and it's a good source of income."

"You're still leasing it to the Byler boy?"

"I am, though he's hardly a boy. He turned twenty-two this year, and he's a hard worker. I think he'll do well farming. I know he'll do better than I would. Never did have much experience planting or rotating crops, though I've learned enough about both in my travels. I do think I'm somewhat handy with a family vegetable garden." He said the last with a wink.

Emma didn't know what to think of that, but she suddenly wondered if it would look proper for her to be alone in Danny's house with him. Her cheeks flushed at the thought, because it was ridiculous. They were well past the age when they needed to worry about chaperones.

"Well, you've done a *gut* job here. I think your parents would be proud."

"I wish I'd come home and made improvements while they were both still alive."

He'd crossed the room to stand next to her. Emma couldn't resist. She reached out and rested her hand on his arm. "Your *mamm* wouldn't have allowed new appliances in her kitchen. Like Mary Ann, she was always a bit stubborn."

The worry lines between his eyes vanished. "*Ya*. One Christmas I offered to paint the hall. You would have thought I'd suggested knocking a wall out. She informed me the hall was fine as it was, and if I was lacking for things to do, I could help her wash the baseboards."

Emma walked to the doorway between the kitchen and the sitting room. The desk was neater than the last time she'd visited. Now the spiral notebooks were organized on a bookshelf, and the top of the desk was clean except for a gas lantern, a pad of paper, and a pen. Her curiosity was winning over her vow to not ask.

Danny watched Emma as her gaze darted back and forth across his work area. She worried her *kapp* strings as she stood there, something she only did when she was uncertain what to say or do next.

He'd known Emma so long, she seemed like an extension of himself. Now that he was home, he couldn't quite understand how he'd survived without her all the years he'd spent traveling. Danny had left, with his father's blessing, when he was seventeen. It had hurt him to leave Emma, but he'd known it was the right thing to do — for her sake. She deserved a normal Amish life, with a husband who stayed in one place. When he'd tried to explain that to her, after they'd been attending singings together for over a year, she'd listened with tears running down her face. He'd returned home occasionally for a holiday or because he was in the area researching, but he'd spent the majority of the past thirty-three years away. It seemed like a lifetime. He had never regretted that decision, but watching Emma, seeing her in his home, he also knew it had been the right time to return home.

"Do you still write every day?"

"*Ya.*"

"What do you plan to do with it?" She turned and studied him. She wasn't being nosy. She wanted to know. "Do you expect to receive an *Englisch* contract to write a book?"

"Haven't thought much on that."

"If you did, would you —" The words died on her lips, and the vulnerable look in her eyes tore at his heart.

"I won't be leaving again, Emma. I'm here to stay. This is home now."

She nodded but didn't respond.

"Right now I'm working with the Menno-Hoff. They offered me a grant to share some of the things I observed in my travels. It's important that we record our history. I believe I can offer an accurate telling from the inside."

"Why?"

"Perhaps it will help the next generation." He shrugged. "I'm not sure I know why. I only know that I'm supposed to be doing it."

She nodded as if she understood.

"Let me fetch that sleeping bag."

He found it, then walked her back out to the porch.

"I wasn't meaning to be nosy."

"Of course not. Emma," — he waited until she turned toward him — "you can ask me anything you want to know."

Now the smile he was so accustomed to broke through. "You always knew what you

wanted to do, Danny. Even at seventeen —
all you were interested in was jotting down
things in your notebook."

"I was interested in you." His pulse raced
as that memory came back to him full force.

"When you were sixteen. At seventeen,
you only had eyes for your books."

"I suppose so." The memory of what was
lost, what they'd almost had together, sank
between them, drawing some of the color
from the day.

"Remember the time you were supposed
to be checking on the goats your *dat* had?
You were moving them from one pasture to
the other —"

"And I left the gate open, the side gate,
while I was writing a piece about a typical
day in the life of an Amish lad."

"The goats were in Mary Ann's garden
before we saw them."

"*Dat* gave me extra chores for a week."

Emma reached out and touched his arm,
as she had in the kitchen. "You were doing
what you were called to do. Your *dat* understood, and your *mamm* too."

"Did you understand, Emma?"

She tore her gaze away, studying the setting sun and their two properties. "After a
while I did. I led the life I was supposed to
live, and so did you."

Danny nodded, but he didn't like the period she put on that observation.

There was still plenty of light to see the area between his place and hers. In truth, the Eicher property had always been the better of the two lots. His house was set back from the road a good space. The northwest section had a small pond where her boys had spent many an evening fishing. It was shielded from the street by a stand of white elms. They were seven, maybe eight feet tall. Beyond the pond was a low spot that ran the length of their property line. An optimist would call it a creek, but water ran in it only once or twice a year. Even with all the rain they'd had, it was muddy but not wet. Long ago his parents had put a wooden walk across a four-foot portion, which provided easy passing from one place to the other.

What he could see now, what he hadn't realized but had been suspecting, was that Mary Ann's garden had practically grown to the property line.

"Indiana evenings are a pretty sight." Danny's voice was low. Shadow's tale thumped against the porch floor, and Emma clasped her arms around the sleeping bag.

"Your neighbor is on the verge of encroaching upon your property."

His laughter filled the night, joined the songbirds, and caused Shadow to bound down the porch steps.

"I'd be happy to walk you back home."

"Don't be silly. There's no need."

Danny hadn't been thinking about whether she needed someone to walk her home. He'd simply wanted to prolong their time together. He stepped away, flustered and unable to remember what they had been talking about.

"Thanks for taking the sleeping bag to him. I wish he'd picked my barn instead of yours."

"Danny, we need to talk to this boy. I'll take your sleeping bag, and I'll leave it for him, but I'm going back out there later tonight. He's going to tell me what his situation is."

Instead of arguing with her, Danny reached down and patted the top of Shadow's head. The dog looked sublimely happy. Affection could do that.

"What time?"

"Thought I'd set my alarm for midnight."

"Okay." He nodded and rubbed the back of his neck. "I'll meet you on your back porch."

"Are you sure?"

"It's because of me you're providing lodging, and now food, to the boy. I don't blame you for wanting to call the bishop that first night. What with you and Mary Ann being over there alone —"

"This isn't about us being alone. It's about what's right for the boy. If he runs from us again tonight, I'll go straight to the bishop in the morning."

Danny's shoulders slumped, but a smile tugged at the corners of his mouth. "Mary Ann thinks we're supposed to minister to the boy."

"She told you that too?"

"While you were inside fetching her a glass of water."

"She brought the subject up at dinner as well. Seems she recognizes something special in this boy, or perhaps she thinks it would be a *gut* way for us to give back to the community. Either way, in a few hours we'll see if she's right. We'll see if he's willing to let us help him."

Without another word, Emma turned and walked back across Danny's property, skirted the pond, and stepped onto the small wooden walkway over the low point. Suddenly she stopped and clutched the sleeping bag to her chest. He was about to start after her, to make sure she was all right, when a flock of birds rose from the garden as one, flapping their wings and catching a draft to carry them out into the night. Danny's heart knocked against his ribs, and he chided himself for worrying over her. Emma Hochstetter was a capable woman, and she'd been taking care of herself all the years he'd been gone.

That wasn't quite right though. She'd had Ben and Eldon then. Last spring, as the green beans were climbing and twining through the trellis he'd helped Ben build, her father-in-law had died. He was nearly ninety, and he'd been sick for over a year. His passing was a great loss, but not unexpected. Six weeks later she found Ben in the barn, near the horses he loved so much. Her husband, and Danny's friend, had suffered a fatal heart attack.

Not to say the entire year had been all gloom and doom. God sprinkled in a few blessings as well, perhaps to assure Emma and Danny He had not turned away.

All of Emma's children — Edna, Esther, Eunice, Harold, and Henry — were happily married. And her oldest granddaughter, named Mary Ann after her two great-grandmothers, had been baptized into the church. Three more grandchildren had been born, which brought Emma's total to twelve. Each was a bright spot in her life, even little Thomas, who was quite the mischief-maker at age four. Danny enjoyed watching them at the Sunday socials. Having a grandchild was something he would never experience. These days, he understood more fully than ever what things he had sacrificed to follow his dream.

CHAPTER SIX

Emma was lying on her side with her eyes wide open, waiting.

As she waited, she remembered things from the evening and prayed about the worries that weighed on her heart.

When she'd left Danny's, crossed the bridge, and walked through the garden, she'd looked up and seen Mary Ann in the kitchen, silhouetted against the window by the gas lantern on the table. Mary Ann might be old and increasingly frail, but Emma still considered her to be her parent in the faith. If she said they were to minister to the boy, then Emma would take her word that it was to be so. The fact that Mary Ann and Danny both felt that way confirmed that God had a purpose in what was happening.

But something more was flitting through her heart.

Emma thought of their garden, pictured it

in her mind, and considered the idea of a sanctuary. What did that mean? Was it so complicated, or was it merely a place where people could rest? A place where they could heal?

Before she'd walked inside, Emma had turned and studied the garden. In the moonlight, it looked less like something that had grown out of control and more like something Mary Ann had planned over the years. A place she'd cared for patiently and tenderly and that was now coming into its real purpose.

But what was that?

And why did Nancy Schlabach and her two boys suddenly come to mind?

Shaking away the many questions, she'd wound her way back through the garden and to the barn. No sign of anyone, so she checked a final time on the horses and left the sleeping bag in the back stall.

Closing the barn door firmly, she'd made her way up the back porch steps and into the kitchen. She needed to go to bed early since she was going to set the alarm for midnight.

Now, watching the tiny hands of the battery-operated clock move, she knew that she wouldn't sleep until this thing was settled. So she waited, and she prayed, and she saw the moment the time switched from 11:58 to 11:59. She reached for the clock and turned off the alarm before it could sound.

It had seemed smarter to lie on top of her quilt in her dress. When she rose, she only had to fasten on her *kapp* and lace up her shoes. She was able to do both of those by the light of the moon spilling in her bedroom window.

Unlike Danny's home, Emma's was two stories. The extra bedrooms had been a blessing when all the children were home. Even now they were frequently filled with grandchildren, especially during summer break and weekends.

She crept downstairs, careful not to disturb Mary Ann, and snagged her shawl from the mudroom to ward off the night's coolness.

When she reached the back porch, Danny was already waiting.

"Any plans for how to do this?"

Emma shook her head in the darkness. "Can't be too hard."

"Coming from you, I'll believe that. You do have five *kinner* and twelve —"

"Soon to be thirteen. Don't forget that Esther is expecting again."

"Thirteen *grandkinner*." Danny whistled

softly. "You've had a full life, Emma."

"As have you, and let's not talk as if we're done yet."

They'd reached the back side of the barn. She knew when they opened the door, the hinges were going to squeak. If the child was a light sleeper, he'd be alerted by the noise.

"Don't let him scoot by you," Emma whispered.

They needn't have worried. A minute later they stood at the back stall, peering over the half door at the snoring adolescent. Even Danny's flashlight didn't waken him, but when Emma rang the bell she used to call in the horses, the lad jumped as if he'd been struck.

Seeing that his way out was blocked — they hadn't bothered to open the stall door — he sat up and pulled his jacket tighter around him. The thing was threadbare and couldn't have provided much warmth, though he had been tucked deep into Danny's sleeping bag.

Danny repositioned the beam of the flashlight so that it wouldn't be directly in the boy's eyes. It was clear he was a boy, though he might have been edging toward sixteen. He still had the look of Danny's pup, as if he hadn't quite grown into his hands and feet. Emma recognized the age. Her boys had gone through the same final growth spurt, and it seemed to take a few years before everything evened out.

His dark-brown hair hung in his eyes, which looked hazel to Emma in the dim light. He was much too skinny, she could see that well enough. Average height. Not much to tell the bishop as far as description.

"What's your name?" Emma opened the door and entered the stall. Danny remained in the doorway, still blocking the boy's escape path.

"Why should I tell you?" His voice was soft but somewhat ragged, as if he were aiming for belligerent but unable to pull it off.

"Because you're staying in my barn. Apparently you have been for a few days." When he didn't speak, she added, "And you've been eating my cooking. You can at least trust me with your name."

"Joseph."

He didn't provide a last name, but then, Emma hadn't expected he would. She'd coax it out of him before they were done.

"Joseph, we'd like to talk to you a minute." Danny picked up a wooden stool once used for milking and carried it into the stall. He sat on the upended oats bucket and left the stool for Emma.

"What about?" The panic in Joseph's eyes nearly broke Emma's heart. She'd been prepared to dislike him, to throw him out, to call the bishop and the police. As she studied him, she realized that Danny had been right. This way was better.

"Why are you here? Where's your family?"

He stood and began stuffing his things into a backpack. "Not going back there. You can't make me either. I'm nearly seventeen now. No use trying to make me go back."

"Son, we're not trying to make you do anything."

Joseph flinched at Danny's use of the word *son.*

"Would you mind sitting down so we can talk?"

Joseph didn't look any more at ease, but he zipped the backpack and sat.

Emma closed her eyes and prayed for wisdom and patience, then she cleared her throat. "Where are you from? I don't think you live in Shipshe, or I'd recognize you."

"Goshen."

"How did you get here?"

"Walked on the Pumpkinvine Trail."

Danny glanced at Emma, his eyes questioning. She nodded. It was a fair distance, but doable.

Since he was answering, Emma decided to dig for more information.

"My *dochder* lives in Middlebury. It's a nice town. Why didn't you stop there?"

"I did, but after a while I moved on. It's best not to stay in the same place too long. I should have left here last night." Dismay flooded his eyes, and Emma got the impression he was fighting back tears.

When he told them his last name was Lapp, a fairly common name among Amish folk, Danny spoke up again. "Won't your parents be worried about you?"

"Why would they? I'm a burden to them. One more mouth to feed in a home that's already too crowded. They're probably glad I'm gone." Bitterness filled his voice, which cracked, accentuating the fact that he was teetering between boyhood and manhood. "I never did anything right anyway. You can't make me go back. You can't, and I won't."

Emma checked Danny's reaction. He shrugged.

She stood and straightened her dress. Her toes were nearly numb, as were her fingers. She'd learned enough so that she'd be able to sleep. Joseph wasn't sick, and he didn't seem to be planning to rob her blind during the night. Anything else could wait until morning.

"That's it? You're just going to let me . . . . let me stay?"

"Breakfast is at six thirty. We'll talk tomorrow about how you can earn your keep until we figure out what to do."

Joseph's mouth fell open, but he didn't argue.

They were leaving when Danny paused and turned back. "You're welcome to come to my house. I live next door and have an extra bedroom."

"*Nein.* I'd rather stay here."

"Suit yourself." Emma put her hand in the crook of Danny's elbow and tugged him out of the stall. "Morning will be here soon. We best get to sleep."

Instead of talking outside the barn, she invited Danny into the house, set the kettle on the stove, and brewed them both a cup of decaffeinated herbal peppermint tea.

Danny was quiet as she moved around the kitchen, gathering cups, saucers, and a slice of the leftover lemon cake.

"I believe your gift is feeding people, Emma." The words were said in jest, but the look in Danny's eyes was solid admiration.

It occurred to Emma that if you served a man a piece of cake, he would believe you could solve the problems of the world. Give him cake in the middle of the night, and he'd likely burrow in and refuse to leave.

Did she want Danny to leave?

He looked completely at home in her kitchen.

"I wasn't much of a cook when I first married Ben. It didn't take long for his mother to teach me, to ensure that I had the basic skills. That first year, I think *Mamm* was afraid that she'd be called home to heaven before the lessons were done. I suspect she was motivated by the fear that her son would be left here to starve with a well-meaning but unskilled cook for a wife."

"Were you that bad?"

"I burnt my share of casseroles, and bread was completely beyond me." She sat at the table, ignoring the cake — though she wanted some. She'd learned long ago that late-night snacking meant disaster for her waistline. Emma had heard an *Englisch* woman at the market commenting on how nice it would be to be Amish — to not worry about your figure or the gray in your hair. It was true that they believed vanity to be a sin, but most women she knew worried at least a little about their weight. Emma could stand to lose five or ten pounds. Hopefully that concern was for health reasons and not because of vanity.

Why was she even worrying about such things? Emma had enough on her plate at the moment without counting her sins at forty minutes past midnight.

"After a few years I understood that cooking was *Mamm*'s special talent, and she wanted to share it with me."

"I'm glad she did!"

They sat together in the near darkness. She had lit one of the gas lanterns but had turned it to low. No use disturbing Mary Ann, not that she could see a lantern in the kitchen. She had a way of sensing such things though, and Emma knew she needed her rest.

It surprised her that she was so comfortable with Danny. Around most folk, even Amish folk, she was often seized by the urge to make some sort of conversation. Danny appeared content to silently enjoy the tea and cake. Emma wanted a few moments to process what they'd learned in the barn.

Finally he carried his plate to the sink, rinsed it, and returned to the table.

"It's good of you to allow the boy to stay," Danny said as he sat back down.

"I'm only doing the Christian thing. I hardly deserve praise for it."

"But you do." He leaned forward, arms

folded on the table, his eyes locked with hers. "Because you spoke to him with compassion, and you offered him kindness, which sometimes is as important as a place to sleep."

Danny's words flowed over her, settling some of the questions in her heart. "What do you think happened to Joseph? To cause him to leave his home?"

"Hard to say. I didn't notice any bruises on the boy, but sometimes abuse takes other forms. It's not something we see a lot in our communities. It is present though, same as any other group of folk."

"You saw things like this? While you were traveling?"

"*Ya,* and it's handled differently in each community it seems. Overall I'd say the bishops provide *gut* guidance, attempting to provide help for the families. Sometimes . . ." He stared down at the old oak table. "One place I stayed in for about a year had a case like this. The *dat* needed help for his moods, needed some of the *Englisch* medicine — truth be told. But they wouldn't hear of it, and the community decided to sweep the entire situation under the rug."

"And?"

"And it didn't work. Something like this,

ignored, will always fester until it sickens the body of believers."

Emma thought about that, thought of the day last summer she'd caught a splinter in the palm of her hand. She had been in a hurry that afternoon, and then tired by the time she fell into bed. She had thought she could ignore it for a day. When she woke, the spot was swollen and warm to the touch. It had festered and was much more painful to treat than if she'd dealt with it immediately.

Ignoring things rarely worked.

"What if he's making it up?" Emma rubbed her forehead as she envisioned the boy sleeping soundly in the barn.

"That's possible. You know more about Joseph's age group than I do —"

"The fear in his eyes seemed real."

"It did indeed."

"Tomorrow we'll feed him properly and set him to work, and then I'll walk down to the phone shack and call the bishop."

"I can do that for you."

"You don't mind?"

"Shadow enjoys a morning walk." He reached across the table and squeezed her hand, sending sparks zipping like fireflies through her nervous system. "I want to help however I can."

She walked with him through the mud-room to the back porch.

Emma didn't know what caused her to utter her next words. Perhaps it was the feeling she'd had back at the table — when Danny had touched her hand. "I still miss him."

Danny turned and looked at her. "I'm sure you do."

"At times I still expect to see Ben walking across the field, carrying his water jug and raising a hand to wave when I come out onto the porch."

"His life was complete, Emma." Danny didn't move closer, didn't reach out to touch her this time, and she was grateful for that. At the moment, she felt as fragile as the specially carved glass figurines sold at the shops in town.

"Ben would be glad you're helping the boy." He added, almost as an afterthought, "He'd want you to be happy. You know that, right?"

Emma nodded, then whispered a good night.

As she watched Danny make his way home under the May moon, she thought about the deep ache she'd endured since Ben's death. For the first six months, it had seemed as if some foreign object was lodged under her right rib. Strange that despair would choose such a specific place to hide. She'd rub at the spot, wondering why it wasn't on her left, near her heart.

Now the ache was gone, though the memory lingered. It had somehow softened over the last year, and though she missed Ben every bit as much as the first morning she woke after she'd found him in the barn . . . she could now smile at their memories, their time together, and the love they'd shared.

Like the green garden that had replaced the snow outside her window, life had moved on.

She remained on the back porch, thinking of Ben, and Danny, and the boy in the barn. She stood for a long time, watching Danny as he made his way in the moonlight, crossing from her property to his. Long after she could see him, she stood there, until the coolness of the late hour forced her inside.

CHAPTER SEVEN

Emma was standing at the stove frying bacon and scrambling eggs when Joseph knocked on the back door. He came inside when she called out to him, but he stood in the doorway between the mudroom and the kitchen, as if he was unsure what to do next.

Glancing his way, Emma could see he'd attempted to wash, though the water outside must have been quite cold. His hair, several inches too long, was combed down. He'd also put on a different shirt and pants, so he must have had at least two sets. He didn't look particularly healthy — a little too thin and a little too pale. But he didn't appear to be sick either. Mostly, he gave the impression of a lasting misery.

Mary Ann shuffled into the room as Emma carried the plate of bacon to the table. They had spoken earlier about Joseph, when they'd each had their first cup of *kaffi*. She had told Mary Ann about their late-night meeting. Mary Ann approved of Joseph staying and even had some ideas of chores he could do.

"You must be Joseph." She patted the seat beside her. "Sit. Sit and eat. Do you drink *kaffi* or milk?"

"Either is fine." Joseph didn't make eye contact with Emma or Mary Ann. Instead he stared at the table. His stomach growled when Emma set the bacon in front of him, causing *Mamm* to laugh.

"The sound of a growing boy is a blessing indeed. *Ya,* Emma?"

"It is, *Mamm.*" She placed *kaffi* and milk in front of him. He reached for the milk and then stopped himself, tucking his hands under the table.

Emma returned with a plate of eggs and biscuits.

They bowed their heads, and Emma silently prayed for Joseph. How long had it been since she'd been so worried about someone else? Someone outside of their family? Yet it seemed God had brought Joseph to them for a reason. After all, he could have stopped at any barn. She prayed for wisdom, for guidance, and that Joseph wouldn't decide to run when he learned what chores he'd be doing.

Mary Ann reached for a hot biscuit, breaking it open and releasing steam and the rich, yeasty smell. "My *dochder* makes the best biscuits around, Joseph. And her pies are *gut* too."

Joseph watched them begin to eat, then hesitantly reached for his glass of milk and downed it in a single long drink. As Mary Ann passed him each plate, he took a minimal amount. Emma could guess easily enough that he wanted more. The child had manners.

"It's only the three of us, Joseph, and I cooked extra for you. Fill your plate."

He wasn't speaking much, but then again, he was completely focused on his food. She let him enjoy the meal, then refilled his glass of milk and cleared her throat.

The massive amount of calories he'd just consumed would be hitting his stomach, so she guessed he'd be less likely to put up too much resistance when he heard their plans for the day.

She thought about offering him some of the lemon cake.

In the end, she decided the extra sugar might push him over. The last thing they wanted was him in the bathroom chucking up his first meal in several days.

"Let's talk about your situation, Joseph."

Mary Ann had moved to her rocker in the

corner of the kitchen and was leafing through her Bible. She acted as if she wasn't listening, but Emma knew she'd hear every word they said. And she'd jump in if needed. Bolstered by her presence, Emma ignored the panic on Joseph's face.

"I gather from what you said last night that you're not ready to return home."

"I'm never going back there."

"Never is often longer than we imagine," Mary Ann said.

"It's not something we need to decide now. But there are a few rules you'll need to agree to."

Joseph's glance darted left, then right, but he remained in his seat.

"First, you do the chores I ask of you. There's not a lot of work around here, but there are some regular tasks you can help me with. Once those are done, there are a few things I've put off since my husband passed."

"What if I don't . . . don't do them well enough?"

Joseph was talking to the table, his eyes glued to the spot where his plate had been before Emma set it in the sink.

"Will you do them to the best of your ability?"

"*Ya.*" He raised his eyes to hers, then

flicked his gaze toward the back door. " 'Course I will."

"Then it will be done well enough."

Joseph shrugged, but Emma thought she detected a small light of hope in his eyes.

"I will not tolerate alcohol or smoking in my barn. Drink too much and you could knock over a lantern. Leave a cigarette smoldering, and we could lose the entire thing. I understand that you're on your *Rumspringa* —"

He flinched at the word.

"A phone, something like that, is your decision to make."

"How would I pay for a phone?" He looked as if Emma had suggested he purchase an *Englisch* car.

She waved away his question. "What I'm trying to say is that I understand the difficulties of your age, but I won't allow the drinking or the smoking. Any sign of that, and you'll have to move on."

Joseph hunched his shoulders and jerked his head up and down at the same time. He resembled a box turtle, which would have been funny if the expression in his eyes hadn't tugged at the heart so fiercely.

"There's only one other thing, and I expect you won't be happy about it. Can't be helped though."

"Why won't I like it?"

"Because it involves our bishop. I gather you'd rather others not know you're here, but I have a responsibility, Joseph."

"What will the bishop do?"

"Simon is a fair man. I expect he'll want to meet with you, and then he'll probably insist on contacting your parents."

"My parents?" Joseph jumped up, and the sound of his chair scraping against the floor echoed across the kitchen. "My parents don't care. They don't want me, they don't miss me, and there's no chance they'd insist I come home."

She doubted that was true, but telling Joseph that would make matters worse. "We'll have to trust that Simon does the right thing, the best thing for everyone involved."

"What if he makes me go back?"

A sigh escaped from deep within her. "No one can make you do anything, Joseph. Unless you've broken the law —"

"I haven't!"

"Then there's no need to worry. You're welcome to stay here, but my responsibility is to notify our bishop and then trust his decision on whether to contact your parents."

Joseph rammed his hands into his pockets. "What chores did you want me to do?"

"Are you *gut* with horses?"

"Ya."

"Then let them into the field and clean out their stalls. Once you're done with that, give them a *gut* brushing and check their hooves. All the supplies, including a hoof pick and conditioner/sealant, are in the barn."

He nodded once, brown hair flopping into his eyes, then turned toward the back door.

"God's mercies are new every morning, child." Mary Ann's voice was as soft as the May breeze coming through the kitchen window.

"I don't know anything about that."

"Perhaps you will learn." Mary Ann reached for his hand, patted it once, and beamed at him.

"We'll have sandwiches for lunch. I'll ring the outside bell when they're ready."

Joseph had no response for either of them. As he clomped through the mudroom and down the back porch steps, Emma watched him from the window.

"What happened to him, *Mamm*? What could cause such bitterness in a fellow his age?"

"Many things are capable of wounding a young man. Maybe the cause isn't as important as the cure."

"And what would that be?"

"What you're doing — a place for him to rest, a full stomach, prayers that he find his way."

Emma hoped her mother-in-law was right. It had been years since she'd had a teenage boy under her roof. If she remembered correctly, it wasn't all pansies and roses.

CHAPTER EIGHT

The rest of the morning passed quickly.

Esther, her youngest, came by with items from the co-op.

Mary Ann had pulled three baskets full of produce from their garden — cabbage, chives, onions, and spinach. Esther had her boys carry into the kitchen what they received in return: milk, eggs, and mangoes. Mangoes!

"Can't say we've received much fruit, other than apples in the fall."

"Paul Byler, you remember him . . ." Esther tucked her blonde curls into her *kapp* as she spoke. Ever since she was a small girl, those curls had fought being corralled. Now Esther was the same height as Emma.

"Sure. He has that furniture shop out in back of his house."

"Right. An *Englischer* stopped by to pick up his order of four rocking chairs yesterday. He was so pleased with the work, he paid in cash and left four crates of mangoes. No idea how he came by the crates of fruit. He did tell Paul that he enjoyed trading, and he was a trucker by profession, so maybe he'd been down south."

"We're happy to have them. They'll work nicely in the sandwich spread I'm making." Emma reached down and caught Daniel and David in a hug. The twins had recently turned eight, and they stood for the affections from their *mammi,* but just barely.

"So where's the boy?"

"Boy?" Emma smiled as she played ignorant.

"You know who I mean, *Mamm.* Do you really think it's wise to let him stay?"

"My, but news travels fast."

"Danny called the bishop, and Verna was in visiting when the call came through."

Emma nodded as if that made sense. "Danny likes the idea of Joseph staying, and so does your *mammi.* Joseph seems harmless enough. Right now, he's cleaning out stalls if you'd like to go meet him."

"Nein." Esther patted her stomach. She was six months along with the next *boppli.* "Stall smells make me feel a little sick."

When they left, Emma spent the next hour giving the bathrooms a good scouring. They were fortunate to have two — one upstairs and one down. She had to remind herself to be grateful as she scrubbed the floors, tubs, and toilets. Her mother had grown up with outhouses. Danny had once mentioned some Amish communities still used them. Was it Wisconsin or Kentucky? It seemed Danny had been to visit districts in over a dozen states. Sometimes the places merged together in her mind, but she loved hearing his stories.

Satisfied with the smell of bleach and the shine of her bathroom faucets, she stored her cleaning supplies beneath the sink and headed to the kitchen. She was halfway through making the sandwich spread — mangoes, onions, green tomatoes, cucumbers, and carrots — when she realized *Mamm* wasn't in her corner rocking chair. She wasn't in the sitting room either. Drying her hands on a dish towel, she looked out the window, and that was when she saw her.

Her heart stopped beating.

Mary Ann was lying between the row of okra and the calico aster plants. Motionless.

Emma must have screamed as she ran down the back porch steps because Joseph appeared at the corner of the barn. One glance and he began to dash toward them. He made it to Mary Ann's side at nearly the same moment Emma did.

"*Mamm.* What happened? Are you —"

"I'm fine."

"You're not fine! Let me help you stand."

With Joseph on one side and Emma on the other, they lifted her from the ground. When had she become so thin? Emma probably could have carried her by herself, except her hands were trembling so badly she would surely have dropped her.

A small groan escaped Mary Ann's lips when she tried to put weight on her right ankle.

"Put your arm around my shoulder, *Mamm.*"

"*Danki.*"

Joseph's brow was furrowed when he looked at Emma.

The bump on her forehead was beginning to swell, and it was obvious she'd sprained or broken her ankle.

"Help me take her inside."

Mary Ann felt well enough to make a joke about being more trouble than a newborn donkey. Had they ever had a newborn donkey? Emma couldn't remember, but if her *mamm* was joking, perhaps the injuries weren't too severe.

Emma prayed as they helped her into her rocker. *Don't take her now.* That was her prayer, and she would have readily admitted it to anyone who asked. Yes, she realized how selfish her petition was, but she'd had too much grief in her life in the last year. The thought of losing one more person, one more piece of her world, caused tears to splash down her cheeks.

"I'm fine, Emma. I fell is all. Then I couldn't get back up."

"How long were you there?"

Mary Ann had begun to shake, so Emma hurried to the mudroom and pulled her shawl off a hook. "Joseph, fetch her a glass of water, then please bring me the quilt on the back of the couch."

Mary Ann pulled the shawl around her shoulders and patted Emma's hand. "Less than an hour —"

"An hour?" Her heart triple-skipped. What if it had happened in the rain or the cold or the dead of night? The last was a ridiculous worry. Mary Ann didn't putter about after dark.

"Lying on the ground gave me time to study the soil and see how the garden is blossoming. It's coming in *gut,* Emma. Our garden, it's a real blessing."

Emma's tears started falling again. Not because of what had happened or fear for Mary Ann's injury, but simply because she'd glimpsed the future — *Mamm* putting aside this life to follow *Dat* and Ben. Given a choice, Emma knew she would want to pass from this life to the next in the place she loved most, their garden.

"Should I go for Danny? Or your doctor?" Joseph shuffled from one foot to the other.

She'd almost forgotten Joseph was there, waiting, holding the log cabin quilt and wanting to help.

Emma swiped at the tears on her cheeks.

"Ya." Emma accepted the quilt and placed it gently across Mary Ann's lap. "Go next door and ask Danny to call a driver."

"I don't need —"

"Let's allow Doc to decide what you need, *Mamm.*" It could have been the tremor in her voice, or possibly the fear that flooded her eyes, but Mary Ann agreed without any further argument.

Joseph was back by the time Emma had brewed Mary Ann a cup of lemon tea.

"Danny said he'd have someone here soon."

"Danki." Emma reached for his hand as he moved back toward the mudroom. "You were a big help, Joseph. *Gotte* sent you here at exactly the right time."

He said nothing, but his cheeks flushed a deep red. As he walked back outside, she thought he stood a little straighter.

"He's a *gut* boy." *Mamm* had opened her Bible and was thumbing through the Old Testament until her hand rested on the book of Isaiah.

"How do you feel?"

"Fine. My foot, it's old, Emma. Like the rest of me." She cupped her hand around Emma's cheek. "Don't worry, dear. Today isn't the day the Lord will call me home."

Emma pulled out a chair and sank into it.

"My heart stopped when I saw you, saw only your foot sticking out from the garden row. I was terrified that, that —"

"Don't fear death, dear." *Mamm*'s eyes filled with something Emma didn't understand — memories or kindness or maybe hope. "It will be a glorious day when I see Ben and *Dat* and my own parents again. So many of my friends have passed already. It will be a *wunderbaar* day when I see our Lord."

Emma's tears started in earnest then. She knew that what Mary Ann was saying was right, but she couldn't imagine enduring it.

"*Gotte* will give you strength, and He won't leave you alone. You have that promise." Mary Ann tapped the worn pages of her Bible. "You have it right here."

The sound of car tires crunching over

gravel drifted through the open kitchen window. How had Danny managed to find someone so quickly? He must have run all the way to the phone shack.

They helped Mary Ann into the car, moving her carefully since her ankle had swollen to twice its normal size. Emma slid in beside her, reminded Joseph he could find lunch fixings in the refrigerator, and thanked Danny. She could tell he wanted to say something. Maybe he wanted to comfort her. But the driver, a sweet neighbor named Marcie, was already pulling away.

CHAPTER NINE

Three hours later they drove back down their lane in the breezy May afternoon. Emma saw Bishop Simon's buggy before they'd even reached the house. Had he come to see Mary Ann? Or Joseph?

Marcie insisted on helping them into the house. Emma paid her for the ride, though she seemed embarrassed by that.

"I wouldn't have wanted to load her into a buggy, and you stayed while we found the supplies the doctor had ordered. You've been a real blessing." Emma pushed the money into her hand and reminded her they'd need a ride again the next week, so the doc could check on how *Mamm* was healing.

She could tell Mary Ann was about to fall asleep standing, so she helped her to the downstairs bedroom and lowered the shade to block out the afternoon sunlight.

"I'd rather be upstairs," Mary Ann

mumbled as she removed the pins from her *kapp*.

"*Ya*, but the stairs are a bad idea. Doc said so."

Mary Ann's eyes twinkled. "All of this special care. I'm going to be spoiled."

"Rest, please. After dinner I'll bring down whatever you need from your room."

Mary Ann shooed Emma away as she folded back the Lone Star quilt and lay down on the bed.

Emma was washing potatoes in the sink when she looked out the window and saw Bishop Simon walking toward his buggy. She'd forgotten he was visiting! Stepping out onto the back porch, she called out to him. He turned, waved, and then made his way back across the yard.

"I heard about Mary Ann. I didn't want to disturb either of you if you were resting. How is she?"

"*Gut.* Come in. I can make tea or —"

"A glass of water would be fine, and maybe one of your chocolate chip cookies if you have any made."

"I do!" Emma brought the entire cookie jar to the table along with two glasses of water. She thought about resisting, but the day had been too nerve-racking. One cookie could go a long way toward improving her outlook.

"What did Doc Burnham say?"

"He cautioned me to keep an eye on the bump on her head."

"Does she have a concussion?"

"He doesn't think so." Emma pulled the instruction sheet from the stack of supplies they'd purchased while in town. "I'm to watch for balance problems, vomiting, dizziness, or severe mood swings."

"And what of her ankle? The boy told me it was painful for her to stand on."

"Doc x-rayed it. There's no break."

"Praise the Lord."

"He does want her to wear a boot to keep it from twisting again. The sprain could take several weeks to heal, especially for someone her age. And she's to use the cane he gave her several months ago."

Simon reached for another cookie. "Mary Ann has a reputation for being stubborn."

"It's true."

"Do you think she will follow Burnham's instructions?"

"She likes Doc, and she promised to behave herself."

Silence settled over the table as they enjoyed the sugar, chocolate, and touch of cinnamon in the cookies.

When Simon pushed away the jar of cookies, Emma knew he was ready to discuss Joseph. Simon was rather young to be a bishop, having only turned forty a few years before. He was slight of build, with a few strands of gray appearing in his dark beard. His eyes were a deep brown, warm and kind. He was a good leader, and he guided their community with compassion and grace.

"Danny called and told me about the boy. He explained what you learned from him last night."

"And you came to speak with Joseph?"

"I did." Simon hesitated, stroked his beard, and then continued. "I also spoke with the bishop from his district in Goshen. I thought it might be best if I had a little background on the family before I came out to see him."

"You found his family already?"

"Bishop Atlee knew exactly who I was speaking of, even before I'd finished describing the boy."

"So the family did report he was missing?"

"*Nein.*" Simon sat back and studied the kitchen.

It looked the same as any other Amish kitchen, so Emma knew he was trying to separate what he should share and what should remain private. One of the reasons Simon was a good bishop was he kept as much private as possible. No one liked to have their troubles aired in public. Though when a confession was required, it could hardly be avoided.

"The parents didn't report anything, but there's been some trouble with the family before. In fact, in the last year — as the economy has become tighter — it's worsened."

"What sort of trouble?"

Instead of answering, Simon leaned forward. "You're doing a *gut* thing allowing the boy to stay here, Emma. He might not be ready to go home anytime soon."

"Did he tell you that?"

"He didn't tell me much of anything, but I could see that he's comfortable with you. He needs a place to stay, a place where he can work, worship, and find *Gotte*'s plan for his life."

"And he couldn't do that at home?"

"From what Atlee told me, no."

"They didn't . . . they didn't hurt him. Did they? They didn't hit him or —"

"There are many ways of hurting a child that don't involve physical violence. But no. It's not what you're fearing. Joseph's father is apparently a very hard, very strict man."

"He hinted as much."

"Atlee has tried to counsel him, remind him that our ways are more compassionate. But Joseph's father was raised by very harsh parents, and he thinks it is the only way. Apparently the community knew it would only be a matter of time before the boy left . . . and probably his siblings as well."

"Can't someone step in? Social services or —"

Simon held up his hand, palm out. "I can't share all of the specifics. I can tell you that the family has been thoroughly investigated, and nothing against the law is going on in the home."

"So the other children will stay."

"*Ya,* for now they will." Simon stood. "Should I go down the hall and see Mary Ann?"

"She's resting. Hopefully she's asleep."

"Then tell her I will be praying for her healing, and I'd be happy to stop back in a few days to check on her."

"*Danki.*"

Emma walked him to his buggy. Glancing toward the barn, she saw Joseph with one of Ben's horses. He was brushing the gelding with solid, gentle strokes. The horse looked completely satisfied, if a horse could wear such an expression.

"There is one more thing." Simon had already climbed up into his buggy. His eyes had become even more serious than before. "Nancy Schlabach . . ."

Emma might have cringed at her name. Surely nothing had happened to the young woman or her boys.

"We're going to have to move her out of their home until Owen can be treated for his condition. He won't go to any of the facilities we've suggested. Or at least he won't at this point, but it's no longer safe for her or the boys to be there. Another incident and the police will be involved."

"What can I do to help?" The words popped out of her mouth before she'd fully considered them. She already had a crippled mother and a runaway boy under her care.

"I've been looking for a place for them to stay — a safe place within our community." He motioned out the front of his buggy, toward their garden and Danny's pond. "This would be a *gut* place, if you're willing to have them."

Emma swallowed the excuses that threatened to rise to her lips. "Of course."

It would be selfish to talk of any difficulties she might have when that poor woman and her children were in danger.

"The Lord bless you, Emma. You know it

is possible that *Gotte* is going to use you, use this place, to care for others."

Emma didn't know what to say, so she remained silent.

"I'll be in touch." And with that, he murmured to his horse.

Emma watched as they made their way down the lane.

Had she just agreed to house a woman and two small children? Had she agreed to care for more if the need arose? Their community didn't have any more problems than other Amish groups, but in her mind's eye, she pictured a long line of folks making their way down the lane and to their front porch.

A feeling of panic bubbled in her stomach, but she pushed it down.

As the Good Book says, "Each day has enough trouble of its own." Certainly that had been true for the past twenty-four hours. No need to borrow problems from the next day when she had quite enough already! But the same Scripture said something about God's provision. Emma walked into the kitchen, picked up Mary Ann's Bible, and paged over to the Gospel of Matthew.

"Do not worry about your life, what you will eat or drink; or about your body, what you will wear. Is not life more than food, and the body more than clothes?" She sank into the chair and continued reading. "Look at the birds of the air; they do not sow or reap or store away in barns, and yet your heavenly Father feeds them. Are you not much more valuable than they?"

For the first time since she'd spied Mary Ann lying on the ground, peace flooded her heart. She didn't know how long it would take Mary Ann to heal. She didn't know what Joseph's problems were. And she couldn't begin to understand what help Nancy and her boys needed.

But God knew.

God knew, and His grace would pull them through.

CHAPTER TEN

Danny waited as long as he could to check on Mary Ann the next day. He'd been tempted to stop by in the morning, when he'd taken Shadow on his early morning walk, but he'd resisted. Then as he worked trimming the bushes and flowers bordering his house, he thought about going over. Perhaps they were both resting though, and he didn't want to disturb that. Finally in the afternoon, after he'd rewritten the same page three times, he called it a day and gave in to the desires of his heart.

He didn't want to be a pest, but he needed to assure himself that Mary Ann was healing and that Emma was coping with the latest emergency. She'd appeared quite shaken the day before. Thinking Shadow might be able to bring a smile to her face, Danny called out to him, and the dog obediently fell in step behind him.

The dog's training was coming along well,

better than Danny had expected. As they walked toward Emma's, Shadow emitted an occasional whine — no doubt wanting to chase the birds rimming the small pond or take off after the rabbit that hopped across their path. Shadow fairly quivered in anticipation of a good romp, but he stayed at Danny's heel. Perhaps on the way back he'd allow him a good run.

He found Emma and Mary Ann in the garden. No big surprise there. Mary Ann was wearing the big black boot, which stuck out from under her dark-blue dress. She looked good, her color back and her customary smile adorning the wrinkles on her face. She reminded Danny of his own mother, and he understood firsthand how important she was to Emma.

Emma, on the other hand, looked as if she had spent the day chasing after one of her grandchildren.

"I was successful keeping *Mamm* indoors and resting for the morning, but by afternoon she was a force to be reckoned with."

"She does love her garden."

"I can hear you both," Mary Ann called from her bench, where she sat with a shawl around her shoulders. "Surely I can't run into trouble by sitting in the garden. The flowers are beginning to bloom, and I want to enjoy their color and breathe in their scent."

Emma was feeding the roses with the old coffee grounds she kept for just that purpose. Danny knelt beside her, and they worked the old grounds into the dirt with a hand trowel.

"Trying to stick close to Mary Ann?" he asked in a low voice.

"Why do you say that?"

"You've practically dug up that rosebush. I thought the idea was to use the tool thingy to revive it, not kill it."

Danny knew all about gardening, aerating the ground, and applying fertilizer. But he enjoyed the look Emma gave him whenever he played like he didn't.

"I am trying to stay close and keep an eye on her. Though the bump on her head has gone down nicely, she's still quite wobbly on her feet."

"How's the ankle?"

Emma stole a peek at Mary Ann, then refocused on the rosebush. "The swelling is better, but the bruising is worse. It's a deep purple now. Doc warned us it would be."

They continued in their fertilizing efforts, working side by side in the afternoon sun. Clouds were building in the west, and Danny guessed they'd have rain again before morning. After initially saying hello to Mary Ann and Emma, Shadow had plopped down on his belly, content to lie on the warm ground and occasionally yelp at the butterflies.

"How's our lad?"

"Joseph has been cleaning up Ben's office. Since he insists on sleeping in the barn, he can at least move out of the horse stall."

Danny was about to reply when Joseph walked down the path separating the roses from the vegetables.

"Did I hear a dog?" His question was directed toward Danny and Emma, but his smile was for Shadow. It was the first smile Danny had seen from him, and it made him look his age — a young man who should be enjoying life.

"You did indeed." Danny stood and called to his pup. "Joseph, meet Shadow. Shadow, down."

The smart little pup had been moving toward Joseph at a lopsided gait, but he dropped to the ground at the word *down.*

"How'd you teach him that?" Joseph knelt beside the dog and rubbed the spot between his ears — black silky fur that was still a bit loose. The dog would grow into his skin in the next few months. He'd be a big one. That was plain to see.

Danny could also see that Joseph was smitten.

"Shadow is a quick learner. Do you like dogs?" Danny stood with his hands in his pockets, beaming at the boy and dog.

"I do."

"Ever have one?"

"Nein." The next words were a whisper. "We weren't allowed."

Danny seemed to consider that for a moment, then nodded his head. "Some Amish don't approve of keeping pets."

"And then there are the puppy mills." Joseph's gaze darkened.

"There are. I saw a few while traveling, but not as many as you might think. Between *Englisch* regulations and pressure from our communities to treat animals with kindness, the mills seem to be disappearing." Danny frowned, remembering the few he had seen, but then that memory was replaced by another. "I also met a lot of Plain families who did have dogs or even cats that they kept as pets. Mostly they stayed outside, of course. Not too many house pets among people like us."

"So you taught him yourself?"

"I did. I can show you how later, if you'd like. It's fairly simple. You have to be consistent, and the occasional treat goes a long way."

"I'd love to learn."

"Excellent! Say, Shadow would probably enjoy a visit to the barn while we're finishing up here."

"Come on, boy."

Shadow trotted at Joseph's heels. The two were gone without another word.

"That was nice of you." Emma scooped more grounds out of the can and worked it around the base of a rosebush that was beginning to blossom pink.

"Seems as if maybe he missed some of the things of a normal childhood." Danny knelt beside her and began weeding.

Emma had shared with him and Mary Ann all that Bishop Simon had told her the day before, all they knew of Joseph's home life, which wasn't much.

"A dog can heal many broken places of the heart."

Emma looked at Danny in surprise and he had the sense she was about to ask how he knew that, but Mary Ann interrupted them.

"I'd like my bench moved."

"Moved? Moved where?"

The wooden bench had sat in the same place for as long as Danny could remember. It had always been at the end of the row of leafy vegetables. The path of hard dirt made a bend in front of her seat. It provided a perfect spot to study the wildflowers to the right, the roses to the left, and the leafy vegetables directly in front. Behind the bench was a large stand of mint, which gave off the loveliest of scents after a rain.

"Perhaps we could move it over between the herbs and the marigolds."

"But, *Mamm* —"

"It's no problem." Danny helped Mary Ann into a standing position.

She clutched his arm with one hand and her cane with the other, balancing precariously on her black boot.

"Emma, why don't you stand here with her while I move the bench?"

The place she had pointed to was a mere three feet away. Emma moved to Mary Ann's side and studied her as Danny picked up the bench, carried it to the new spot, and made certain it was settled firmly.

"Are you feeling confused, *Mamm*? Mood swings? Dizziness? You could have a concussion after all."

Mary Ann looped her left hand through Emma's arm. With her right she tapped the ground with her cane. "Don't worry so, Emma. A change of view is helpful at times."

Change of view? She could throw a pebble

from the new spot to the old. Danny helped her to the bench, waiting to make sure she was satisfied with her *new view.*

He had to resist the urge to laugh. Emma looked both concerned and put out at the same time, but she remained the patient daughter-in-law. Wrapping Mary Ann's shawl around her shoulders, she returned to the row of roses and had crouched down to continue her chore when Mary Ann spoke up again.

"We should plant something new there."

"Plant something?" Emma stared around at row after row of garden in bloom.

"I know." *Mamm* clapped her hands. "Transfer a little of the rosemary there. It can grow nice and tall. The tiny lavender blooms will look lovely next to the roses."

Emma stood, dusted the dirt from her fingers, and put her hands on her hips. Watching her made Danny want to pull out a notebook and begin writing about Amish women working hard on a rural farm.

"You want rosemary planted there?"

"Ya."

"And you want it done now?"

"Now would be *gut.*"

Emma was too old to roll her eyes and too well-mannered to stomp her foot. Danny guessed she wanted to do both.

Instead she marched over to the small shed where they kept garden tools.

Finding a medium-sized shovel, she backed out of the shed and into Danny. Her face flushed as he stepped back.

"I've got that, if you'll point out which plant is rosemary."

"You know good and well which is rosemary!" When he only smiled, she added, "We have enough to do, and she wants us to transplant perfectly healthy plants!"

Emma took him to the herb area and pointed out a dark-green bush, which had grown knee-high.

"Doesn't look like an herb." This time Danny was serious. He'd never seen such a big rosemary plant.

"They grow large. Some people even use them for landscaping."

"Does it matter which I dig up?"

"I'd take the one to the right side. It will leave a bit of an empty space, but this garden could use more open area."

Emma stifled a yawn. No doubt she'd risen several times during the night to check on her *mamm*. Danny wanted to tell her to go inside, to rest, but he knew those would be wasted words.

He carried the plant back over to the spot where Mary Ann was waiting. Holding it up, he smiled and asked, "Will this work, Mary Ann?"

"It's perfect. You can leave it here while you dig. Careful with the shovel though. Digging can unbury surprises. A person never knows when he'll hit something hard."

Mary Ann's eyes were wide and focused completely on what Danny was doing. She had the look of a child on Christmas afternoon, when the gift-giving time was about to begin.

Danny pushed the shovel into the rich, dark dirt. Both of their farms had been blessed with good soil. They had very few rocks, and over the years, they'd created pathways for the water to run down each aisle when the rains came.

Placing his foot on top of the shovel, Danny dug up one, two, three shovelfuls of dirt. He glanced at Mary Ann.

"A few more." Now she was leaning forward, hand on her cane and chin on her hand, her eyes locked on Danny and the growing mound of soil.

Danny added a fourth, then fifth shovelful of dirt to the growing mound.

And suddenly his shovel hit something hard, and he heard the sound of metal scraping against metal.

CHAPTER ELEVEN

Emma didn't know what to say when Danny stopped, turned, and looked at her. She raised her shoulders up, then down. Perhaps he could dig to the left.

But Mary Ann had other ideas. "Best see what that is." Her eyes twinkled, and Emma suddenly realized her *mamm* knew what was buried.

She stepped forward to help Danny. Together they dug around the object and lifted it from its hiding place. The thing was rectangular in shape, approximately the size of a large book, heavy, and sealed shut with a combination lock.

Danny handed the box to her. She dusted the dirt off and carried it to Mary Ann.

"It's not for me, Emma. It's for you."

"For me?"

"*Ya.* I've been waiting until the time was right."

"And it's right now?"

Mary Ann reached forward and patted her hand. "Open it." She gave Emma the combination. And how had she remembered that for so many years? But then, Mary Ann's mind had always been clear. It was her body that was failing.

Danny had followed Emma over to stand next to her *mamm*. He bumped his shoulder against hers. "*Ya,* open it, Emma. I've seen a lot of things in my travels, but never treasure buried on an Amish farm."

"It's not trea—" The word hung in her throat when she saw what was in the box. She pulled out the clear, weather-proof sack. It looked like a Ziploc bag but was made of a heavier material. What was inside had been wrapped in wax paper, now crinkled and yellow.

Emma sat on the ground at Mary Ann's feet and pulled the large bundle out of the bag, then unwrapped the paper.

"There're hundreds of dollars here."

"Thousands, actually."

"What? How? *Mamm,* where did this come from?"

"Let's have some tea." Mary Ann stood and Danny instantly moved to her side. "Tea and maybe one of your cookies. Then I'll answer all of your questions."

Danny reached for Emma's hand, helping

502

her up off the ground. When their fingers touched, electricity zipped up her arm. Emma felt confused, more confused than she was about the money.

But instead of asking questions, she followed Mary Ann into the house, put the water to boil, and set out tea, cream, sugar, and cookies. Within ten minutes, they were all gathered around the table. Mary Ann sipped her lemon tea, nibbled on a gingersnap, and then began to tell her story.

"You know about the war. You both have heard the old ones talk of it."

Emma glanced at Danny, and they both nodded. War was not discussed often in their gatherings or their families, but occasionally the topic would come up. When it did, the older folks would describe how they had made it through the years of conscription and service.

Ben's father, Eldon, had been eighty-nine when he died. Emma quickly did the math and realized he was probably eligible for service when he was eighteen, during World War II.

"Eldon had the opportunity to serve with the CPS," Emma said.

"Civilian Public Service." Danny ignored the cookies, something he didn't normally do. His fingers tapped against the kitchen table. No doubt he was wishing for a pen so he could take notes. "Many conscientious objectors ended up working on public service projects — Amish, Mennonite, Quakers, even Methodists."

"We had just married." Mary Ann stared into her tea, a smile forming at the corners of her eyes. "I thought I would die when he packed his bag to leave, but in the end, *Gotte* used that time to bless us. Now I want it to bless you."

"Slow down a minute." Emma reached for the strings of her prayer *kapp* and ran her fingers from top to bottom. The familiar gesture calmed her jumpy nerves. "He worked in the service, versus going to war —"

"Or to jail." Danny's eyebrow arched when she glanced over at him.

"Eldon was assigned to a wildlife camp, tending quail that would later be released in state parks. That was the first year. The second year he worked at a tree farm."

"I didn't think they were paid for their service." Danny finally reached for a cookie, but he didn't eat it, opting instead to break it into pieces on his plate.

"They weren't. Many families struggled because of this, but Jeremiah, Eldon's father, was always looking for an opportunity to better the farm. During the Great Depression, Jeremiah had planted large fields of mint."

"It was quite the cash crop during the 1930s."

"And continued to be for many years. By the time Eldon had left for the CPS camp, Jeremiah was still making a good profit from the crop. Companies used it to make toothpaste, gum, candy, even food flavoring. We conserved our resources, as everyone did during the war, even though we were doing well with the crops. When Eldon returned from the CPS camp, his father gave him one-third of the profits from those years."

"One-third because —"

"Because there were three brothers. All had served in various camps. Jeremiah thought they could use the money to get started with their families, once they returned."

"So why didn't you use it?"

"Eldon and I didn't need the money to start a home. We stayed here, stayed with his parents. He was the oldest, and it was his responsibility. He told me a few weeks after he returned that he didn't mind serving in the CPS. He missed me and his parents, but he was convinced *Gotte* used that time away from home to mature him.

However, he also felt the money from his father was tainted somehow. He was adamant that he didn't want to begin our life together with proceeds made during the war."

"So you buried the money?" The story made no sense to Emma. Who buried money and left it for nearly seventy years?

"*Ya.* We buried it beneath the bench —"

"And near the mint." Danny wore a satisfied expression, as if he'd successfully solved a mystery.

"We didn't want to forget where it was, and we knew that sometimes old people have memory problems."

The clock on the wall ticked as Emma considered all Mary Ann had said. Danny finally began to eat his crumbled gingersnap, then reached for another.

Emma stared at the stack of bills in the box, which now sat in the middle of the kitchen table. "This is a lot of money, *Mamm.* All of it came from a mint crop?"

"*Nein.* You will also find war bonds in the stack."

"War bonds?" She was beginning to feel dizzy.

"Everyone was encouraged to buy war bonds in those days. The local Mennonite community helped us to choose which bonds were not specifically used for war purposes. That way we could help our neighbors but not betray our convictions."

Emma reached forward and flipped through the stack. Finding one of the war bonds, she pulled it out and placed it on the table. "Why didn't you cash them in?"

Mamm smiled and sipped her tea.

Danny offered an explanation. "War bonds were given a ten-year extension, up to forty years."

"Can these still be cashed?"

"Sure. I met a man in Pennsylvania who would take some into his bank once a year. He used it to pay the taxes on his land. A twenty-five-dollar bond issued during World War II is worth approximately one hundred dollars today."

"But these are hundred-dollar bonds —"

"We had no children when Eldon left." *Mamm* stared out the kitchen window. "At first the days seemed so long. Then I began to work in the garden and to sew. I sold the handmade items and canned goods at the local mercantile, and I used the money to buy the bonds."

Emma sipped her tea and tried to process all she was hearing.

"When Eldon returned, we placed the bonds in the box, added Jeremiah's money, and buried it in the garden."

"And you were never tempted to dig it up?"

"*Gotte* has provided all these years." Mamm sat back and sipped her tea.

Emma stared at Danny, but he said nothing, content to smile back at her. This wasn't his family history that had been dug up, but something made her think that it involved him. After all, Mary Ann had chosen to reveal her secret when Danny was present. That couldn't be a coincidence.

Closing her eyes, she pulled in a deep breath. Then she opened her eyes, sat up straighter, and asked the question that had bothered her since Danny's shovel struck metal.

"Why now?"

"I have a feeling you and Danny are going to need it."

Emma nearly choked on the sip of tea she'd taken. "Me and Danny?"

"*Ya.*"

Danny's grin widened and Emma's cheeks warmed to the color of the red roses yet to bloom in the garden.

"*Mamm,* why would we . . . Danny and I aren't . . . That is . . ."

Stuffing an entire gingersnap into his mouth, Danny didn't help her out at all.

"The Lord is calling you, calling both of you." Now Mary Ann leaned forward and pinned Emma and Danny with her gaze. "He's doing something important on this little piece of land, and you two are going to be in charge of it."

"I don't —"

"Can't you see? *Gotte* brought Danny home. He brought Joseph to us. And soon there will be others. The money has been cleansed by nearly seventy years of rain and sunshine. Now it's time for you to use what we have to bless others."

It occurred to Emma at that moment that perhaps Mary Ann did have a concussion, but her eyes were clear and a smile continued to play across her lips. The money on the table was certainly real, though Emma had no idea how much it totaled.

"Don't worry." Mary Ann reached forward and patted her hand.

"But I don't understand what —"

"You don't need to. *Gotte* will provide the answers and the direction you need."

With that, she stood, waving away their offer to help. Leaning on her cane, she stumped down the hall to her new bedroom.

Danny and Emma stared at each other for one minute, then two. Finally he cleared his throat. "She's something else, Mary Ann is."

"I think maybe my *mamm* has misunderstood our relationship."

"Maybe." He smiled down into his mug of hot tea. "And maybe not."

Emma didn't know what to say to that, so she remained silent.

What was the money for?

What were they to do with it?

Had it actually been buried in the garden since the 1940s?

Danny seemed in no hurry to go, and Shadow was still in the barn with Joseph.

Unable to resist, she pulled the bundle toward her and ran her fingers along the time-worn string that bound it.

"Want to help me count?" She suddenly felt emboldened. They had never been poor. Even since Ben had died, they'd been able to meet their financial needs with what was saved.

But this?

With this stack of money they had different options available to them. They *could* use it to help other people. She wondered if Ben had known. What would he have advised her to do? Then she looked up at Danny, and somehow knew he understood what she was thinking.

He reached over and squeezed her hand. Together, they cut the string surrounding the bills and began to count.

CHAPTER TWELVE

Later that evening after dinner, Emma carried fresh sheets and blankets out to Joseph.

He'd pulled down an old cot from the attic and set it up in the corner of Ben's office, which was now quite clean. It still smelled of horses and hay and tackle, but the room was warmer than the stall. He wouldn't need a heater, and she was thankful for that. Heaters in barns worried her. On any farm, fire was a constant fear.

She would rather have him in the house, but Joseph seemed to still need his space. Perhaps a little privacy would allow him to work through the things that still haunted him. Perhaps in the barn, among the animals he obviously loved, he could once again find *Gotte*'s *wille* for his life.

Joseph helped her with making his bed. As they worked, he talked about Shadow and Danny and how he'd like to learn to train dogs. Maybe one day, he would have a place where he could raise litters, train them, and then sell the pups to good homes.

It was the most she'd heard him say.

Perhaps the words and dreams that had been bound inside of him were suddenly freed.

The thought made Emma happy. There had been many days in the last year where she found it was an effort to endure the hours from sunrise to bedtime. Other times the days had merged together, and she found little to look forward to. Seeing Joseph smile made her realize that though her children were grown and living in homes of their own, she could still be a help to others.

Was that what Mary Ann was trying to tell her?

Was that why she'd chosen to reveal the treasure?

Emma had thanked Joseph for his hard work that day and was turning toward the barn door when they both heard the clatter of buggy wheels. Grabbing a large battery flashlight, she and Joseph hurried out into the night at the same moment. The lamplight from the kitchen spilled out across the yard. Emma was able to make out Bishop Simon as he stepped down from his buggy and began to walk toward their door.

"Bishop?" Emma called out as she rushed to meet him. "Is everything all right?"

Joseph was hurrying along beside her. She could feel him tense. Was this about his parents? Were they going to insist he return home?

"I'm sorry to disturb you so late."

"It's no problem. *Was iss letz?*"

"I've brought Nancy and her boys. I'm afraid there's been another . . . incident."

"She's here? Now?"

"*Ya*. Waiting in the buggy."

Emma didn't stay to hear another word. Her pulse had kicked up a notch, and her mind was racing. What had happened to Nancy? Were her boys all right?

Then she walked around to where Nancy waited in the back seat of the buggy with her children. The moment Emma saw her, she knew the details of what had happened weren't important. All that mattered was that they provide this family a safe place to stay.

Nancy's lip was swollen, recently cut open by the looks of it. The black eye Verna had spoken of during sewing circle had turned a deep purple. Nancy's older boy was huddled next to her, his face hidden, pressed into her dress. The youngest was in her arms sound asleep.

"Nancy, *wilkumm*. Let me help you out."

Nancy said nothing, but when she stepped out of the buggy, Emma saw how dangerously thin she had become. The boys wore clean clothes, but when the oldest looked up, the fear in his eyes tugged at her heart.

They moved quickly inside the house. Nancy and her boys sat at the table. Bishop Simon stood at the door, watching the darkness outside. Joseph shifted from one foot to the other, as if unsure whether he should stay.

"Joseph, didn't you offer to help Danny with some home repairs early tomorrow?"

"*Ya.*"

"You best go on to bed then. We're fine here."

He glanced from Nancy to the bishop to Emma, and then he shuffled out into the night.

"Let me find you some dinner."

"It's enough for you to let us stay. You don't have to feed us as well." Nancy's voice was strong and her eyes resolute. How did she manage to hold herself together after all she'd endured?

"Of course I'll feed you, and I trust you will accept my hospitality. Now would your boys rather have cold ham or cold chicken?"

"Both, p-p-please." The oldest boy kept

his hands folded on top of the table. He was close to five years old, if Emma remembered correctly, and he had his father's blond hair.

"Jacob, Emma might need to save some of that food for —"

"*Nein*. It's leftovers and I already have a casserole put together for tomorrow." She placed the platters of meat on the table and added fresh bread and cheese. It wasn't a perfectly balanced meal, but it would do for an evening snack.

Jacob didn't touch the food. Instead he bowed his head and waited for his *mamm* to indicate it was okay to eat. Her eyes met Emma's, and Emma saw the tears she was valiantly holding back. Nancy touched her son's head and whispered, "Amen."

The boy reached for a piece of fried chicken. When his teeth sank into it, a smile covered his face. "Th-th-this is *gut, Mamm*."

Nancy stared at her son, then looked at Emma. *"Danki."*

"Gem gschehne."

In that moment they had more in common than one would have imagined. They were two moms who cared immensely for their children. They were two women whose lives had taken unexpected turns, leaving them alone without their husbands. And they were two members of a community who cared for one another.

Nancy's younger son, Luke, began to fuss, nudging her as if he wanted to nurse.

"You'll be comfortable in the upstairs bedroom, first one to the left. The boys can sleep with you or in the room next door."

Nancy stared at Jacob, uncertainty and worry filling her eyes.

"I'll bring him up when he's done eating."

"All right."

Simon motioned Emma into the mudroom once Nancy had gone. "I have three bags of clothing in my buggy. I'll go and fetch them."

"What of Owen? Will he be looking for his family?"

"*Nein.* He's in town courtesy of the Shipshewana police at the moment."

"The police?"

"Drunk driving."

"Oh my." Emma had heard of folks being arrested for driving an *Englisch* automobile while drinking, but she'd never heard of anyone being arrested while they were driving a buggy!

"Captain Taylor phoned me and asked that I send someone for the horse and buggy, which I've done. They're going to hold him for at least twenty-four hours."

"It was a *gut* time for Nancy and the boys to leave."

"Yes." Simon ran his fingers through his beard. "This is temporary, Emma. I spoke with Owen, and he seems repentant, but I doubt he has the strength to resist his addiction."

"What will you do?"

"Minister to him. Encourage him to seek an intervention at the center in Elkhart or Goshen. After this, I think he will."

"And their farm?"

"Neighbors will care for the animals and his crops. I need you to provide a safe place for them to stay, if you're willing." He hesitated, then continued. "In my opinion, it would be better if Nancy and the boys weren't alone, and Owen will more likely agree to treatment if his family is gone."

"Of course, but I don't know anything about helping an abused woman."

"Love her, Emma. Offer the entire family our Lord's grace and mercy. Feed them. Pray for them. *Gotte* will take care of the rest."

He brought in the bags of clothing, and Emma promised she would take them upstairs. Mary Ann had slept through the entire episode. The less folks tramping up and down the stairs the better.

She tapped softly on her guests' door and then opened it.

Nancy sat in the rocker near the window. Her babe was asleep in her arms. Jacob had carried one of the bags of clothes, which he set down near his mother, kissing her, and then his baby brother, before sitting on the bed.

Emma placed the other two bags underneath the hooks they used for hanging clothes.

Was this all she had left? All she'd brought from her home? But her home was still there. It hadn't blown away in some storm. Perhaps with *Gotte*'s help, Owen would be able to return to it whole and ready to care for his family.

"You're welcome to stay as long as you need."

Nancy nodded and swiped at the tears cascading down her cheeks. Emma's heart broke for her again, so she crossed the room, enfolded Nancy in her arms, and let her cry.

CHAPTER THIRTEEN

Mary Ann didn't seem a bit surprised to have extra people eating breakfast with them the next morning. As Emma placed raisins and brown sugar on the table, then brought the pot of oatmeal from the stove, she couldn't help smiling. A week before it had been the two of them, but their lives had turned and taken an entirely new direction.

Emma's mind flashed back to the afternoon she had knelt in the garden and swiped her dirty fingers against her clean apron. It had left a brown mark, but one that had washed away after two launderings. In a similar way, Christ washed away their sins. He never failed to offer them another chance.

Joseph was talking to Jacob, telling him about Shadow. Luke lay in a cradle Emma had found in one of the upstairs rooms. Often it had been used for her grandchildren, and she supposed one day it would hold her great-grandchildren. Truly, God had blessed them.

Nancy appeared to have rested, but the bruising around her eye seemed worse in the daylight, and her busted lip looked painful. Emma was certain Mary Ann would know what herbs they could put on both to soothe the skin.

The morning passed quickly. Nancy washed the clothes that had been in the bags and hung them to dry on the line. It was funny to look outside and see diapers drying in the May sun. Mary Ann baked a cake and fresh bread, while Emma aired and cleaned Jacob's room. By the time Danny and Joseph joined them for lunch, they once again had a full table.

Then there was a commotion at the back door, and Emma's son stepped inside.

Her oldest, Henry was always the first to check on them when anything out of the ordinary was going on. He had turned thirty recently. He was tall, big enough to handle the horses he worked with, and balding slightly. Although he was a farrier in town, they spoke occasionally about him moving back to the farm. They had rented out the fields after Ben had died, but the barn and yard and house were a lot of work for two women living alone.

They weren't alone anymore.

They had an entire family gathered around them now.

"I heard *Mammi* had fallen." He sat beside Jacob as Emma made sure he knew who everyone was. They had two church districts in Shipshe. Henry and his family were members of the district in town. The rest of them belonged to the country district, which Simon oversaw.

"It's true," Mary Ann said. "Tumbled over right outside in the garden. Emma saved me."

"How are you feeling?"

"*Gut!* The Lord is my right hand, Henry."

"And your foot?"

"Sore, but Doc's cane helps."

They spoke of business in town, Danny's pup, and how Joseph and Jacob had searched for worms in the garden.

"Planning on some fishing, are you?" Henry smiled at the boys.

"*Ya.* Emma and *Mamm* say we can . . . can . . . can cook what we catch."

"Hmmm. I have two boys who might enjoy a little fishing. Maybe we can come out Saturday afternoon."

"If we don't ca-catch them all today."

Everyone laughed, everyone except Nancy, who at least managed a smile.

When they were done eating, Emma rose to wash the dishes, but Nancy stayed her hand. "Let me. Please."

"All right. I'll walk Henry outside then."

They were barely out the back door when he started peppering Emma with questions. "Where is the teenager from? How long is he going to stay here? Why didn't you call me about *Mammi,* and what are you going to do about Nancy and her boys?"

Henry had always been her worrier. It wasn't that his faith was weak, but he tended to agonize over whether he was doing enough.

Emma tucked her hand through his arm. "Goshen. I'm not sure. I would have called, but I haven't had time to walk to the phone shack, and I'm not going to do anything. They're just . . . visiting for a while."

Henry grunted. "I'll slow my questions if you'll slow your answers."

"Fair enough."

They'd made it to his buggy, and they both rested their backs against the black side that had warmed in the midday sunlight.

"It's a lot of changes at once."

"*Ya.* Tell me. A week ago, it was only your *mammi* I had to care for. Now, once again, I have a family."

Henry turned and studied her. "It's been hard on you since *Dat* passed."

"All loss is difficult."

"I should have —"

"You've done all you could and should. You're a *gut* son."

Henry smiled ruefully, then turned back to look out over the garden. "The word in town is that you're going to allow people who are in need to stay here."

Emma was a little surprised, since she hadn't quite decided what they were doing herself. But the Amish grapevine worked well, and she admitted to her son that the idea was growing on her.

Then she told him about the money.

Henry let out a long, low whistle and rubbed the top of his head where the hair had disappeared. "Leave it to *Mammi* to keep a secret like that buried."

"I don't know exactly what she wants me to do. She seems to think we should spend it on some kind of ministry here." When Henry didn't comment, she nudged his shoulder. "How do you feel about that? Rightfully the money would go to you and the other *kinner*."

"We're not *kinner*, *Mamm*. We're adults, and you know that none of us needs the money."

"So you think it's the right thing to do?"

"I think however *Gotte* prompts you is the right thing to do." He turned to her, and Emma was relieved to see the familiar twinkle in his eyes. " 'Course we'll inherit this place one day, so any improvements you make will benefit all of us."

"But would you want strangers living on your property?"

"Can't say. I've never thought about it, and these folks aren't actually strangers, except for Joseph, who Danny assures me is harmless."

She wasn't too surprised to hear he'd talked to Danny already. But when had he found the time? Perhaps Danny had managed to slip into town.

"I'm glad Danny lives so close, *Mamm.* He's a *gut* person, and he cares about what happens to you."

Her cheeks warmed, which was probably due to standing in the sun but might have been caused by the idea of Henry blessing her love life.

Did she have a love life?

Did she love Danny Eicher?

The question confused her more than the new group of people who had eaten lunch in her kitchen.

"We all want you to be happy. If you ever

decided to remarry, we would understand."

"Marry?" The word caught in her throat, causing her to blush even more.

Henry bent and kissed her cheek, then he climbed into his buggy and promised to come by on Saturday with his wife and children. "I'll even stop by my *bruder*'s and encourage him to come as well."

Emma stood next to the garden, watching him drive away. He was a blessing, all of her children were, and she was grateful to have them close and willing to help.

The rest of the afternoon passed quickly.

Bishop Simon came by, but he stayed less than ten minutes. He told Nancy and Emma that Owen had agreed to go to Goshen.

"While you could go home, I'd feel more comfortable if you'd stay here for at least a week. We can see how Owen is doing and how best to proceed."

"How long will he be there?" Nancy's voice trembled slightly.

"That will depend on him. Technically he could check himself out anytime, which is why I'd rather you stay with Emma. But hopefully he will remain in the facility for the full month."

"Yes. I'll stay." Nancy moved a step closer to Emma.

Emma put her arm around her, glad she had agreed to forgo heading home. Nancy needed time to heal, and the children needed a safe spot. A sanctuary, as Mary Ann had said.

They worked in the garden again that afternoon. Jacob ran up and down the rows, pausing to look at a plant and ask what it was. Luke lay on a blanket next to Mary Ann's bench, staring up at the sky and playing with his toes. While Nancy and Emma sowed beets, lettuce, and radishes, Joseph and Danny built a new trellis to support the tomato plants. The old one had finally crumbled, and at the rate the plants were growing, they'd need the support from the wooden structure soon.

Danny didn't say much, but occasionally Emma would feel his gaze on her. When she'd turn to look at him, he'd blink once and then return to his work.

She still didn't completely understand why he walked over to help them each afternoon. He'd told her once that it was easier to help with their garden than to grow his own. But he could have purchased what few vegetables one man needed.

He said something to Joseph she couldn't hear, and the boy's laughter mixed with the sound of the afternoon birds searching for worms and insects.

She didn't know when, or if, Joseph would return home. But her heart relished the fact that he no longer looked afraid or anxious.

When they'd finished, Emma invited Danny to dinner, but he declined. He started to say something, then shook his head, reached out and squeezed her arm, and walked away.

Which was strange behavior, even for Danny. It was as if there was something he needed to talk to her about, but he didn't know how. And when had Danny ever been at a loss for words?

Words were his tool and trade.

Emma walked into the house, pulled out the spaghetti casserole, and complimented Nancy's salad. But her thoughts were on the man walking through their garden, back toward his home.

CHAPTER FOURTEEN

Danny walked back over to Emma's. It was early in the evening, but he worried, nonetheless, that he would be interrupting something.

He knocked on the back door and waited, his hands sweating as if he were a young man calling on a young girl for a date. This was far more serious than that, and he almost laughed at himself.

Emma didn't look surprised when she answered the door. Had some part of her, some part of her heart, been expecting him? Now that he stood on her stoop, hands in his pockets, and the evening breeze stirring the hair at the back of his neck, he wasn't sure what to do.

"Emma."

"Evening, Danny. Did you forget something?" When he didn't immediately answer, she added, "Would you like to come in?"

"*Nein.* I was wondering if you would like

to take a walk with me. Maybe through the garden and toward the pond. The weather's *gut* and you wouldn't need more than a shawl."

Emma placed her hand to her throat, then glanced back toward Mary Ann, who sat in the kitchen sorting beans at the old table. She waved Emma away. "I'm fine. I don't need babysitting."

Emma smiled at her feistiness and asked Danny to wait a minute. Hurrying across the kitchen, she found a dish towel and dried her hands. Then she kissed Mary Ann on the cheek. "I'll be back soon to help you to your bedroom."

"I can walk down the hall fine, Emma. You go and enjoy the stars."

Enjoy the stars.

Those words echoed in Danny's mind as Emma fetched her wrap and joined him outside.

The garden looked like a sacred place in the moonlight.

Emma smiled, then said, "It was a relief to see Jacob's joy as he ran up and down the paths. A young child should have a place to play, a safe place to discover the world."

"A place where healing blooms."

Stopping, Emma placed her hand on his shoulder. "What did you say?"

"Your garden — look at all the abundance and all the blooms, but perhaps its real purpose is to be a place where healing blooms."

"Maybe so." She removed her hand and continued walking.

The light southerly breeze brushed against Danny's skin as they made their way to the bench — Mary Ann's bench.

"How are the boys?"

"*Gut.* Nancy has them all settled in the room next to hers." Emma stared out across her land, toward Danny's pond.

The moonlight bounced off the water, and he found himself thinking of summer. For the first time since Ben's death, Emma seemed to relax completely. Danny thought that perhaps it was because of the idea of summer and warmer days, or possibly the boys upstairs and the one in the barn, or her *grandkinner.* He could picture them all fishing around the banks of the pond, surrounded by marsh marigold, yellow water iris, and brown-eyed Susan grown tall and thick.

Danny reached for her hand and laced his fingers with hers. She wasn't completely caught off guard, but that didn't stop the words he wanted to say from catching in his throat. So instead he raised her hand to his lips and kissed it. Her expression changed again — what seemed to him a river of joy tinged with a little fear.

She said nothing.

Fortunately Danny's tongue wasn't tied. "Do you think we're too old for courting, Emma?"

"Too old? *Nein.*" She didn't pull her hand away, but she stared at it in the darkness.

"And are we too old to marry?"

"Danny Eicher! Are you asking me to marry you?" She jumped up from the bench and crossed her arms, but he saw that her hands were shaking. Was she amused or worried?

Danny honestly didn't know. He wasn't that good at understanding women. But he did know that this was the right time to say what was on his heart, what had been there for quite some time.

"If I did ask you, what would your answer be?"

Emma closed her eyes and tried to calm the thudding that was her heart. Was she dreaming? Or was she actually in the garden with Danny Eicher? Had he just asked her to marry him?

"You've put the buggy in front of the horse and you know it."

His smile widened as he stood. "I care for you, Emma. You know I always have, since we were youngsters . . ."

"We were children, who had no idea what twists and turns life would take. You left, set off traveling, and I — I stayed here and raised a family."

Danny didn't answer.

Emma realized in that moment that Danny had learned some important lessons while he'd moved about. He'd learned that life wasn't a race, and he could afford to take his time. He'd learned where his home was. And he'd learned how to listen.

She walked to Mary Ann's rosebushes. The buds nearest her showed a hint of yellow. In another week or so the rose hedge would be a dazzling display of yellow, white, pink, and red, and the scent would be heavenly.

Danny stepped behind her. He didn't push, didn't say anything else. Instead he stood close and waited as she studied the roses.

"I loved Ben."

"I know you did."

"And I miss him still."

"I expect you always will. I miss him too. He was my *freind,* and I'm glad the Lord saw fit to bring me home before his passing. I'm glad we had those few months to become reacquainted again."

Turning, she nearly bumped into Danny, who had moved closer. He didn't back up, but put his hands on Emma's arms to steady her.

Slowly, he lowered his head and brushed his lips against hers. She let go then — of all her doubts and fears and regrets. She closed her eyes and allowed hope to seep into the empty places of her heart.

Clasping her hand, Danny turned them, and they began walking toward the pond.

"We could build the *Wilkumm Haus* there, on the southeast side of the pond."

"You've already named it?"

"With a porch across the front and side, so the folks can look out on the garden —"

"Or the pond," she whispered, catching his vision.

"It will be a *gut* place for those in need to come. A quiet place, and a haven of safety."

She stopped suddenly. "Is that why? Is the house why you're asking me to marry you? Because we can build it, we can help those in our community without —"

His lips brushed hers again. Then he tugged on her hand, pulling her toward the pond. "I asked you because of what's in my heart, Emma. What has always been in my heart. It seems *Gotte* had a plan for you and me, one where we care for each other and offer grace to those who need it most."

She shook her head in the darkness. How could God's plan include Ben's passing?

"He would want you to be happy. You know that Ben would. And you would have wanted the same for him if you had gone first. It's not *gut* to be alone, and you do care for me. Don't you, Emma?"

"Ya."

"Ben would want this, and your *mamm* wants us to use the money."

"Your land —"

"And your money —"

"It will take six months, maybe longer." Emma thought of Nancy and the boys and Joseph.

"To build the *haus*? *Nein.* The bishop has hinted around, promising me we would have help for whatever we decide to do. The families here know such a home would be a blessing to our community. Certainly we would be done before the heat of summer, before your *grandkinner* start appearing for their summer stays."

How had he known about their family plans? Perhaps he guessed. Perhaps she'd mentioned it and he remembered.

Emma knew then that Danny was someone who paid attention. Maybe it was a habit born in his writing and carried over into his personal life.

Her biggest worry about creating a safe place, a haven, tripped away into the night. She hadn't wanted to push her own children, or their children, out while she was helping others.

"If we wed, we'd live in my house?"

"I'll live wherever you want, Emma."

"But what of your house?"

"Young Moses Byler is marrying in a few months. He'd be happy to rent it while he works my land. Once he saves up a little, we can decide whether to offer it to him for purchase."

"Perfect." The word was as sweet as a lemon drop on her tongue. "It all sounds . . . perfect."

"Life is rarely that."

"But —"

"But it would be close, and what isn't perfect, we'll work on together."

From the direction of the barn, she heard Ben's horse whinny. The sound was like a blessing sweeping through the night. Sweeping over her heart.

They'd reached the pond and Shadow had joined them. He licked Emma's hand once, then pounced into the weeds in search of night critters.

Emma turned and studied Ben in the moonlight. The quiet, steady look in his eyes convinced her of what she was feeling, of all he promised, and of what God intended.

"Yes."

He seemed about to let out a holler. His eyes crinkled with the smile that spread across his face. He kissed her again, softly, tenderly, and then they turned and walked back toward her house, Shadow trotting by their side.

"You'll still help with the garden, right?"

"Ya."

"Because you do seem to enjoy it, appearing every afternoon as you have."

"The hours weeding and trimming have been the highlight of my day, Emma. But I would have appeared in the barn if you were cleaning stalls. Each day I would wait as long as I could, and then when I could wait no longer, I'd come to see you. The time I spent here in your garden has been precious to me."

"We'll have plenty more."

"*Ya. Gotte* willing, we will." With her free hand, she brushed the butterfly weed as they walked by, sending up a sweet, fragrant odor.

A place of healing, that was what *Mamm*

had called it.

A place where healing blooms, that was what Danny had said.

Both seemed good descriptions to Emma. Sometime in the past year her heart had healed.

She thought of Joseph, sleeping in the barn. Perhaps he would grow comfortable enough with them to share his past. Perhaps with time and guidance and hard work, he would heal as well.

Then there were her guests, Nancy and the boys upstairs.

She heard Luke's cry through the upstairs window, and saw the shadow of Nancy moving to pick him up, then sitting in the rocker. It was the same rocker she'd used to comfort many a child.

Together, they made an odd sort of family, but perhaps it was a family God could use. One God could bless, and one that would endure through the seasons.

Perhaps together they could create a place where healing blooms.

READING GROUP GUIDE

1. Emma is struggling to find purpose for her life. She's content, but she also feels an emptiness because she's not needed in the way she once was. How do the people in her life convince her otherwise? What does Scripture say about our service to the Lord? (Read Colossians 3:23.)

2. We never learn the details of Joseph's history with his family. The author purposely left this out so that you could envision people in your community who need help. The bishop does make it plain that Joseph has not been physically abused. What specific things can we do to help those around us who are experiencing a harsh home life?

3. Mary Ann has kept her secret buried in the garden for many years

until she felt the time was right to reveal the box. What are some reasons that we keep secrets, and how do we know the right time to reveal them?

4. At the beginning of the story, Emma suspects she is too old for romantic love. Read I Corinthians 13:4–7. What does the Bible say about love?

5. Gardens are a place of healing for many of us. Discuss the gardens in your life (past and present) and why they have been special to you.

ACKNOWLEDGMENTS

This book is dedicated to my husband's Uncle Joe. Though he is now legally blind, he still keeps a garden. He's the person to see when I need a cutting or have questions about why something isn't flourishing. His garden is a thing of beauty, and he is an inspiration to me.

Thanks also to my prereaders: Donna, Dorsey, and Kristy. You girls know I love you. Becky Philpott is a joy to work with and a fabulous editor. I'd also like to once again thank Mary Sue Seymour, who is a wonderful agent and a good friend.

I enjoyed this return visit to northern Indiana. If you're in the area, I encourage you to visit the quilt gardens in Middlebury, Goshen, Nappanee, Elkhart, and Shipshewana.

And finally . . . "always giving thanks to God the Father for everything, in the name

of our Lord Jesus Christ" (Ephesians 5:20).
Blessings,
Vannetta

BROCCOLI SALAD

1 head cauliflower
1 bunch broccoli
1 pound bacon
1 package (2 cups) shredded cheddar cheese
1 1/2 cups salad dressing (recipe follows)
1/2 cup sweet-and-sour dressing (recipe follows)
1 teaspoon salt

Cut cauliflower and broccoli into small pieces. Cut up bacon and fry; drain on paper towel. The dressings can be added the day before, but wait to add the bacon and cheese until ready to serve.

SALAD DRESSING

1 egg plus water to make 1/2 cup
3/4 cup cooking oil
1/2 cup white sugar
2 teaspoons salt
1/2 teaspoons dry mustard
1/4 teaspoons garlic salt

In saucepan, cook:

1 1/2 cups water
2/3 cup flour
1/4 cup vinegar

The result will be very thick. Mix with first ingredients. Beat well.

SWEET-AND-SOUR DRESSING

1 cup white sugar
1 cup vegetable oil
1/4 cup vinegar
2 teaspoons mustard
1 tablespoon salad dressing
1 teaspoon salt
1/4 teaspoon pepper
1 teaspoon celery seed
1/4 cup water
1 medium onion, minced

Beat all ingredients well before adding onions.

from *A Taste of Home*
from the Schlabach family

BAKED CHICKEN BREASTS

Chicken
Salt and pepper
Butter
Cracker crumbs

Salt and pepper the chicken. Melt 2 or 3 sticks butter. Dip chicken in butter, then roll in cracker crumbs. Bake on cookie sheet at 350° for 30 to 45 minutes. Serve on a bed of cooked rice. Also good with mashed potatoes and vegetables.

from *A Taste of Home*
from the Schlabach family

AMISH TOMATO FRITTERS

1 cup all-purpose flour
1 teaspoon white sugar
1 teaspoon sea salt
1 (28 ounce) jar canned tomatoes
2 tablespoons minced green chilies
2 tablespoons minced onion
1 teaspoon Worcestershire sauce
3 eggs
Canola oil for frying
Additional salt

In a large bowl combine flour, sugar, and salt. Drain tomatoes and cut them into 1/2-inch pieces. Add green chilies and onion to the flour mixture.

In a small bowl beat eggs and Worcestershire sauce, then add to the flour-tomato mixture. Stir lightly until all items are mixed together. Heat 1/4 inch of oil in a skillet over medium heat. Drop teaspoons of batter into oil, patting down with back of spoon. Fry until golden brown and then flip over. Place on plate lined with paper towel to remove excess oil. Sprinkle fritter lightly with salt while still hot. Keep warm and then serve.

Makes 30 to 35 small fritters.

Note: You can substitute stewed tomatoes with green chilies and onion, or Rotel tomatoes with green chilies and onion, for canned tomatoes.

TOMATO AND CUCUMBER SALAD

5 medium tomatoes, cut into bite-size pieces
1/4 red onion, peeled and thinly sliced
2 cucumbers, peeled and cut into bite-size
  pieces
2 tablespoons extra-virgin olive oil
1 teaspoon balsamic vinegar
1 pinch garlic powder
Coarse salt and black pepper

Mix vegetables in a bowl, then dress with olive oil, vinegar, and garlic powder. Add salt and pepper to taste. Retoss right before serving.

SANDWICH SPREAD

6 onions
6 mangoes
6 green tomatoes
6 cucumbers
6 carrots
1 pint vinegar
4 cups white sugar
3/4 cup flour
1 cup prepared mustard

Grind first five ingredients and put in salt water overnight. Drain, then boil 25 minutes in 1 pint vinegar and 4 cups sugar. Add 3/4 cup flour and boil 10 minutes longer. Allow to cool. Stir in mustard. Put in jars and seal.

from *Mutschler Sampler of Authentic Amish Cookery*

BLACK BEAN SOUP

1/2 cup olive oil

3 cups diced yellow onions

8 cloves garlic, peeled and crushed

2 pounds black beans, soaked in water overnight

1 meaty ham bone or 1 pound salt pork

6 quarts water

2 tablespoons ground cumin

1 tablespoon dried oregano

3 bay leaves

2 teaspoons black pepper

1 pinch cayenne pepper

6 tablespoons chopped fresh parsley, divided

1 medium-size red bell pepper, stemmed,
seeded, and diced

1 tablespoon brown sugar

1 tablespoon fresh lemon juice

2 hard-boiled eggs, chopped

Sour cream (optional)

Heat oil in soup pot over medium-low heat. Add onions and garlic and cook over low heat until vegetables are tender, about 10 minutes.

Drain beans and add them, the ham bone or salt pork, and 6 quarts water to pot. Stir in cumin, oregano, bay leaves, black pepper, cayenne, and 2 tablespoons parsley. Bring to a boil, reduce heat, and cook, uncovered, until beans are tender and liquid is reduced by about three quarters (approximately 2 hours).

Transfer the ham bone or salt pork to a plate and cool slightly. Pull off any remaining meat with your fingers and shred finely. Return meat to pot.

Stir in remaining 4 tablespoons parsley, bell pepper, brown sugar, lemon juice, and eggs (boiled and chopped). Simmer for another 30 minutes, stirring frequently. Taste, correct the seasoning, and serve very hot. Garnish with a dollop of sour cream.

KATHERINE'S PINEAPPLE CHERRY CRISP

1 cup canned crushed pineapple
3 tablespoon minute tapioca
1 cup sugar
2 1/2 cups (pitted) cherries
1 tablespoon lemon juice

Combine and cook until clear, stirring constantly.

Mix crumbs together:

1 cup flour
1/2 cup butter, melted
1/4 teaspoon baking soda
1 cup quick-cooking oats
2/3 cup brown sugar

Put half of crumb mixture on the bottom of 9×13-inch baking pan. Add cherry and pineapple mixture, then cover with remaining crumbs. Bake at 400° for 25 minutes.

ROSEMARY'S CHEESY SALMON CASSEROLE

1/4 cup chopped onions
2 tablespoons margarine
1 can cream of mushroom soup
1/2 cup milk
1 cup shredded cheddar cheese, divided
4 cups cooked macaroni
1 (8 ounce) can salmon
1/2 cup buttered bread crumbs

In medium saucepan cook onions in margarine until tender. Stir in soup, milk, 3/4 cup cheese, macaroni, and salmon. Pour into baking dish. Bake at 250° for 25 minutes. Top with bread crumbs and remaining cheese, then bake 5 minutes longer.

ABOUT THE AUTHOR

Vannetta Chapman is author of the best-selling novel *A Simple Amish Christmas.* She has published over one hundred articles in Christian family magazines and received over two dozen awards from Romance Writers of America chapter groups. In 2012 she was awarded a Carol Award for *Falling to Pieces.* She discovered her love for the Amish while researching her grandfather's birthplace of Albion, Pennsylvania.